the Doomed Disciple

GOD DOESN'T WRITE TRAGIC ENDINGS

Paul Campbell

THE DOOMED DISCIPLE
GOD DOESN'T WRITE TRAGIC ENDINGS

This is a work of fiction. Though these characters and places are based
on historical people, events, and locations, all are used fictitiously.
The historical facts as we know them can best be found in Scripture.
For more information on my own research, please visit www.traitorbooks.com.

ISBN (paperback): 979-8-35093-417-5
ISBN (ebook): 979-8-35093-418-2

Published by Bookbaby
www.bookbaby.com

Books by Paul Campbell

THE CALLAHAN CHRONICLES:

Grayscale

Gray Matter

Grayhound

Blue Blood

OTHER WORKS:

The Doomed Disciple

SHORT STORIES:

(Available for free at www.traitorbooks.com)

The Gardener

Blue Tiger

The Angel of Dijon

Saint Nicholas Day

This book is dedicated to the hopelessly lost.

Job 19:10

and the One who came to save them.

Luke 19:10

Part 1

I

"**Y**ou're fired." The words produced less of a shock than perhaps they should have, but Judas knew his master to be an intelligent man. Joseph did not own half of Arimathaea by accident. Judas's termination was unexpected but not undeserved. He knew his actions would eventually come to light, but he always imagined it in some distant future on his own terms, after he had made arrangements elsewhere.

Instead, the easiest mark in Judea had blindsided him. Joseph had kept his suspicions a secret. *That* was surprising. Joseph was many things, but he was *not* naturally suspicious.

"I understand," Judas replied calmly.

Joseph stared at him, clearly expecting more. In Judea *everything* was a negotiation. No price was fixed, no wage was set, no decision was in stone until both parties had sufficiently haggled. A termination merely meant an opening to renegotiate terms. Joseph expected him to either defend his innocence with adamant protests or repent in tears, beg forgiveness, strike his breast, and possibly even rend his garments, all while swearing to never offend again. If nothing else, to beg for mercy. Anything less would be a blatant admission of guilt. But Judas would not beg—especially since he was actually guilty. He refused to humiliate himself by pleading for mercy he did not deserve or offering up promises he would not keep.

"That's all you have to say?" Joseph asked, leaning back onto the cushions behind his large, wooden desk. He was rich enough to afford the finest marble imported from the furthest reaches of the Empire, but the man preferred humble wood—expertly designed and ornately carved, but still wood. The walls were lined with scrolls, books, and oil lamps, but little else hinted at the man's vast fortune. Joseph was rich but not extravagant. He was truly a good man, but good men could not always do what was necessary.

"*That's all you have to say?!*" Joseph shouted, rising from his position behind the desk to stand eye-level with Judas, who stood silently in front of him. Joseph was considerably older than Judas, and though his curly black hair had started to turn ashen, he still held the vigor of a man far younger. He took a calming breath and looked at Judas closely, studying his young steward to find any possible reason to excuse his actions. "Five years you've kept the records here. I put you in charge of *my entire estate*. All the farmers who lease from me come to *you*. I gave you a great honor by raising you to your position, and you repay me by skimming off the top. *Why?*"

The man still expected a negotiation. Judas was certain if he begged forgiveness and promised never to steal again, Joseph would reinstate him. Judas would not do that. He would not lie, he was not sorry, and he would steal again.

"How long?" Joseph asked quietly, finally giving up on an explanation.

"Three and a half years."

"Three and a h—*Why?*" he asked again, his rage crumbling into the pain of betrayal. "I don't understand. Do you have debts? Were your wages insufficient? If you had only come—"

"My wages were more than generous," Judas replied simply.

"And yet you have been stealing from me. I... I am at a loss for words. How could you do this after everything I have given you? I treated you as a friend! No, you *were* a friend. I *trusted* you! And you repay me with betrayal! How could you?" he asked.

Judas remained silent. What could he say? Nothing that mattered.

"Do you realize the penalty for thievery, especially on this scale?" Joseph asked hoarsely.

"Yes," Judas said quietly. *Capital* punishment: A quick death if your master was *incredibly* merciful, a very slow one if he was normal. The Roman Empire did not tolerate thieves. Crucifixion was common.

"And still you persist in your stubborn pride?" Joseph asked, tears forming in his dark eyes even as his anger rekindled. "I gave you a position second only to myself, and you stabbed me in the back! And you won't even defend your motives?! Tell me the men who brought these accusations are lying. Tell me! Give me a *single* reason to show you mercy!"

Joseph would never have made the accusation if he was not already certain. He had undoubtedly checked—and double-checked—the reports. Both men knew any defense would be a blatant lie. And still, Judas's master held out hope. Even as Joseph's eyes grew moist from the pain of betrayal, he *still* wanted to negotiate. Joseph was a good man and refused to grasp the idea that others were not so. He had probably been swindled countless times before, and still he wished only to see the good in people. He would learn today. Judas respected the man too much to take advantage of him with a fake apology, no matter how desperately the man wished to hear it. Judas had no excuse, and he would give none. He straightened. "I have nothing left to say."

The silence smothered them. Judas stood firmly while Joseph tugged at his robe in irritation. His robes were of the finest Egyptian linen and imported silk from the furthest reaches of the Empire—one of his few luxuries. "I could reduce your wages and use the difference to begin repaying the debt," Joseph said quietly, beginning the negotiation with or without Judas.

"In about three hundred years."

"Only until Jubilee," Joseph insisted.

Judas gave him a condescending stare. "Nobody goes by that anymore. Face it, Joseph. You aren't getting your money back."

Joseph threw up his hands. "It's not about the money! You..." He settled himself again. "If word of this gets out at all, you will never work again. If you at least *try* to settle the debt, you could work here. I can explain away why you were moved to a different position, and no one would have to know. You could *repay the debt*. Keep your honor and reputation. Remain an honest man! Please, Judas! We can fix this. No one would have to know."

Judas almost gave in, but his resolve hardened. It was better that Joseph learned from him than some less scrupulous source. "Don't you get it, Joseph?!" he spat. "I'm *NOT* an honest man. Stop pretending I am!"

Joseph reeled back from the cold reaction his mercy produced as the truth finally soaked in. He stiffened, his face growing hard. "Get out of my sight," he said coldly, covering fury that boiled from the hot pain of betrayal. "Turn in your accounting books and go. You have until sundown."

For research notes, see chapter 1 in the reference section.

II

The day was warm when Judas stepped out of Joseph's office and into the central courtyard of his home. The weather was finally cooling from the dry months, but summer still lingered as fall approached. Smells wafted from the kitchen in preparation for the noonday meal, and Judas's stomach rumbled. He had eaten at Joseph's table often during his time as the man's steward, and he would miss the sumptuous meals: not only the fresh produce from the man's farmland, but also imported delicacies and spices from his trading enterprises. Joseph funded three merchant ships that sailed from Joppa, and he made the most of them.

Judas glanced at the house servants bustling about the courtyard as he left. None paid him any mind. They were used to him meeting with the master. From their perspective today was no different. Joseph's comment bubbled up in Judas's brain: *You could keep your reputation.* Joseph had confronted him in secret. So far as anyone else knew, Judas still held his job. He still had a chance to leave on his own terms.

"Zed!" he called as he passed the stables, motioning for one of the servants to follow him as he continued. A plan was forming in his mind, but he didn't have much time. Zedekiah quickly set down his shovel and hurried over.

"Sir?" he asked, wiping his brow with the back of his arm, smearing the dust and sweat.

"Send messengers to every farmer who leases from our master. I must speak to them *all*—individually—today. No time to waste. Send them to my house. I'll meet them there." Zedekiah was a household servant, but he had been in Joseph's employ long enough that the other servants followed his orders. Plus, Zed had an ample supply of discretion—and he owed Judas a favor.

"Right away, sir," Zed replied, hurrying off to fulfill his commission. Judas continued on toward his home at a quick walk. It wasn't his home, exactly; it was the house of whomever happened to be steward, and it belonged to the estate. Judas was the steward, so he lived there—at least for the next few hours. It was about two miles away and closer to the fields than the master's mansion so that the steward could manage and supervise the workers more easily, and they could have quick access to answers or redress if the occasion warranted. Normally, Judas didn't mind the walk, but today it was all he could do to keep a dignified pace. Men of position did *not* run. Messengers ran and beggars ran. Running was a direct affront to polite society—plus it would warn the farmers that something was wrong.

Judas kept a dignified pace until he reached his dwelling. He quickly shut the door of his simple, one-room house and began gathering his things. He didn't have much: an extra cloak, a coat for winter, and a little money he had kept back for emergencies. Everything else came with the position, and although Judas had been embezzling from his master since nearly the beginning, he was not about to stoop so low as to steal household supplies. He would leave this little house as it had been. However, he did take some food. He stuffed everything into his bedroll and quickly rolled it up. It looked a little thicker than usual, but nobody would be the wiser.

He checked the bright rectangle of light on the floor that streamed in from the window. He still had plenty of time before sundown. He turned his attention to the accounts, settling himself down at his own simple desk that doubled as his table. He brushed off a few crumbs from breakfast and opened the most recent tallies.

He hesitated for a moment and glanced over the entries. Everything looked in order. Somehow, Joseph had stumbled upon a discrepancy between the numbers Judas reported and the numbers the farmers paid. Looking back, it wasn't surprising. Joseph was constantly among the workers. He often hired day laborers himself. But Judas hadn't cheated the day laborers. He couldn't quite hit on how his master had discovered the change—not that it mattered now.

He flinched at the sudden knock on his door. "Sir?" Zed's voice came through the wood. "Samuel of the olive grove is here, sir."

"Excellent, Zedekiah. Send him in. Send in the next when he leaves."

"Yes, sir," Zed said, opening the door and ushering Samuel in. Judas wasn't surprised to see the old olive farmer here first. The groves were nearby.

Samuel was an old man, but hardy. There was not a servant in Joseph's house that looked the least impoverished. Joseph was a generous master. Judas had nothing bad to say about the man except that he was far too trusting. Perhaps that would change. "You want'd t' see me, sir?" Samuel asked, standing with his hands clasped in front of him.

"Yes, come in, Samuel. Quickly, now. Have a seat," Judas replied, glancing again at the creeping square of light slowly inching toward sundown. "You lease land from Joseph, yes? He will be going through all his holdings with a fine-toothed comb in the next few days. How much is required to lease his land?"

Samuel licked dry lips and dropped his gaze. "Well, it's been rather harsh these years. Wit' increas'd taxes from Rome, an' 'em flies this year..." He drifted off.

Judas had no time for the usual negotiations. "How much do you currently owe Joseph?" he asked, cutting directly to the chase.

"Oh. Well. A hun'erd measures of oil... sir," he admitted. "But the hot summer'll take care of 'em flies. If the God of our fathers looks fav'rably on next's harvest, should almost cover what's due. I don't see need to be concerned over—"

"Here it is," Judas said, cutting him off. He spun the book so it faced Samuel. "Samuel ben Simeon. Deficit: one hundred measures of oil." He tapped the entry. "See it?"

"I do, sir." The workers were another matter, but the farmers who leased Joseph's fields could all read and write—at least enough for business, if not for the study of the Torah. Judas was an educated man, but not all Jews were so lucky. If every Jew could read, the scribes would be penniless.

Judas pushed a quill and inkwell toward the grizzled farmer. "Cross it out and write fifty."

"What?" Samuel said, stunned.

"Cross it out and write fifty!" Judas repeated, eyes continuing to glance toward that creeping square of light. He needed more time.

"Me, sir?"

"Yes, you!" He sighed, forcing down his impatience. Farmers were not accountants. "You must write it in to prove that we both agreed upon this sum. It's my account book; if there is an error, the blame will fall to me. But there will be no error, I assure you. Your debt is reduced. Congratulations. Joseph knows it has been a hard year. Take the blessing and go! I haven't time to explain every detail."

Samuel still struggled to process what was happening. "But... Tha's nearly a year's wages!"

"Yes. You gain a year gratis. You're a hard worker, and you deserve it. Now, write it in quickly! I have other people to see!"

"Yes, sir!" Samuel said, quickly taking the pen and crossing out a year's salary from Joseph's income. "Blessings be on you and your master's house!" He stood, nearly in tears, and hurried from the house.

Judas waited a moment for the next farmer to enter, until he grew impatient. "Zed! Next!" he shouted.

Through the mud brick walls of his house, Judas saw Zed flinch in his mind's eye. He smiled to himself as Zed threw open the door and practically tossed another farmer inside.

"Jonathan. Good to see you," Judas said before the man could collect himself. "Sit down, if you please. Quickly. How much do you owe?"

"How much do I owe?" Jon asked stupidly.

Judas sighed irritably. "You lease land from Joseph. Each year, he receives a portion of your crop based on a set sum or the equivalent in coin, etcetera, etcetera. The harvest is over except for some late pomegranates. You've had ample time to sell the crop. What do you owe?"

"Well, that's true, but Joseph has never expected payment immediately. I've always—"

"The ledger says a hundred measures of wheat. Is that correct?"

"Now, I may come up a little short on that," Jon protested. "Wheat's down this year." *Again with the bargaining.* Usually, Judas relished the back-and-forth, the challenge of making a deal which convinced both parties *they* were the ones getting a bargain. Today, he did not care.

"Doesn't matter. Cross it out and write in eighty," Judas said, tapping the entry with a nervous finger.

"I—what, sir?" Jon said, looking up at him sharply.

If every farmer was going to be so tedious, Judas would never get done in time. "Consider it a bonus for faithful service."

"Sir! Even with the drop in wheat prices, that's—"

"Nearly a year's wages," Judas finished, nodding to speed things along. "I know! Put your sign by the entry to make it official. Give an offering at the Temple or something, but do it quickly and *go!*"

"Right away," Jon said, never one to question good fortune. "You're acting awfully strange today, Judas," he added as he made his mark. "Everything all right?"

"Quite alright. We can catch up another time. I have other men to see."

"Yes, yes. I hear you. I'm leaving now," he said cheerfully. "Do give Joseph my eternal thanks."

"Your benefactor already knows of your gratitude," Judas replied with a sly grin. Jon gave him a puzzled look but stepped out without further comment. He was a sly one, that Jon. He would be the first to put the pieces together.

"Next!"

The other farmers came and went in similar fashion as the square of light continued inching up the wall. It had nearly reached the level of the window when the last farmer left. Judas had given each man an additional year's salary. Joseph's income would be practically nothing over the next year, and it was all recorded properly in the official books. Joseph would discover the fraudulent entries when he opened them—probably this very evening. Joseph could easily prove that the changes had been entered without his consent, but the farmers were already celebrating their good fortune, which they assumed Joseph had approved. Joseph could demand that the fraudulent entries be corrected, but it would turn the farmers against him. They would forever view Judas as the man who had given them the reward and Joseph as the man who had stolen it from them. Joseph would sooner die than lose his farmers' adoration.

The only option left was to eat the cost. Once the farmers heard of Judas's termination, they would realize Joseph had been totally unaware of Judas's illegal generosity. Joseph would have every right to demand what was his, and the farmers would be forever indebted to him for *not* demanding it. The only risk was on Judas himself. The farmers were innocent. When Joseph learned Judas had repaid his mercy by stealing even more, the fury and embarrassment of being double-crossed twice might just push him over the edge.

The risk was high, but Judas was desperate. Without some leverage, his reputation would be ruined. No one would trust him for anything besides hard labor. He would be no better than a slave. He hadn't the strength for manual labor, and he was too proud to beg—not that anyone would show mercy on a known swindler.

If he was right, half the farmers in Arimathaea would owe him a lifetime of favors. They were not Joseph, but neither were they paupers. Even if they didn't trust him, they would admire his daring. Better to have a good swindler work for you than against you. He would have allies.

But if he was wrong... Joseph had clout with Roman magistrates and Sadducees alike. He could have the Romans hunt Judas down and send him to the galleys or throw him on a cross to rot. Both outcomes were unthinkable. One meant a life of misery, trapped in the belly of a Roman ship, rowing unceasingly to aid their war machine until an enemy ship tore into the hull and dragged you under, still chained to the darkness of the cramped hull. The other...

He shuddered. There was no turning back. He plucked up the ledger and snatched his makeshift pack. Opening the door, he reeled back as he nearly collided with Zed.

"Sorry to startle you, sir!" Zed said quickly. "There's a man here to see you."

Judas recovered himself. "Another farmer?" he asked. He thought he had seen them all.

"Ah, no. A visitor. One of the messengers saw him walking through the fields, and he mentioned a debt. You manage our master's books, and the messenger knew you were calling everyone in today..."

Judas glanced at the light on the wall that had turned a dark gold. He still had a few minutes. Sundown happened officially when the first star was visible. Perhaps it would be better to let a little darkness fall before Joseph discovered his scheme. "Very well, send him in," Judas said. He set the account book back on his desk and stuffed his bedroll behind it. He really didn't have time for this, but the man was here, and turning him away would only raise suspicion among the servants. Judas would not dare raise Joseph's suspicions until after he had slipped away in the night.

The man stepped into the small room, and Judas looked him over. His calloused hands showed him to be a craftsman. His clothing was of sturdy quality but unremarkable. He was a craftsman of enough skill to afford a decent cloak, which meant he did more than scrape by, but little more—certainly not anyone Joseph would be expecting as an honored guest. The visitor was merely a tradesman with an unsettled bill—somewhere around Judas's own social status—but there was something striking about the stranger that piqued his interest.

The man smiled kindly. "I am sorry to bother you. I understand you have had a busy afternoon." The man was in his thirties, the best Judas could guess, several years older than himself.

Judas cleared his throat and did his best to summon what politeness he could muster. Thankfully, business transactions did not require the same hospitality as genuine guests. He should simply send the man away; he was only a simple worker. But there was something inexplicable about him that Judas found fascinating. "I have a few minutes. Please, sit. Can I offer you some water?"

"Please," the man said. Judas stood and retrieved the pitcher, which still held water, and reached for a cup. His hand hovered over the cheesecloth. He glanced back at his guest. No, the man was no Pharisee; he wouldn't need to strain the water for unclean insects. He filled a cup and set it in front of the visitor.

"Zedekiah said you were here about a debt?" Judas asked, opening the account book again and glancing through it. Joseph often loaned money to people, with little interest as to whether they paid it back or not. It had been a constant annoyance for Judas, who had been required to keep track of all those outstanding loans. Of course, since Joseph could never possibly remember every debt, it was easy to simply erase an entry when a debt was paid and use the money for his own ends. "I don't recognize you," he told the stranger. "You're from Arimathaea, yes?"

"No," the man said, shaking his head. "From Nazareth."

For research notes, see chapter 2 in the reference section.

III

"Nazareth, eh?" Judas asked, giving his visitor a closer examination. "You don't look like a Nazarene."

Judas's visitor took a long drink of water. "See a lot of Nazarenes around here, do you?" he asked with a grin. Nazarenes hardly ever ventured into Arimathaea. It was too close to Samaria's southern border. The only way to reach it without a lengthy detour was to travel straight through Samaria, and no sensible Jew would do that. It was bad enough just meeting the occasional Samaritan on the road without being surrounded by entire cities of them.

"You'd be the first," Judas replied. "I find it odd that you have traveled all the way here just to settle a debt. Does Joseph owe *you* money?" he asked skeptically.

This provoked a hearty laugh. "It's an unsettled debt of my father's. Joseph and he were old friends. I have decided to quit the family business, and it would not be right to leave my family with the added workload along with the responsibility of an unpaid debt. I was hoping to see Joseph personally and find some way of repaying his generosity. We make ends meet, but nothing more. Nazareth is a poor village."

"Which may be the nicest thing anyone can say about the place. I don't blame you for leaving," Judas said before stopping himself. "I mean no offense," he said by way of apology. He mentally kicked himself for speaking without thought. Nazareth was considered a backward village even by backward Galileans. The town had no schools, no public works, no industry, nothing to commend it to anyone. The people scraped by—mostly farmers—and kept to themselves. They were intensely proud—though nobody could figure out exactly *what* they were proud of—and disliked intruders. They had all the self-satisfied piety of the strictest Pharisee—without the manners. There was nothing more offensive than a poor man thinking he was better than everyone else, and Nazareth was a whole village of them.

"It's not exactly a tourist destination," the man admitted with a kind smile.

"Thank goodness, or Jerusalem might go bankrupt!" Judas joked, trying to save face. "So, tell me what name this debt would be under," he added, quickly navigating away from any further insult of his guest's hometown.

"Joseph bar Jacob, of Nazareth."

"Joseph borrows from Joseph," Judas chuckled. "We really could learn from the Greeks about having a wider variety of names. This may take a minute to track down. Do you know the approximate date the loan was given?"

"About thirty years ago now. Just after Archelaus received governorship of Judea. My father lost everything on the journey from Egypt. Joseph gave him enough money to restart his business in Nazareth, but our family never quite managed to make enough to repay it."

"And until the Messiah finally breaks the yokes from off our necks, you never will," Judas replied, scanning the ledger for the correct entry. "Don't get me wrong; I admire my master greatly. He is an honest and generous man, but the Roman occupation ensures that the rich stay rich and the poor stay poor."

"Poverty is not the curse people think it is."

"God's people were not created to beg," Judas replied darkly without taking his eyes off the pages. He failed to find the entry. "Do you recall the amount?"

"Two minas, originally, but with usury costs—"

"Joseph never charges usury," Judas said distractedly, finally pinning the correct entry with his finger. "Still, that's a lot of money to risk carrying about without protection. You did *bring* the money?"

"No. Truthfully, I am not sure how I can repay the debt," Joseph's son admitted. "I have no money, but I cannot leave my family under this debt."

"I understand your feelings," Judas said. "You could work off the debt. It's not quite a year's wage. Subtracting cost of living expenses..." Judas considered. "It's not impossible. Joseph is generous. You could work it off in a year or two if you worked hard and didn't eat much."

The man shook his head. "My Father's business can't wait."

This remark took Judas off-guard. "Wait, wait, wait," he said, leaning back and appraising his guest with amused confusion. "You came all the way from Nazareth to repay your father's debt, but with no money and no time to work it off? You *must* work off the debt; without money, you have no other option!"

"God works the greatest miracles when we have no other options."

Judas raised his eyebrows at this presumptuous remark, but he was impressed by it rather than incensed. "Bold, aren't you?" He chuckled. "You'd be better off begging Joseph to forgive your debt. He's a gracious man." He laughed again. "But no, you are like me. We are too proud to beg, so we gamble on the grace of the Almighty."

"It's not a gamble if you know who He is," the man replied quietly.

Judas looked up sharply. He had gambled his life against the mercy of Joseph of Arimathaea. If Judas was right about his generosity, all would be well. If he was wrong... He studied his guest, and behind the stranger's kind eyes he saw an intellect that unnerved him. A pang of fear sliced into his chest. Had his guest somehow discovered his scheme? No, it was impossible. His eyes again flicked to the window, which revealed a dark sky well into twilight. He only had a few minutes.

He slapped the table. "I like you! I don't know what your game is, but you play it flawlessly." He dipped the quill in the inkwell and crossed out the entry. "Congratulations…?"

"Jesus."

"Jesus bar Joseph. Your debt is paid in full. Sign here."

"You would cancel the debt of a man you hardly know? Without your master's permission?" Jesus asked.

If you only knew… "I know exactly who you are," Judas said. "You're the kind of man who leaves his home with no money to repay a debt that isn't even his! You're bold and willing to take a chance. You're a gambler. I like that. However, I do want one thing in return."

"Oh?" Jesus asked.

"You said your father and Joseph were old friends?"

Jesus smiled. "Yes, they grew up together. I think they liked having the same name."

"Dine with Joseph tonight. I'm sure he would love hearing about your family. Zedekiah will show you the way. Don't bring up anything about me repaying your debt until *after supper*. Simple enough, yes?"

"Simple enough, and yet simple requests often have complex motives."

Judas stiffened. "My motives are my own. It's best not to question blessings, don't you agree?" he asked with a smile. He stood, not waiting for a reply, and gathered the books for Zed to return to their rightful owner. "It's been nice talking to you, Jesus, but I have other appointments."

Jesus let the subject go. "Thank you for your hospitality and your generosity. I will tell Joseph that his steward is a man of great kindness."

"After supper," Judas reminded him.

Jesus grinned. "After supper. Until we meet again, my friend."

Judas nodded absently as he quickly gathered the accounts into his arms.

Jesus noted his burden with a knowing glance and opened the door for him without comment.

"Thanks," Judas said. Zedekiah waited patiently in the growing darkness. Judas handed him the accounts, which Zed took unquestioningly. "Zed, this is Jesus of Nazareth, he will be dining at the master's table tonight. Make sure he gets there safely and leave these accounts for Joseph to review in the morning."

"You won't be coming, sir?" Zed asked.

"Not tonight, Zed."

Zed nodded obediently and led Jesus into the gathering twilight toward the master's house. Judas watched until he could no longer see them in the growing darkness, then he retrieved his pack from inside, closed the latch, and slipped into the night.

For research notes, see chapter 3 in the reference section.

IV

"The time is here, friends! The kingdom is coming! *Now* is the time for repentance! Now is your chance. You may not get another! Come forward. Yes! Come and be cleansed. Be ready when the kingdom comes!"

"Rather eloquent for a savage, isn't he?" Judas asked his comrade, watching the wild man preach while half-submerged in the muddy water of the Jordan river. The wild man beckoned eagerly as a man stepped from the crowd of listeners on the bank and waded into the water. The new man spoke softly to the wild preacher for a few minutes and was then promptly dunked into the muddy water. The wild man pulled him back up, and the two embraced. The recently submerged then waded back out to join a group of equally soggy comrades who had undergone the same treatment. They doled out quiet congratulations to their new comrade with apparent cheerfulness.

Judas winced as his companion slugged him in the shoulder. "He's no savage," the man replied, as if Judas's words had been a personal insult. "Essenes are well-educated."

"This dunkard is no Essene, Andrew," Judas said. "You probably don't see many of them in Galilee. Essenes are hermits, but they live in communal camps and their ideas of ritual purity make even the Pharisees seem lax by comparison. An Essene would never interact with the unclean public like this, but you're right; he *is* educated. For a savage."

"Don't call him that!" Andrew snapped. "John is no savage. He may be unconventional, but he knows the prophecies better than anyone."

"I suppose a Galilean fisherman is the perfect judge of such things," Judas replied sarcastically. It was now over a month since he had left Arimathaea. He had traveled to Jerusalem and struck up an amusing camaraderie with Andrew bar Jonas, a fisherman from Galilee. Judas had decided to stay for a while, doing his best to stretch his meager savings until Joseph's anger had time to cool. "Ever since I met you during Tabernacles, you've been begging me to come see this baptizer—you've been out here every day since! Well, he is rather entertaining," Judas admitted.

"Nobody knows where he's from," Andrew replied, ignoring Judas's sarcasm. "There are some..." Andrew glanced around cautiously. "There are some who believe he is Elijah, here to announce the Messiah—or the Messiah himself!"

"Ahhh..." Judas said. "That's why you dragged me all the way out here into the desert. Do you think he'll call down fire from heaven?"

"It's not like you had any other pressing plans, Judas," Andrew said hotly. "Now that you've seen him, are you convinced?"

"That this baptizer is Elijah? No," he said with a chuckle.

Andrew was probably a shrewd businessman in Galilee, but in Jerusalem, he was a bit of a yokel. It was common practice for Jerusalem residents to rent their rooftops for Tabernacles at grossly inflated prices. Andrew had been in the process of falling for such a scam when Judas had rescued him. Now, Andrew owed him a favor—which Andrew was attempting to repay by forcing him to sit through the summer heat listening to an educated savage. Andrew's naivety was almost endearing. Almost.

"I don't think he's *the* Elijah, but he knows things. The first time I saw him," Andrew lowered his voice again, "there was a man. He came to be baptized like everyone else, but John... John *refused* to baptize him! John has said from the beginning that he was only here to prepare the way—there would be another. I *saw* him, Judas. I saw *Him!* John did baptize him, and—"

"You've told me before, Andrew. There was a dove, and then the man slipped away into the crowd and disappeared. You've been coming back ever since, hoping to see him again. You've told me the story a dozen times."

"I said it *looked* like a dove—and he didn't 'slip away.' You know, as many times as you claim you've heard this story, you don't seem to have listened to any of them," Andrew replied, only half-joking.

"What if he doesn't return?" Judas asked. "He could have been from Egypt for all you know. He probably came to see John out of curiosity like everyone else. Are you planning on staying in Bethabara indefinitely on the off chance he returns? Eventually, your brother will get tired of doing your share of the fishing."

"He's not Egyptian. I know a Galilean when I see one! You didn't see what I saw. John knows him. John's whole ministry is focused on *him*. Eventually, their paths will cross again."

Judas smiled patiently. "If he's from Galilee, that's probably where he is! Why not return and look for him there?"

"Why come all the way here if you don't believe a word I say?" Andrew asked by way of reply.

"Because if this *dunkard* is half as smart as you say, there is going to be quite a show."

Andrew creased his brows. "What do you mean?"

"Well, my friend, while you were out here looking for a Galilean in the middle of the Judean wilderness, I've been making friends in Jerusalem. Word has it that the Sanhedrin is upset with synagogue attendance. They put together a committee to learn the cause, and the reason why is dressed in nothing more than a rough camel's hair cloak and a leather belt," Judas said, nodding significantly to the wild man. "He's gathered a lot of interest from all classes, and what interests the people interests the Pharisees."

"Their involvement will only mean trouble," Andrew said darkly.

"They teach religion; it's their job. It's not illegal for others to gather disciples, but Pharisees are the experts. People want to know their opinion on things."

"And what is their opinion on John?" Andrew asked.

Judas grinned and glanced at a group of well-dressed men pushing their way toward the crowded riverbank. "I think we're about to find out."

"Are those...?"

Judas nodded as the group pushed their way through the crowd. The shine of metal sparkled in between the fine linens of the rabbis and the dirty cloaks of the commoners. "Romans. Looks like the Sadducees are interested, too. They brought the Temple Guard."

Andrew started to his feet. "We have to—"

Judas pulled him back down. "Relax. We aren't doing anything. They won't arrest him unless he says something to incriminate himself."

"But the soldiers—"

"The Sadducees won't leave Jerusalem without them," Judas assured his friend. "Too many Jews don't like that they work so closely with Rome. They hold the power in Jerusalem, but they don't have the people's respect. The Pharisees do."

"Snakes!" John cried suddenly, interrupting his sermon and high-stepping rapidly out of the water. "There's a nest of snakes here!" The crowd parted in fear at his sudden outcry. Venomous snakes were common in the Jordan Valley, and they occasionally took to water. The bite of a viper was deadly. John ejected himself from the water with impressive speed and danced through the crowd right into the Sanhedrin committee. He froze, his face mere inches from the leader. His panic vanished immediately. "Snakes!" he cried again, staring unflinchingly into the Pharisee's face. "Who invited these snakes?"

For research notes, see chapter 4 in the reference section.

V

Judas chuckled. "Told you there would be a show."

"This is not good," Andrew muttered, more to himself than to Judas.

"Luckily, insulting religious authorities isn't illegal—technically. The man has guts."

"We represent the authority of the Sanhedrin!" the Pharisee replied hotly. "To determine what sort of *teacher* you are." He spat, as if he was anxious to get the taste of the word "teacher" out of his mouth. He retreated a step back to the protective barrier of the Sadducees' guard. Judas recognized the lead Pharisee: Nahum was a rabbi of one of the wealthier synagogues and had been for several decades. He had more reputation than wealth, but the one was as valuable as the other. The six soldiers of the Temple Guard belonged to the two Sadducees lingering at the back of the group. The two factions kept a tenuous truce. Pharisees were known for their strict adherence to the law in every minute detail, but they knew how to play a crowd. Most were upper-middle class and were still considered men of the people. They could be found in any village big enough to have a synagogue. Sadducees, by contrast, were almost exclusively high class. Often rich and always influential, they controlled Jerusalem. Although many in the priesthood tried to maintain neutrality, the majority of priests were Sadducees. They were content to interpret the law in ways which created the least friction between Jewish law and Gentile society. They often worked closely with Romans and Greeks in an effort to smooth the edges that divided Jew from Gentile. This penchant for siding with Gentile authorities alienated them from the poorer populace—a vacancy which the Pharisees filled all too eagerly. Both groups had influential members within the Sanhedrin and fought tirelessly to gain the majority.

"This is a place of repentance!" John shouted, not giving an inch. "Who warned *you* about the impending doom?"

The priests were taken aback at this hostile reception. They were used to deference and humility from practically everyone. Even Herod knew not to push the Sanhedrin *too* far.

Nahum rallied. He was smart enough to realize that John the wild man was immune to intimidation. Unfortunately, he broke the first rule of confrontation: do not engage. "The *Temple* is the place of repentance. We are the Chil—"

"Shut it!" John shouted, reaching down and plucking up a river stone that looked about ten pounds. "Don't even *think* to use that excuse! '*Children of Abraham*'!" he said in mocking disdain. "God can make Abraham more children from these *rocks!*" He threw the rock down dramatically. The two soldiers stepped back quickly, muttering curses as they dodged to keep their toes intact. "Repentance requires *action*," John continued, now addressing the crowd. "Actions are the fruit that prove the root; without it, you're *fruitless*—good for nothing but the ax, cut up for firewood and burned." John was pacing now, still in full control of the crowd, despite the intruders. Judas was starting to think this show might actually be entertaining enough to repay the favor Andrew owed him. Judas slipped closer through the crowd, motioning for Andrew to follow. He wanted to hear this.

"What can we possibly do with Roman taxes crushing us?" someone asked from the safety of the crowd. Several of the Temple Guards cast a glare in the voice's direction but quickly shifted their focus on John to see what answer the preacher might dare while mere inches from Roman steel.

"The answer is simple," John replied with no hesitation. "We help each other. If you have an extra tunic, share it. If you have extra food, share it. God gives all of us something extra. It's our job to give that extra to those who lack."

"Can't share with people who spit in your face when you try and speak to them," came a spiteful comment from further back in the crowd.

John spotted the heckler easily. "Tax collector, yeah?" he asked, appraising the man carefully. The man was better dressed than most of the crowd and stood slightly apart from it. The crowd waited for John's answer. He sighed. "Tax collectors: thieves and traitors. To be a tax collector is to willingly and repeatedly commit the vilest of sins." John turned back to Nahum, the Pharisee, who was stewing in silent rage. "Did I get that pretty close?" John asked sarcastically. "Or is there something you want to add?"

Nahum opened his mouth to reply, but John intentionally cut him off. "What could you *possibly* do to repair *that?!*" he asked the tax collector loudly. The crowd waited for his answer. Judas stole the opportunity to inch closer, but a Roman hand stopped him. The soldier shook his head coldly.

"Number one," John continued, taking a deep breath. "Don't cheat people." The crowd waited, expecting further demands, but there were none. "Simple!" he repeated. "Repentance is for everyone." He cast a significant glance on the priests as well as the Roman Guard. "Everyone."

"You have suggestions for us, too, then?" one of the guards asked half-sarcastically, but obviously impressed enough with John's answers to risk a dark glare from one of the Sadducees.

"Ah," John said with a kind smile. "An excellent question. You have been given power over the life—and death—of the common man. How to be sure that you do not abuse such power?" John asked thoughtfully. "Do not use your position as a threat and make no false accusations."

The solider seemed surprised at this answer. "That's it?" he asked.

Judas chuckled. Any sensible rabbi had an entire list of infractions against soldiers in general and Roman soldiers in particular. Tax collectors were the worst sinners by the *quality* of their sins, but soldiers were a close second by sheer *quantity*: drinking, gambling, Sabbath breaking... The list was endless. Despite this, the priests needed them.

"Maybe... don't complain about your wages?" John added with a shrug, seemingly incapable of recalling anything else.

This finally pushed Nahum over the edge. He stepped forward angrily, fighting to summon a response, but John cut him off again.

"Alright," John said in a calming gesture. "Since we've opened this up for questions, it would not be fair to deny you the opportunity. Go on. You came here to ask me questions; ask away."

Nahum smoothed his *tallith*, the prayer shawl that Pharisees wore practically everywhere and that set them apart from their less pious inferiors. Finally realizing that he had lost control of the crowd—or more accurately, that he never had control to begin with—the old Pharisee cut right to the point. "Who are you?" he asked.

John sighed. "You know who I am, Nahum."

"This is an official inquiry into the claims you make about yourself," Nahum clarified through clenched teeth. "*Not* a social call. If your father was alive... You're a *disgrace* to the priesthood," he spat in a harsh whisper, too quietly for any but the closest to hear.

"I'm not the Christ," John replied loudly, answering the unspoken question.

Nahum relaxed visibly. He was still annoyed, but relieved at John's answer. *Strange.* The Pharisee actually thought this wild man *could be* the Messiah, and he was greatly relieved to hear differently. "Elijah, perhaps?"

"No," John replied with a chuckle.

Nahum smirked. "You're clearly attempting to summon the imagery of a prophet, dressed as you are, living in the wilderness. Are you a prophet, then?"

John shook his head. "Do you want to know who I am?" he asked. "Go back and tell the Council that you heard a voice in the wilderness saying 'Prepare for the king!'"

Nahum relaxed further with this announcement. "So," he said calmly. "You're not claiming to be anyone specific. You're just another common sensationalist looking for the coming Messiah like so many others."

"I am common," John agreed humbly. "Not even qualified to clean *his* sandals. But you're wrong. The Messiah isn't coming; He's *here*. In this very crowd."

For research notes, see chapter 5 in the reference section.

VI

The crowd exploded in tumult at this shocking revelation. Andrew, who had been quiet for most of the confrontation, suddenly seized Judas's arm. "He's here!" he cried, going on tiptoe to scan the crowd. "We have to find him!" He pushed into the crowd, not waiting for a response.

Judas shook his head. Every man, woman, and child of Israel was eagerly waiting for the Messiah, but losing one's wits was not the proper response. There were upwards of five hundred people in this crowd, and it would be impossible to find anyone in the growing chaos—which was John's intention. The Temple Guard was doing its best to keep a safe perimeter around Nahum and the other priests, and rough hands pushed Judas back. He chose a dignified retreat before the truncheons came out—or worse.

He fell in behind the soldiers as they pushed a path through the crowd for the Sadducees. It was the fastest exit, but still took several long minutes before Judas found a point high enough to survey the masses. The wild man's rough camel-hair cloak should have been easy to spot, but he had already disappeared amid the chaos. Andrew could tire himself out in this mess and hope for a miracle, but Judas knew the only sure way of discovering the identity of Andrew's hoped-for Messiah was through John. Luckily for Andrew, Judas's curiosity was piqued.

He knew finding Andrew in this crowd was just as impossible as Andrew's own search, so he left. It was a short trek from the river back to the village of Bethabara. Judas wasn't about to trudge the whole twenty-some odd miles back to Jerusalem when he could simply go to Andrew's rented guestroom. The owner paid him no mind after he explained that he was here to see Andrew. He was enjoying his third cup of wine kindly provided by the hosts, who kindly added it to Andrew's rent, when Andrew finally stumbled in, exhausted, dusty, and disappointed.

"Curses on curses!" Andrew growled, tossing his cloak onto the floor. It landed with a puff of dust as Andrew collapsed onto a woven mat next to Judas. The small household had no servants, but the lord of the house signaled to one of his younger sons, who hurried over to remove Andrew's sandals and wash his feet while the lord brought another bowl of water to wash his hands and face. The water refreshed Andrew but did little to cool his temper. "I was *this* close! *Bar kassoris*, he was *there!* I could have been standing right next to him, and he slipped—Why do you look so pleased with yourself?" he demanded, giving Judas a hard glare.

"This has been the most entertaining afternoon I've had in a long time, Andrew. I'm glad you invited me!" Judas replied with a wide smile.

"Why didn't you help me look?" Andrew asked with a glower. He dismissed the lord and his son with an insulting level of gratitude, which was overlooked, given his mood. They retired, leaving Judas and Andrew alone in the guestroom.

Judas sighed sympathetically. "First of all, I have no idea what John's Messiah even looks like. I assume he's Jewish? Besides, you can't catch fish by chasing them. Even I know enough about fishing to understand *that*."

Andrew gave him a quizzical look. "You catch fish with fishing nets. So what?"

"How do you know where to throw it?"

"Well, if you're day fishing, you throw the net into the boat's shadow, otherwise the fish will see it. Night fishing is easier, but you have to know the lake—where the biggest schools are found—and keep that knowledge to yourself, otherwise the other fishermen will find out and over-fish the spot. If you're indescribably lucky, you might stumble on an underwater spring. If nobody else has found it, you could practically retire just fishing that..." He paused. "What in Sodom's burning *peripsema* does this possibly have to do with John?!"

Judas chuckled. "Now, now, Andrew, there's no reason to use that kind of language. My point is, you have to know where to throw the net. We have no idea where John's successor is. We know nothing about him, and we know hardly more about this John himself. So," Judas continued, "what do you do if you don't know where to throw the net?"

"You find another job," Andrew snapped. "Get to the *koprios* point!"

"You bait the water, and the fish come to you."

"Thank you," Andrew replied sarcastically. "You're so helpful."

"I'm offering you my help, *raca*," Judas said laughingly. "This John is quite a character. Whoever his successor is, I can convince John to tell us."

"You?" Andrew scoffed. "You've seen him once! I've been following his ministry for over a month. He camps in the wilderness—nobody knows where—and he hasn't given a straight answer to anyone since he baptized... baptized *him*—who, I might add, hasn't been seen since."

"Until today," Judas corrected.

"Even so! John didn't point him out. John just said he was in the crowd—knowing the announcement would provoke enough chaos for them both to escape unnoticed. John knows me, but he won't tell me anything! I've asked!"

"I know people."

"You don't know anybody in Bethany!"

"I know how people think, Andrew. You're throwing your net, but you aren't throwing any bait! You've been asking for information without offering any incentive. How does John know you're sincerely interested and not just asking from idle curiosity—or worse?"

"You don't mean that," Andrew said, paling. "No son of Israel would even think of betraying the Messiah."

"John is keeping him secret for a reason, Andrew. Antipas has spies everywhere, just like his father. The Herodians take threats *very seriously*. Try and find a Bethlehemite turning thirty this year."

Andrew scrunched his brow. "What do you mean?"

"No one talks about it. I suspect it was too painful. Herod had every male child under two in Bethlehem killed on a whim because he suspected an heir to the Davidic throne. The entire matter was hushed up, struck from the official records, and mostly forgotten after his death. You wouldn't have heard about it all the way in Galilee. Your parents might have, but only by rumors."

"Oh," Andrew replied, his irritation snuffed out under the weight of such a tragedy. "That's terrible."

"And that's not the only incident. Antipas's own brother was strangled because his father, Herod, feared a coup. How do you think Antipas will react to a challenge from someone outside the Herodian line? Now do you understand why John has to be so careful?"

"I see your point," Andrew admitted slowly. "So, does this mean you believe me? You think John is telling the truth?"

Judas chuckled. "I believe *you* believe it. But John is an interesting man. If you're so determined to find this Messiah of his, I'll help you."

"Do you really think you can?" Andrew asked, sitting up.

"I guarantee it."

"You'll talk to him tomorrow?"

Judas shook his head. "Definitely not."

"Oh, right. You'll want to gather your things from Jerusalem. That will take all day."

"Tomorrow, I talk to Nahum."

"Nahum? The Pharisee? Why?" Andrew asked in confusion. "He came to question John. He knows even less than we do!"

"Nahum knows everything we need to know about John to convince him to trust us. Nahum just doesn't know it."

"What about your things?" Andrew asked. "This could take some time. If you leave things in Jerusalem, they have a way of leaving you and finding new owners."

"You mean those things?" Judas asked, pointing to a sack sitting quietly in the corner.

Andrew gave him a flat look. "You brought all your things here expecting my invitation. What would you have done if I hadn't invited you to stay?"

Judas grinned. "I told you; I know people."

"You're exasperating," Andrew replied with a snort. "I'm going back to Galilee. At least I know how fish think." He shook his head, but his foul mood had passed.

Judas laughed. "You can catch men as easily as fish. Stick with me, Andrew! I'll teach you how."

For research notes, see chapter 6 in the reference section.

VII

Nahum was an easy man to find. Bethabara, or Bethany, as the locals called it, was not a large town, and a contingent of Pharisees visiting from Jerusalem would not go unnoticed. The trick would be in convincing Nahum to speak with him alone. Luck was on his side, however, as there were no homes in Bethabara large enough to house the entire Sanhedrin committee and their guards. Rabbis were always honored guests, but they would need to split up if they wanted to sleep indoors.

Judas left the guestroom before the family woke. He and Andrew's hosts were early risers by necessity, as simple farmers, and Judas congratulated himself on being the first to wake. Andrew would sleep late. Most fishermen worked the sea at night, and although Andrew had been off the sea for more than a month, he still slept late. The family would be long gone by then, but they would be sure to leave him some breakfast.

Judas had other plans. He walked through the quiet streets, picking his way carefully in the dark until his ears picked up the quiet murmur of voices from the center of the village. A thin glow of lamplight crept out from beneath the thick curtain over the door of the synagogue. Pharisees were always early. Not everyone came to synagogue for morning prayers, but the *Habarim* were sure to be here morning, noon, and night. They were always the first to arrive and the last to leave. Judas had often lingered at synagogue in Arimathaea simply to watch the show when several particularly pious types would try to outlast each other.

Today, he was not here for entertainment. He paused at the door to carefully wipe the dust from his feet. He pulled his *tallith* up to cover his head. It was worn and cheaply made, but it would do. His *tefillin* were no better, but he had to wear them, or Nahum would never take him seriously. Unlike the Sadducees, Pharisees did not shun the poorer classes, but their religious obsession made them look with disdain upon any Jew who didn't at least *try* to keep the whole Law, however poorly. Pharisees tended to act superior, but they weren't exclusive. They were always willing to teach.

Judas saw Nahum immediately upon entering. He had hoped to beat him here and make a decidedly positive impression, but the Pharisee had come earlier than anticipated. There were some local Pharisees from Bethabara as well as Nahum's group visiting from Jerusalem. The locals were not nearly as well-dressed as Nahum and his entourage, but it was evident that they were trying their best to make a good impression. Judas settled himself on a wooden bench to quietly wait for the synagogue's rabbi to start the official devotions, then thought better of it and decided to stand and say some prayers of his own while he waited. Not that he put much stock in public prayers, but Nahum clearly did.

The synagogue slowly filled as Judas recited morning prayers that had been drilled into his brain from his schooling as a youth in the *bet ha-midrash*. He didn't worry about repeating himself as the long minutes dragged on; Pharisees would sometimes repeat the same prayer for hours. Who would dare to assume they could improve upon the great traditions?

Finally, daybreak began to overwhelm the power of the oil lamps, and Judas was surprised to note that it was a visiting Sadducee who led the devotions. No wonder the Pharisees were here so early; the local rabbis had snubbed them and were instead giving the honor to a Sadducee. The Pharisees would never openly complain, but they would be sure to arrive far earlier than the Sadducees, proving themselves the more pious and, therefore, the more appropriate choice.

Judas listened to the Sadducee's service and silently gave thanks for his incredible luck. He would have no trouble ingratiating himself with Nahum now. He waited until the services were over and intentionally slipped past the Sadducee without thanking him for his reading. The Sadducee was busy with others and didn't notice the slight, but Nahum did. Nahum gave Judas an appraising glance as he approached. "Shalom, rabbi," Judas said, bowing slightly. "I look forward to hearing your reading on Sabbath. Do you know what scripture you will teach on?"

Nahum's face darkened. "No, friend. We will be leaving for Jerusalem later today. I will not be here for the Sabbath reading."

Judas let his face fall with supreme disappointment. "Oh... I am greatly saddened that I missed your service yesterday."

"We only arrived yesterday. I have not had the honor of teaching in this synagogue," Nahum replied politely but with evident agitation.

Judas went for the kill: "You are obviously the leader of this committee. You are the oldest and most educated. Clearly, you are devout, for you were here even earlier than I, and still you were passed over for the honor of leading services. I naturally assumed the rabbi here must have selected you for a more honorable service, but as you are leaving so soon... How could he have made such a simple oversight?"

Nahum sighed. "The situation here is complicated. Rabbi Caleb made a wise decision under the circumstances."

Judas nodded in understanding. "You mean John, the dunkard. Rabbi Caleb dislikes you questioning John. He profits from the crowds John is attracting and therefore considers you a threat. After the way you handled John yesterday..." Judas decided to lay it on thick, "I'd say he has good cause."

Judas's moniker for the wild man brought a smile to Nahum's lips. He chuckled quietly. "Yes, I do mean John 'the dunkard.' John has many sympathizers here, and Rabbi Caleb is wise enough not to anger them."

"I suppose," Judas admitted, "but it seems to me that one should never hesitate to speak truth simply because it is unpopular. I was there yesterday, and I saw the way you cornered John into answering your questions—clever, by the way. Rabbi Caleb would look bad if he refused to let any of the visiting rabbis teach, but he couldn't let you teach for fear of looking like he condoned your questioning. The rabbi is shrewd to not openly condemn John, but John's disregard for the Law is alarming. He called you a viper! I understand John is the new sensation, but that is no excuse. We have enough Sadducees twisting the Law as they see fit, but to offer baptism to a tax collector while calling our Brotherhood venomous snakes... It's unthinkable!"

"Certainly, I agree with what you have said, but John's is a unique case. It requires some finesse."

After the debacle at the river, Judas almost asked the Pharisee when he planned to start utilizing the required finesse, but he bit back the reply. "John isn't the first sensationalist to make claims on Messianic prophecy," he countered. "John is the newest in a long line—nothing special." There was a delicate balance between agreeing with people to gain their trust and arguing enough that they defended their position.

For a moment, Judas thought he might have pressed too far. Nahum's lips pressed into a thin line, but finally, he motioned for Judas to follow him into a secluded corner. He leaned close, speaking in a low whisper. "John is a special case. He has... history. It's why I was selected to lead this committee. I knew his father."

"I'm sensing there is more to this story."

"There is," Nahum replied with a nod. "John's father was a priest— served in the Temple, well-respected in the Sanhedrin. We both served in Abia, so I knew him somewhat. It was about thirty years ago, just before John was born. Zacharias was quite old, even then. There was an incident while he was offering incense. He was inside longer than usual."

"Doesn't seem so odd," Judas replied.

"He didn't speak afterward for nine months—not until his son's naming day. He claimed to have seen a vision while in the temple, prophesying the birth of his son."

"And you believe it?" Judas asked.

Nahum sighed. "It's easy to dismiss this type of claim. Zacharias would never have lied, but old men can become senile. His wife actually giving birth to a child at her age... Well, it does summon up imagery of Isaac, the promised seed of Abraham. The symbolism is striking—and hard to dismiss."

"If his father was a priest...?" Judas asked.

Nahum shook his head. "Zacharias died before John was old enough to serve. John was well-educated in the *bet ha-midrash*, but he left the school after his parents died. No one knew what had become of him until recently, when he reappeared from the wilds dressed like a prophet from centuries ago and summoning up Messianic imagery."

"And yet he has rejected the priesthood and mocks the teachers of the Law."

Nahum's face grew dark. "Yes. Considering his history, it is deeply disturbing. Especially since he is not naming himself the Messiah. He's obviously not asking for money or position. He has no discernible motive other than repentance, but his form of 'repentance' stands opposed to everything the Law represents. You see the problem."

"John is turning the Law into something it isn't, which countless others have also tried, but his birth and lineage give him a level of legitimacy that makes him into something far more dangerous."

"Far more dangerous," Nahum agreed with a sigh. "But," he shrugged, "this is a decision for the Sanhedrin, not you and I. Besides, I am growing hungry, and Rabbi Caleb has provided a grand breakfast for our visiting committee before we return to Jerusalem. You may come as my guest if you like."

Judas smiled to himself. He had been hoping for a better breakfast than Andrew's hosts could provide. He would have helped Andrew from sheer curiosity, but sometimes success was its own tasty reward. "I would be most honored, rabbi," he said, bowing graciously. "Perhaps, after everyone finishes their obligatory fawning over the morning's service, I could persuade you to give us your insights on the words of the prophet, Isaiah. John referenced a passage, I believe, and I would greatly enjoy your insight—if you have time before your return to Jerusalem."

Nahum smiled kindly as the two men left the synagogue for Caleb's house and breakfast. "Yes, I would be happy to give you my insights. What passage was it, if you recall?" Nahum asked, subtly testing to see if Judas's knowledge of Torah was genuine, or if he was simply using the question as a ploy to gain Nahum's confidence.

Why must it be one or the other? Judas smiled. "It begins, 'Comfort, comfort ye my people, saith your God...'"

For research notes, see chapter 7 in the reference section.

VIII

Judas was fuming by the time he finally left Bethabara for the Jordan. Tired, sweating, thirsty, and fuming. The breakfast had gone wonderfully. Judas had managed to ingratiate himself adequately with the other rabbis. Nahum's exposition on the prophecies of Isaiah had gone over splendidly, and Nahum knew it. After, Nahum had made a special point of introducing Judas and asking for his opinion on various subjects. Judas was no rabbi, but his formal education at least gave him familiarity with the subjects, and his knack for reading people did the rest.

And then he had been accosted by a tent squad of Roman legionnaires on their way to Machaerus. Romans could be brutal and ruthless, but usually, Roman soldiers were hardly more than a nuisance. By law, any subject of Rome was required to carry a soldier's gear upon demand. Legally, a man was only required to carry the soldier's pack a single mile, so the man would not be forced to travel too far out of his way while the soldier was still given a short rest from carrying his heavy equipment. The law benefited the soldiers without putting too much hardship on the people they protected—in theory. It was part of the "tax" paid to the soldiers for fighting to maintain the Pax Romana. Low-level grunts like legionnaires were rarely cruel, but when they were out from under the nose of their *decanus*, soldiers had a penchant for abusing their authority. The law was intended to mean that a man could not be forced to go more than one mile out of his way, and that was how it was typically enforced, but there was a loophole for those cruel enough to exploit it. The law applied to the demands of a single soldier on a single Roman subject. When you had carried a soldier's pack for the obligatory mile, he could demand no more. But a second soldier...

Eight soldiers. Eight Roman pigs had each forced him, one by one, to carry their packs for the required mile. They had come into Bethabara with expectations of finding eight sturdy Jews to carry their packs, but with all the working men in the fields, Judas had been the only Jew on the roads, and the soldiers were tired. He had walked eight sun-cursed miles toward Machaerus, before they had let him come back. Their *decanus* would never have dared allow such blatant exploitation from his legionnaires, but what the squad leader didn't know wouldn't hurt them.

Judas was hot and thirsty, but he was too angry to feel the fatigue of the last sixteen miles. His throat was parched, but he marched through town without stopping for a drink, heading for the river where he had first seen John. He was fuming with the kind of anger that would only end when he finally reached his goal.

The wild man's camp was impossible to find, but John would preach in the same area for several days before moving on. Judas had met John for the first time yesterday, but he certainly knew of the man; John's ministry was well-known. John stayed mostly in Judea, but he traveled all along the Jordan and its tributaries.

Sure enough, John had taught in the same place, but Judas was too late. The crowd was already breaking up. Judas saw Andrew on the outskirts as he approached, obviously trying the same technique as yesterday to spot John's successor—and failing. Andrew did spot Judas, though. He rushed up, ecstatic. "He was here again! I'm sure of it! He can't be..." Judas marched right past him. "Judas! Where—did you hear me?! Judas!"

Straight into the crowd, Judas pushed until he reached the river. John was gone, having disappeared into the crowd or the underbrush. Judas didn't care. He stepped into the mud of the river, soaking his clothes, and waded out to where the muddy water turned clear. He sunk his face into the cool water and took a long drink. And then another. Finally, he let the cool water wash away the dust and mud on his feet and the anger steaming from him.

Andrew stared in shock from the riverbank. "Where *have* you been?" he asked. "You disappeared before breakfast, and the first thing you do is stomp right through the mud you were complaining about yesterday! What's gotten into you?"

Finally freed from his anger and his thirst, Judas straightened and started back to solid ground. "I was planning on being here, but instead I— agh!" He slipped on a rock and went down with a splash. He righted himself quickly and exited the river, now completely soaked.

Andrew burst into laughter at this unfortunate accident. "You're supposed to have *someone else* baptize you," he said between bouts of laughter. "Still," he laughed, "I'm sure John would appreciate the enthusiasm!"

"So," Judas said, not at all amused. He pulled up his robes to step out of the muddy water and collect what was left of his dignity. "Here again, huh? That's a good sign. It means he's staying nearby."

"Yes, but who knows for how long?" Andrew countered. "He might disappear tomorrow! It's been over a month since his first appearance!"

"Do you know where John is staying?" Judas asked politely.

"Well, no! But—"

"Then we'll never find him tonight. We'll return tomorrow, Andrew," Judas said consolingly, giving his friend a soaking wet embrace. Andrew pulled away. "Don't sulk," Judas added, "or I'll baptize you, too."

"We can't!" Andrew lamented. "John's moving on. He's not preaching tomorrow, and John's the only link we have! If you had only been here, we could have... You should have been here instead of rubbing noses with those Pharisees!"

"Relax, Andrew. It couldn't be helped," Judas said soothingly. "The Roman guard forced me into service. I would have been here if I wasn't dragging their gear halfway to Machaerus!" He paused as Andrew's words sunk in. "What do you mean, he's not preaching tomorrow?"

"He's moving on! He only stays in one area for a few weeks. No one knows where John will go. *John* probably doesn't even know where John will go! And I can't keep following him without money. I have to go back to Galilee. It's hopeless. We've missed our chance." Andrew kicked a rock in frustration.

Judas grabbed his shoulders. "Andrew, look at me. Have a little faith in my abilities, would you? I'm not giving up and neither are you. I didn't spend all morning with a bunch of pompous Pharisees for nothing! Listen, the Sanhedrin has been gathering reports for a long time. They've been watching John's movements for six months."

"That doesn't mean they know where he will be next!" Andrew cried angrily.

Judas chuckled. "Of course not. The rabbis study Torah. I study people." He grinned.

"You mean..." Andrew's eyebrows rose.

Judas nodded. "John—savage that he is—is still a son of Levi. He is a man of order and precision. He's crafted his movements carefully to look random, but they aren't." He grinned. "I know where he's going."

For research notes, see chapter 8 in the reference section.

IX

"This is crazy. You know that, right?" Andrew asked. "He's not coming. Just admit you were wrong."

Judas sighed contentedly. "I admit nothing," he replied, shifting to a more comfortable position as he leaned against the trunk of a tree. The two men had risen early, which had instantly put Andrew in a poor mood, and followed the Jordan north toward Galilee. "He'll be here."

Andrew grumbled something impolite under his breath and reached into their empty satchel, looking for more food. Lunch had come and gone hours ago.

"John's options are limited. He has to pick a place close enough to civilization to gather a crowd but also where he can slip away unseen. This is the spot. He'll be here to survey the area by sundown, before the Sabbath starts. He'll go into town tomorrow and announce at the local synagogue his intentions to preach here over the next few weeks. The following afternoon, he'll have a crowd."

"Unless you're wrong—which you are. There's no possible way you can predict someone's movements from hearsay—especially someone like John. He's too unpredictable."

Judas shrugged. "He's *predictably* unpredictable."

"Oh, sure. I've been following him for a month, but you meet him once and you know how he thinks," Andrew said with enough snark to wrap the statement up two or three times.

Judas dropped the subject, and the two sat in silence until Andrew decided to refill their empty waterskins from the river. He stood to stretch, but Judas snatched the back of his cloak and yanked him down again, clamping a hand over Andrew's mouth to stifle his surprise as the larger man tumbled to the ground. Andrew gave him a puzzled look, until Judas pointed to a familiar form moving toward the riverbank from the opposite shore. "Wait until he gets closer to the river, then come from the road. I'll circle around behind. He shouldn't be alarmed, but if he runs, I'll follow."

"Are you sure about this?" Andrew asked.

"Will you trust me for one single time?" Judas asked.

"Ugh... fine," Andrew said with a shake of his head.

"Just give me a few minutes. I'll have to swim across, and I'll need a head start—John is likely a far better swimmer than me."

Andrew eyed Judas's scholarly frame with a skeptical expression. "Shouldn't *I* be the one swimming across? I'm a fisherman, after all."

Judas slapped his forehead. "Of course! Why didn't I think of that? Maybe it's because you're a head taller than me, and John would hear you stomping through the brush like an ox from a mile away."

Andrew stiffened. "I can be quiet when I want."

"Good!" Judas whispered. "Now is your chance! Shh!"

"John! John!" Andrew shouted in reply, standing up too quickly for Judas to snatch him back down. John looked over in surprise but broke into a smile at seeing Andrew's face. "See? He's not going to run. Have some faith," Andrew said, giving Judas a soft kick as he crouched out of sight.

"Ow!" Judas grumbled. "I do have faith, but I also like to have a backup plan. Uh... hello, friend!" he said, dusting himself off as he stood up and saluted John.

"What's going on there?" John asked suspiciously, starting toward the two men.

"Oh, just a... theological dispute," Judas said, plastering a smile on his face. John must have noticed the tussle. "Right, Andrew?" Judas asked, slapping him on the back.

"Uh... right!" Andrew said uncomprehendingly.

Judas brushed dirt from his friend's cloak. "Actually, John, we came to see you."

"To see me?" the wild man asked in surprise. "Here?"

"Yes," Judas said, correctly guessing that John's surprise came more from being found than from being sought. "We saw you in Bethabara. Andrew has been following your teachings for over a month."

John smiled politely. "I see," he said slowly. "And you followed me here?"

"On the contrary," Judas said quickly. "Nothing knows this wilderness like you, except a wild goat. No, Andrew and I have been waiting here most of the afternoon in order to meet you."

"Why here?" John asked, narrowing his eyes. "What made you think I would be here?"

"You did! The Pharisees can't seem to find you, but you're more predictable than you realize." Judas shrugged apologetically.

"Can't say anyone's called me that before," John admitted.

"You move to small towns away from Jerusalem after a feast and slowly make a circuit back to Jerusalem before the next. Generally, you move only a town or two over from wherever you preached last, but when things with the Council get too heated, you break pattern and move either north or south a full day's walk along the Jordan, while they look for you nearby. You spoke with them in Bethabara, so a day's walk north puts you... here," Judas said with a smug grin.

"I'm not preaching today," John said coldly. "Come back after Sabbath."

"Please!" Andrew interrupted, who had been following the conversation with growing perplexity. "We are sincere followers, and we have only one question," he begged.

"My life is private for a reason," John said curtly, turning to leave. "Good day."

Judas attempted to repair the damage Andrew's indelicacy had done by gambling everything on one play: "We already know everything about you, John ben Zacharias."

John froze. "Where did you hear that name?" he asked quietly.

"I know your birth was predicted by an angel as your father ministered in the Temple. I know you were born long after your parents had given up hope, just like our forefather, Isaac, and I know you are *not* the Messiah."

"No," John said, turning slightly. "I'm not the Messiah." He turned again to go.

"'The voice of him that crieth in the wilderness,'" Judas quoted. "'Prepare ye the way of the Lord.' You're not the Messiah, but you *are* his messenger."

"'What shall I cry?'" John asked, turning to Judas with piqued curiosity as he continued the quote from Isaiah.

Judas chose to skip the typical answer provided by the ancient prophet and moved ahead a few lines. "'Say unto the cities of Judah: Behold your God!'"

John stared at him in surprise at this unexpected answer.

"*You* are God's messenger," Judas continued, recognizing the growing excitement in the wild man. "Your purpose is to proclaim the Messiah's coming! Fulfill it! 'To whom then will ye liken God? Or what likeness will ye compare unto him?'"

Andrew paled visibly at this quotation, which was high blasphemy given the unspoken undertones of the conversation. "Those questions are meant to be rhetorical!" he said nervously.

"Are they?" Judas asked, not taking his eyes from John. Judas knew he had struck the right chord in John's mind. The wild preacher's excitement was reaching a crescendo at Judas's recognition of his ministry's true purpose. John took a deep breath, and Judas recognized the hesitation. Even now, John weighed the risk of revealing the Messiah's identity, but both men knew the words Judas had spoken were far too bold to be the words of a Sanhedrin spy.

John hesitated, and his eyes wandered to the roadway beside the river, where the occasional group of travelers could be seen on the northern road from Bethabara. A small group had attracted his attention, and his eyes widened. "There!" he said, pointing to a man in the passing group. "'Lift up your eyes and behold who has created these things!' There is your Lamb of God!"

At first, the coincidence seemed too great that the very man they sought should appear on the road at that exact moment, but the look on John's face was impossible to fake, for John was struck by the same supernatural timing. Judas's eyes searched the group as they passed, trying to find which of the men John had indicated. Then his eyes locked on John's Messiah, and the coincidence doubled.

Judas recognized him.

For research notes, see chapter 9 in the reference section.

X

Andrew's face lit with excitement. "Let's go!" he said, running after the group of travelers without a second glance.

Judas smiled politely at the man who had trusted them with this revelation. "Thank you, my friend. You've done well." He bowed gratefully to the wild man.

"God's peace be with you," John replied, watching Andrew disappear with a somewhat wistful expression.

"It will get worse, you know," Judas said, watching the preacher. "Seeing your followers leave you for *him*. Eventually, all eyes will turn to him."

John smiled and nodded thoughtfully. "I hope so."

Judas was impressed. John cared nothing about his own popularity. He was perfectly content to fade into the background once his job was done. It took an extraordinary man to get such a drink of fame and pass it to another without a hint of jealousy. Judas looked at this educated savage with new admiration. "You're an extraordinary man, John," he said in a moment of rare honesty. "Shalom."

He left John to his solitude and ran to catch up to Andrew before the country fisherman caused too much damage. Andrew knew the man's face and there was no telling what he would blurt out once he got a chance to talk to John's Messiah. This was a delicate situation for which Andrew was unprepared. Blessedly, Andrew was following along at the back of the group, hesitant to approach the man he thought to be the Messiah.

Judas fell in beside him at the back of the group. "I don't know what to say!" Andrew said in a low whisper. "What do you say to... to *him?!*"

It was quite a dilemma, Judas had to admit: how to introduce yourself to the One on whom hung all the hopes and dreams of a nation from the last fifteen hundred years?

Judas had no such dilemma. "Watch and learn, my fishy friend," he said, slapping Andrew on the back. "Jesus!" he called. "Jesus bar Joseph!"

Jesus turned, and a flash of realization crossed his face as he recognized Joseph of Arimathaea's former steward. Judas was shocked at the carpenter's gaunt face. The man was thin—terribly thin. He must have fallen on hard times, and Judas's stomach clenched as he wondered if the man's suffering was somehow related to Judas's own underhanded dealings. It was possible that Joseph had vented his rage—which should have been focused solely on Judas—on Jesus instead. For a moment, he hesitated, wondering if Jesus might be less than pleased at seeing him, but Jesus's thin face broke into a wide smile. "Judas!" he said cheerfully. "It's good to see you, my friend. How are you?" he asked, genuine concern in his tone.

"How am I?" Judas asked in shock. "How are *you?* You look like you haven't eaten since I saw you over a month ago! What happened? Did Joseph—I mean, I hope he didn't force you—"

Jesus raised a hand. "Joseph of Arimathaea and I parted on good terms. I did not have to slip away in the night," he said knowingly.

Judas's stomach flipped. Jesus knew about his deception. "Did he..."

"He honored the cancellation of my father's debt."

"Of course he did," Judas replied, hiding his relief. "He's an honest man, and you were totally ignorant of the deception."

"But *you* cannot claim ignorance," Jesus replied.

Judas eyed him curiously. "No..." he admitted, trying to discern Jesus's point. "But Joseph and I were parting on bad terms anyway, so you gained, and I had nothing left to lose."

Jesus sighed. "That isn't the point. You had no right to forgive debts that were not your own."

Judas gave him a condescending stare. "You aren't feeling guilty, are you? I know your father and Joseph have history, but Joseph won't miss that money! Talk all you want about the letter of the law, but I'm stealing no food from hungry mouths. Joseph can afford to lose the money, while you can't afford to pay it. Are you not grateful in the slightest?" he asked, somewhat incensed.

Jesus smiled kindly. "I am grateful for your *desire* to be generous, but being generous with another person's money isn't generosity. It's theft."

"Your debt was forgiven!" Judas said defensively. "The end result is still the same."

Jesus nodded in consideration. "Except that I left Joseph on good terms, and you did not."

Judas had to admit the carpenter made a good point. "Sometimes," he said thoughtfully, "villains must do what good men cannot. David's hands were covered in too much blood for him to build the Temple, but he did what was necessary for its completion. Without him, it would never have been built."

Jesus hummed thoughtfully. "Is that what you want to be, Judas? A villain?"

Judas sighed. "It's not about what I want. It's about what needs to be done. I'll make that sacrifice if I have to."

The conversation died as Andrew finally got up the nerve to approach. The travelers were moving in the same direction, but not all as one group. Andrew caught up and looked at Jesus with unbridled admiration.

"What can I do for you?" Jesus asked politely, noting Andrew's expression.

Andrew answered by summoning up a very good impersonation of a gasping fish.

"This is Andrew bar Jonas," Judas said, chuckling. "From Galilee. He catches fish. You might be able to tell by the resemblance."

"Welcome to the conversation, Andrew," Jesus said with a hearty smile. "I much prefer you up here rather than skulking in the rear." He glanced at Andrew's and Judas's packs. "Are you boys staying somewhere nearby? It will be sundown soon."

"Well, we were staying in Bethabara, before—"

"Where are *you* staying, teacher?" Andrew broke in, unthinking.

Jesus chuckled awkwardly at this bold question.

Judas quickly intervened. "We will make arrangements at the next village." He licked his lips, trying to find a tactful way of approaching the subject. Jesus was clearly starving. He had no food for himself, let alone guests, and any honorable host would be obligated to offer his last morsel to a guest. To force that social expectation upon a man in Jesus's condition was unthinkable. "We have no food, but we can buy some in the next village, and you are welcome to stay with us wherever we camp."

"It's almost Sabbath," Jesus replied. "The shops will be closed." He laughed. "Stay with me. I have a house nearby. And," he added, with a sly smile, "it has plenty of food for all of us."

It was Judas's turn to look like a fish, as he tried to process how a man with plenty of food could look so thin. Perhaps the man had some wasting disease, but surely the Savior of Israel would not be some diseased wretch. The man looked healthy otherwise, but he was *so thin*... Perhaps John was wrong, but something about the man's demeanor made Judas think otherwise.

"I've been away from home for a while," Jesus said. "I had some things I needed to do, but now I am ready."

"Ready for what?" Andrew asked.

Jesus smiled. "Come and see."

For research notes, see chapter 10 in the reference section.

XI

Judas and Andrew spent the Sabbath with Jesus bar Joseph. The man had a simple home which he had likely built. He was clearly a skilled craftsman. Jesus had prepared a simple meal of bread and vegetables for supper, and all three men had dug into it as if they were starving—which, one of them was.

Jesus's apparent starvation was inexplicable. His house was well-stocked. Judas knew it would have been rude to ask outright and Jesus had chosen to remain silent on the subject, though he had easily spoken on many others. The man was highly intelligent, but it was clear his knowledge came from personal observation rather than rabbinical schools. The man was completely unassuming. He had treated Judas and Andrew as equals even though Andrew was far less educated.

Andrew had managed to make it through the entire day without putting his foot in his mouth, which was impressive. He was convinced that Jesus was the Messiah simply because John the dunkard was convinced. Judas was less certain. If Jesus was the Messiah, he was not the Messiah *yet*. Thin as he was, the man was in no condition to raise an army or to lead one. Judas was unsure if John simply considered Jesus to be the best candidate or if John had some special knowledge. There were signs tied to John's birth. There might also be signs regarding the birth of Jesus, but Jesus had said his family moved to Galilee from Egypt. Andrew might not know the prophecy foretelling the Messiah's birth in Bethlehem, but John surely would. Why would John place the Messianic mantle on an Egyptian? It made no sense.

Andrew, simpleton that he was, had begged Jesus to come with him to Bethsaida to meet his brother. Jesus had agreed, which might indicate that Andrew was smarter than he acted—at least regarding diet. The Jonas brothers were successful fishermen, and Jesus would benefit from a diet rich in fish. It was hard to bulk up on vegetables. Andrew had forgotten to invite Judas in his enthusiasm, and Judas hadn't pushed the subject. He had needed to return to Jerusalem. There was precious little work for an educated man in backwater Galilee. So Jesus had accompanied Andrew to Bethsaida, and Judas had returned to Jerusalem to pursue temporary work—and other things...

It was odd how often Judas's thoughts returned to the Nazarene. He glanced around the constricting walls of the dark alley where he waited. He didn't often frequent the slums of the lower city. Even in Jerusalem, there were places where wise men—and Roman guards—would not dare go.

He waited in the shadows with nothing but a waning moon to light the dark street. Judas kept his eyes on the ends of the narrow alley, watching for danger. He flinched in sudden alarm as a dark form appeared beside him with a soft thud. While watching the street, he had neglected the rooftops.

The man's face was covered, and his tunic was shortened to allow him ease of movement for fight or flight. His cloak was tucked into his belt but open in the front, giving him a perfect place to hide his long dagger while also leaving it within easy reach. The man didn't reach for the dagger, but Judas knew he didn't need to. They both knew it was there, and they both knew the man could put it anywhere he wished before Judas could react.

"You have money?" the man asked gruffly.

Judas pulled back with a start. "Where's the Canaanite?" he demanded. The man stiffened, and Judas hastily continued before the dagger came out. "Simon—he's my usual contact." Simon was no less dangerous than this new *Sicari*, but Judas had known the Canaanite long enough to render him predictable. This new man...

The man relaxed and lowered his mask, exposing a face that was no less fearsome than the mask itself. "Simon is gone. I'm your contact. I was told you only made drops during the feasts. Why now? Did you come into some kind of unexpected windfall?"

"Not exactly," Judas admitted. "Joseph discovered the skimming. I won't be able to send money for a while."

The man growled. "Pity. We valued your support."

"I still support your mission!" Judas said passionately. "No Lord but God! I may not be able to give much, but I will find other work. I'll find a way to help."

"You know how you could help," the man said darkly.

"I'm no assassin," Judas said tiredly. "I want to break the yoke of Rome as much as any Jew, but I know my limits. You fight with swords and daggers. I fight with numbers and letters. I was not made for battle. I must support the resistance in other ways."

"Apparently you can't," the man spat.

"I didn't *want* to get fired!" Judas huffed. "Do you know the penalty for theft of that scale?! My life was at risk just as much as yours!"

"Better if you had died. You've outlived your usefulness. You failed, Judas. You failed Israel. We need men who are not afraid to do what is necessary. Many men are willing to sympathize with our cause and reap the rewards, but few are willing to get blood on their hands. What about you, Judas? Are you willing to do what it takes or not?"

"I would do anything for Israel!" Judas seethed. "But I know my limitations. I'm no fighter, and I'm no assassin. But... I'll be staying in Jerusalem for a while. I might be able to get information for you. I'm good with people. I have connections from my time under Joseph. I know Pharisees. I can infiltrate their circles."

"Really?" the man asked, his question riddled with sarcasm. "We don't kill Pharisees. We kill traitors. Pharisees are not generally included in that group."

"What's your name?" Judas asked.

"Simon," the man said sardonically.

Judas gave the man a humorless glare. "I liked Simon. You're not him."

"Call me Ishmael," the *Sicari* replied.

"A strange name for an Israelite," Judas mused aloud.

"It suits the purpose—not that you will use it again. You are useless to us, Judas."

"Joseph had many connections to the rich and powerful—connections I can use! I know that information will be useful to your superiors. Take me to your commander; I'm sure he'll see things differently."

Ishmael laughed coldly. "No one sees the Son of the Father until he has shed the blood of Israel's enemies. But I'll be sure to pass along your recommendation," he added mockingly.

"What happened to Simon?" Judas demanded.

"He disappeared. That's all you need to know. As you said, you're no assassin." Ishmael turned and crawled back onto the rooftops by bracing against the two walls of the narrow alley.

He disappeared before Judas could even process the feat of speed and agility, and with Ishmael also disappeared Judas's hopes to finally do something meaningful. Israel was drowning in Roman debt and corruption. Not only were they being taxed into poverty, but also being absorbed by the Roman state. The people were forgetting what it meant to be Israel as Greek culture slowly digested them. Judas felt the same way. Everything was crumbling around him. He had lost his position under Joseph and his position within the Resistance in one fell swoop, though he hadn't realized it until now.

But hope remained. The Messiah was still coming—might even be here. The *Sicarii* fought to ensure there would still be an Israel when the Messiah came. They waited for him as much as any son of Abraham. Ishmael put no value on Judas's skills, but when Judas returned with proof of the Messiah's true identity, the leader of the *Sicarii* would be forced to admit his value.

Judas wasn't useless. He was going to find the truth. He was going to find the true Messiah.

For research notes, see chapter 11 in the reference section.

XII

"*Jesus?*" the old man asked.

"Yes," Judas said. "The carpenter, Jesus ben Joseph. What do you know about him?"

The man gave a spiteful laugh. "Mary's *bastard*, you mean. He's no son of Joseph. I liked Joseph—watched him grow up—respected him. But then he met Mary. She was trouble. Everybody knew it but him. She's a *pacifist*," the man spat, more forcefully than Judas had expected, but this *was* Nazareth. They hated the Roman occupation as much as the *Sicarii* did, but they would never stoop to assassinations to break it. Their consciences wouldn't let them take their hatred that far, even though they wanted to. This conundrum produced a level of anger that permeated just about every social interaction in the small community. It was no wonder Jesus's peaceful amiability hadn't thrived here.

"*Ben Zonah*," the old man snarled. "Jesus is probably half-gentile himself. Mary got herself pregnant while she was engaged to Joseph, but the whole town knew it wasn't his. Probably some Roman's *mamzer*. Joseph was a good man, except he was too weak to do what needed done. Should have stoned her outright, but nobody could prove who the father was, and Joseph had a soft spot for his whore. Nobody dared touch her while he was around. Why'd you say you were asking questions?" The man was naturally suspicious of any stranger asking questions, as everyone in Nazareth was.

Thankfully, Judas was pretty good at finding ways around that. "Official Sanhedrin inquiry. When a man quits his job to become a rabbi, the Sanhedrin will often look into his background." Judas had no idea if Jesus had any intentions of becoming a teacher, but the excuse was plausible, and one which would get the old Nazarene talking.

"Ha!" the man said disdainfully. "Always did act like he was better'n us. Not surprised. Good riddance, I say. His brothers are alright, though. Do good work."

"He has siblings?"

"Sure, but Mary treated Jesus special, like he was better'n Joseph's other sons. Like his *mamzer* father had something Joseph didn't. Joseph let it slide. She treated him alright besides that, but... I just never could quite forgive either of 'em. She broke Joseph's heart, an' he married her anyway. For any respectable man to marry a woman who did that... Look," he said with a heavy sigh. "Jesus never gave nobody cause to hate him. He keeps the Law, but he's just... He don't fit in. Don't belong here. Makes people down-right uncomfortable."

"I can believe it," Judas said graciously, without giving the man any hint as to his own feelings. "One thing I don't understand: I was told Joseph moved to Nazareth from Egypt, but you're saying he grew up here?"

"Yep," the old man agreed, leaning back against the side of his house. Nazareth didn't have city gates per se, but the houses which bordered the main road into town had benches, which sufficed. It was where anyone went who wanted information about a given place. Old men often lingered around the city gates to offer information and advice. It gave them an important role, even if they could no longer work. Today, though, there was only one. "Joseph was respected," the man said, nodding his wrinkled head. "It's Mary that ruined him—thought she was better'n us, and he let her get away with what she did. But it's bad luck to speak ill of a widow," he added in a rare moment of humility.

Judas nodded in commiseration. "Too many Roman sympathizers in the cities down south."

"Right!" the man said. "It's those Sadducees, you know, trying to keep peace with the Romans when there's no peace to be had."

"I have it on good authority that Joseph moved to Nazareth from Egypt," Judas said, struggling to keep the man on topic.

"Huh. You know, he never did say where he went," the man said, scratching his beard, where all his hair had migrated to spend the winter of the man's life.

"What do you mean?" Judas asked, curiosity piqued.

"Joseph grew up here, but his family's from Bethlehem. Had to go back for the census. You wouldn't remember that—happened before you was born."

"About thirty years ago, wasn't it?"

"Yep," the man grunted, unwilling to discuss matters pertaining to Roman rule.

Judas sat for a moment, putting together the pieces. "Was this before or after Jesus's birth?"

"During, most like. Mary was near ready to deliver when they left."

"So Jesus was born here while Joseph was away?" Judas asked.

The man grunted and shook his head. "Nah. Took her with him."

"*Took her with him?*" Judas asked. "A woman in her condition on such a dangerous journey? That's unheard of! Why would he do that?! Women aren't required to present themselves unless they are widows or have none to represent them."

The man shifted uncomfortably. "Suppose he knew what would happen if he left her behind," he said, somewhat reluctantly. "You know what the Law requires. Some folks aren't so lenient as me."

Judas instantly grasped the implication. "She would have been stoned."

"It was a long time ago," the man admitted. "We all saw what it did to Joseph when he found out. He was all heart, Joseph was. Couldn't bring himself to put her away, but we knew it broke him inside. General consensus was that he'd be better off if someone did what he couldn't bring himself to do. He knew what would happen if he left her here alone. Didn't return for some years. Left his house and business to rot. Left all his tools... Strangest thing. Never said where he went. Guess it was Egypt."

"I guess it was," Judas said, his mind furiously throwing the facts together into a startling picture. "Joseph went to *Bethlehem* for Caesar's census? Why Bethlehem?"

"It's David's city. Joseph's of that line."

Judas paled. "It's possible Jesus was born there?" he asked with bated breath.

"Well, unless she gave birth on the road. Can't imagine she'd have held out long. They stayed here in Nazareth for weeks, hoping she'd give birth first, until they was afraid they'd miss the census. Finally gave up and went anyhow. You're asking awful specific questions. Why's the Sanhedrin interested in this?" the man asked.

"Just gathering information," Judas said numbly. His mind was elsewhere. The time of the census lined up perfectly with Herod's murder of the innocents. The prophecies predicted the Messiah's birth in Bethlehem as the heir to David's throne. If Jesus had been born in Bethlehem... Joseph might have fled to Egypt to escape Herod's paranoia, not daring to return to Nazareth. But if Jesus *was* the Messiah, Herod's paranoia would be well-founded. Joseph's son would be an heir to the Davidic throne. Perhaps John had put together these same pieces.

But Jesus was *not* Joseph's son. Surely, John would be smart enough not to promote a known bastard as the Messiah. It made no sense, and yet the coincidences were too striking to dismiss. Herod had killed all children under the age of two in Bethlehem only a month after the census. Why then? Herod had been a madman, to be sure, but something must have triggered such a violent response. *Response to what, though?* Joseph and Mary would have still been in Bethlehem at that time, recovering from the birth. Joseph might have risked his wife's life once, but he would not risk the journey again so soon—not with a newborn and not without good cause.

They must have been warned. Why else would Joseph abandon his home and business? Something must have forced him to escape the country to save the child's life. Jesus might well be the only man his age who could claim Bethlehem as his birthplace. No other explanation made sense. The birth in Bethlehem, Herod's attack, the link to the Davidic line, the signs surrounding John's birth and his link to the priesthood, the wild man's absolute certainty that Jesus was the coming Messiah: it was all too much to ignore, but... a *bastard?* It made no sense—but Judas suddenly realized it *could* make sense, and the implication nearly struck him down. It was impossible. It was insane! It was perfect. Joseph had gone to extreme lengths to protect a child that *wasn't his.* What if Joseph knew something about the child no one else did?

Prophecies were often figurative. One such prophecy in Isaiah had always been taken as symbolic with some esoteric meaning, but what if it *wasn't* symbolic? What if it was literal? It was impossible, but still... Israel's own *history* was impossible. What if the *single greatest sign* of the Messiah's arrival was one no one believed?

"The Lord himself shall give you a sign. Behold, a virgin shall conceive, and bear a son, and shall call his name Immanuel."

For research notes, see chapter 12 in the reference section.

XIII

As winter settled in, Judas buried himself in his work. He was convinced that Jesus was the promised Messiah, but he had no idea how to process that knowledge or what to do with it. Perhaps Jesus himself didn't know. John the dunkard had put his ministry on hold for the winter, as the cold weather and heavy rains made outdoor sermons and baptizing an unpleasant affair. John had disappeared, and Judas didn't have the time or money to track him down again. Now that he was back in Jerusalem with steady employment, he could not travel whenever he pleased. The dreary days slipped by, and as Passover approached with the coming spring, Judas found himself busier than he had ever been in his life.

It was an honor to be selected for a position working in the Temple. Judas was no priest, of course, but during major feasts, especially Passover, the Temple required additional staff. Millions of Jews from all over the Empire came to offer their sacrifices in the Temple. Of course, the chances of a sacrifice remaining unblemished on any lengthy journey was infinitesimal, so the Temple provided priest-verified unblemished sacrifices for sale on the Temple Mount. This solved one problem and created another. The millions of Jews who came from every corner of the globe—Parthians, Mesopotamians, Cappadocians, Pamphylians, Egyptians, Cretans, Arabs, and many others—all brought Parthian, Mesopotamian, Cappadocian, Pamphylian, Egyptian, Cretan, and Arabian money, all of which needed to be exchanged for the official Temple currency: the Tyrian shekel. For that, the Temple needed money changers—lots of them—even men who might have been fired from their previous stewardship for questionable reasons. Anyone with the memory to quickly recall exchange rates and the skill to catch counterfeit coins was welcomed with open arms. Judas was such a man.

The actual wages for money changers were hardly above poverty levels. It was a tacit agreement between the Temple and the changers that their wages could be supplemented by whatever they could negotiate out of their customers. Some money changers stole from everyone equally as much and as often as they could, while a rare few kept strict adherence to customary rates and were forced to supplement their meager income with a clear conscience and an empty stomach.

Judas preferred the middle path. He cheated only those who could afford it, but those who could afford it were also the ones smart enough to catch him. He liked the challenge. If a poor family came through, he would give them a reduced rate or "accidentally" give them too much change. Often, they would discover the mistake and rush back, insistent on returning the money. Strange, how poor people were usually the most generous. Judas enjoyed helping them nearly as much as he enjoyed cheating some pompous fool into overpaying. He usually ended up giving away most of what he managed to gain, leaving him little better than the rare few who cheated no one. But since his rude reception by Ishmael, Judas's desire to fund the Resistance had waned, and he had no family to support. He could afford to scrape by.

The Temple was a hurricane of activity on the feast's preparation day. Judas was stationed on the south side with the other money changers among the giant columns of the Royal Stoa. He was on the outer row, and in the precious seconds between customers, he had a good view of the southern Court of the Gentiles, which was packed with people and animals. Every sacrifice had to be inspected, signed for, and turned over to the priests for keeping until the big day. Everything on Passover had to proceed quickly and smoothly, which took an enormous amount of preparation. Even the many Jews who preferred the simplicity of purchasing a sacrifice had to be sure they could pay for it with the Temple's preferred currency, which meant standing in long lines for someone to exchange their silver or bronze for Tyrian shekels, and then selecting a sacrifice from the ever-changing rotation brought through the Court of the Gentiles for just such purposes. The sacrifice was then marked with the name of the buyer and returned to the Temple's holding pens to wait for Passover. It was a writhing mass of organized chaos, and the walls echoed with the cries of sheep, goats, and bulls amid the countless voices of men haggling over price and arguing with the money changers.

"Yes," Judas explained to one such man. "The *issar* is usually equal to a shekel, but the silver content fluctuates, see?" Judas said, indicating his scales where he had placed the Italian coin against the balance of a certified shekel-weight. The *issar* was noticeably lighter. "It's a little over three-fourths. You can add to it, or I can give you back one denarius, one drachm, and one, two... three leptons," he said, plucking up the certified weight and replacing it with the coins as he added them one by one.

"Your weights are heavy!" the man said angrily.

Judas sighed tiredly and scooped the coins off the scale. He placed a Tyrian shekel on one side and returned the shekel weight to the other. "No," he said, nodding to another booth some distance away, "Ezekiel's weights are heavy. Mine are just fine. Here's what I recommend," Judas continued, glancing at the man's clothing, which showed no evidence of wear. "You can purchase a pair of doves for a handful of leptons and still have money left over."

"No!" the man snapped. "I want a lamb! But you're cheating me, you thief! Give me a Tyrian shekel or I'll summon the guards!"

Judas smiled calmly. He had guessed right about the man's pride; he was rich enough to afford a lamb and would never survive the shame if he presented a lesser sacrifice. He just didn't want to pay full price. *Why were the rich always the stingy ones?* "Bring the Levites, then," Judas replied, calling the man's bluff. "I'm sure they'll be very interested in how you were attempting to steal from the Temple. It would be tragic if you were in prison and unable to make the required sacrifice for you and your family." He gave the man a mockingly sympathetic glare.

The man huffed, practically steaming at the ears, and angrily slapped another *issar* onto Judas's booth. Judas gave the man his change with a smile and pointed him to the pen where he could select and purchase a sacrifice.

The man stormed off, and Judas had a moment to scan the crowds as the next man stepped from the line. The crowd shifted, giving Judas a rare view into the center of it, and his eyes instantly locked on a familiar face. Time stood still. Of course, it was natural that the man would be here—every Jewish male was required to present himself at the Temple for Passover—but there was something off about the scene. As the crowd shifted back into its normal chaos, Judas suddenly realized what had given him the strange feeling; Jesus of Nazareth stood in the middle of the milling crowds but separate from them. He wasn't going anywhere, but he wasn't standing in line, either. He just stood, watching and... braiding something?

"Hey! Accountant! I need an exchange!" The angry voice of his next customer snapped Judas out of his trance.

"Of course, my friend," Judas said, shaking off the eerie feeling and casually checking the man's worn cloak. "Silver or bronze?"

The man never had a chance to reply, as a loud crack reverberated off the stone walls. The entire Temple Mount fell silent at the sound, and the suddenly quiet courtyard shook with a furious roar that gave no room for hesitation: "*Get. These. Things. OUT!*"

For research notes, see chapter 13 in the reference section.

XIV

In the stillness, the voice seemed louder than the crack of the whip. All eyes turned to find the source of the disturbance, but seeing only a single man without so much as a sword, the crowd dismissed him, and in another moment, business returned to normal. Jesus wasn't the first lunatic to make a spectacle of himself in the Temple and he would not be the last.

Judas was curious what the man would do after such a flippant dismissal. Jesus was highly intelligent, but calm and unassuming. Yet, the tone of his voice had left no room for disobedience.

"Hey! Are you going to do your job or not?" the man at Judas's table demanded. Judas held up a finger, waiting. For a moment he thought Jesus might give up, but then another crack sounded, followed by the frightened bellow of a bull, bitten by the sharp whip.

Instantly, Judas saw movement in the crowd. The bull rushed to escape the biting whip, and the crowd rushed to escape the bull. Another crack followed the first, and this time, screams erupted from the milling crowd. In moments, the chaos had spread, and the multitude became a mob rushing for the exits.

"Out!" the voice roared, loud enough to still be heard over the roar of the terrified crowd. This time, the crowd responded. Laymen and Levites alike fled from the madman. Many of the priests rushed for the safety of the Inner Temple, while some joined the crowd rushing for the exits—including the stairs leading to the Triple Gate, which was reserved for use by priests only. The crowds cared for nothing except escape from the frightened animals and the biting whip.

Without thought, Judas climbed onto his table, clearing it of coins and weights with a kick. His booth was right beside one of the massive pillars of the Royal Stoa. He braced himself against it as the panic spread through the crowd, and he found his table jostled from all sides. He ignored them, his eyes riveted on the unassuming man from Nazareth, who now looked more like a conquering king than anyone Judas had ever seen. Gone was the weakened body of a starving man. In its place was the form of a man born to command, his rage tightly controlled and fueling his unyielding determination. Thickly corded muscles, forged by the work of a hammer, now set upon another purpose with equal dexterity, snapping the whip left and right. Judas watched, dumbstruck, and all his previous doubts shattered. *This* man, Judas would follow into battle against the very gates of hell. He watched as the Messiah forced a space through the panicking crowd and marched straight for the vendors of the sacrificial lambs.

The gate of the enclosure surrendered to him as a swift kick smashed the wooden barrier into splinters. The sheep and the shepherds both fled as another crack of the whip sped their flight. Several feet away, the men selling doves stood petrified beside their carts, which were stacked with cages, each holding a pair of Temple-certified doves for sale. Jesus spun on them, and they flinched under his fiery gaze, even though they were out of the range of the biting whip.

"Get them out," he commanded. The anger radiating from him gave them no room to wonder what might happen if they refused. "This is *my Father's House,*" he said calmly, even as the rage pounded through him. "*Not a village bazaar!*" He raised his whip, but the men needed no further urging.

They snatched the handles of their carts and rushed for the nearest exit, dragging their carts behind and throwing their avian captives into disarray.

It was only then that Judas noticed a few men on the outskirts of the rushing mob who were not fleeing, but instead herding the mass of people and animals toward the exits. The crowds continued to thin as fast as the gates would let them, and Jesus turned his wrath on the money changers. He grabbed the nearest table with one hand and flung it away as the stunned clerk still sat behind it. Jesus again lifted his whip as a rain of coins pelted the ground, and the stunned man snapped into action. He threw himself away, which tipped his chair backwards, and he went sprawling amid the scattered coins.

Judas couldn't help but chuckle at the fate of the man whom he knew to be one of the most notorious filchers in the bunch. The other clerks, warned by this sudden attack about the reception they would receive, quickly gathered their things and fled, leaving their tables and anything they couldn't quickly grab. By this time, the mob had flooded down the stairs, leaving only a trickle of stragglers behind with the broken sheep pen, abandoned animals, and anything else dropped in the mad rush for the exits. As the crowd dwindled, Jesus's followers made their way back. There were only four. Judas looked for Andrew, but the four men were strangers.

Jesus continued down the line, cracking the whip at anyone who dallied too long at snatching up money from their tables. "Get all this out," he said as soon as his followers were within earshot. "The animal pens, the tables. I want everything gone." With the money changers on the run, Jesus's mood calmed considerably, though he still held the whip at the ready. He watched as the last of them rushed for the exits, joining the few stragglers still running for the stairs. He marched through the columns of the Royal Stoa, watching the clerks' retreat, until he came to Judas's table. He paused, noting the feet resting on the top of the table, and looked up, his gaze cold and hot at the same time. He blinked in recognition, and the fiery gaze flickered. "Judas?" he asked. "*What* are you doing?"

"Um..." Judas hadn't actually considered what Jesus would do once he arrived at his booth. There was a good chance Judas would get a taste of the whip for lingering, but he could not take his eyes off the man who had dominated his thoughts for so long, and who now dominated the Temple as well. Jesus raised his eyebrows expectantly, and his hand tightened around the leather whip. In an instant, Judas's decision was made. He straightened himself.

"You're going to need help dragging all this out before the Temple Guard arrives," he said bravely, his eyes breaking away to glance across the court to the Antonia Fortress, built against the opposite wall.

Jesus watched him carefully as he made this remark, then gave a slight nod. "In that case, there's no time to waste."

The following few minutes were a rush of activity as Judas helped clear away all evidence of the Temple's Passover preparations. He was breathing hard by the time the last of everything had been cleared away into storerooms or simply thrown down the wide stairways. The Temple's Outer Court was strangely empty. Empty, but not silent. Shouts rose up from the garrison, and across the long courtyard, Judas could see Roman soldiers marching quickly from the Tadi Gate on the north wall, just east of the Antonia Fortress.

"Master..." one of the disciples said in warning. "I think it's time to go..." The watchmen stationed at the four corners of the Temple walls had alerted the garrison, and it was only a matter of time before the Roman guards cut off all avenues of escape.

"I see them, Nathan," Jesus replied calmly. "We'll take the Shushan Gate across the valley to the Mount of Olives. Let's go." The small group nodded and started for the eastern gate.

"Wait!" Judas said, pulling the group to a stop. "They'll have horsemen on the way by the time you cross the valley. The mount's too open. You'll never cover enough ground before they spot you."

"It's the only exit we can reach before the Guard closes it off!" Nathan argued.

"I'm sure that head start will be a great relief as they are trampling you with their horses," Judas countered sarcastically.

"If we give ourselves up willingly, it might gain us a quick death," another follower suggested.

Jesus suppressed a smile. "Nobody is dying today, Thomas."

"Right! Herod will want to torture us first," Thomas realized.

"I think Judas may have a suggestion," Jesus said with a chuckle.

"Don't look at me!" another disciple protested, throwing up his hands. "I'm a follower, not a leader."

"Not you, Judas," Jesus said, smiling at his disciple. "*This* Judas," he said, indicating Judas with a gracious smile.

"Hello," Judas said with an impatient smile, glancing nervously at the oncoming soldiers.

"Well, in that case, call me Thaddaeus. It's my Greek name," the other Judas replied helpfully. "My father was a Greek, but he fell in love with a—"

"Another time," Jesus said, cutting him off as kindly as he could for some quick introductions. "Nathanael, Philip, Thomas, and, ah... Thaddaeus, then, and Judas. You have a suggestion, Judas?"

"Kiponos," Judas said, pointing to the gate on the western wall. "It'll take us to the Upper City. We can lose them there."

"But... that gate is always guarded," Thaddaeus said. "It's all palaces and mansions. Herod's palace is there! We'd stick out like lepers!"

"Exactly," Judas said. "Which is why the garrison won't bother sending troops there! It's also just far enough away that the posted guards won't be looking for us."

"That's a brilliant plan, city boy—except the watchmen will have signaled them by now," Nathanael protested.

"Probably," Judas shrugged. "But it's far enough away that they can *claim* ignorance—and that's the important part." He smiled and snatched up a handful of Tyrian shekels from where they littered the floor—more than enough for a hefty bribe. "Let me handle this, farm boy."

"Are you—are you *stealing* those?" Nathanael asked, eyes widening. "Master, he's—"

"They're not for me," Judas said angrily. "They're our ticket out of here." He glanced at the Temple Guard, who were advancing across the long courtyard at a rapid pace. The window of escape was rapidly closing. "It's now or never," he said impatiently.

"Maybe the guards are friendly..." Philip mused aloud, watching the oncoming soldiers. "Master, I could run and ask them if they are friendly."

"Are you sure about this?" Jesus asked, ignoring Philip. His tone implied far more to the meaning of the question than just the reliability of Judas's plan.

Judas nodded solemnly. "I am."

"*He's* coming with us?!" Nathanael demanded. "You can't trust him! He's a thief!"

"What will happen to my body?" Thomas wondered despondently. "I don't have money for a tomb..."

Jesus held a hand out to quiet his disciples as he addressed them. "Trust is a decision, Nathan, not a reaction. Thomas, you are not dying today; have a little faith. Philip, I admire your enthusiasm, but you must learn to control it. Thaddaeus, someday you're going to have to find a midpoint between saying nothing and saying everything. Judas," he continued, "do you know the way?"

Judas slowly nodded as he gazed at his Messiah. "I do now."

For research notes, see chapter 14 in the reference section.

Part 2

XV

"He did *what?!*" Judas asked. "I thought Herod liked John!" Judas was again standing by the entrance into Nazareth talking to a man he hardly knew. This time, though, the man was a stranger to the village, like Judas himself. All the Nazarenes were at synagogue. Judas had been called away by the messenger before the start of the weekly service. It was Jesus's first official reading of Torah in his hometown, and Judas was missing it.

"Herod didn't *like* John. He found John amusing," the messenger clarified. "It was less amusing when John marched into Herod's palace and publicly insulted him! Nicodemus thought you should know immediately."

Judas groaned in frustration. "I knew it! I knew John was planning something stupid! This is bad. We're not ready—not ready by far." Judas had been one of Jesus's disciples since the Passover incident—over seven months ago now—and still no plans for the war against Rome. Nicodemus had witnessed the Temple cleansing as well, and the same fire that had captivated Judas had captivated Nicodemus. Nicodemus was a Pharisee of Pharisees, a *Haber*, and hesitant to outwardly support the upstart preacher, but he provided Judas with valuable intelligence—and funding.

"There is good news," Nicodemus's contact said, squeezing his woolen cap nervously. "Herod's fascination with John remains—and Herod fears the people. John is in no immediate danger."

"Madness calls to madness," Judas muttered. "John has the madness of the wilderness, while Antipas has the madness of his father. Who is to say whether he will be killed tomorrow or released? The Herods are impossible to predict."

"Still, it might be for the best. There have been... tensions... between your master's disciples and John's."

Judas smirked. "That's why we left Judea in the first place. Galilee is rustic, but the men here are strong. They will make good soldiers, with the right leader. John and Jesus aren't competing. They're cousins, after all." Judas paced, chewing his nail in thought. "No, perhaps we can use this. Jesus is... He *is* the One; I am sure! But... he lacks focus. He wants to teach people, but we have enough teachers. We need a *king*."

"That is not for me to decide," the man said humbly. As a Greek, the Jewish Messiah meant little to him.

"You've done well, Jason. Thank you for coming all this way."

"Is there anything Nicodemus should know?" Jason asked. He was a free Greek and therefore not required to keep the Sabbath prohibitions on travel. Jews could travel for only half a day's walk on Sabbaths, and Jason had likely run most of the way from Jerusalem.

"Nicodemus should bide his time. The *Habarim* will be the hardest to convince. We will remain in Galilee for a few months. By the time Passover arrives again, maybe things will settle down. Do you need any money?" Judas asked, reaching for the money bag. As the only one of their small group with experience as a money changer, Judas was the natural choice to manage their meager funds. The other disciples did not know about his questionable history as a steward—yet.

"No," Jason said quickly. "In fact, Nicodemus sent this for you." He pulled a small bag from inside his cloak and handed it to Judas. "He overpaid me for the journey and said to give you whatever was left."

"Take this," Judas said, pulling out a few coins for himself and giving the rest back to Jason. "For the return journey."

"I was hoping to buy some bread before I left, rest for a bit, get some water..."

A sudden flood of angry voices exploded from the direction of the synagogue. Both men glanced sharply at the sudden disturbance. "Not today, you won't," Judas said grimly. "And not here. Nazareth doesn't like strangers, least of all foreign ones. Here." He quickly slipped off his own waterskin. "I don't have any food. You should go." Judas glanced nervously in the direction of the angry shouts. "Before whatever that is gets here."

Jason nodded and started back down the road at a steady, loping jog. Judas watched him for a moment, then turned to investigate the disturbance. He was certain of the culprit, but not the cause. Jesus had been invited here. Surely Jesus's own hometown knew what to expect from the man.

Apparently not. Judas followed his ears, which were taking him away from the synagogue and toward the outskirts of the little village. Nazareth was built on the side of a long, sloping hill, which terminated in a low, jagged cliff. Judas broke away from the cluster of houses on the upper side and pulled up short as he saw a murderous crowd swarming their way up the hill to the edge of the cliff, pulling someone with them.

Judas's stomach lurched. The hill was too far to see who the crowd was dragging to the top, but it wasn't hard to guess. Judas wasn't the only observer; a group of bystanders, mostly women, hung back, watching the proceedings with mixed emotions. Some watched eagerly, others in horror. Judas recognized Jesus's mother in the crowd, her hands clenched in worry. "Where are they?" Judas asked. She pointed to the swarming mob, which had reached the top of the cliff. The drop wasn't dizzying, but the jagged rocks at the bottom would ensure anyone thrown off it would be hopelessly broken.

Even if he lived, the crowd could throw rocks down upon the broken victim, ending what little shred of life persisted.

"Don't go!" Mary said quickly as Judas started forward. "They'll kill you, too."

Judas clenched his teeth. Mary was right. They needed an army. Unfortunately, in the seven months since Judas had joined Jesus, they had added only one other disciple—hardly enough to stop an angry mob, although he might come close. Judas looked again, and his eyes widened as he saw Jesus slip through the back of the mob. A few moments later, more figures pulled away, and Mary's sigh of relief was audible even among the angry cries of some of the other onlookers. The mayhem was too great for the mob to hear the warning cries about the escape of their victim. Despite their outcries, none of the passive onlookers moved to stop Jesus's escape.

"I hope this won't become a trend," Judas said quietly, joining Jesus after he had said a hurried goodbye to his mother. Jesus slipped among the buildings to escape the eyes of the mob with Judas on his heels.

"First the Temple, now this? What happened in there?" Judas asked.

"A theological disagreement. A prophet is welcomed everywhere but his own country," came the clipped reply.

"Can't believe I'm saying this, but I *actually miss Samaria!*" Judas muttered to nobody in particular. "At least nobody tried to kill us in Sychar."

"If you'd heard what he said in there, you wouldn't be so surprised, City Boy," Thad said under his breath, falling in beside Judas from an adjacent street. As Judas was the only one of their group not from some rural area, Nathanael's nickname for him had stuck. Judas embraced it, knowing that it reminded them of his more urbane skillset. The other disciples quickly joined them, converging again after slipping away one-by-one.

"He was reading a Messianic prophecy from Isaiah," Thad continued. "You know the one about the acceptable year of the Lord and the day of vengeance? He *skipped* the parts prophesying the destruction of our enemies—skipped right over them! You know that's got to be the Nazarenes' favorite part of that entire prophecy! Then he told them, 'You're hearing this prophesy come true, as I speak it!' Let me tell you, they were none too pleased about a local carpenter proclaiming himself the Messiah!" Thad shook his head in amazement and let out a low whistle. "'Theological disagreement,' my plow-dragging ass."

"Whew…" Judas said, wincing. "Bold. Wait," he said, suddenly realizing that their group was still short by one. "Where's the new guy? Where's Little James?"

"Causing a distraction," Thad said quickly, then threw up his hands as Judas gave him a shameful glare. "His idea!"

"You left your younger brother in the middle of that mob *by himself?!*" Judas asked angrily. "I've been saying from the beginning that we need more men, but nobody listens to me. Jesus finally calls someone with potential and you abandon him to—"

"Sorry I'm late, master," James said, his heavy footsteps giving away his arrival before anyone saw him. "Little" James bar Alphaeus was a giant of a man, used to solving problems with muscle, rather than mind. Judas wished they had two or three thousand just like him.

"No permanent damage, little brother?" Thad asked cheerfully, slapping the big man on the back proudly.

"Only their pride," James replied.

"He meant you, you big oaf," Philip said laughingly.

"I suspect the only thing that could hurt Little James is a shepherd boy with a sling and five smooth stones," Judas said with a chuckle.

Little James gave him a puzzled look.

"He means you're a giant. Like Goliath?" Thad explained. Despite the near-death of their master, the small group was in high spirits. Their master had escaped without a scratch, and if the Messiah was saved, Israel was saved.

"Goliath was a Philistine. I am a Jew," Little James said in confusion. "I keep the Law."

"Of course you do," Judas said consolingly. The man was endearingly simple at times. The ideal soldier.

"Where are we going?" Nathanael asked, always straight to the point. The man had one direction: forward. In seven months, Judas had managed to find out almost nothing about his past.

"Isn't there some way we can smooth things over?" Thad asked in concern, turning to Jesus. "Your family lives here! What about your mother? She's a widow. What if they go after her? I can't believe your family didn't…"

"My mother will be fine, Thad," Jesus said. "She's been part of this community too long for them to hurt her. But it's time we moved on. There are many more villages in Galilee."

"So, where to?" Nathanael asked again.

"That's a good question," Jesus said, hiding disappointment behind his words. "I had hoped to spend a few days here with my family."

"Come to my home in Cana," Nathanael suggested. "It's within a Sabbath day's walk."

"You live in Cana?" Thad asked in surprise.

"Yes," Nathanael replied simply.

"We were there for a whole wedding, and you never thought to mention it?"

Nathanael shrugged. "We were guests of the bridegroom. Why would I need to offer my home?"

Judas remembered that wedding. It was the first proof he had seen that Jesus could do more than any ordinary man. Water had become wine—wine like no one had ever tasted.

"We should stop by," Philip said thoughtfully. "They might still have wine!"

"No one else mentioned it either..." Thomas mused, studying Nathanael. "In fact, I can't remember anyone speaking to you at all."

Nathanael sighed. "No one did."

"But... why not?" Thad asked.

"Because they know who I am."

For research notes, see chapter 15 in the reference section.

XVI

"Wait, *the* Tolmai? The one who...?" Thad asked.

"Yes," Nathanael said, resigned to having his life's story spilled out in front of him. "I am Bar-Tholomew. It means 'the son of Tolmai.'"

"Didn't he..."

"You don't have to talk about this, Nathan," Philip cut in. Everyone knew Philip and Nathanael went way back. Judas had tried pulling some of Nathanael's history from Philip, but the man had refused to speak of it.

"Philip is right," Jesus said, interrupting. "Your history is not what defines you." Usually, Jesus let his disciples work things out on their own, choosing to lead by example rather than admonition, but on rare occasions, he did step in.

Nathanael's jaw clenched as their group neared Cana. "Yes, I do." He took a slow breath. "If I would dare to call you friends, then you deserve to know. My family comes from royalty, long ago—pagan royalty. Talmai, my father's namesake, was the king of Geshur. His daughter married King David. We're descendants of Absalom. The ultimate traitor. My father was a high official in Herod's court. He embezzled from the royal treasury. Herod had him killed—publicly. Herod had many men killed wrongfully, but my father was not one of them. My family has a long history of cheating and thievery, and my father only reinforced it." His voice was husky, but it hardened as he continued. "I've lived under it my whole life. I've always been seen through the haze of my father's betrayal. I cannot escape his shadow. All despise me the minute they learn my name! I was named Nathanael, but my true name is Bartholomew, son of Tolmai. That's what everyone hears, no matter what I say. That's the name everyone knows."

Little James put a giant hand on Nathanael's shoulder. "You are a good man," he said gruffly.

"Everyone *knows* I come from a long line of cheaters," Nathanael continued. "I've never stolen from anyone, but they all clutch their money closer when they see me. Everyone! My whole life. They call me a pagan because of my Gentile lineage. They call me a thief because of my father. I'm not a *true* Israelite. I *can't* be honest; my blood is impure! They have spat that in my face so much, I could—and then Jesus..." He angrily bit back a sob. "When Philip told me he'd found the Christ, I didn't believe him. But then the first thing Jesus said to me... He said: 'Now, here's a *true* Israelite, and not a dishonest bone in his body!' And the fig tree..."

"And I meant every word, Nathan," Jesus added with a smile, wrapping his arm around Nathanael's neck in a friendly embrace. "I'm sure Nathan was just about to tell everyone that he would understand if none of you wished to be his friend and offer to leave if anyone wished. *He* might understand, but I would not. So if you cannot stand to be friends with an honest Israelite, *you'll* be the one to leave." He smiled kindly. "Nathanael is not the only one with a troubled past." Jesus gave Judas a subtle glance. "It is the future that matters."

"I think you're an asset to the team, Nathan," Judas said quickly, deflecting attention away from himself and giving Nathanael an encouraging smile.

Nathanael's dark countenance flickered with a smile. "Well, I'm no city slicker like you, Judas, but I do my best."

The others voiced similar sentiments as the group reached Cana and the customary welcoming party of city leaders, beggars, and the merely curious who ventured out whenever a large group was seen approaching. As the two groups exchanged the customary greetings, Judas pulled Nathanael aside. "What did you mean about the fig tree?" he asked. Nathanael had little taste for social formalities on his good days, so while the rest of the group ingratiated themselves with the men from the city, Judas decided to take advantage of this rare window into Nathanael's history.

Nathanael smiled wistfully. "I was seven," he said, swallowing. "My mother had gone to Herod to plead for my father's life. Herod granted her my father's wealth, but not his life. I remember it so clearly. A servant found me and told me my father was dead." He pulled his gaze back and looked at Judas with misty eyes. "I was sitting under a fig tree. It was the last moment of my life where I was seen as anything more than the son of a traitor. That moment. He knew. Jesus knew." He shook his head and smiled. "He called me a true Israelite, and I asked him how he knew me. He said he saw me under the fig tree. Can you explain that?"

Judas shook his head. "Can you explain the wine?"

Nathanael gripped his arm. "He said I would see greater things! In fact," he stifled a chuckle. "I think he might have called me gullible..." He shook his head and smiled at the thought, his dark mood clearing. "Let's see if Jesus has got a better offer than the guestroom of a thief."

"Probably depends on if he's planning on making more wine," Judas said with a wink.

Nathanael caught Judas's arm again, pulling him to a stop. "Judas," he began. "I... I'm sorry. When I first met you at the Temple, I called you a thief. I'm so used to being seen as a thief, I just... I'm sorry. Forgive me."

Judas slapped his shoulder. "I've been called worse, farm boy. Come on." The two men rejoined the quickly growing group of men from Cana.

"Ah!" Jesus said, spotting them. "There he is! I cannot accept any of your gracious offers because I have already agreed to stay in Nathanael's home tonight."

This statement brought a stunned silence, followed by one brave soul stepping back slightly to hide among the crowd before saying, "Rabbi, that man is *Bartholomew*."

"Yes, I know," Jesus replied. "The son of Tolmai has lived in Cana most of his adult life. In that time, has he ever taken anything wrongfully?" Jesus asked, daring anyone to answer.

"Never gave him a chance to," one voice muttered from the back of the crowd, drawing some snickers and muttered agreement.

"'The father eats a sour grape, and the children's teeth are set on edge,' is that it?" Jesus asked.

"It's *your* teeth'll be set on edge if you trust Bartholomew at all," the same voice muttered.

"If you deny a man the chance to prove himself, you are the guilty one," Jesus shot back. "Don't be so quick to condemn others, or they will be equally quick to condemn you."

The argument stopped abruptly as a man pushed himself through the crowd with desperate force. The crowd parted grudgingly as the man thrust himself into the space between Jesus and the surrounding crowd. He looked about wildly, his desperate mood at odds with his expensive clothing. He breathed heavily, as if he had been running. Men of standing never ran—that's what messengers were for. Running was undignified.

"Which one is Jesus of Nazareth? Is it you?" he asked, naturally turning to the tallest of their group.

Little James shook his head and pointed a meaty finger at Jesus. The man rushed for him. James took a step forward in case the man meant trouble, but Jesus held out a hand.

The man dropped to his knees, covering his robes with dust. "Please," he said. "My son is very sick. He won't last the morrow. I just heard you were here. I was on my way to Nazareth to find you..."

"Do you know this man?" Jesus asked, turning to Nathanael.

"Yes," Nathanael said thoughtfully. "I've seen him. He's from Capernaum—a nobleman with ties to the Hasmoneans."

"Yes!" the man said quickly. "I have money! I'll give you everything if you just come with me to Capernaum—if you can heal my son."

Jesus raised his eyebrows.

The man hastened to explain. "Everyone heard about what you did here—at the wedding. If you can make water become wine, you can make the sick become well. Please, I beg you. Hurry, or he'll die before you reach him!"

Jesus looked at the man sadly. "No."

The man's shock was palpable, as was the crowd's. "Without signs and wonders, they don't believe," Jesus muttered. "You want to see results before you believe me, right? You act the same way with Nathan here," Jesus continued. "You want to see proof of his honesty but refuse him any opportunity to display it. Many times, belief must come first."

The man stared, still kneeling in front of Jesus, unsure how to respond to this cold dismissal. The crowd was quiet, but Jesus made no move to fill the silence. Finally, the same earlier naysayer spoke up. "Well, this man's giving you a chance to prove yourself, like you said. If you refuse, what's that prove?"

Jesus smiled. "Good question. But proof doesn't always come first." He knelt down, meeting the nobleman at eye level. "Go home," he said kindly, pulling the man to his feet. "Your son will live."

The man stared at him for a long moment. "You're not coming?" he asked hesitantly.

Jesus cocked an eyebrow. "Do you believe me?"

The man wavered for a moment, struggling to decide if the rumors surrounding Jesus were worth the gamble of his son's life.

He made the gamble. Catching Jesus up in a tight embrace, he nodded. "Yes!" he cried. "I do believe. I do! Thank you!" He kissed Jesus on each side of his face, then rushed away through the crowd, departing as suddenly as he had come.

Jesus smiled. "Belief," he said, more to himself than the crowd. "Belief comes first."

For research notes, see chapter 16 in the reference section.

XVII

J esus left Cana the following day, saying it was better to leave "before anyone finds out." Whether that meant finding out that Jesus had healed the man's son or that he hadn't, Judas did not know. At this point, he had no idea exactly what Jesus was capable of doing, but Judas was certain he was the promised Messiah. The only problem was turning a mild-mannered carpenter into a warrior. It had worked with the Maccabees. Swinging a sword was not so different from swinging a hammer. Jesus only needed the right motivation.

No one in Cana would listen to anything Jesus had to say until they knew for sure if he had accurately predicted the boy's recovery in Capernaum. Jesus had spent nearly a week bouncing from village to village, teaching in synagogues and fields to anyone who would listen. Jesus did no recruiting. Mostly, he taught people to see things from a new perspective and announced that the kingdom of heaven was imminent. It was a far cry from raising a standing militia, as Judas had first hoped, but it was a start. Jesus was silent on specific plans, but his confidence was catching. The carpenter had an air of certainty about him that bled into everything he said, but he was quick to silence any talk of overthrowing Rome. It was unsettling. If Jesus was to be Israel's Messiah, he would require a drastic change of focus. The fire that

Judas had first seen in the Temple was still burning in Jesus's eyes, but it had lessened to a tender warmth for the oppressed. Did the man not understand that the greatest need of the oppressed was the destruction of the oppressor? The healing balm must come *after* the chains were broken.

It was the morning of the preparation day when Jesus finally turned his steps toward Capernaum. All week, Judas had been itching to learn if the nobleman's son had been healed. His mind was plagued with indecision. Surely, the Messiah would not lie, but the impossibility of it all... If Judas had been wrong about the Messiah's identity—no, he was certain! Wasn't he?

Judas was uncertain—until the crowds found them. Jesus and his disciples had walked the seaside from Gennesaret, enjoying the early morning sun, and were just reaching the Capernaum docks when the crowds swarmed in. They came from all three sides, and at that moment, Judas knew for sure. He knew even before the first word was spoken. The boy was alive. The boy was *alive!* Judas hardly had time to consider the implication as the crowds pressed in, and Jesus found himself forced backward along the dock. They were quiet enough, anxious to hear what Jesus had to say, but they would push him right into the sea with their zeal.

Judas cast about for a solution, scanning the dock and the several fishermen scattered about. Providence supplied. "Andrew?" he called in surprise, recognizing a familiar face among the sun-dried seamen, back from their nightly fishing and working over their nets to repair tears and remove the weeds and trash that would inevitably tangle in the fine netting. "Andrew bar Jonas!"

The fisherman turned at hearing his name, and his face shifted from confusion to recognition, surprise, elation, and finally understanding as he fully grasped the dilemma in which Jesus had found himself. Andrew tapped another man on the shoulder. Judas guessed him to be Andrew's brother, Simon. Simon instantly saw the problem, and the two men dragged their boat back out. With expert skill, they rowed it to the end of the dock, just in time to catch Jesus as the eager crowd drove him off the end of the dock.

Jesus stepped lightly into the boat, giving himself some breathing room from the pressing mob. He paused long enough to greet his friends. "Hello, Simon. Night fishing again, I see. Any luck?" he asked with a smile.

"Not a *koprios* thing," Simon muttered, obviously tired. "*Skubala bar skubalos.*"

"I'm sorry to impose."

"Where you wanna go?" Simon growled, knowing that he was obligated to offer help to his friend, but none too happy about the idea of prolonging an already long night into an even longer morning.

"Just row out a few feet. I can address the crowd from there. I won't keep you long."

Simon grunted in annoyance but rowed out a few yards. Jesus took a seat near the back of the boat while Simon and Andrew took turns manning the oars, stabilizing the boat while Jesus taught. His sermon was a short one, just long enough to satisfy the crowd without putting further strain on the already tired fishermen. The other fishermen were still cleaning nets or sorting fish when Jesus dismissed the crowd. He only convinced them to leave by telling them where he was going. It was a temporary solution, but it gave him and his disciples some breathing room to decide their next course of action.

As the crowd slowly drifted away, Judas assembled the others for a consultation but turned with confusion to find Simon rowing Jesus *away* from shore. The six disciples watched in silence at this oddity until Little James began chuckling to himself.

Judas gave him a questioning glance.

"He's going fishing," the big man said, still grinning. He pointed, and true enough, Simon reluctantly picked up his net and threw it out. The nets were large and bag-shaped, with thin webbing, weighted on one side, so even a slight current would pull the fish into the center of the net where they could be hauled up. Simon waited as the net disappeared, a tired smirk on his face. Even Judas knew if Simon had caught nothing all night, there was no chance anything would present itself during the day, and especially so near the docks.

Simon reached down with one hand to retrieve the net and nearly fell out of the boat as the net refused to give. Simon tried again, his face growing increasingly mystified at the obstinate net. The ropes refused to do more than groan under the strain. As the Jonas brothers struggled to solve this dilemma, Jesus sat calmly, watching their efforts with a bemused expression.

Giving up on hauling in the net themselves, Andrew began waving his hands, silently pointing to another group of fishermen still on the docks. If the two fishermen had somehow discovered a new spring, where fish were known to gather, they could not risk the other fishermen learning of the exact location. Sound carried far over the water. With renewed vigor, Simon began slowly rowing the boat closer, dragging the heavy net behind like an anchor, while Andrew continued to discreetly summon his comrades.

Judas caught the idea and weaved his way through the clusters of fishermen, pointing to various groups until Andrew's excitement reached full pitch. He stopped behind an older man and several young men sorting fish and repairing nets. Andrew gestured excitedly as Judas pointed to one. Judas tapped the younger man on his shoulder and pointed across the water. Andrew went wild, pointing at the net urgently. The young fisherman tapped another man on the shoulder, and they went for a nearby boat.

The two men rowed silently to keep from drawing attention and pulled up along Simon and Andrew's boat. By now, Simon had managed to get the boat within a few yards of the shallows, and the four men worked furiously from both sides to pull up the net, straining desperately. Simon staggered as one of the ropes snapped, but he snatched up another part of the net with quick hands. The fishermen had gathered up the edges of the net, so that both boats could work to pull it up evenly. The nets were large, and a good draw would yield perhaps fifty or a hundred fish, but good draws were rare. Most nights, fifty fish might be the entire catch, or like tonight, it might yield none at all. The four fishermen had pulled up only about a foot of net when the fish appeared. The net was full—totally full. So full that the net could only bear the weight while submerged. Hundreds of fish. *Thousands* of fish. Enough fish that a person might retire on the profit. A fortune.

The fishermen tied off the net and began scooping fish by the handfuls into the boats. The boats filled faster than the net emptied, and by the time the net was empty, the fishermen were forced to abandon the boats to lessen the weight and swim to shore, pulling the loaded boats behind them.

Simon collapsed as soon as he hit shore. By now, other fishermen had taken notice, but the four men were too tired to care. They must have been exhausted, but it was shock that stopped Simon, rather than fatigue. His knees sunk into the sand as Jesus stepped lightly from the overloaded boat. "Leave!" he said hoarsely. "I don't deserve this. You shouldn't have done this! You know I can't repay you! I don't have—"

"No reason to panic," Jesus said. "You don't need to repay me. You're done catching fish; from now on, you catch men."

Judas nudged Philip with a grin. "That's my line," he said proudly. Philip gave him an odd look, not knowing that Judas had told Andrew the same thing when they had first started looking for the Messiah.

"Who are your friends?" Jesus asked, nodding at the two fishermen who had rushed to help the Jonas brothers.

"This is James, John, and their father, Zebedee," Andrew said, drawing the older man over from where he had stood gaping at the two boatloads of fish barely floating above the surface.

Jesus introduced his six disciples and then turned to the old fisherman with a question. "Do you have the manpower to process this catch without the help of these men?"

"We hire day laborers to help with processing," Zebedee said, still somewhat in shock. "This catch..." He shook himself out of his daze. "Yes," he said, clearing his throat. "The hired men and I can take care of it. Are you..."

"That is their choice, but my invitation remains open," Jesus said, turning his gaze back to Andrew and Simon. Andrew looked to his brother, who hesitated, licking his lips. "Rabbi... I have no education. The only trade I know is fishing, and… well, clearly you don't need a fisherman," he said with an incredulous laugh.

"I don't *need* you, Simon," Jesus said. "I *want* you with me—all four of you." He smiled. "Andrew, you found me, but you didn't want to abandon your brother to support his family alone. I can't promise you safety or prosperity, but I can promise that what you will gain is far more valuable than a few fish." He kicked the side of the boat with his sandal.

Zebedee chuckled. "'A few,' he says."

The four fishermen exchanged a look, then glanced at the old patriarch, who gave them a silent nod.

"We will," Andrew said.

"All of us," James said. "We will follow wherever you lead."

"Anywhere?" Jesus asked, his eyes twinkling.

"To Rome itself," Simon said, forcing his tired frame to stand a little taller.

Jesus nodded approvingly at this declaration and his eyes sparkled with mischief. "All the way to Rome? That's brave of you. Would you visit your mother-in-law?"

Simon made a puzzled face. "My moth… Why?"

Jesus smiled. "Because you're exhausted and wet, your house is closer than Andrew's house in Bethsaida, and you smell like wet fish. Shall we?"

For research notes, see chapter 17 in the reference section.

XVIII

The crowds had worsened by the time Jesus reached Capernaum with his disciples, now ten in number. Judas was nearly beside himself with anticipation. Jesus had practically doubled his following, and his fame was spreading. It couldn't be long until the Messiah finally took his place on the throne and moved to conquer Israel's enemies like David of old.

There were now several hundred people swarming the gates of Capernaum, eager for Jesus's arrival. The disciples switched to crowd control, making a path for Jesus to reach the city. Judas let the larger Galileans go first. He moved beside Jesus as the group pushed their way through the throng. "Master," he said excitedly, "I am thrilled that you are finally seeing the value in recruitment. I do not know what assets these fishermen bring in regard to strategy," he said jokingly, "but they will make fine soldiers."

"I'm not looking for soldiers, Judas," Jesus said.

"I know!" Judas replied in frustration. "That's what I'm saying! You should be. Even Gideon had his faithful three hundred."

"Are you so certain of my mission, Judas, that you want to decide how I am to fulfill it?"

"Yes! I know the prophecies! I am your man. Together we can achieve great things!"

Jesus smiled. "Yes. Together, we can." He gripped Judas's shoulder. "But you must trust me. I need you to follow me, Judas. Not guide me."

"I do trust you, master. It's just..." Judas hesitated. "I think you may not understand the world outside Galilee. You can't *preach* Rome into surrendering. And what about your cousin, John? Do you think Antipas is going to release him? To ascend the throne of David, you must first take it from Herod. It is impossible—but not for you. I *know* you can succeed, but wars require soldiers."

"This is war of a different kind. It requires soldiers of a different kind. Be patient, Judas. You'll see. But if you want soldiers," Jesus said, eyes twinkling, "here's one now."

Judas looked around the dense crowd but saw nothing out of the ordinary, save for the massive frame of Little James, who pushed through the crowd like a Roman trireme. But then the crowd parted as another procession met them, pushing through from the other side.

Jesus's small group of peasants, smelling of fish and road dust, met a pristine group of Pharisees, bureaucrats, and city elders. "Jesus of Nazareth," the leader said grandly. "I am Levi ben Judas, a Pharisee and high elder of Capernaum. You must come with us."

"I must?" Jesus asked, his mouth twisting into a skeptical grin.

The man drew himself up, his lip stiffening in irritation at this cold welcome. "A Roman centurion has requested your presence at his home. It would be unwise to refuse."

Jesus raised his eyebrows. "And why would I go to the house of a Roman?"

Levi, the high elder, relaxed slightly and gave a commiserating smile. "I understand your distaste for Rome. I understand completely, but Centurion Rufus is a Jewish sympathizer. He funded the construction of Capernaum's largest synagogue. He has renounced the gods of Rome and fears the true God. He is an ally to all of us—not just the Sadducees."

Jesus nodded. "All that is commendable, but it does not answer my question."

Another elder, with hair just beginning to gray, spoke up. "He heard rumors about some of the... *events*... surrounding your ministry," the elder said. "Though I am sure you would be the first to acknowledge the exaggeration of these reports, Centurion Rufus is quite convinced. A servant of his has severe palsy, and Rufus has taken it into his mind that you can somehow remedy it. So that relations with the centurion remain friendly, we must ask you to humor his request, however ill-founded." The man gave a patronizing smile.

Jesus's face grew serious. "His servant is sick? Why didn't you say so? Lead the way!"

"We understand your reluctance," Levi the Pharisee said as he started forward into Capernaum's richer district. "Centurion Rufus will do you no harm. Do not feel pressured to try and live up to the rumors surrounding you. He understands completely how stories of this nature can become something they are not. Be polite. That is all we ask. His servant does not have a contagious disease, so there is no risk of uncleanness by simply looking in on him."

"You've visited him, then?" Jesus asked.

Levi paled slightly. "Well... no... Centurion Rufus fears God, but he *is* still a Roman! To enter a Gentile's house would defile me, and as a Pharisee, I must remain clean at all times. However, *you* do not adhere to such high standards, and it would greatly benefit our city and our synagogue if you would do this small thing."

Judas leaned close, dropping his voice so none could hear but Jesus. "It could be wise to gain the favor of a Roman centurion. He might be able to slip us important information."

Jesus hummed thoughtfully. "I think you could learn much from this centurion. Watch him carefully."

Judas nodded, relieved that Jesus was finally starting to see the value in his advice. "I will."

"Good," Jesus said, grinning mischievously.

"Rabbi," Levi spoke up again. "We're getting close to the centurion's house. Perhaps it will make a better impression if the crowds and the... fishermen... wait here?" he said, clearly wanting to use a different term, but trying his utmost to be polite.

Strangely, Jesus agreed. "Yes, there's no need for them to go further."

"Ah, good," Levi said, relieved. "If you'll just—"

Jesus ignored the Pharisee, turning instead to greet yet another group of men coming to meet him. Everyone but Jesus stiffened as the group approached, and the crowd dropped into uneasy silence. These were Romans. They were off-duty soldiers and wore togas instead of the red and gold armor of the Roman guard. None were armed, but their movements betrayed their status. They marched in double file, a squad of eight soldiers, led by a *decanus*. Off-duty or not, they could have any Jew arrested on the slightest whim.

The *decanus* dropped to one knee and placed his fist on his heart. His eight soldiers mirrored his movements. "Commander," he said quickly, dropping his gaze in respect as he addressed Jesus. "My centurion begs me to say that you are not required to come to his house. He knows that entering a Gentile home would be offensive to a Jew. He only asks that—"

A commanding voice cut him off. "That will do, Patrobas." It was the centurion himself, also dressed in an off-duty toga. He walked calmly up to his squad and gripped the *decanus's* shoulder as he knelt before Jesus. Patrobas looked at his commanding officer with perplexity at the interruption. Rufus said a few quiet words to the man in Latin and dismissed the squad.

The centurion was tall, even by Roman standards. He was obviously a veteran; his entire demeanor radiated a constant readiness for combat. He carried himself and his scars with noble pride. Judas did not know whether the Roman had been assigned here or had chosen Capernaum as a place to retire, but he was obviously still in charge of the local garrison.

As soon as the *decanus* moved away, the centurion's military austerity collapsed. He dropped to the ground, giving no heed to his reputation. "I'm sorry," he said. "I'm sorry, I know I shouldn't even dare speak to you, but I *know* what you can do! I saw Jude's son with my own eyes! He came to you in Cana about the seventh hour, if you recall? I was with his son when he awoke! I've never seen anything like it. I know I am unworthy to ask for anything. I sent the elders to speak with you, but..."

"I know," Jesus said kindly. "Some things are too important to trust to anyone else. You could not rest until you were certain that you had tried everything to convince me."

"Yes!" Rufus said, standing up and reaching for Jesus without thinking, before restraining himself. "Yes, you understand! I command men, and they follow my orders, but..."

"But something this important must be done personally. I understand—more than you know."

Judas listened to this exchange with growing perplexity. Jesus was being more than polite; he was actively being *friendly* with this Roman. Capernaum's elders appeared as shocked as Judas. For the life of him, Judas could not discover the reason for this camaraderie, even if Jesus was planning on using the centurion as a spy. Well, Jesus did say that Judas could learn much from the Roman. Perhaps Jesus was goading him.

"Let's go see this servant," Jesus said, extending his hand.

The centurion reeled back. "No!" he said quickly. "Please, I would not ask you to defile yourself. I know a commander when I see one. I command men, but you... You *command*. I demand nothing. You are free to act as you see fit, but if you would only..." The centurion's eyes glistened, and he struggled to compose himself into an attitude more befitting a Roman officer. "Only say the word."

Jesus's face split into a wide grin, and he turned to address Levi and the other city elders. "Did you hear that?" he asked proudly. "I'm telling you, this man believes harder than any Israelite I've ever met! Abraham could throw a family reunion for all Israel, and people would be thrown out just to get *this* man a seat! Rufus," he said, dropping the centurion's title, as if they were old friends. It was a daring move for a Jew, but Jesus was nothing if not daring—in some ways, at least. "Your wish is my command."

For research notes, see chapter 18 in the reference section.

XIX

That night was Judas's first taste of genuine fame. The healing of Jude's son was known to the entire town, and now with the display of two more miracles in a single day, the town went wild. All Capernaum turned out to see Jesus, and when the crowds realized there was not enough of him to go around, they turned to his disciples. Within an hour, everyone in Capernaum knew Jesus's name, as well as the names of Judas and the other nine. The four fishermen were asked to tell and retell their story a hundred times over. When Zebedee arrived, they swarmed him too. Rufus threw a feast for the entire city in honor of Jesus, and they welcomed the Sabbath by eating a good portion of the Jonas brothers' enormous catch. Zebedee was quick to assure everyone that there was still plenty more. Even the Pharisees and city elders had loosened up enough to join the festivities.

Rufus and the other Roman soldiers had respectfully kept their distance, choosing to celebrate apart from their Jewish subjects, but the groups occasionally mingled. Apelles, the centurion's formerly-paralyzed servant, now healthy—and a surprisingly good dancer—was as much a celebrity as anyone. In addition, Jesus cared little for social rules of separation, as he had proven beyond doubt by meeting the woman in Samaria at Jacob's well— alone. Jesus mingled with everyone in spite of the Pharisees' admonitions.

All Jews, but especially Pharisees, avoided Romans nearly as much as they avoided Samaritans. Jesus avoided nobody, which often led to trouble.

The night passed without any dire incident. Capernaum was more welcoming of Jesus than Nazareth by far, and it stood to reason, as Jesus had healed two of Capernaum's men without even seeing them. If that same ability could be applied to soldiers in combat, then perhaps Jesus's disinterest in raising a large army was understandable. Why expend resources for massive armies when a few highly trained operatives could be sent in without risk of injury? Judas knew he must learn to think differently with Jesus, as Jesus could do things no ordinary man could dream.

By the end of the night, the Pharisees and scribes had been so impressed with Jesus's conversation that they had agreed to let him teach in Capernaum's new synagogue. It had taken some subtle prodding by Rufus, who had built the synagogue and therefore had some limited influence, but it hadn't taken much to convince even the Pharisees. They were anxious to see what sort of teaching a man might have who could heal disease with only a word.

So, after a short nap at Zebedee's house—Simon had carefully avoided inviting them to his own home—Judas was spending the morning in synagogue, listening to teachings that he had heard repeated over the last several months and hoping that this time they would not be dragged away and thrown to their deaths. At least Capernaum had no cliffs. Even as often as he heard them, Judas did not grow tired of Jesus's sermons. All his life, Judas had listened to doctors of the Law give their opinions on scripture and argue between themselves about the meaning, but Jesus... Jesus did not argue. He knew. It was this confidence that had likely gotten him thrown out of Nazareth. Confidence was essential in a military commander, and Judas was anxious to see it used somewhere besides a Torah room.

Judas was relieved to see the receptiveness of Capernaum's spiritual elite. They sat in stunned silence but listened with fascination rather than offense. The entire synagogue listened with rapt attention—all but one. Judas always stood near the back. He preferred to study people rather than Torah, and his focus kept returning to one man, who was growing increasingly agitated. At first, Judas had taken it for nothing more than a nervous tick, but the man continued to grow worse, biting his fingers, holding his head, and moaning softly.

Suddenly, the man exploded, unable to endure his misery a moment longer. "*SHUT UP!*" he screamed, causing everyone to flinch in surprise at this unexpected outburst. "Get out! We don't *WANT* you here!" He clutched his head and stumbled back, staggering to remain upright. He stabilized and pointed a shaking finger at Jesus, who taught from the central podium. "Why are you *here?!* You've come to *DESTROY* us! I know!" The madman was now gasping for air, working himself into a frenzy.

No one moved to stop the lunatic. People watched in horrified silence at this sudden madness.

"I know!" the man shrieked. "I know *who you are*. You're God's Holy—"

"Quiet!" Jesus snapped, his tone impossible to ignore. The man quieted instantly, though he still stood, wheezing and swaying slightly. Jesus stared into the man's eyes. "Hello, Shelumiel," he said sadly. "It's been a long time."

The man snarled. "That's not my *NAME* anymore!" he shrieked. "I am *MASTEMA!* And *YOU*... I'm not the only one with a new name, am I, *Jesus of Nazareth?*"

"So that's how it is," Jesus said calmly, still filled with sorrow and still the only person in the room who had any expression on their face other than shock. "Hostility is not welcome here. This is a place of peace. *Get. Out!*" His sadness hardened into undeniable command.

The madman let forth a violent shriek of rage, and Judas feared the maniac might try to kill Jesus with his bare hands. The man lunged forward, hands curled into claws and reaching for his enemy's throat. He took two steps and collapsed in front of the podium.

The synagogue erupted. One of the elders rushed for the fallen man. "Jacob? Can you hear me? Jacob?"

"It was demons!" another man hissed, shying away from Jacob's unconscious body. "Always was touched in the head, was Jacob."

"Yes, it was," Jesus said calmly. "Jacob will be alright now."

The elder turned. "You... That demon *knew* you. He *obeyed* you! You merely commanded and... Who *are* you?!"

"Well," Jesus said, looking around at the dumbstruck crowd. "I think it's safe to say the services are over."

Levi, the high elder, stepped over, smiling awkwardly. "Yes, I believe it would be best if we broke for the afternoon—let people recover from the excitement. You are welcome at my table, rabbi."

"Thank you," Jesus said, "but I've made plans to eat at Simon's house." He smiled at the sun-tanned fisherman, whose face dropped in surprise.

"Ah, master?" Simon said quickly, licking his lips. "I would love to, but this is really a bad time. You should take Elder Levi's offer."

"But Simon, your house is just across the street," Jesus said, pointing.

Simon was growing more uncomfortable, and Judas wondered why. The fisherman had been keeping Jesus out of his house since yesterday. He was hiding something. Jesus ignored him and left the synagogue, heading for Simon's home. Judas followed, supremely interested in what the fisherman was hiding.

"Master," Simon said through clenched teeth, reluctantly following. "I'm not prepared to serve guests. *Please!*"

"That's alright. I'm not hungry," Jesus replied.

Simon finally broke. He swung around to plant himself in front of the door before Jesus could enter. "Alright!" he said, holding up his hands. "It's not that. It's not." He sighed heavily, rubbing his forehead. "It's my mother—I mean, my wife's mother. She has a fever. My wife is staying with her, but the elders are concerned it might spread, so they are both quarantined until it is certain that the fever is not contagious. You can't go in!"

"Ah, I had wondered. She's been quarantined?" Jesus asked, raising his eyebrows.

Simon drooped. "I haven't been inside for three days."

Jesus's brows drew down in concern. "Why didn't you tell me?"

"She's quarantined! It's the Law! There's nothing anyone can do but wait it out."

Jesus shrugged. "I don't feel like waiting. Besides, I know there will be questions about what happened in the synagogue, and I'm not ready for *that* conversation. A quarantined house might keep them at bay."

"Fine," Simon said in exasperated resignation, opening the door to allow them in.

Jesus paused in the doorway. "Are you coming, Judas?"

Judas hesitated. "No, rabbi. I'm going to scout the city. I'd like a plan in case things get out of hand."

"Wouldn't that be a better job for a local?" Jesus asked with a wry smile.

"I'll take the Zebedee brothers. They'll show me around, but I'd like to get a feel for things myself."

"You sure this isn't about not wanting to enter a quarantined house?" Jesus asked with a smirk.

"It's not that," Judas lied. "I just don't want a repeat of what happened in Nazareth."

"Alright," Jesus said with a shrug, "Don't keep the Zebedee boys out too late."

For research notes, see chapter 19 in the reference section.

XX

It was late in the evening by the time Judas was satisfied with his exploration. He had spent much of the time vetting James and John, and their bravado had been a pleasant surprise. Like himself, they were certain Jesus was far more than some magician but were also perplexed at his reluctance to take his rightful place on the throne of David. They were eager for revolution, but like simple fishermen, they were content to let Jesus decide the time and place. Judas was unsure if Jesus would *ever* take that step without being pushed into it. He had no doubt that Jesus belonged on Israel's throne. His only doubt was whether Jesus would be willing to take the necessary steps to reach it. Thankfully, Jesus had Judas to take those steps for him. Judas just had to figure out how.

James and John returned to the synagogue, but Judas lingered on the outskirts of Capernaum. He wanted to see things after dark in case they needed to slip away under cover of night. Capernaum did not seem hostile, but fame carried its own risks. However friendly Rufus was now, he was still a Roman, and any Jew who gathered a following would be viewed with suspicion—miracles notwithstanding. If Jesus's reputation continued to explode, the eyes of Herod and Rome would be on him long before he had anything resembling an army. Then again, perhaps the man didn't need one.

Judas returned to Simon's house sometime during the third watch. After the celebration the night before, he expected Capernaum to be asleep by this late hour, but such was not the case. The dark streets had been quiet, but only because everyone was here at the synagogue. The crowds were more organized this time. Judas maneuvered to the synagogue door, moving easily enough as most everyone let him pass, recognizing him as a disciple. He found Philip and Nathanael at the door, letting people in only a few at a time as others slipped out.

"City Boy! Where have you been? Isn't this great?" Philip asked, grinning from ear to ear. "He's been at it since early afternoon! I can't believe it! Look at these people!"

Judas looked and furrowed his brow. "They look diseased," he said with a grimace, leaning close to Philip's ear. "Everyone in this line looks like there's something wrong with them. What's going on?"

"Yes!" Philip said, beaming. "That's it! But look at the ones *leaving.*"

There was no one leaving just then, so Judas slipped inside. The other seven were inside, managing the people who came and went, while a separate crowd stood near Jesus. Jesus sat on a stool in front of the podium, speaking to a hunchback. The people behind him were mostly elders and Pharisees. Judas saw Levi among them, and Jacob, the recently possessed man. Jacob looked calm enough, watching Jesus with unrestrained awe. Simon and Andrew stood on either side of Jesus, and Judas noticed two women nearby, one younger and one older. Judas guessed them to be Simon's wife and mother-in-law. Both looked perfectly healthy.

Jesus stood and pulled the hunchback into a strong embrace. As stooped as the man was, it seemed an impossible feat, but the man melted into it. Judas did a double take as the man stepped away a moment later. He was *taller.* Jesus had pressed the man into his arms, and during the short embrace, the man's spine had *straightened.* He grabbed Jesus up in another embrace, thanked him, and launched himself toward the doorway with a spring in his step.

"They're going to kill him."

Judas flinched and found Thomas standing beside him.

"Look at him. They're pulling the life right out of him."

Judas looked closer. Jesus's head and shoulders slumped, as if his spine had somehow taken the man's infirmity. Jesus sat back down, nearly collapsing onto the stool. The next petitioner stepped up, but James the fisherman held out a hand. He waited until Jesus recovered enough to motion the next man forward. The man burst into a coughing fit and covered his mouth with his sleeve until the fit released him. Jesus gripped the man's arms, locked eyes with him, and took several deep breaths, encouraging the man to mimic his actions. The man's breaths were shallow at first, with a growling rattle at the base of them, but each grew progressively deeper until he was taking great lungfuls of air, even though the rattle persisted.

Jesus collapsed back on the stool, and the man embraced him, kissing his forehead as he spoke his thanks with a clear, deep voice. Little James ushered him away, but the rattling of his breathing lingered. Judas realized that the rattle no longer came from *him*, but from Jesus.

"You're right," Judas said, realizing Thomas's pessimism was correct. "He can't keep this up. I'll take care of it."

Judas maneuvered his way through the line of people. "Rabbi," he said, kneeling down so he could look Jesus in the eyes. "You can't keep this up. You have to rest."

Jesus looked up, his face haggard. He sat swaying on the little stool and struggled to focus on Judas. The man was barely conscious, and his breathing still held a concerning rattle, though it did sound slightly better up close. "Judas..." he said in belated recognition. "You didn't miss the party... after all..."

"Rabbi, you need rest. You must stop."

"No!" Jesus said, reviving himself. "Can't stop. Not now."

Judas gripped his shoulders. "Do you see how many people are here? There's more outside! You'll collapse before you heal them all!"

"Then that's... when I... stop," Jesus replied weakly. "Next!" he called, more forcefully than Judas had thought possible in his condition. Judas relented, recognizing that no amount of persuasion would work. He stood back to watch as the people continued to trickle in. The night wore on, and the lines never seemed to thin. Three times men with demons came, but Jesus refused to let them speak until he had cleansed them. A blind man was led in and walked out alone, eyes dazzling. Jesus's voice was the first sound a deaf woman heard, and she understood his words perfectly. A man limped in on crutches, only to abandon them.

As wonderful as the miracles were, each healing took its toll. Judas continued to try and get Jesus to stop, but as promised, Jesus continued until he collapsed. He was unconscious when the two Jameses carried him out. Simon's house was the closest, so they took him around the back to the narrow guestroom—hardly bigger than a closet, but enough room to sleep. There was still a line of people waiting in the street, but Judas and the other disciples got them moving toward their own homes, or wherever they planned to stay—many were not from Capernaum.

The dark sky was beginning to glow by the time everyone was settled. Philip and Thomas managed to squeeze into Simon's house along with Andrew on beds of straw laid out in the stable. The two goats which usually lived there were sent to Zebedee's house along with Nathanael and Thad, who were bunking with James and John. Little James got Zeb's guestroom to himself, since he was too large to squeeze in anywhere else.

That left Judas. Capernaum was so filled with visitors that every house and rooftop in the city was full. Many of the sick had fallen asleep on the street outside the synagogue, partly because there was nowhere else to go and partly so they could be first in line the following day. Judas had planned to sleep on Simon's roof under a makeshift tent, but in the end, he gave it to an old woman who was shivering from the cold night.

With nowhere to sleep, Judas sat down in front of Simon's house, staring at the people wrapped in their robes and forming lumps on the dusty street. There were still so many. Jesus could not bring himself to turn them away, even if it killed him. Judas knew the numbers would only grow, as those healed returned to their own villages and word spread. There would be more by the end of the day. There was no stopping them, and there was no stopping Jesus from healing them until he dropped dead. Jesus needed an intervention. Their Messiah would burn himself out and leave Israel in total darkness unless someone stopped him. There was only one solution, and only one person who knew it.

Judas had to kidnap the Messiah.

For research notes, see chapter 20 in the reference section.

XXI

J esus groaned and sat up, pulling off his blanket and blinking in the bright sunshine. He wrinkled his brow and took a look at his surroundings. "Where are we?" he asked, stretching himself with a groan.

"South of Mount Tabor," Judas replied, glancing back. "You sleep okay?"

Jesus examined his bed, which lay in an ox cart. "Not bad," he admitted. "Why am I in a wagon?"

"I... uh... kidnapped you," Judas admitted. "Are you angry with me?"

"Should I be?" Jesus asked.

Judas spun on his seat, letting the oxen drive themselves for a few minutes. He pointed at the sun. "It's almost noon. If I hadn't gotten you out of Capernaum, you'd have started healing people from the first light of dawn and still be healing them now—or dead from trying. I probably saved your life."

Jesus considered. "I'm not angry, Judas, but I wish you had talked to me."

"I did!" Judas exclaimed, throwing up his hands. "I talked to you as soon as I saw you! You refused to listen! You worked yourself unconscious! I had to take matters into my own hands."

"By stealing an ox cart?"

Judas grimaced. "I didn't steal it! I woke up Paulus—he's a servant of that centurion you healed. He loaned it to me. He's a Roman, but at least he won't tell the whole synagogue the first chance he gets."

"I have four new disciples in Capernaum who need my guidance. You didn't tell them where we were going?"

"We would have never gotten everyone out. *You* are my first priority. I barely got you out! We'll go back, master—but not until you've rested. We need you."

"So do they."

"Exactly," Judas said. "We all do. And it's my job to make sure you live long enough to keep being needed for a very long time, alright? Now, I know you must be starving, so I brought food. It's behind the seat. I'll get off the road if you want to stop, but I'm not going—*skubalon!*"

"There's no reason to use that kind of Greek," Jesus chuckled. "What is it, Judas?"

"Philip," Judas snarled, catching a glimpse of the man running down toward them from the top of a hill. "I knew he'd be the first to find us."

Judas turned the plodding oxen toward a small village not far off the road. "We can rest here. Maybe whoever is following Philip won't see us and think he's just stopping at the village to ask around."

Judas pulled the oxen around the side of a crumbling stone wall. "Can you walk?" he asked, stepping off the cart and moving around the front to tie the oxen to an olive tree.

Jesus looked to heaven and shook his head. "I'm fine, Judas. Really."

"Alright," Judas said, putting a tight cinch in the knot. He didn't like the idea of leaving the oxen here, but by now everyone in Capernaum would know to look for an ox cart. Maybe Philip could return it.

Judas heard the running footsteps before Philip appeared around the crumbling wall. "Judas!" he said, somehow barely out of breath. "Have you seen him? Where is he?"

"Seen who?" Judas asked.

"Jesus! Who else?" Philip asked. "Thought he was with you! Woke up this morning and you both were gone."

Judas spun. "He was right..." He saw Jesus's retreating form disappear around a low hill heading for the front of the village. "He's impossible to manage," Judas growled, taking off after him. "Where's everyone else?" he asked as the two men started after their quarry.

Philip laughed. "You can't imagine the uproar in Capernaum when they heard Jesus was missing. To tell the truth, I was a bit panicked, myself," he admitted jovially. "Now, Thomas..." Philip cracked up, laughing. "Thomas was the only one who took this in stride—said he figured it would happen eventually."

"I have yet to discover what sort of benefit Thomas brings to our group," Judas admitted. "The Lord bless him."

"I think it's his sense of humor," Philip said, barely keeping a straight face. "Anyway, the whole town set out to find you. We split into pairs."

"You came alone?"

"Teamed up with Simon," Philip said. "We wanted to pair the new boys with someone who's been around, so Nathanael took Andrew, Thad paired up with John, and we threw the two Jameses together. Thomas stayed behind because he didn't see any point in looking, but I think that's just his way of saying he wanted to wait in case Jesus returned."

"And Simon is...?" Judas asked as they turned the corner of a building.

"Went on ahead when he saw the village. I can keep a steady pace, but that fishmonger can *run!* I'd eventually outlast him, you know, but still... I'd send him to the hippodrome if I could find a saddle in his size."

Judas paused as a loud wail broke the stillness of the day. It started high and dropped in pitch until it ended in a dreadful moan. More voices joined the first, until the entire village was filled with the pitiful sounds. "Mourners," Judas said. "Not professionals, though. Probably just family. No surprise, as small as this village is. You know the name of it?"

Philip shrugged. "Nain, maybe? Ask them," he said, nodding his head to a small line of people making their way from the village. "But it's impolite to ask during a funeral. Is that..."

"It is," they said in unison, spotting Jesus at the same time. He was about a hundred feet ahead of them, heading straight for the funeral procession.

"Maybe he wants to pay his respects. It's not uncommon for strangers to join a procession," Philip said thoughtfully.

Judas had seen enough funeral processions to know how they went. The burial ground would be somewhere outside the village, and the deceased would be carried on a bier, wrapped in a shroud. The family would guide the procession, followed by men carrying the bier. If the family was wealthy, they would hire professional mourners to wail—often for days. The family went in front, while professional mourners always followed directly behind the bier, followed by the friends of the deceased, and then by whoever was curious enough to follow. This procession had only one woman in front of the bier; she had no family to mourn her loss. The rest of the village followed along behind, mourning the loss for her, but the absence of professional mourners meant the woman was too poor to hire them.

No money. No family.

As a stranger to the village, Jesus should have joined the crowd following along behind, but he instead stepped up beside the old woman, moving into stride with her as she took slow, heavy steps. To lead such a procession was to claim blood ties to the deceased. It was a bold declaration for anyone to make, let alone a stranger. By claiming to be her only living relative, Jesus would be legally obligated to provide for her welfare. Judas held the money, and he knew they could not afford this.

Jesus walked with the woman for a time, then dropped back. The four men carrying the bier paused, unsure whether to wait for this stranger to continue in the procession or to move on without him. Jesus took advantage of this pause and stepped up to the bier, resting his hand on the forehead of the corpse that lay under the shroud.

Judas stared in disbelief. "What is he *doing*? It's not like he can heal someone that's already—"

The corpse moved.

Judas flinched, watching from a hundred feet away. The effect was even more startling up close, and the men carrying the bier reeled back, dropping it in shock. The body crashed to the ground and sat up in confusion at such a rude awakening. The former corpse pulled the shroud off his face and looked around in bewilderment. Jesus knelt beside him, but Judas was too far away to hear his words. It couldn't have been much, because in the next instant, the woman rushed to the young man and threw her arms about him.

The boy is alive! Judas stared in wonder, his mind spinning with possibilities. Not only could Jesus heal disease, but also *raise the dead!* His armies would be unstoppable! Soldiers killed in battle could rise to fight again. And again. And again. Even Rome and her legions could not stand against an army that death itself could not stop. Suddenly, victory seemed within easy reach. So long as the Messiah lived, Israel would be unstoppable.

He shook himself out of his dreaming as a man bumped into him. He noticed that, yet again, a crowd was gathering. This little village, whatever its name was, wouldn't produce much of a crowd, but it would not be long before everyone knew. Judas trotted up to Jesus through the gathering crowd. Simon appeared from the crowd a moment before Judas reached them. "Master!" Simon said. "Where have you been?! Everyone is looking for you!"

Jesus grinned mischievously. "Judas decided that I needed some time away." He gave Judas a knowing look. "But he was right. We need a break from the cities." He turned to Simon. "We'll cut through the wilderness back to the sea. Tell the others to meet us there."

"They'll find us," Simon predicted. "Not just in Nain, but Capernaum, too. If Philip and I hadn't run the whole way, we'd have a crowd with us. There's no way we'll all be able to slip away from Capernaum undetected."

Jesus nodded thoughtfully. "Take the two boats. You can fit everyone, right?"

"Sure—more, if they don't bring much stuff."

"Good," Jesus said. "Take everyone first thing in the morning. We'll watch for you from the shore. And Simon," he added, "Can you return an ox cart for me?"

For research notes, see chapter 21 in the reference section.

XXII

"Can you believe this crowd?" Judas asked, staring at the people littering the hillside below.

"After Nain, I'll believe anything," Philip admitted. "Didn't take them long to find us."

"We aren't the only men who fish Galilee, you know," Andrew said. "Someone must have followed us by boat and reported back."

"Couldn't have picked a better spot!" Philip said cheerily.

Judas had to admit that the incurable optimist of their party was right. The hill where they stood sloped down on their left toward the sea of Galilee, and the view in the setting sun was breathtaking. The late autumn day was cool, but not overly so, even with the breeze coming off the sea. Jesus stood at some distance along the ridgetop, dismissing the crowd in the deep sun of early evening.

After leaving Nain, Jesus, Judas, and Philip had met the rest of the disciples coming by boat and camped by the seashore for one blissfully quiet evening. It hadn't taken the crowds long to find them again. People had started filtering in at dawn, and by mid-morning, it was a multitude. The previous night's sleep had refreshed Jesus somewhat, but he still looked tired. He had spent most of the day teaching from Simon's boat, just like he had at the Capernaum docks, but as the day wore on, he had moved to the top of the hill, where the majority of the sick and diseased had been taken. Half the afternoon had been spent in healing them and the other half in sending everyone away. Miraculously, Jesus had healed everyone there. Most people capable of traveling any distance were relatively healthy, so it hadn't been terribly taxing, but Jesus was still far more exhausted than he pretended.

More would come tomorrow as word spread, and the infirm had more time to reach them. Judas wasn't sure what Jesus had planned, but surely by now even Jesus was starting to understand the relentless power of a crowd. They would eat away at him, bit by bit, until there was no Messiah left to save them.

"Hey," New James said, trotting over from where Jesus stood speaking to the few stragglers who refused to leave. "Jesus said to prep the boats. We're taking off as soon as he can get away." Andrew nodded and moved to help. Of the four new disciples, Simon, James, and John, had clustered around Jesus from the start, not knowing anyone else. Andrew had gravitated back to Judas due to their previous friendship while hunting down John the dunkard.

Jesus finished dismissing the rest of the crowd as the four fishermen reached the boats. From his vantage atop the hill, Judas saw someone step from a hiding place behind the boats. The fishermen reeled to a stop. From here, Judas could see nothing about the man except that his face was covered. Bandits were common despite Rome's death penalty. Theft was difficult to prove without witnesses.

The leader of the *Sicarii*, known only by the title 'Son of the Father,' was notorious for stealing from supply caravans—even military caravans—and leaving no witnesses. Judas's funds had kept the *Sicarii* from needing to steal so frequently, but since Joseph's money had stopped, the Son of the Father was again forced to steal from foreign merchants and even rich Jews to supply his soldiers. He was smart enough to attack only when he outnumbered the enemy. This lone bandit must be desperate to steal from poor fishermen.

Strangely, the man had no weapon. Surely four burly fishermen could handle one unarmed bandit, but the men kept back, not daring to get within striking range. Jesus and the other disciples stepped over to where Judas and Philip watched this strange confrontation.

"What is it?" Nathanael asked.

"Looks like a poor attempt at thievery," Judas said with a chuckle, content to watch the action play out from a safe distance. "Too bad for him I carry the money."

"That's no thief..." Nathanael muttered, studying the bandit carefully.

Jesus started down without a word. The others followed. Down below, Andrew broke away from the confrontation and ran to meet them halfway up the hill, leaving his three friends to face the thief alone. "It's a leper!" he said, breathless from his run. "He says he won't leave the boats until he speaks to you. What do we do?"

"Abandon the boats," Judas said quickly. "He can't wait there forever. We can come back for them once he gives up and leaves."

"It can't hurt to see what he wants," Philip remarked carefully. "So long as we keep our distance..."

"I know what he wants, and he's not getting it!" Judas said angrily. "Healing ordinary infirmities is one thing, but I've seen what happens when Jesus heals someone! He takes on *their sickness!* We absolutely cannot risk the Messiah catching leprosy. It's too dangerous! The disease is highly contagious and has no cure. There's a reason lepers are quarantined—a good reason!"

Disease was often associated with sin. Sin was simply disease of the spirit rather than the body. Since the soul was comprised of both body and spirit, physical maladies were often seen as evidence of spiritual ones. Leprosy was the worst of all. The disease was feared, and with good reason. It often took years to develop beyond a certain stiffness of the joints, or a simple rash that refused to heal. By the time the sufferer thought to seek treatment, the disease had already taken root. All a sufferer could do was wait for their body to slowly digest itself from the inside, turning them into inhuman lumps of suffering flesh as their body ate itself away. Their hair, fingertips, and noses would go first, then their ears, fingers, and eyeballs, until their hands were no more than lumps and their faces melted into shapeless monstrosities. Eventually, the inner organs would rot, or the person would starve from an inability to feed themselves. Contact with a leper was strictly forbidden for safety reasons. That was why lepers lived in colonies. No sane person would dare risk exposure to the terrible disease. Lepers had to fend for themselves. In colonies, the less-advanced cases could tend to those unable to do for themselves.

This leper was alone. Most men would kill a leper before risking exposure, but the fishermen seemed content to let Jesus sort it out so long as the leper kept his distance. Simon and James hovered several yards away from the boats, right hands resting on the long, thin knives they used for filleting—both fish and thieves, probably. Not that a quick death was any kind of threat; a quick death would be a blessing for a leper.

The leper turned toward them as they reached the edge of the circle which the fishermen had formed to keep a safe distance between themselves and the afflicted one. The three fishermen had pulled their tunics up over their faces to prevent themselves from breathing the polluted air. As Judas and the others reached the edge of the circle, they did the same—all but Jesus. He left his face unmasked and stepped through the circle of distance required by social custom, entering the unclean space.

This shocking move brought an explosion of protests, but none would dare step forward and risk entering the zone of contamination. If the Messiah became unclean, it would be as terrible as his death. The Messiah *must* remain pure. An impure Messiah was unacceptable as much as a Passover lamb with a blemish. It simply could not be. If the Messiah became unclean, he would cease to be the Messiah. Judas shuddered in horror at the thought. Jesus *was* the Messiah, but leprosy was a deadly contagion. It was far different than healing a cough or a cripple.

The risk was too great. Judas lunged, rushing forward to grab Jesus's cloak and drag him back before the leper had a chance to unwittingly destroy Israel's one last hope. The desperate man had no idea what his selfish desires put at risk, but Judas did, and he would rather risk his own slow death than see the Savior of Israel destroyed by disease.

Jesus stepped lightly aside, and Judas found himself rushing headlong for the leper. To even be near a leper would render one ritually unclean, but to touch one... For a moment, Judas knew he was going to become a leper, but Jesus caught the back of his cloak and halted his headlong plunge into abomination. "It's not your time, Judas," Jesus said, calmly pushing him back. "Although I admire your enthusiasm." He glanced back, giving Judas a mischievous grin. "There's nothing to be afraid of," he added, although Judas couldn't be sure if Jesus was addressing him or the leper.

"So," Jesus said kindly. "You're the one holding our boats hostage. What's your name?"

"Jacob," the man said hoarsely, his face still covered with a cloth wrap, masking everything below his eyes.

This brought a grin. "Ah, Jacob. Quite the coincidence! You won't let me go unless I bless you. Is that right?" Jesus asked

"No! No! It isn't that way. I just... I had to try. I know what you can do. I will leave if you ask! I know what you are risking by even speaking to me. But if you wish it, I know you can heal me. You can cleanse me of this disease, but if you say no, I will leave. I swear it."

"Show me your face," Jesus said kindly. Jacob hesitated. Jesus smiled encouragingly. "It's alright. You don't have to be afraid."

Haltingly, Jacob took the cloth wrap and, fumbling with numb fingers, pulled it down around his chin. There were gasps from some of the disciples. They had probably never seen a leper up close. Judas had. The man's condition was terminal, but not terribly hideous. His nose was half gone and his mouth was deformed, but his eyes were clear and he still had enough fingers to remove the cloth around his face. He was moderately healthy and still had decades of suffering to look forward to.

Judas was frozen. Half of him desperately wanted to drag Jesus away from this awful danger, but the other half held him fast, desperately hoping. *Could it be possible...?* Jesus never flinched from the hideous face. He reached out a hand. The man shrank back instinctively. He had likely not been touched by a living person in years—not unless he had helped others who were even more deformed and desperate than himself.

Jacob trembled as the hand reached for his face and took a stumbling step back, his entire being fighting by habit to avoid the touch of another. He looked ready to flee at any moment, but his shaking form stood still as the hand reached up and palmed his jaw. Jacob stiffened.

"I am willing," Jesus said, pulling him slowly into an embrace. Jacob remained tense. "I am not made unclean. You are made clean."

As Jesus spoke the words, Judas saw the man's face shift. It was startling to see. Jacob's body *obeyed*. His body, once too weak to defend itself against this invader, was now suddenly energized with power, not only to stop the spread, but to repair the damage already done—with unbelievable speed. The man was growing back before their eyes.

It was over in moments. The man was in more shock than the disciples—too shocked even to offer gratitude, though his eyes were filled with it, flooding over with sparkling drops of thanks. Jesus gripped his shoulders. "Don't tell anyone about this," he commanded. "Not a word. Go to the Temple, get your certification from the examiner, and make the proper offering of thanks."

This statement shook Jacob out of his shock. "Examination?" he asked. "I don't need any examination! I can feel it! I see it!" he cried, holding up his hands.

"You can, but others may not believe without proof. Go," Jesus replied. The man did not hesitate, but took off for Jerusalem at a run, laughing and crying with unbelievable glee.

Jesus waited a moment as if expecting some response, but no one could bring themselves to say anything. "Boys!" he said finally, breaking them out of their daze. "Don't we have some boats to prep? We need to leave before sunset."

For research notes, see chapter 22 in the reference section.

XXIII

Judas sat huddled in the middle of the small fishing boat, clinging for his life as another swell threw the boat up before casting it back down into the deep trough below. "...'ve got ... back! ...ind's too ... ong!" James yelled from the other boat, barely visible in the stormy darkness. The cold wind ripped away half his words before they reached Judas.

Simon shook his head, straining against his oar to keep their boat from smashing into James and John's boat—again. "Can't turn back!" Simon yelled. "We'll capsize with this wind on us! We've got to push through!"

James's dark form disappeared as another wave dragged the boats apart. The Jonas brothers manned the boat carrying Judas, and the Zebedee brothers manned the other. They had squeezed Little James, Philip, Thomas, Nathan, and Thad into the boat with James and John, leaving Simon and Andrew with a slightly lighter load, only carrying Judas, Jesus, and all the gear, leaving Jesus enough room to stretch out on top of it. The healing had finally taken its toll, and they had arranged a space in the boat for Jesus to stretch out and get some rest. At least, that had been the plan before the sea unleashed its fury upon them.

"I knew this was a bad idea!" Simon shouted into the wind, groaning with effort as he struggled to steer the boat into another oncoming swell. The sea of Galilee was known for sudden squalls. Fishermen rarely ventured too far from shore, especially at night. Jesus had been insistent, however, and the two boats had struck out to cross the sea just before sunset.

Healing the leper had drained Jesus, and he had fallen asleep on their makeshift bed as soon as the boats had been loaded. His exhaustion was evident because even in the tossing waves, he slept on. "Keep bailing water!" Simon screamed, not taking his eyes off the black waves.

The night was dark and cold. Judas could barely see at all. One hand gripped the rail with terrified determination, keeping him partially steady in the small craft as the other searched desperately. He fumbled in the bottom of the boat, splashing in the frigid water that continually came over the sides, feeling for the collapsible leather bucket that was essential to every traveler. He had dropped it somehow, but he had no idea when. He could barely keep himself inside the rolling boat, even with one hand clamped firmly to the side. His efforts to bail water were poor at best, but it was better than going overboard. The water was too cold to survive for long, and his robes would only succeed in dragging him under. His searching hand found the bucket behind Simon's seat, half buried under Jesus, who slept on in the back of the boat, stabilized by the packs and kept above the rising water—for now.

Judas took a desperate breath as his stomach flipped and he suddenly lurched forward. The boat slid down the wave and into another trough, careening sideways. "*LEAN!*" Simon shrieked as the boat tilted precariously. Judas threw himself against the high side then back again as the boat rolled first one way and then the other. The boat stabilized as another wave struck, and the Jonas brothers pushed against the oars, straining to straighten the boat before the wave bowled them over.

Jesus slept on. "Wake him up!" Simon screamed, straining to be heard above the whipping wind. "Wake him! We can't keep this up!" They should have reached shore long ago. Galilee was only a few miles across, and they had been rowing for hours, but without gain. If anything, the wind was slowly pushing them back toward their starting point. Judas was ready to collapse from the strain, and he could only imagine the point of exhaustion that the fishermen were enduring after hours of constantly fighting the oars with both hands and bracing with their feet to keep from being thrown into the frigid water. All Judas was doing was holding on. "You've GOT to bail water!" Simon yelled again. "We're sinking!"

They weren't technically sinking—yet—but every drop of water inside the boat made it harder to steer and easier to capsize. Judas couldn't keep up, and the Jonas brothers were on the point of collapse; anything that could be done to help them must be done. If Simon or Andrew collapsed, they were all dead. Judas prepared to die and released his death grip on the side of the boat. He crawled shakily back, hoping that a sudden swell wouldn't toss him out. Simon leaned to one side as Judas reached behind him and shook Jesus.

The man slept on. If he could sleep through this, Judas would need something more to wake him. Desperate, he threw the bucket. It smacked Jesus on the head and bounced out of the boat. Judas cursed, but the sacrifice worked. Jesus woke with a start. "Wake up!" Judas screamed. "We're sinking! Help bail, or we're dead!"

Jesus sat up and gripped the boat as another wave made them lurch sideways. Judas threw himself down until the boat stabilized. "You have a bucket?" Jesus asked.

Not anymore... Judas's stomach dropped. "We're going to die!" he shrieked. Jesus looked around calmly, a strange expression on his face. "Do something!" Judas cried. "Don't you care that we're going to die?!"

Jesus rubbed his face and stood up. Judas's eyes widened in terror. He could barely stay in the boat on his knees, gripping the gunwale, and Jesus was *standing*. All it would take was one sudden swell, and their Messiah would be lost forever in the tossing waves.

"Enough!" Jesus yelled, shouting into the darkness. "Be still."

This absurd demand seemed to indicate that Jesus was possibly madder with desperation than even Judas. If the Messiah was grasping at straws, they were certainly doomed. There was no way...

The wind stopped. The waves still rocked, but without the wind whipping them up, their force lessened, until the desperate tossing of the boats transformed into a gentle rocking. As quickly as it had started, the storm was over.

Simon and Andrew sagged in their seats, exhausted, until a whoop from the other boat roused them. "Land!" James shouted. "I see land!" The clouds had broken enough to see a dim outline of the horizon ahead.

"Can't be far!" John added. "Less than a mile." The fishermen heaved to with renewed vigor as the dark shoreline came into sight.

As the boats found a landing point on the shore, a dim dawn light slowly brightened the rocky cliffs of the eastern shoreline. As soon as the fishermen had the boats on the shore, they collapsed. Judas set to work salvaging their wet belongings from the bottom of the flooded boat, too cold to rest.

"Where are we?" Little James asked, a massive hand shielding his eyes from the ever-brightening shoreline.

"Don't care," John mumbled. "It's land."

"Looks like Gergesa, maybe?" Nathanael mused. "We have any dry clothes?"

"Nope," Judas said, stripping off his cloak and wringing it out. "We'll just have to stay here until everything dries, including us."

"Great idea," Andrew mumbled from his bed of grass. It had been a long night for all of them, but especially the fishermen. Jesus was the only one who had gotten any sleep. No one spoke of their brush with death or the miraculous escape. They still struggled to process that their master could heal leprosy, let alone command the wind itself! None knew how to process *that* terrifying reality. A mortal man who held the power of God—it was dreadful and wonderful all wrapped into one.

"You boys get some rest," Philip said. "We'll spread out everyone's clothes to dry and then see if we can't get a fire going or hunt up a village and see where—what was that?" he asked, as a bone-chilling shriek filled the quiet dawn.

John's head shot up from the grass. "No... No! It can't be..." He shot to his feet, exhaustion gone. "We've got to go! Right now! Get everyone back in the boats."

"What is it?" Thad asked skeptically. Judas could relate to his reluctance. He wasn't about to throw all their wet things back in the boats without good reason.

"John figured out where we are," James moaned. He raised his left hand but didn't stir from his supine position. "Gadera is that way. They bury their dead by this sea. Their cemetery isn't far from here. There are *monsters* here," he said mockingly.

"Stories fishermen tell when they can't catch any fish," Simon groaned. "It's fine. I'm not moving."

Another shriek exploded over the quiet shore, sounding closer.

"Not moving!" Simon repeated.

"Second that," Andrew mumbled.

"It's not stories!" John cried. "I met a guy who saw them! They stay in the tombs and attack anyone who gets close. They're animals!"

"If they were real, Rome would have crucified them by now," James growled. "Go to sleep, little brother."

"They *tried!*" John protested angrily. "Rome can't capture them. They rip the chains right off!"

"Right," Simon groaned. "They rip off *iron chains*. They live in tombs. All you need to add is that they cut themselves and eat the flesh of small children who forget their prayers."

Another shriek came, followed closely by a second. These were *much* closer. Judas's brow drew down as he caught the glimpse of a dark form against the horizon of a nearby hill. Something *was* coming, whatever it was. John saw it too and rushed for the boats. "Leave the gear. We have to go *now!*" he cried in panic, anxiously struggling to drag the sodden boat back to the water by himself.

A guttural cry sounded close by, then turned into a shriek, followed by a hoarse groan. John froze.

"Too late," Thomas said quietly as two large men rushed toward them from the shadows. John dove into the boat. His fellow fishermen leapt to their feet, but not before two madmen rushed them. The madmen were naked and covered in cuts. Spittle flew from gaping mouths, showing teeth that seemed unnaturally long. Little James was already on his feet and threw his entire weight at the intruders. Little James was probably twice their size, but the first lunatic planted a hard fist into his chest with an inhuman hiss, and Little James flew backward as easily as a pillow. The big man struck the ground hard and crumpled.

The Jonas brothers didn't hesitate. They rushed the maniac. Andrew reached him first and swung his knife, missing the man by a hairsbreadth. The man didn't even flinch and snatched Andrew's throat, throwing him back as easily as he had Little James. This gave Simon an opening, however, and he slashed at the man's arm with his own knife, leaving a deep cut. The man twisted, snatching Simon's wrist with his injured arm and wrenching it. Simon struggled to break the madman's grasp but failed completely. The man slowly turned Simon's wrist until the long blade of the knife pointed toward the madman's other arm. The madman eagerly slid his arm across the sharp blade, giving himself a second cut to mirror the one Simon had given him, smiling as he did it, before throwing Simon away with a chilling laugh.

"Stop!" Jesus cried. "Leave him!"

The madman spun instantly, eyes locked on Israel's Messiah. His lip curled into a snarl. "What do *you* want, *Jesus*? You son of a—" His throat clenched. "Son of God Most High?" he asked, forcing out the words painfully.

Judas recognized the greeting. The man was possessed. Both men were. The second man hung back in the dawn shadows, shoulders hunched and eyes glowing.

"Please," the first man begged, his voice breaking from the deep snarl into a fearful whisper. "Please... Don't hurt me."

Jesus released a breath. "What's your name?"

Both men laughed.

"Can't tell?" the first hissed in a slithering voice, his confidence returned.

"Can't... quite decide?" asked the other, almost overlapping the first.

"Can't nail it down?" the first cut in.

"Too many choices?"

"Too many guesses?" The two were nearly talking over each other.

"One name isn't enough."

"So many options."

"So many choices."

They paused, suddenly speaking in unison: "*So many demons.*"

"Call us 'Legion,'" the first spoke up again.

"Legion," the second echoed. "We are many."

"So many."

"An entire army."

"An army of demons."

"Rome cannot stop us."

"No one can stop us."

"*I can.*" The words came out with such force, even the disciples fell back a step. The two demoniacs fell to their knees, all bravado gone in an instant.

"Please," the first begged. "Please, do not send us to the deep."

"The swine!" the second spoke, his face still hidden in the dim light.

"Yes!" the first agreed. "The swine!" He pointed to a distant hill where several Gentile swineherds watched a large group of pigs. "Let us enter the swine."

"The swine," the second echoed again.

Jesus watched the men carefully, his brow creased with sadness. There was always some strange sense of loss about the Nazarene when he dealt with demons. "I will allow it," he said, and his tone left no question that it was indeed an act of mercy, rather than any fearful attempt to pacify the monsters. They were no threat to him, and they knew it. "Now *go.*"

They went. Both men screamed—a scream longer than Judas thought the human body capable of producing. Finally, the men collapsed. They were bleeding, weak, and disoriented.

Judas had seen Jesus cast out enough demons to know the aftereffects by now, and with the number of demons inside these two... He snatched two tunics from the spread where they lay drying, not caring whose they had been. He brought them over. "Here," he said, offering one to each. "You'll need—" His voice caught in his throat as he got near enough to see the men's faces. Neither was a pure Jew. The first was a local, someone from Gadara or Gergesa most likely, but the second...

The second was a Canaanite. Judas finally found his voice as he stared into the wild and unkempt face of his former *Sicarii* contact. "Simon?"

For research notes, see chapter 23 in the reference section.

XXIV

"I don't remember much..." Simon the Canaanite said. "What month is it?"

"Kislev," Judas answered. "I haven't seen you in over a year! How did you get here—get like... this?" Judas was reluctant to explain how exactly he knew Simon the Canaanite. Some Jews supported the *Sicarii*, but not many. They stole to survive and used spies and assassins to do their work; none could stand against Rome in open warfare. Their methods were too cruel for most to condone, but their hit-and-run tactics were based on the actions David had used to escape Saul and defeat the Philistines. Still, of the few Jews who recognized the *Sicarii*'s importance, Jesus was not among them. He had many views which opposed tradition, but in this he would certainly side with the majority. Jesus avoided violence like leprosy—except that Jesus did not avoid leprosy. The Messiah was a mass of contradiction.

"I was sent here by the Son of the Father," Simon admitted.

Thad sucked in a breath. "The Underground," he said wonderingly, throwing another log on the fire. Everyone had heard the name of the Underground's notorious leader, but nothing else was known about the mysterious man. He had no mercy for Romans or Roman sympathizers.

"He sent you to kill the beast?" John asked without thinking.

The other demoniac dropped his head at this title. Jesus put a comforting hand on his shoulder. "That evil is gone, Lucius. You have nothing to fear from it now."

Lucius nodded. The two madmen had washed themselves in the cold waters of the sea after coming to their senses. By the time the disciples had given them some of their extra clothes and let them comb their hair and beards, the two men looked remarkably presentable—even their wounds had been healed. A stranger would be unable to tell which of their group had been the two so recently insane.

"*Kill* him?" the Canaanite asked. "No. I was sent to *recruit* him." He shook his head. "Come on, what would you think? Rumors of a man living in the wilderness, whom the Romans cannot capture? A man who could not be killed or bound with chains? It was a prophet with the strength of Samson! I came to find the Messiah! I found... something else. The rest is a blur. I... I can't remember."

"You pledged yourself to me—well, to them," Lucius said quietly, continuing the story. "I remember that. You said I was despised and rejected, a man of sorrow; everyone hid their faces from me. You said that with my strength, it proved me to be your Christ. *They* reveled in your belief."

"They were right, though," Simon countered. "In a way." He looked at Jesus with renewed wonder. "I *did* find the Christ. He's just... not who I expected."

Jesus chuckled. "Join the club."

"Hey," Simon bar Jonas said nervously, nodding toward the hill behind them. "Company."

Coming down the hill was a group of city officials bordered by a double squad of Roman soldiers. Behind them came the swineherds who had been tending the pigs—before the demons had stampeded the entire herd off a cliff and killed them all.

"That's them!" one of the swineherds said, pointing. "I don't know how they did it, but it's them, for sure! Spooked the whole herd. They gotta pay for damages, or you're gonna arrest 'em. Hope you brought irons for..." He paused to count. "Thirteen!"

"We'll take it from here, Janus," the leader replied. He stepped up to their group with a patronizing smile. "These men claim you are responsible for the destruction of their entire drove of pigs—about two thousand. They—" The official's face went white. "*Lucius?*"

"Governor Cyrus," Lucius replied, smiling. "It's good to see you well."

Governor Cyrus might have replied in kind, but he was overcome with shock. The Roman soldiers paled, and the swineherds retreated a step. "It *is* you," Cyrus whispered. "How..."

"It was him!" Lucius said eagerly, pointing at Jesus. "He freed me!"

Jesus stood and smiled politely. "I am also to blame for the death of your herd. The demons begged to be sent into the swine, and I decided to allow it."

Governor Cyrus let out a nervous chuckle, half terror and half disbelief. "I've personally seen that man—if man he was—snap chains like twigs," he said, pointing cautiously at Lucius. "We've captured him while he slept and chained him. Each time, we find our chains shattered—not cut, nor worn away—*shattered*. I sent an entire garrison of soldiers to kill him, and the two who survived fled in terror. Now we find him here, clothed, calm, and lucid. And you say the demons who tormented him killed the swine because you 'allowed' it? You *allowed* it?!"

"They asked nicely," Jesus said with a slight shrug.

"They... asked..." Cyrus laughed nervously. "Two years Lucius has plagued this region. Not only attacking others but himself as well. He has the strength of a thousand men! And you..."

Jesus nodded. "Yes. Do you want me to pay the damages?"

Cyrus's already white face turned an even lighter shade. Judas could easily imagine the thoughts which assaulted the governor's head; Cyrus knew what to expect from the screaming madness of the demoniacs, but this man, who had healed their rage with only a word and who now stared back at him with such quiet calm, Cyrus could not comprehend. It was obvious that Jesus terrified him.

"That... that won't, uh, won't be necessary... Will it?" Cyrus asked, turning desperate eyes on the group of swineherds. Cyrus was a sensible man and knew better than to demand anything of someone with such power. The swineherds also realized the danger in angering such a man and quickly relented. No one dared upset the man who held such impossible power.

"Wonderful!" Governor Cyrus said nervously. "We have no, uh, no reason to detain you here, since there are no pressing charges. You are... are free to return to... wherever you wish. Free to... leave." He smiled again, more nervously than before, as he gestured hopefully toward their boats. "We wouldn't want any... uh, complications."

From their point of view, the longer Jesus stayed, the more risk there was in them doing something to upset him, but none would dare to openly demand anything from him. They could only make subtle hints and hope he decided to leave on his own.

Judas watched their response with growing pride. This was how the Messiah should be received. These heathens recognized the power of the Christ while Jesus's own city had tried to kill him. If Jesus showed just a fraction of his power, this type of response would not be such an isolated event. Perhaps now, Jesus finally realized how to provoke an appropriate response to his kingship.

Jesus chuckled to himself. "No, no, we wouldn't want that," he mildly replied. "My friends and I were just leaving."

"Just leaving?!" Simon bar Jonas cried. "We just got here! I've been rowing for—"

"We were *just leaving*," Jesus said more forcefully.

Simon groaned.

"Yes," Cyrus said quickly, breathing an obvious sigh of relief. "Excellent. That would be best. Godspeed in your travels, be they near... or far. Preferably the latter," he added under his breath.

"You're coming with us," Judas said, gripping Simon the Canaanite on the shoulder. If Jesus chose to pacify these heathens rather than reveal his true power, at least Judas could gain an ally within the ranks of the *Sicarii*.

"Yes, please," Lucius replied. "Take us with you."

"Your place is here, Lucius," Jesus said kindly. "You have family here. You've been gone a long time. They need you. Gergesa needs you. I'm going to be coming back. When I do, it's your job to make sure they want me here. Alright?"

Lucius nodded. "Alright. Yes. I am your man, whatever you command. But I know nothing about you. What do I tell them?"

"Tell them what you do know." Jesus smiled. "You've already made a fine start."

For research notes, see chapter 24 in the reference section.

XXV

Two things happened when Jesus and his disciples reached Capernaum. The first was that the four fishermen, who were by this time totally spent, went home to find some dry clothes and a bed. The second: a crowd appeared.

As soon as word spread that Jesus was lunching at the house of High Elder Levi, he was swarmed. Tired as he was, Jesus was probably the least tired of their group, as he was the only one who had gotten any sleep the night before. The six disciples who hadn't spent all night rowing for their lives were placed on crowd control.

Levi's house had a large dining hall, as well as separate rooms for sleeping, cooking, and the study of Torah. A low wall joined the main house with several outbuildings to create a large, central court. It was quite the contrast from the simple one-room houses that were common among the lower classes. After lunch, Jesus had commandeered the large dining hall for teaching, as it had a wide window looking into the central courtyard. The courtyard was packed and had been for hours.

"When will you report back?" Judas asked, letting the late afternoon sun warm his back. He and Simon were watching the crowd from the roof. Like most houses, the roof was almost flat, with a low wall around the outside as the Law commanded. From this vantage, Judas and Simon could keep an eye on everyone and speak without fear of hungry ears. Simon the Canaanite had been absorbed into their group without complaint, though the other disciples were reserved around him. He made them nervous, and like Judas, he didn't fit in with the Galileans. Simon was fully restored to himself, but he still exuded a certain dangerous energy. Simon was a weapon.

Simon considered the question quietly. "I don't think I will," he said finally. "I joined the Underground to free Israel from Roman rule—to prepare her for the Messiah. From everything you've told me—everything I've experienced myself—the Messiah is *here!* Why would I return to serve the one who calls himself Son of the Father when the Father's true Son is here? The only reason I would go back is to tell them that the man for whom they fight has come!"

"They might not want to hear it," Judas said.

Simon creased his brow. "What do you mean?"

"Jesus is... not what I expected. Not what you expect either, I imagine. He has shown no interest in breaking the Roman yoke. In fact, he is friends with the centurion here. Don't get me wrong; I believe in him, but... he has no initiative. He is perfectly happy to travel, teach, heal, and nothing else. As wonderful as that is..."

Simon pursed his lips. "What are you saying?"

"We need Gideon, Samson—well, perhaps not Samson—but David, or Moses! If anyone could march into Rome itself and give Caesar ten kinds of plagues, it would be Jesus, but he does not."

Simon shrugged. "Be patient, Judas. Moses was a shepherd for forty years. You have been with Jesus for only one. When the time is right, I am sure he will act."

Judas laughed. "You've been with him for only a day, and yet you trust him more than I. I've missed you, Simon. Jesus needs your abilities."

"I hope not," Simon said quietly.

Judas furrowed his brow. "What do you mean? Of course he needs you! You're the only one of us with any experience in combat."

Simon shook his head gravely. "You don't understand what he saved me from. I pray you never will. When I first joined the *Sicarii*, the idea of killing a man sickened me. But I was told that it was right—it was for Israel—so I forced myself to do it, to love it. I was sick with it. I never imagined the Messiah as a Prince of Peace. I thought peace could only be achieved through bloodshed. If Jesus never asks me to pick up a weapon, I will be glad of it. I shudder to imagine the man I was. Violence took me hostage. It was peace that freed me."

"But the war hasn't even begun. Battles must be fought. You know the prophecies!" Judas protested.

"What of you?" Simon asked, quickly changing the subject. "Do you still work for Joseph?"

"I was... fired," Judas admitted. "He learned I had been taking his money, but I never revealed where it went. I managed to slip away without ending up on a cross. That brought me here. Strange, isn't it? The very tragedy which broke my ability to help Israel led me to her savior."

Simon grinned. "Perhaps you do understand."

Judas did understand. Simon would not be the ally he had hoped him to be. The man had seen horrors, Judas was certain, and his hesitation was understandable, but what use was a soldier who was afraid to fight? Perhaps Simon's fear of violence would fade with time. "I cannot even begin to—who's this?" Judas asked, spotting a head appear on the stairway leading up to the roof from the outside wall. "Who are you?" he asked the stranger.

"I did not mean to disturb you, friends," the man said meekly. "We were seeking a way to see Jesus. You see..." He continued up the stairs, and Judas saw that the man was carrying the front end of a woven mat, bent with the weight of the man lying on it. Another man bore the other end, and in the middle was a man who appeared paralyzed from the waist down.

"Hello," the man on the stretcher said, lifting a hand in greeting. "We could not even enter the courtyard, it was so packed. Had to come around back."

High Elder Levi's house had an outer stairway that lead straight from the garden to his roof, where he—or his servants, more precisely—could store and access their tools without needing to spread dirt through the house by entering a backdoor or walk around the wall to the front entrance.

Judas and Simon exchanged a look and shrugged. Who were they to decide who could or could not stand on High Elder Levi's roof?

"Alright," Judas said. "Can't see from here, but you can listen. Set him down near the front."

The men set their friend down in a corner where he could listen, then turned to go. Judas and Simon migrated to the opposite corner where they could still speak privately in hushed tones. "Have you ever met the Son of the Father?" Judas asked quietly, unable to let the topic rest.

"His identity is closely guarded even in the Underground. But he reveals himself to those who succeed in killing a Roman official without detection." Simon hesitated. "I've met him," he said quietly, almost reluctantly. "I was good at what I did, Judas, but... what I did was not good."

"You fight for Israel! The methods may be brutal, but the result is noble."

"You saw the reward I received," Simon said grimly. "If the Messiah calls me to fight... I don't know if I can. I have too much blood on my hands already."

"You will!" Judas said encouragingly. "The Messiah did not forget you in Gadara, and he will not forget you now. We will find a way to—Hey!" he exclaimed, as he heard a loud thwack behind him.

Both men spun at the sudden noise as another thwack struck the roof. The paralytic's two friends had not left but had instead stolen two picks from High Elder Levi's gardening tools and were attacking the rooftop with a vengeance. Like most Judean roofs, it was supported by several wooden beams laid in parallel, covered in layers of woven straw, and sealed with a thick layer of clay.

"We must"—*thwack*—"reach"—*thwack*—"Jesus," one man said in between swings. He paused, raising his pick menacingly. "Do *not* try and stop us."

Simon raised an eyebrow. The men didn't know what sort of man they were threatening—at least, what sort of man Simon had once been. He and Judas shared a look. Judas nodded toward the two men, but Simon just chuckled. "I'm not going to stop you," he said with a grin.

"*What?*" Judas asked through his teeth. "You're going to let them vandalize this man's roof?"

Simon nodded nonchalantly. "I admire their ingenuity. Come on, Judas, these are two men who will stop at nothing to find help for their friend, and without anything resembling a plan, they set about it. You, of all people, should admire that—or relate to it," he muttered. "Besides, this high elder is a pompous ass, and he can obviously afford to fix the roof. Plus," he added, "there are visiting Pharisees here, as well as disciples sent from John."

"Go on..." Judas said, starting to catch Simon's drift.

"Jesus hasn't healed a single person all day. John is in prison, and his disciples are here to find his successor. The Pharisees are the voice of the people. Any movement to unite Israel must have their support, and the only way an outsider like Jesus will ever gain their support is if he shows them what he can truly do."

"Jesus does nothing for show. He takes intentional steps to avoid it," Judas countered.

"But he will not turn away men who have tried so hard to reach him, will he?" Simon asked. "Especially not when the man falls right into his lap." A soft crunch sounded as one of the picks broke through the layer of clay and punched into the straw, creating a small hole.

"We're going to get blamed for it anyway," Judas admitted. "Might as well put on a show."

Simon smiled. "I'll stop anyone from coming up the stairs. You help them lower him down." The men set to work. Shouts from below sounded as those inside suddenly noticed the attack on the roof. It wouldn't be long before someone was sent to investigate.

Judas found a length of rope and set about tying it around the paralytic's bed, but the paralytic stopped him. "I can hold the rope," he said. "My arms are strong. They are my legs as well. I'm Caleb."

Judas clasped the man's hand. "Judas."

Once the first pick breached the roof, it didn't take long to enlarge the hole. The beams were a little less than a cubit apart but wide enough for a thin man to slip through. Judas knew Simon couldn't buy them much time without resorting to violence, so he quickly gripped Caleb's mat and pulled him over to the hole, swinging his legs into it. Jesus's teaching abruptly stopped as two thin legs appeared through the hole in the roof.

Caleb's two friends grabbed the rope to help support his weight. Judas pushed Caleb into the hole as his weight dragged the mat with him. The mat slid through the hole and landed on High Elder Levi's ornate dining table, which was now littered with clay dust and broken straw.

"His name's Caleb," Judas said through the hole, smiling. "Sorry to interrupt. He wants to ask a favor."

"Hello, Caleb," Jesus said, glancing at the hole as the man slowly came to rest on Levi's low table. "Impressive."

"That's destruction of property!" Levi cried, still sitting at his table, surrounded by visiting Pharisees from all over Galilee. He hadn't moved to investigate the attack on his roof. Either he felt the damage was already done, or he had sent servants in his stead.

"I will work to repair the damages!" Caleb said quickly.

"You're a cripple," Levi replied coldly. "What kind of work could you possibly do?"

Caleb ignored this question. "Rabbi," he said, focusing on Jesus. "As a child, I broke the fifth commandment and was crippled. My father taught me to build, but I ignored his instructions and broke my back by falling from a roof. I have carried this sin and this guilt ever since."

Jesus inspected the intruder. "Your friends punch a hole in Elder Levi's roof, and you publicly promise to repay the debt even though you have no means. Risky, don't you think?" Jesus asked.

Caleb smiled hopefully. "*You* can provide the means! And when I am whole, and my debt settled, I can finally be free of this sin."

"I have even better news," Jesus said, his eyes twinkling with mischief. "Your sin is already forgiven."

This bold statement brought several gasps from the Pharisees. They didn't speak, but it was evident that this statement made them extremely uncomfortable. No man held the power to forgive sins.

Jesus turned on them, his eyes still twinkling. "Oh, right," he said in mocking forgetfulness, smacking his forehead. "That's blasphemy! Only God has the power to forgive sin. It's so easy to assume the worst, isn't it? It's even easier to lie about something that can't be proven. We can't *see* sins, but when the sin is removed, the curse is lifted. Isn't that what you teach? So, here is your proof:" He turned to Caleb. "Stand up, take your mat, and walk home."

Caleb's face brightened, and he maneuvered himself with his hands to the edge of the low table, letting his atrophied legs flop to the floor. He looked at Jesus questioningly. Jesus nodded. Judas's position on the roof gave him a unique vantage, and as Caleb's feet hit the tiled floor, his shrunken legs thickened as forgotten muscles suddenly bulged with new vigor. Caleb gasped and stood, releasing the table. The crowd was as silent as stone, watching Caleb reach down for his mat without hesitation, then stand again with perfect balance. "Thank you," he breathed.

"Go on," Jesus said, nodding toward the door. "I know your father's old tools are aching to be used again. You have a roof to fix."

Caleb's look of wonder broke into a huge grin. "I do!" he said. The crowd parted for him, gaping as the former paralytic walking out on two firm legs. The silence lasted for a long minute, then exploded into chaos as the Pharisees began arguing among themselves as to the implications of this momentous feat. Some argued that the healing did indeed prove the veracity of Jesus's claims, while others contended that sin and sickness were not the same and one did not prove the other. Between these were other factions, all arguing from one idea to another.

High Elder Levi watched the chaos with growing concern. He approached Jesus. "You should go," he said. "My brethren will consider what you have said, but as someone outside our sect, your presence will make them uncomfortable. You've proven your point, now you must give them time to digest it."

Jesus nodded. "Thank you for your hospitality, Levi." He turned to go and met a solid wall of people standing in the courtyard. Judas whistled through the opening in the roof, catching Jesus's attention. He wiggled the rope. Together, he and Caleb's friends pulled Jesus up through the narrow hole.

"If we hurry, we can slip away before the crowd gets themselves out of the courtyard," Judas said, knowing that even though the front of the crowd would see Jesus's escape to the roof, it would take time for the back of the crowd to let them out.

"Excellent," Jesus replied. He turned to Simon. "Judas always has a plan when we need to escape. Right, Judas?"

"Uh... right!" Judas said, slightly late.

"And don't worry about the others," Jesus replied. "They already know where to meet us."

"Excellent!" Judas said with relief. "Ah... Where is that, exactly?"

"Levi's house," Jesus replied.

Judas blinked. "Master, *this* is Levi's house."

"Different Levi."

"But... there's only one other Levi in Capernaum. That's Matthew-Levi, and he's..." It was just like Jesus to utterly stain his reputation by dining with a sinner and ruin the perfect opportunity to convince the Pharisees of his Messianic identity. The man was infuriating.

"A tax collector, I know," Jesus replied.

"A *tax collector!*" Judas emphasized. "Do you realize what that will do to your rep—clearly not, or you wouldn't suggest it!"

Jesus nodded. "The only house in all Capernaum where we might be left alone."

For research notes, see chapter 25 in the reference section.

XXVI

"We will be leaving Capernaum for Jerusalem soon, for the Passover," Jesus said, using his bread as a scoop to dip into the large bowl of lentils in the middle of Matthew-Levi's table. "I mentioned this to Matthew-Levi earlier."

"Just Matthew is fine," the tax collector said.

"Matthew," Jesus corrected. "We want you to join us."

"We... do?" James asked skeptically.

Judas agreed with James' reluctance, but he would never voice that opinion openly—not in the man's own home. It was Jesus who had decided to eat here. Eating at a tax collector's house was bad enough, but openly asking the man to travel with them would put a black mark on Jesus's already sinking reputation. Of course, Jesus did not care about such things. Which meant someone else had to.

"Yes," Jesus said, glaring at James, and passing his severe gaze to the other disciples who sat cross-legged around the low table. "*We do.*"

Questioning your rabbi's decisions was grounds for dismissal, but Jesus kept an open dialogue with his followers. He welcomed questions—usually—which meant those few times when he refused to be questioned, no one dared complain. He had never forced anyone to leave, but there was always a first time.

"We spoke earlier today at your booth," Jesus reminded Matthew. "You said you would give me your decision tonight."

"Yes," Matthew said quickly. "I must admit you took me by surprise. I didn't truly know what to say. No Jew has asked me anything—anything polite, that is. Of course, my answer is yes!"

Jesus leaned back on his left elbow into a more relaxed and informal dining position. "Excellent," he said cheerfully.

"Yes, just perfect," Simon bar Jonas muttered under his breath.

Jesus caught the comment and gave him a mockingly wide grin.

The other Simon, strangely enough, seemed to take no issue with Matthew's inclusion. The *Sicarii* had a long history of hating and even killing any Jew who collaborated with Rome, and tax collectors were high on that list—not only for aiding Rome, but also for the large sums of money they collected. The Canaanite should be the most incensed at the invitation, but he had remained strangely silent.

One of Matthew's servants entered the room, interrupting their meal.

"Yes, Eubulus?" Matthew asked. All of Matthew's servants were Greek. No self-respecting Jew would ever work for a Roman collaborator unless they were sold into slavery and forced into servitude in a foreign land.

"There are Jews outside, demanding to speak to your guest," he said, extending a hand toward Jesus. He cleared his throat. "They seem... *pious*," he added, struggling to find a way to politely explain the attitude of the Pharisees toward those sub-human wretches who stole from Israel under the Roman title of *publicanus*.

Matthew had likely never even spoken to a Pharisee. The only time a Pharisee would even acknowledge the existence of a tax collector was for the purpose of paying taxes, and a Pharisee would send a servant or hired man to keep himself from being defiled by the sin of the traitor. Matthew glanced at Jesus, unsure how to respond.

Jesus smiled wickedly. "By all means, let them in!"

Eubulus cringed. "They will not enter."

Jesus's face fell in mocking disappointment, and he made a sad noise.

Judas sighed. "I'll see what they want. Nathan, you want to come?" he asked, knowing Nathanael was the only other of their group who had any sense of decorum. Jesus may not care what the Pharisees thought, but Judas knew their support was essential to ascend the throne of David.

"Eh, why not, City Boy?" Nathanael asked, pushing himself to his feet and heading for the door.

Outside, Judas and Nathanael met a group of the visiting Pharisees from High Elder Levi's house. John's disciples had come as well. Not all the visiting Pharisees had dared come this close to the house of a *publicanus*, but a few had. It was a good sign. They were interested enough in Jesus to risk at least this much.

"How can your master eat with... *these* types?" one asked in greeting.

"Tax collectors and sinners!" another interjected. "Gluttons and drunks!"

Judas took a breath. It was not the greeting he had hoped to hear. He was expecting questions like this but had no answer for them. Nathanael appeared no better capable of explaining their master's actions. Much of Jesus's behavior was maddeningly inexplicable, but his origins and the power he possessed proved him the Messiah, regardless.

"Doctors don't visit the healthy," came a voice from behind them. Judas turned and found Jesus leaning in the doorway, smiling kindly. "They visit the sick. You are doctors of the Law, yes? Have you visited this house before?"

The Pharisees paled, but Jesus's words had drawn the interest of John's disciples, who drew closer.

"Of course not!" the Pharisee replied vehemently before calming himself. "We choose to keep ourselves pure. It is difficult, and sacrifices must be made, but God has given us a higher calling."

"Higher?" Jesus asked. "Really? Is there no higher calling than what God desires? Go back to school and study the meaning of the phrase: 'I desire mercy and not sacrifice.' I didn't come to call the righteous to repent, but sinners. We'll compare notes when you finish."

Judas was struck by this simple, yet profound answer. So quickly, Jesus had taken the Pharisees' ideas and turned them on themselves, leaving the doctors of the Law as speechless as Judas and Nathanael.

"Why do you never fast?" one of John's disciples asked in the sudden stillness. "We fast often, as do the Pharisees, but your disciples never do."

"Come on," Jesus said with a shrug. "Fasting is for times of mourning and distress. When the bridegroom is with his friends, they feast! There will be plenty of time for sadness and fasting when the groom is gone and sorely missed. Are you hungry?" Jesus asked. "You can come in, if you like. There's plenty of food."

John's disciples hesitated but actually considered the invitation. Judas remembered that John was not any harsher on tax collectors than he was on anyone else. He viewed it as simply another occupation, no worse than any other, but old habits died hard.

They never had a chance to decide, as one of Capernaum's elders rushed up to the group and dropped to his knees, bowing his head to the ground in an act of worship. To worship a mere man was blasphemy, yet none moved to stop him. Judas recognized him from the several times they had met the city elders. He was younger than most, with only a few gray hairs around his ears. "My Lord, please," he said quickly. "You must come."

"Stand up. There you go," Jesus said, pulling the man to his feet. "Goodness! What is it, Elder Jairus? What's wrong?"

"My daughter," he said, pain evident in his voice. Judas remembered that the man had only one daughter, born late in his life. She was now about twelve, and the entire town adored her. "She fell ill shortly after you left. I went after you and returned as soon as I heard you were back in the city. You must come. It's the fever Simon's mother-in-law had, but it has attacked my daughter with much strength. Please come!"

Jesus nodded. "Let's go."

Jairus quickly led him away, and Judas fell in behind with the other disciples. As usual, the discussion with the Pharisees had drawn a crowd, and it grew as the men made their way through the warm light of evening that filtered in through the westward streets. The crowd grew, and despite the disciple's best efforts, people pressed in. It was impossible to move with any speed and still keep them back.

Jesus suddenly gasped and stopped short. The crowd slammed to a halt behind him, piling up on each other at the sudden stop. "Who touched me?" he asked.

The disciples shared a puzzled look. "Do you see this crowd?" Simon bar Jonas asked, suddenly squeezed in beside Jesus with hardly room to move his hands. "People crammed in tighter than fish in a net, and you want to know who *touched* you?"

"Spread out," Jesus said. "We go nowhere until I find out who it was." The disciples pushed out, creating a circle around Jesus. Little James was the most effective at this task, while Judas's efforts were hardly more than a polite suggestion.

A woman hesitantly stepped from the crowd, reluctant to draw attention to herself, and prepared for a stern rebuke. "I'm sorry, master," she said, shrinking from the many eyes now focused on her. "I... I had a problem—a bleeding issue. For twelve years, I have been unclean. Shunned. No doctor could heal me. Twelve years, I haven't been touched by... And I heard of you. I knew I could not touch you, or I would make you unclean, but I thought, 'if I can just touch the edge of his cloak...'"

"Cheer up, dear one," Jesus replied softly. "My cloak did nothing. Your faith has healed you. Go in peace." He gave her a kind smile and turned back to Jairus to find the elder speaking with a messenger who had squished his way into the thick crowd.

"It's too late," the messenger said. "Your daughter... She is dead, Elder Jairus. We didn't know where to find you, or we would have informed you sooner. Your wife has already made arrangements. The mourners are there. There's no reason to bother the good teacher further. It's over. I'm sorry, sir."

Jairus's face turned pale as a look of dread washed over him.

Jesus quickly stepped over to the men, cutting into the conversation. "No!" he said firmly, gripping Jairus's arm. "It's not too late. Don't let this fear inside, Jairus. Don't let it smother your belief. Do you trust me?"

Jairus looked at him with tears in his eyes, filled equally with hope and dread. His gaze broke away to glance at the eager crowd of strangers, hesitant to make a spectacle of himself in front of so many.

Jesus instantly understood the situation. "James, John, Simon," he said, picking out three of the four fishermen. "You're with me. Little James, Thad, Andrew: make sure we are not followed. Everyone else, go back to Matthew's and make sure we have everything ready. We leave for Jerusalem at first light."

For research notes, see chapter 26 in the reference section.

XXVII

"How does he fare, Joanna?" Judas asked. "Any hint of release?" He idly examined an apricot, careful to avoid looking at the woman who stood beside him, also apparently shopping for apricots at one of the markets in Jerusalem's Upper City. The man running the apricot stand was a disciple of John, and Judas often used his booth as a way to discreetly exchange information—and money.

Joanna shook her head. "John has many loyal followers, and his imprisonment has only further convinced the populace that he is a true prophet. They ensure his needs are met. Even Herod often summons him to ask his opinions, but his wife took John's rebukes on their marriage personally. She wants him dead, but Herod fears the people's response should he give in to her demands. John's imprisonment is a shaky compromise that keeps both Herod's family and his throne secure."

"Several of John's disciples have been traveling with us," Judas commented, "keeping John informed about the welfare of his cousin, I suppose."

"It is not Jesus's welfare that concerns me," Joanna said. "John is... withering. Not outwardly, but my husband speaks with him often. John didn't expect to be in prison long. He thought Jesus would rescue him, or," she lowered her voice to a mere whisper, "or overthrow the dynasty. I believe Jesus is the Christ, but I do not understand why he hesitates."

Judas nodded in commiseration. "John's disciples asked as much. There are many who share these concerns, myself among them. The man is headstrong. He does what he wants and takes no heed for the consequences. If there was only a way to direct that iron will into the right direction, Rome would shatter. A Nazarene should be the first to take up arms, but no. Jesus turned his own village against him! At least he has finally seen the value of more followers—or rather, he is finding it harder and harder to escape them."

"This is for him," Joanna said, placing a small bag among the apricots. "We do what we can to support him."

"I thank you," Judas said. "Most of my informants demand money, rather than give it. You are a rare jewel, if your husband will allow me to be so bold." Jesus had made many enemies, and Judas considered it his job to keep informed about their plans. Someone had to. He waited a moment before nonchalantly picking up the bag and placing it in his pouch. "How do you manage to get so much silver?" he asked, noting the weight of the bag.

Joanna smiled slyly. "My husband is not the only one with connections."

"I see!" Judas said. "Tell Chuza to contact me immediately if he hears anything. Jesus has made enemies, and the Herodians are no doubt among them. As Herod's steward, your husband may be one of the first to hear rumors."

Joanna nodded. "I may hear of it before him. You men always seek to be seen, while we women are invisible. I have heard plotting—Sanhedrin plotting."

"You're talking about what happened at the pool, aren't you?" Ben, the apricot vendor, asked, leaning forward, eyes wide. "The Sanhedrin was *not* happy. Another incident like that and the *Haberim* will push them to make a formal declaration."

Judas grimaced. The *Haberim* made even the strict standards of an ordinary Pharisee seem lax. They were obsessed with the Law and became even more zealous during the feasts. Passover was the most solemn of feasts, when the Law was at the forefront of everyone's mind. Jesus had broken the Sabbath by healing a paralytic and then demanding the man carry a burden. Even worse, he had been observed. It wasn't the first time Jesus had ignored Sabbath laws, but this time, leading members of the Sanhedrin had personally questioned the healed man, and several members of the Council were *Haberim*. The healed man hadn't known Jesus by name, but it was only a matter of time before the Sanhedrin learned of Jesus's identity. No amount of bribery would prevent that.

"I have *tried* to make Jesus understand! He *must* have the Sanhedrin's support if he is to gain the people's support!" Judas said in frustration. "But... increasingly," he admitted, "it seems he is gaining the people's support *in spite* of the ire he draws from the religious leaders! Perhaps he intends to overthrow them as well, creating a new priestly dynasty as well as a new kingly one, much like the Maccabees. Either way, he is rapidly growing more famous and more *infamous*."

"There is one thing you should know," Joanna said quietly. "You asked if my husband has heard rumors... There are whispers in the court that Herod fears an heir—a child who escaped his father's soldiers thirty years ago. So far, John has remained tight-lipped about his cousin, and I don't think Herod even knows Jesus exists—yet—but if the Pharisees target Jesus, they will certainly turn Herod's paranoia on him. He is the proper age..."

Judas paled. Herod was right to fear. A child *had* escaped thirty years ago, and *Jesus was that child*. "If your husband or any of your friends hear *anything*, you tell me," Judas said, daring to lock eyes with the woman. She instantly grasped his desperation. "Jesus is... I have seen him raise the dead, send demons away in terror. He *is* the Messiah, and I believe in his power, but..." He shook his head. "We *cannot* get this wrong. If we allow this Messiah to fail, we will not get another."

Joanna nodded solemnly. "I will find a way."

"Thank you," Judas said. "And your husband. May God grant him safety. Herod has eyes and ears everywhere. Chuza must take care."

"Chuza reveals his secrets to none but me, and I am but a woman. We are no threat to anyone," Joanna said lightly.

Judas chuckled. "Let us pray the Herodians continue to think so. Shalom, sister," he said, giving a *prutah* to the vendor and plucking up two apricots.

He hurried off down the narrow street toward the Temple. After washing quickly in one of the ritual bathhouses—and slipping off his sandals, as was required—Judas entered the Temple through the Double Gate, which led up an underground stairway of uneven steps to the plateau. The steps were designed that way, so no one could rush to the Temple but instead had to walk carefully, deciding with each step if he was truly prepared to continue moving forward.

Judas took his time, considering the implications of a clash between Jesus and the Sanhedrin. Judas had never seen Jesus break the Law in any respect, but he kept it in his own way, ignoring the traditions of the elders. Often, his ideas were in total opposition to theirs. His rapidly growing popularity meant that he was quickly becoming a threat the Sanhedrin could not ignore. Those who fought to take power would also fight to keep it. Saul of old had forced David into a position where he had to fight, and the Sanhedrin would eventually place Jesus in the same position—unless Herod beat them to it. The Pharisees had no love for Herod and his Hellenistic tendencies, but nothing could unite rivals faster than a mutual enemy. Jesus was quickly becoming that enemy.

Upon reaching the Temple Mount, Judas found his master easily. The Outer Court was packed, but a noticeable cluster was centered around a specific point of Solomon's Porch, which ran along the east wall. Judas glanced behind him and smiled at the empty spaces between the columns of the Royal Stoa, where he had changed money the year before. The priests had quietly moved the location after last year's *incident*. The changing tables had moved to the street below, and the sheep market had moved next to the Pool of Bethesda, where Jesus had healed the paralytic over whom the Sanhedrin was making such a fuss. Judas smiled at the thought. The Pharisees would never openly admit they had made changes based on the actions of a rogue, but the facts were impossible to hide.

Judas had no trouble passing through the crowd of people. Even in his worn traveling clothes, people recognized him as a disciple. He smiled politely at Simon, James, and John. Ever since the incident with Jairus's daughter, Jesus always had them nearby. Whether he simply preferred their company or didn't trust them out of his sight, Judas did not know, but his apparent favoritism was beginning to cause tension with the others.

"Judas, you're back!" Jesus said. "You remember Samuel, don't you?" he asked, indicating an unkempt man of nearly sixty, who was bouncing from one leg to the other with childlike energy.

"How could I forget?" Judas asked, staring at the former paralytic in renewed wonder. No matter how many miracles he witnessed, each was as wondrous as the last. "Sam, you look like you could run all the way to Marathon on those legs. How do you feel?"

Samuel's face split into a wide grin. "My legs feel even better than they did forty years ago! I can't believe it! I forgot to even ask his name!" He gave Jesus an apologetic smile, tears in his eyes. "But he found me again! Jesus found me!" he repeated, eager to use the name of the man who had restored power to his legs after so long. "Everyone will know it!"

Jesus caught his shoulder as the man started a jig. "Not so fast, Samuel," he said with an amused smile. "I must ask you to not reveal my name to anyone."

"Oh?" Samuel said in surprise. "Why... why not?"

"Soon, Samuel. You'll be able to tell everyone you meet, but for now, tell no one. Not yet."

"But... I cannot lie. The Sanhedrin will surely question me again!"

Jesus nodded. "I would not ask you to lie. If you are questioned, answer truthfully, but do not offer additional information and do not tell anyone who does not specifically ask you. Alright?"

Samuel hesitated at this strange request. A beggar's occupation was to provide the rich with an opportunity for generosity, and in exchange for their coins, the beggar would loudly and publicly extol the virtues of the giver. This give-and-take provided the unfortunate with something very much like employment, while giving the giver a way to improve his reputation in society. For Jesus to request Samuel to abstain from this natural response was almost unthinkable.

Jesus smiled understandingly. "You are no longer a beggar, Samuel. There is no obligation to me. Your obligation is to God. Keep to His paths, or you may find yourself somewhere worse than you were before."

"Obligation?" Samuel cried. "It is not from obligation! I can hardly contain myself! I will hold my tongue—because you ask—but you can be sure my greatest desire is to tell everyone I meet! If I am asked, I *must* speak!"

"Yes," Jesus said thoughtfully. "You must." He brightened. "Which is why we are leaving Jerusalem before the Sanhedrin has a chance to question you further."

"No rush, then!" Andrew said with cheery sarcasm. "Before they question him again, they first have to argue over every word he said the first time!"

"Right! Who knows how long that will take," his brother chimed in.

"Probably days and days," John added.

"Slightly less than that," Judas said, watching a group of Pharisees approaching from the Sanhedrin's council hall beneath the Royal Stoa. "Based on their current pace, I'd say we have about two minutes."

For research notes, see chapter 27 in the reference section.

XXVIII

"We can't leave Jerusalem now!" Thad protested. "It's almost dark!"

"And the middle of the feast!" Philip added.

"There's no law against traveling during the feast, so long as we eat no leaven," Simon the Canaanite countered.

The other disciples still acted uneasy around the former demoniac—even more uneasy than they did with Matthew, the former *publicanus*. Tax collectors made all Jews uneasy, but at least they were predictable. Simon was something else entirely. Judas considered them both worthy members—not for a *typical* rabbi, but Jesus was hardly typical. He did not need students of the Law. Jesus needed warriors. Matthew was highly intelligent and had a phenomenal memory. He would make an exceptional *actarius*. Simon had connections in the *Sicarii* and understood the undercurrents Jesus was forced to navigate. Even as a pacifist, the deadly creature which was Simon Zelotes was somewhere waiting to be resurrected. The man refused to even carry a weapon for fear of what he might do with it, but when the time was right...

While the disciples argued, Jesus steered them closer to the outer gates. It took them over an hour to even get close to the city wall. "Oh, Judas," Jesus remarked conversationally. "We met Chuza at the Temple while you were gone. He said his wife had something for me. Did she find you?"

"Yes," Judas said. "No news about your cousin, I'm sorry to say. It seems if he is ever to see the light of day, it will not be while *Herod* reigns." He gave Jesus a significant look, which Jesus ignored.

"Did you get the silver?" Nathanael asked. Their money had been stretched terribly thin of late. Their numbers—and their enemies—were growing faster than their donations.

"Yes," Judas said. "Twenty-eight pieces."

John grunted and eyed Judas suspiciously. "Chuza said it was thirty."

Judas shrugged. "I didn't stop to count it." The truth was he had stopped to count it, and taken out one, leaving twenty-nine.

"Twenty-eight is an odd number for a guess," James muttered, coming to his brother's aid.

"I'm a professional. I can tell much by the weight of the bag," Judas countered. "I might be off by one." If they did insist on counting it, finding twenty-nine would ease their suspicions, since Judas's prediction would then be proven wrong. It wasn't the first time Judas had needed to dip into the mutual funds, and it would not be the last. Bribes were an essential expense in the search for information. Some, like Joanna and Nicodemus, slipped him information because they believed in Jesus. But other informants told Judas their secrets because they believed in payment. It was a necessity that the fishermen from Galilee did not understand. They expected the money to be spent only on food and supplies. Thankfully, Judas carried the money and could spend it as he saw fit—so long as he kept it a secret.

The conversation moved on as they passed through the Roman checkpoint at the northern gate. Entry into the city was still allowed after dark, but it was more carefully scrutinized, especially during the feasts when the Romans felt particularly outnumbered. They were only a few steps past the gate when three men pushed through and rushed after them.

They were Pharisees and by the look of them, quite intent on some goal. Judas could only guess. "Which of you is Jesus?" one demanded.

Judas recognized him. "Nahum," he said in greeting, dropping back from the group to speak to the Pharisee. "Allow me to introduce you." He held his hand out to direct the man.

Nahum relaxed slightly, seeing Judas. Judas had spent a long day convincing Nahum that he was a fellow Pharisee in order to get information back when Nahum was investigating John the dunkard. "Judas, right?" Nahum asked. "*You* are following this... man?" he asked, hesitant to give Jesus any title of respect.

Judas nodded. "Yes. Rabbi Jesus is unconventional, it is true, but a man of surprising wisdom. I believe his teachings worthy of consideration." Judas was hesitant to show his total allegiance to the rogue preacher and risk alienating Nahum completely, but if he could sway the Pharisee's opinion toward the positive, it would be enough. "Jesus!" he called. "Can we spare a moment? This is Nahum, a leader of the Pharisees here in Jerusalem."

Jesus paused to take a slow breath and nodded. He returned with a smile on his face. "How can I help, Nahum?"

Nahum cleared his throat. "We just came from an interview with Samuel, the paraly—*former* paralytic. I'm afraid there is no room for doubt on *that* front. He has been paralyzed for thirty-eight years. *How* he came to be restored is more complicated. He believes *you* healed him—two days ago, on the Sabbath. Do you deny it?"

Judas gave him a pleading look. *Deny it, or at least make up a decent excuse!*

Jesus caught the look, and his eyes twinkled, which was always a bad sign. "Do you not say that God upholds all, even on the Sabbath, and so breaks His own Law?" Jesus asked.

The three Pharisees stiffened. "The Law was given to *us* by *God*—not the other way around!" Nahum said coldly.

Jesus shrugged. "A son will do what he sees his father do. Whatever the father does, the son will do as well. To honor the father, you must also honor the son. Isn't that right?"

Nahum wavered. "Yes..." he said reluctantly, agreeing with these obvious rules of society but nervous regarding the point Jesus was going to make.

Clearly, this response was not what Jesus wanted. His jaw clenched, and he took a long breath. "The Sadducees don't believe in the resurrection of the dead, but you know better," he began.

Judas could tell he was warming up for a tirade. This would not end well.

"The Father raises the dead," Jesus said, pointing upward, then pointing to himself. "So does the Son! The time is coming when the dead will hear the voice of the Son and will live. The Father is the source, naturally, but He has given that life to His Son. You investigated John, yes? John told you the truth, but I don't need *him* to prove my identity. The Father has given me a job to do, and I am going to do it."

Judas listened in horror. Jesus was excusing his behavior by claiming a legal exemption reserved only for God. Judas believed every word, but to speak of such things to leading Pharisees was spiritual and social suicide—blasphemy in the highest degree! Whatever interest or goodwill Judas had managed to gain among the Pharisees was now gone forever, but Jesus wasn't finished.

"If that is not enough, study the scriptures, and you'll find me there, also," Jesus continued, digging himself even deeper. He paused as the Pharisees' faces grew redder with each new word. "You aren't interested in hearing this, are you?" he asked, realizing for once that his words were not being taken well. "You didn't come here to celebrate a man walking on his feet for the first time in thirty-eight years! You aren't here to rejoice with God over His children's joy. You came to accuse me!" He didn't wait for a response. "You know what? I don't care. I didn't come here to be honored by you. I came to represent *my* Father. You Pharisees pretend to care about God's honor, but all you truly care about is your own! You came here to accuse me, but don't worry, *I* will not accuse *you*—though Moses does. You focus so much on the Law of Moses, but you don't really believe it. If you did, you would believe me. So, since we *both* know you don't truly care about the Law, let's drop the accusations, shall we?"

The two other Pharisees were nearly red, but Nahum had passed into purple.

Still, Jesus was not finished. "Yes, *I* healed a man on the Sabbath day. *I* told him to carry his bed away from the pool, because a healthy man cannot live among the diseased—your own laws of quarantine demand this! Had I told him to remain, you would accuse me of commanding him to break quarantine laws! There is no right answer with you, is there? So hear this: A son will always copy his father. *My Father* works, so *I work*."

Jesus turned and stalked away, leaving the trio of Pharisees staring after him in silent fury, his words too shocking to even illicit a coherent response. Judas stared after him in similar shock. Jesus had burned every bridge between himself and Israel's religious leaders with fire from heaven itself, licking up even the water underneath. For a moment, Judas hesitated, struggling to decide if he should follow Jesus or try to smooth things over with Nahum. Finally, knowing the impossibility of ever again gaining Nahum's allegiance, he gave up and hurried after Israel's impossibly frustrating Messiah.

"Well," he said shakily, rejoining the eleven and moving back into step with Jesus. "That was..."

"Blasphemy?" Jesus asked.

Judas whistled. "*I* would not say that."

"But *they* will," Jesus predicted.

"There's no coming back from this," Judas said in rising frustration. "You insulted the Sanhedrin, made them look like fools, and placed yourself on equal footing with God! You couldn't have said anything worse if you had tried! They didn't like you when all they knew about you was rumors! We will envy John the Baptist by the time the Sanhedrin is done with us. We'll all have permanent targets on our backs, and it isn't like we are hard to find!" Judas waved a hand at their core group—now twelve in number, thanks to the recent addition of Matthew, the *publicanus*. Only the twelve were with Jesus now, but their group often included many others who were regularly employed and followed Jesus in their free time.

"You're right, Judas," Jesus said calmly, raising his voice so that his twelve followers could all hear. "The Sanhedrin will try to stop us. It is time to accelerate our plans."

"Yes!" Judas said. It was about time Jesus announced some solid plans for retaking Israel. "We will consolidate our forces, create a base of operations, and start an official campaign."

"No," Jesus said, deflating Judas's hopes of a rapid ascension to power. "Gather around," he said, motioning to his disciples. "It will take several months for the Sanhedrin to reach a formal decision, but we shall start preparing now to be ready. When Tabernacles arrives, they will surely be hunting us, so we will travel in groups of two. Our message of good news will spread seven times faster, and the Sanhedrin will run themselves dizzy trying to keep up."

"With all due respect, master, I disagree," Judas countered, frustrated yet again in his attempt to focus Jesus in a more important direction. "Your miracles are what sets you apart from every other teacher in Israel! Splitting up will not have the impact you think and will only leave you exposed. The Sanhedrin will know exactly which traveling preacher to hunt down because only you can do the wonders you do, while we won't even be there to protect you!"

"You can't protect me, Judas, nor do I need it," Jesus replied. "But you are partly right—my miracles *do* set me apart. But you are also wrong. The Sanhedrin *won't* know which group to follow. What My Father does, *I do*, and what I do, *you* will do! You twelve have seen me heal the sick and cast out demons, and it's time for you to do the same. We're not building armies, Judas. We're building bridges. It's time to go to work."

For research notes, see chapter 28 in the reference section.

Part 3

XXIX

"The Sanhedrin is divided, but you are right; many within our ranks seek to kill him—with or without a trial. Of the *Haberim*, I alone support him, and I can no longer do so openly." Nicodemus paced in agitation. He held a high place within the Sanhedrin, but his allegiance to the Messiah would ruin him if it was exposed. "It's good you came dressed as you did. I must be extremely careful with whom I am seen."

Judas smiled. He had apportioned some of the disciples' money to purchase himself new clothes in the style of the Pharisees. It had taken a noticeable chunk from the mutual funds, but with the Sanhedrin growing more hostile by the day, Judas needed to blend in.

"Annas is the main voice speaking against Jesus, with Nahum a close second," Nicodemus continued. "But Annas has recently made several subversive comments which reached Pilate's ears. There are rumors that Pilate may force him to step down. If I can push for someone more lenient to take his place, there is a chance... but it is slim. It is an impossible task! Jesus has intentionally pitted himself against the Council! I don't even know how much longer I can retain my own position. If my allegiance is discovered... But his scheme is brilliant!" Nicodemus admitted. "They've gone positively mad trying to find him over the last several months. No sooner do they investigate a healing in Judea, than another sprouts up in Galilee, and then Perea, or the Decapolis! Have you...?"

"Yes!" Simon exclaimed. He was not dressed as a Pharisee, but he could pass for Judas's servant if they were noticed. Judas had practically begged to be paired with the Canaanite, and Jesus had agreed. The three sets of brothers—Simon and Andrew, James and John, Thad and Little James—had naturally been paired together, as had Philip and Nathanael, who were old friends. That left Thomas to be paired with Matthew, the *publicanus*. Matthew was nice enough and was honest—if a *publicanus* could be called honest—but the man could not keep a secret. Judas had hated to make such a fuss about getting paired with Simon, but it had to be done. He had nothing against Matthew, but Matthew's former occupation would make many of Judas's contacts nervous or even downright hostile. Thomas had accepted his fate with typical resignation, as if he had expected to be paired with the tax collector all along. Perhaps the two would force each other out of their respective shells.

"It is incredible!" Simon continued. "To think that I, a man once possessed by demons, can now free others from the same fate! It fills me with awe and humility I am honored beyond comprehension."

"Not only can Jesus do these mighty works, but he can give this ability to others!" Judas said excitedly. "It is... it is far more than any man has done in the past! Not Samson, Joshua, Elijah—not even Moses!"

Nicodemus cleared his throat. Claiming anyone was better than Moses was almost blasphemy. "That is remarkable, but reasonable if Jesus *is* who he claims to be. The Son of God would possess the same abilities as the Father. He said as much to Nahum, so I'm told. Yet, my compatriots refuse to see it. They will never believe anyone is of God who also rejects God's Law. But so far, Jesus has managed to find such simple and clever ways of explaining the Law that the lawyers cannot pin any charge against him. It frustrates the *Haberim* so! Still, *he* may have such answers, but *I* do not. If I am to hold back the fury of the Council, I need help. I need someone of influence who believes as I do—who has experienced Jesus's power on a personal level and who also has connections. But the rage of the Council prevents any scholar from daring to even consider Jesus as anything more than a blaspheming pariah." Nicodemus huffed in frustration. "It is too late to hope for the Council's full support, but if we could cause a schism... But I cannot do that on my own! If I could find an ally, just one..."

Judas hesitated for a long moment. "I may..." He hesitated again. "I may be able to gain you an ally."

Nicodemus raised his eyebrows in surprise. "Really? Who?"

Judas shook his head. "I shouldn't say. I don't want to give you false hope." He shrank from even considering the idea, but it had been boiling inside for a long time and he could ignore it no longer. "Do not rely on support appearing any time soon, but I will make inquiries."

Nicodemus nodded. "Understood. Say no more until you are sure. I will keep searching for open-minded allies and attempt to undermine Annas's authority when possible, but I will be no help if things come to a head. I will gladly speak out in support of Jesus, but if I am outvoted, I will lose what little influence I have left. After that, I will be useless."

Judas sighed at the daunting task before them. "We will see what can be done."

The men parted ways, feeling no better than when they had met.

"What's your plan?" Simon asked as the two disciples made their way through the streets of Jerusalem. "Talk to Nahum again?"

Judas had selected central Judea when the disciples split into pairs so he could keep informed regarding the Sanhedrin's plans and Herod's plans as well. Herod was currently distracted with a hedonistic birthday celebration and too drunk to do any plotting, but it was better to plan for the worst should his suspicious nature suddenly focus on Jesus of Nazareth.

"No, no," Judas said quickly. "Nahum was publicly humiliated. He is no friend to us—not anymore."

"You don't know any other Pharisees—or Sadducees for that matter," Simon mused. "Except for Joseph... Would you dare—after what you did?"

Judas chuckled nervously. *Joseph of Arimathaea...* Judas had gambled on his mercy one too many times already. "I know another Pharisee," he said. "One of the *Haberim*, in fact—at least he was. Someone with both the contacts and the craftiness to exploit their full potential. Unfortunately, he's also been banned from all Sanhedrin gatherings—both official and unofficial."

"Banned? Why?" Simon asked.

"We have to split up," Judas said, ignoring the question. "We were sent to not only confuse the Sanhedrin, but more importantly, to gather followers."

"We were told to remain together," Simon reminded him as the men continued toward the poor district of the Lower City. Judas had to remain vigilant here, where Roman guards did not patrol and thieving guilds ruled supreme. This new Simon would be no help in a fight. Judas had hoped to talk some sense into his friend after spending some time together, but Simon's reluctance to fight was tenacious. The man was... different. Gone was the daring patriot who would strike down any enemy for the sake of Israel. The man was broken—no, broken was not the word. The man was... reforged. It was not fear of the demons which held back the deadly rage. His burning hatred for Rome was quenched and in its place was a strange tranquility. The man was... at peace. During their time together, Judas had grown more certain that the man had lost all interest in military conquest. When the demons had been cast out, they had taken the Zealot with them, leaving behind only Simon the man.

"Yes," Judas said. "But you must contact the *Sicarii*. They will be suspicious of me. See if you can meet the Son of the Father; get him to consider Jesus's qualifications. Show them what Jesus can do—*what we can do!* Even if they disagree with his methods, perhaps we can recruit them, should the need arise. You are the only disciple Jesus has with any hope of stopping an assassination. And I'm not even sure you are still capable of killing an assassin," Judas said, eyeing his friend for any response, "even if he was sent to kill the Messiah. It would not hurt to have an underground network of skilled warriors as allies—even tenuous ones."

"Perhaps," Simon said skeptically. "Or it may prove that placing Jesus under their focus will only put him in more danger."

"It's not him I worry about," Judas replied. "The *Sicarii* fight to liberate Israel. We follow the Liberator!"

"The *Sicarii* are thugs who only fight to legitimize their thievery. They are not who I once thought them to be."

"They need guidance!"

"Judas, I..." Simon hesitated. "I do not cherish the thought of returning there. I am a new man now. I do not wish to resurrect the old one."

"Jesus called you for a reason, Simon. Perhaps he needs you for this very purpose. Belief," Judas said, recalling Jesus's words from almost a year ago. "Belief comes first."

Simon nodded. "So be it. I will try. And where will you go?"

"Bethany," Judas said. "I'll meet you back here when I am done. I have my own dark past to face."

"And what makes you think a former *Haber* will be any help—or that he will listen to you?" Simon asked.

Judas took a deep breath. "Because in this tangled web we call society, *he* is the spider. Plus," Judas added, wincing slightly, "he's my father."

For research notes, see chapter 29 in the reference section.

XXX

Judas met a servant on the path long before he reached the large house on the outskirts of Bethany. The man didn't recognize him, and Judas was forced to introduce himself.

"You're his..." the servant asked skeptically.

"His son. Yes," Judas said.

"My name is Antony. I have served the master for some years, and I have never met you. Sir," he added a bit late.

"I have been away on business," Judas lied. "Confirm with Eli if you don't believe me."

"Eli? Is that a Jewish name, sir?"

"Eli? The chief steward? My father would never fire him!"

"Your father hired all *Greek* servants some years ago, sir." Antony said with a thin smile.

"All Gr... Oh..." Judas said in realization. "Of course he would have to..." Greeks were far less concerned about Jewish laws of ritual purity. "That must have chafed him something terrible."

"Would you like me to announce you, sir?" Antony asked in a dull tone. "I can lead you to the window where he speaks with his visitors. You cannot enter the house, sir. Your father is..."

"I know what my father is!" Judas snapped before calming himself. "Tell me *where* he is."

"He is in the guest house. He isolates—"

That was all Judas needed to know. He started up the hill. "Go to the east window!" Antony called after him

"I will speak to him *alone*," Judas said, turning to give Antony a hard stare before continuing up the hill to the large house. There was now a smaller house that Judas didn't remember built next to the one from his childhood. This must be the guest house. There was a large window in the nearest wall, covered with a thick curtain from the inside. As Judas approached, a courier slipped a packet across the wide sill and down behind the curtain, then rang a bell attached to the outer wall.

Judas passed the courier as he left on some other errand. Judas gave the window a cursory glance but ignored Antony's recommendation and walked around to the other side. He found a door, which was unlatched, and stepped inside. The interior was brightly lit by an open skylight and richly decorated. At a high desk, a man stood with his back to the door, his shoulders hunched as he pored over the many papers littering the desk. Beside him, a small hearth crackled with a low fire. The man considered one of the papers, then tossed it into the fire with a shriveled claw.

"Hello, Simon," Judas said.

The man didn't turn. "My only son returns at last," he said coldly. "I often wondered if I would see my son again before my sight was completely taken from me. What *powerful* desperation you must feel to find yourself here!" He laughed harshly. "Is it money? You swindled enough from Joseph of Arimathaea that I can't imagine you need more yet! Especially since the *Sicarii* have no further interest in you." He laughed again: a spiteful, humorless sound. "Yes, I know where the money went. I know many things. Is your *new* master demanding money? He doesn't seem the type." Simon continued to study the papers on his desk, his head covered by an expensive *tallith*.

Judas's skin crawled, not only from the scent of rot clinging to the room but also from the things his father could discover from inside his prison. "I don't want your money," Judas spat, the words coming out harsher than he had intended. He paused, struggling to reign in his roiling emotions. "I didn't come to demand anything, Simon! I came to share good news."

Simon snorted in derision. "Oh! How delightful," he said sardonically. "Good news for whom? *You?*"

Judas stifled his emotions, deciding to ignore them completely rather than try and sort them out. There were too many, all jumbled together. "Good news for you—for Israel! I found the Messiah! He's here! After four thousand years, he is *here!* Israel's future is safe!"

Simon turned, nearly stumbling in his attempt to turn quickly as his feet and knees struggled to obey his commands. "Am I supposed to care?!" he asked angrily, pushing back the *tallith* from his head with a gnarled claw. "Does it look like I have any *future* to save?"

Judas blanched in spite of himself, shrinking from the face that had once been his father's. The leprosy had taken an awful toll. One eye was completely gone, eaten away by the voracious disease. The other was partly shrouded under a growth of skin as the naked eyebrow slowly melted downward. The nose was nothing more than a hole. Only the mouth remained nearly as Judas remembered it: a last holdout of what could now barely be called a face. The hair and beard had long since fallen out, leaving pale skin covered in lesions, some oozing, others scabbed over.

"Yes, take a good look!" the monstrosity said. "Do you not recognize your own father? You stopped calling me 'Father' long before my face rotted." He smiled cruelly as Judas dropped his gaze, unable to keep his eyes on the horror before him. "All my life, I have followed every precept of the Law! Look at me!" Simon shouted. "Do you see what a lifetime of service to God has earned me? God has cursed me! I have kept every precept—even now! The Brotherhood has done nothing for me. They come only when they need my secrets. Even my own son left me to rot as soon as that dreaded word was spoken: *leprosy!* I was forced to buy Greek slaves because my own servants—the few who cared enough to stay—could not remain without breaking *God's Law*. I have served God with all faithfulness, keeping myself pure from all contamination, and in return I receive this curse—a mockery! I cannot go to synagogue. I cannot even touch my own scriptures, for my hands will defile them! In a vicious stroke of irony, I have become the unclean thing which God commands us not to touch! I am forever cursed by God's own hand to break His Divine Law by my very existence! He stole my wife's life quickly and steals my life slowly. He has given me nothing but evil! Everything I have gained is by *my* hands." He held up his arms. "What is left of them." His right hand was eaten down to a misshapen stump. His left still retained some semblance of fingers, gnarled and bent at odd angles into a barely serviceable claw, which Simon must manage to use somehow.

"You don't understand," Judas pleaded. "I found the Messiah. The Savior of Israel!"

"Then tell Israel!" Simon snapped. "I don't care about Israel. Israel does not care about me! I care for nothing except living out the dregs of my miserable life in relative comfort. Israel's corruption is what sustains me. My mind connects the pieces that my spies collect. I sell truth and lies to the highest bidder. The *Haberim* have abandoned me, but they cannot live without me."

"If your spies know so much, then they've seen what I've seen!" Judas exclaimed.

"Oh, yes! Jesus the Nazarene!" Simon said mockingly. "Yes, I've heard of the many ways he's managed to upset God's ordained teachers and mock His Law! He is celebrated for mocking God's Law, and I am a mockery for keeping it! He heals unworthy sinners and ridicules the worthy shepherds! A fine Messiah he will make, spitting in the face of everything God commands!" Simon turned from Judas with a grimace and snatched up the letter that the courier had dropped through the window during Judas's approach. Simon pinned one corner to his desk with his withered stump and used the claw to unfold it.

"What *God* commands?" Judas cried. "The best doctors of the Law cannot lay a single accusation upon him! His answers stop them cold! Are you so certain that it is *God* who commands, or is it man? You trained me in the best schools; I *know* the Law, but he... he *understands* it! The Messiah has come to *break* the shackles we ourselves have placed upon our neck! He is here to save us, not just from Rome, but from ourselves!"

Simon crushed the paper in his claw and threw it at Judas from across the room. "*Save* us? You expect *Jesus the Nazarene* to save us?" he spat. "He couldn't even save his own *cousin!* You see?" Simon asked acidly as Judas spread the crumpled paper. "John was beheaded this very afternoon."

Judas paled, scanning the quickly scribbled note. "No... Herodias's daughter..."

Simon smiled cruelly. "Yes, apparently Antipas made a drunken proposition to Salome, and Herodias seized the opportunity. With so many witnesses present, Antipas was forced to make good on his promise, however brash and insincere it was. John's head is still warm."

Judas sunk to the floor. "Oh, John..."

Simon sighed. "The whole country will know the story by tomorrow. This information is worthless—unless you think your Nazarene might retaliate... *That* information might be worth something." He gave Judas a calculating glance.

Judas shakily stood to his feet. The tragic news had smothered his anger. A good man had died—died for no reason—and his father only saw it as information to exploit. The man was diseased, inside and out. Judas looked with pity upon his father's misshapen face. "Do you care for nothing besides yourself?"

"Do *you?!*" Simon shot back. "I know you didn't come back to *care for me* once I finally lose all ability to feed and clean myself! No, you came only for *yourself!* I know about the Pharisees' plot to kill your 'master.' It's obvious why you came: you're seeking an advantage only *I* can give. You're no different than anyone else, coming here only when it benefits *you!*"

"I didn't—I came here to give you hope!" Judas exclaimed. "Hope I could not give before, because I did not have it myself!"

"Hope is an illusion!" Simon cried angrily. "It's a lie! Nothing is true! The Law does not bring life! The wicked are blessed while the righteous die. Jesus is a charlatan preying on the idiotic hope of the masses. How can he save Israel when he can't even save his own family?! His father is dead. His cousin is dead. He will be next! There is nothing you can say to change my mind. You will leave here with *nothing* because I have nothing left to give you or God or anyone else!" The room fell into a terrible stillness as Simon's diseased body failed to summon the energy necessary to sustain his anger.

"You're right," Judas said, staring at the floor, unable to lift his eyes to look on what little was left of his father's face. "The Law does not bring life." He forced his eyes to look at the diseased husk of his father. "Only God can."

Simon grimaced. "Then God has abandoned me."

"No!" Judas said forcefully. "No, the *Haberim* have abandoned you! God has not. If you cannot find life following the rules of the Brotherhood, then it is time to look elsewhere."

Simon's face darkened. "That is almost blasphemy. They are God's shepherds."

"They *abandoned* you! God has sent a true shepherd!"

"Who? A peasant from Nazareth?" Simon asked, his voice rising angrily.

"Yes!" Judas shouted.

"Prove it!" Simon roared, spittle flying from his diseased mouth.

"He sent me!" Judas cried, rushing forward in desperation.

"No!" Simon exclaimed, staggering back as Judas did something he had never done before.

He embraced his father.

"Please," Simon said again, moaning in desperation but too weak to pull away. "This is *my* curse. Please, don't touch me! I will not let my only son carry this curse, *please!*"

"No," Judas said, pressing his cheek against the oozing sores on his father's face. "I will not let you go, Father." His eyes were squeezed tightly shut, but still the tears formed as he prayed with such desperation as he had never felt before. "I will not let you go until you bless me," he whispered.

"I bless you!" his father cried, pushing against him. "I bless you! *Please!* Go, or you will be made unclean! Please, my son," he begged, fear overwhelming his anger as he realized his son's deadly exposure to the horrible disease.

"I will not let go until you bless me," Judas whispered again, making the same plea Jacob had made centuries before. Jesus had always insinuated that belief was necessary for healing, but Judas's father did not believe. "*I believe*," Judas whispered. He felt no change in the sickly skin pressed against his cheek. Still, he held on, clinging to the hope that God would answer and that his own belief would be enough for them both.

Slowly, he felt a shift, but not the healing for which he so desperately hoped. His father relaxed into the embrace, breaking down into sobs at his son's desperate act. Slowly, his deformed arms lifted and returned the embrace. "I missed you," he said raggedly.

"Sorry I'm late," Judas whispered.

Simon choked out a laugh between his tears, and Judas felt his father's fingers clutch the back of his robe.

Fingers.

Both men froze. Judas was the first to pull back, his heart frozen in fear and awe. His father reached up with his hand and with strong, straight fingers, brushed tears from the side of a thick, fleshy nose. He stared at Judas with unspeakable wonder from two sparkling eyes.

Judas stepped away from the embrace, feeling suddenly awkward. It was wonderful, but it was too much, too fast—for both of them. For the first time in his adult life, Judas thought he might actually *love* his father. He needed time—they both did. "I should go," he said shakily. "I must tell Jesus of John's death."

Simon nodded. "I... I must... think this over," he said, dumb with shock.

Judas took his father's new hands in his own. "Search the Scriptures," he said, tears glistening. "You can touch them now. You'll see. He *is* the One."

For research notes, see chapter 30 in the reference section.

XXXI

"I knew John was popular, but this..." Nathanael muttered as another group of sympathizers arrived, joining the milling crowd waiting to gain entrance to Jesus's home in Capernaum. A flickering torch was the only illumination at Jesus's door, but still the crowds came, long after their minds should have turned to sleep. People had been flocking to Capernaum for days, offering condolences, offering advice, demanding retribution. Others simply came to wait, curious to observe what Jesus might do. Many expected a counterstrike against the Tetrarch—not only as payback for John, but for the blood of every prophet before him.

"Most are probably pilgrims, here early for Passover," Judas commented. "Only about half are driven by love for John. The other half come out of hatred for Antipas."

Jesus chose this moment to push his way out of the house. He looked as haggard as they all felt. None of them had even been able to eat in the chaos since John's death. The news had spread like wildfire, and all the disciples had returned to be with their master as he grieved, but so far, Jesus had been given no opportunity to grieve. John's many supporters, as well as his own, had all gravitated to the man they knew to be John's successor—and something more.

"We're done here," Jesus whispered. "We all need rest. I sent the fishermen to prepare the boats. We'll slip away one by one." Jesus patted the two men on the shoulders and slipped away into the night. The people would expect him back. It was ridiculous for a man to leave his home during the third watch.

Nathanael left a few minutes later. Judas was the last to arrive at the docks, careful to arrive unseen. They set off across the sea in silence. This time, there were no storms, and the disciples took a short break from rowing to finally eat the food which Matthew and Thomas had prepared. They were all famished, and the food disappeared in minutes. It was dawn by the time they arrived on the opposite shore, a lonely patch of wilderness somewhere south of Bethsaida. It was prime grazing land for shepherds: lush, grassy hills, and not a village for miles. After days of stress with no food or sleep, the promise of a respite from the crowds seemed too good to be true.

And it was. As the shore came into view, the grassy hillside was already packed with people. "*Bar alopex!*" John said angrily, slapping his oar against the water. The boats pulled to a stop about a hundred yards offshore. "How did they find us?"

"It's got to be nearly a thousand people!" Philip said in wonder.

"We'll just go somewhere else," James muttered. "Got to be somewhere around here people won't go. Hey, Canaanite, you know this area. Any ideas?" he asked, turning to Simon Zelotes, who sat in the Jonas brothers' boat with Thad, Little James, Nathanael, and Matthew.

"Look at them," Jesus said, staring tiredly at the crowd. They stood on the bank, staring back at the boats expectantly. "They have no idea where to go. Sheep with no shepherd."

"They must have guessed where we were going and ran around the whole north shore!" Andrew exclaimed. "That's got to be, what? Five miles at least!"

"Wherever we go, they'll find us," Thomas moaned from beside Judas.

"I can't abandon them," Jesus said piteously. "Not now."

"Yes, you can!" Thomas replied. "We abandoned them last night! They followed us here!"

"This is better," Jesus said. "In the open. I can address everyone at once—take care of everyone's expectations and give them the direction they so desperately need. Row in to shore."

Reluctantly, the disciples did. They spent the rest of the morning getting the crowd under control. By the time noon came and went, the crowd had swelled to over three thousand, and by evening, that number had doubled. Jesus spent the day teaching and healing but carefully avoided any promise of vengeance for John's death. Instead, he focused on giving them principles they could apply in their own lives. By the time evening began to fall, none of them had eaten anything since the previous night, including the crowd.

"Rabbi?" John asked. Judas found it strange how James, John, and Simon had somehow managed to become the inner circle within the inner circle. He had asked Andrew about it once, but the fourth fishermen had shrugged it off, and Judas hadn't wanted to risk appearing petty. "Don't you think it's time we send them away?" John continued. "It's almost evening, and there are no towns nearby. They'll have to make arrangements to stay somewhere and get food."

"They came to us," Jesus replied. "That makes them our responsibility. You won't send them away hungry; I won't allow it. Give them something to eat."

James choked back a laugh. "We have no food."

"Judas carries money. Philip knows this area. Where's the closest place to buy bread?"

Philip blanched. "A year's wages wouldn't buy enough food for this crowd! We don't have that kind of money, and we'd have to scour the countryside just to give everyone a handful of crumbs!"

"Philip!" Jesus said jokingly. "Where is your optimism when we need it? We don't have time to hunt down food from every village. What do we have on hand?"

"From what I can gather, no one thought to bring food," Nathanael said. "They just... came. We've got upwards of six thousand people and not a crumb among them."

"Except for that shepherd's kid," Andrew said, chuckling to himself.

"What shepherd's kid?" half the disciples asked simultaneously.

"Oh, just a boy I saw earlier. A hired hand—likely talked his way into staying while the shepherd took the sheep back to town. He had food," Andrew said with a shrug, knowing the unhelpful nature of this trivial information.

"Perfect!" Jesus said without a hint of sarcasm. "Ask him if he will share."

Andrew cocked an eyebrow. "Right," he said sardonically. "We'll just split his bread six thousand ways."

"Andrew," Jesus said sternly, "bring the food or bring the boy, but bring me something. Everyone else, get this crowd organized. Form the men into ranks."

"Ranks?" Simon asked in surprise. "As in... military formation?"

Jesus nodded. "Groups of fifties and hundreds, even ranks. This crowd wants to see my response to Herod's banquet? Well, this is *my* banquet. Herod showed his true colors. My turn."

For research notes, see chapter 31 in the reference section.

XXXII

"Now is the time," Judas said, handing a barley cake to a sturdy-looking man. "Do you think it an accident that he has organized you into fighting ranks? Herod's days are numbered."

"Are you sure?" the man asked skeptically. "I've been following Jesus for some time now. I've never heard him say anything about war. In fact, often he seems to say the very opposite. Not that Herod doesn't deserve it, but..."

Judas nodded. "Jesus is hesitant to start a war, but he knows what he needs to do! He assembled us here for a reason. He once told me that belief comes first. Well, perhaps he is waiting on us! *We* must act first! When we take the first step and declare him king of Israel, *then* he will become that king! But we must act first."

The man nodded. "Yes," he said thoughtfully. "Yes, I believe you speak the truth."

Judas slapped him on the shoulder and continued to move down the line, handing out bread from the pouch at his side. He had seen Jesus place two barley cakes into his pouch with his own eyes. He had taken several hundred out. Simon came behind him, passing out dried fish. Judas didn't know how many Simon had given out, but it was far more than the single fish that had been placed there.

The men Judas fed were equally amazed, as none of the disciples ever returned to refill their pouches as they worked their way through the ranks. Though they had no uniforms, the men looked like an army, all neatly organized into companies. There were five thousand men. Enough to take Jerusalem. Even with no training, a group this large could easily overrun Herod's palace and the Antonia Fortress. Of course, Rome would retaliate, but Judas had confidence in their Messiah.

Belief comes first.

The disciples finished distribution and started back through the crowd toward the center where Jesus sat. They collected any uneaten food along the way and ended up filling their pouches again from the leftovers—enough to last them several days apiece. They gathered around Jesus in the lowering gloom and sat down to their own feast. "Not bad for a barley cake," Philip said, lightly punching the boy. "You think this is one your mom made or a different one? How does that work?" he mused, glancing at Jesus. "We started with five barley cakes. Are the thousands we passed out all new ones, or the same five, over and over? And don't get me started on the fish!"

Jesus laughed. "Perhaps one day you can ask my Father, but for now, just enjoy them. It's been a hard week for all of us." He sighed contentedly, staring into the sinking sunset peeking over the water. "This was a good day."

"And it will get better!" Judas said excitedly. He had explained things to the other eleven, and they agreed, as did the majority of the crowd. Jesus had made the first move, and now it was up to them to move forward in faith. It was time.

Jesus gave him a suspicious look. "What do you mean?"

Judas gave a nod to the other disciples, and they stood, raising their fists in salute. "Hail to the king!" Judas cried, quickly joined by the others. In a moment, the crowd took up the cry. Thousands of voices shouted their allegiance to the king of Israel. Judas's heart swelled with joy at the thunderous cry, and he saw on his comrades' faces that they felt the same thrill. The time was now. Israel would be free at long last.

Jesus stood, lifting his arms. The crowd fell silent. He turned to the disciples, but his face did not hold the same pride and joy that radiated from their own. His face darkened with that same quiet rage that Judas had witnessed in the Temple. "What have you done?" he asked quietly.

"It's the perfect time!" Judas protested. "The people are with us! We're too far away from any village to be overheard! Herod's spies don't even know you exist! And the nation will rally behind you to avenge John's unjust death. It's the perfect time to strike. We have two swords among the twelve of us. If you can do the same thing with them as you did with the food—"

"It's late," Jesus said, cutting him off. "Take the boats and go back to Capernaum."

"What!?" John asked, pointing to the other disciples. "It's not fair that we four have to leave with the boats, while they—"

"All of you!" Jesus said. "Go! This is not up for debate." He sighed, clearly agitated, though Judas could not understand why. "I will deal with this."

They went. None dared question their teacher when his blood was up. However he chose to address the crowd's desire to crown him king, he did not want them there to witness it. They spoke little on the way back, each buried in his own thoughts and the darkness around them. As if to match their stormy thoughts, the wind picked up, pushing them back. They were all tired. Their frustration added to their fatigue, which had faded in the excitement of the crowd. The wind continued to increase as a storm slowly settled in. They pressed on. The winds gave the four fishermen a target on which to vent their perplexed irritation, while the others were forced to huddle in the boats with their thoughts. The night crawled on. They made little progress. There was nothing to do but keep rowing until the storm passed.

A sudden shriek broke from the other boat. Judas flinched. "It's a ghost!" Thad cried.

Nathanael laughed. "You ever hear of ghosts on Lake Gennesaret?"

"I saw it!" Thad affirmed. "Just beside us. Look!" He pointed, and a sudden flash of lightning illuminated the dark silhouette of a man against the night sky.

"It's a man, Thad!" Philip said consolingly. "Just a man on the beach. We must be closer to shore than we thought."

"We are *NOT* close to shore!" John cried, catching Thad's panic. "We can't be more than halfway! *Nobody* is walking out here!"

"Then who is *that?!*" Thad demanded, as another crack of lightning illuminated the dark figure, unmistakably human and closer than it had been before.

"It's John's ghost!" James cried. "Jesus won't avenge his death, so it's come for us!"

His declaration caused a general panic as the ghostly apparition moved steadily closer. The panic increased with the shrinking distance until the disciples were nearly on the verge of abandoning the boats for the deadly black water around them.

"Cheer up, boys," the apparition called in a strangely familiar voice over the howling wind. "It's just me. No reason to panic."

The dark shape was now close enough to be visible against the dark water even without the lightning.

"Master?" Simon bar Jonas asked shakily. "If that's you, stay where you are! I'll come out to you!"

Andrew gripped his brother's arm. "*Are you crazy?!*"

Simon took a shaky breath. "Probably. But if that's really Jesus, I'll be able to stand where he's standing. If it's a ghost... at least it will take only me, and you can escape."

"Come on out!" the apparition said cheerily, standing atop the rolling waves.

Simon gulped back his trepidation and swung his foot over the gunwale. Andrew moved to steady the boat as Simon's other leg followed. "I don't feel any sandbar..." he muttered.

"Come out to me!" the apparition called again.

Simon shook his head as if to say, "Here goes nothing," and plunged into the water feet first—or tried. His feet struck the rolling surface with a light smack, and he gripped the gunwale to steady himself. Carefully, he put weight on his feet. He let out a loud whoop that didn't match his nervous movements as he struggled to maintain his balance on the moving surface of the waves.

"Eyes on me," Jesus said, his face illuminated suddenly by a bright flash of lightning. "Slow and steady. Easy does it!" He was smiling.

Judas reached out a hand and plunged it into the water. It yielded to his touch as water always did—and yet somehow it was holding Simon's weight, even as it moved and shifted under him. Simon took another tentative step, then another. Judas wasn't about to test *his* luck on these waters. Even a skilled swimmer would have difficulty staying alive in the rolling surf, especially fully dressed in heavy clothing, as they all were.

Simon continued until he was hardly more than an apparition himself. He had nearly reached Jesus when a large wave stole his focus, and the wind pulled him off balance. His silhouette disappeared with a sharp cry of panic. He disappeared into the spray, his plea for help cut off as he plunged beneath the waves.

Andrew panicked. "He'll sink in those clothes!" he cried, throwing Simon's oar into Big James's hands. "Go! Go!" The boat moved nowhere, as Big James took a moment to consider how best to apply this new tool thrust so quickly into his hands. Jesus rushed forward, unmindful of the waves, and plunged his hand into the dark water to catch hold of Simon's wrist. He pulled him up with surprising strength and wrapped the fisherman's arm around his shoulders as Simon coughed up water.

They made it to the boat with Jesus supporting Simon, who was struggling to get the water to support him again. Simon gratefully clambered back into the boat, and Jesus followed, stepping gracefully from the rolling waves and into the boat, which settled into a gentle rocking as Jesus took a seat. The wind calmed a moment later without even needing a rebuke.

"What happened, Simon?" Jesus asked. "A sailor like you panicking at the first big wave he sees? After everything, you still have doubts? You want to stand with me against waves of Roman soldiers, but you cannot stand against a wave of water. Why didn't you trust me, Simon?"

Simon dropped his head. "I'm sorry. I shouldn't have left the boat."

"No! I wanted you there!" Jesus said quickly. "But you lost your focus. You failed, yes, but you were not afraid to try! I didn't see anyone else leaving the boat," he added, giving Simon a playful nudge. "Don't regret starting something just because it didn't end how you wanted. Failure is nothing more than an opportunity to overcome."

Simon watched his teacher in wonder and spoke the thought on everyone's mind: "You really are the Son of God, aren't you? I mean, we all believe... but... You're not *just* the Messiah. It's not a metaphor. You are *His Son*."

"Let's keep that information between us, alright?" Jesus said, his face curling up in an amused smile. "We wouldn't want another mob trying to crown me king."

"We thought..." Andrew began.

"We thought you wanted to send Herod a message," Simon finished.

Jesus nodded. "I *did* send Herod a message. I had five thousand men ready to storm his palace while he had nothing more than a hangover. He will realize soon enough that he sits on the throne only because *I allow it*. Herod's time will come, but not yet. If you recall, David did not take the throne from Saul by force."

"We're sorry we acted impulsively," James said, gaining nods from the others.

"I know. I understand your eagerness, but you must also learn patience. I explained this to the crowd earlier and managed to keep them from turning into an angry mob, but many still want a war. I will need to continue the topic at synagogue tomorrow. I'm sure many of the same people will be there."

"What are you going to tell them?" John asked.

"I'm going to tell them the truth," Jesus said.

"Oh no," Thomas groaned. "That's what you told them in Nazareth! You remember how that ended?"

Jesus laughed. "I do."

"Well," Nathanael muttered, shaking his head. "Should be an interesting sermon. Let's hope we live to remember it."

For research notes, see chapter 32 in the reference section.

XXXIII

"What are we doing here?" Simon bar Jonas asked.

"Letting things cool off in Israel," Jesus replied.

"Yeah, I know," Simon continued. "We've been hiding in Syro-Phoenicia for months—ever since you told everyone at Gennesaret that you were the bread sent from heaven, and they would have to eat your flesh and drink your blood if they wanted to see your kingdom! I don't know what that means—and I don't want to—but it took us from leading an entire *legion*—eager to liberate Israel—to a handful of people all quite disturbed about your cannibalistic expectations!"

"Cannibalism is no way to gain support," James confirmed. "It reeks of paganism."

Judas had originally been the only one of the disciples who dared question Jesus, but James, John, and Simon were quickly becoming bolder in their respective roles, while Judas had been pushed aside. Generally, Judas preferred to work in the background, but Jesus required constant nudging to keep his focus properly aligned. The fishermen were usually sensible but never subtle. They lacked the finesse needed to subtly steer Jesus in the right direction. Jesus probably kept them around because he knew he could easily outsmart them. Judas could still suggest things, but he was not included in this new inner circle within the inner circle.

"Speaking of paganism," John chimed in. "What *are* we doing here?"

"That's what I asked!" Simon reminded them. "We've been slumming it up with pagans in Greek cities for months! How is this liberating Israel? Pagan cities are bad enough, but why are we at a *pagan temple?!*"

"Multiple pagan temples," Matthew corrected. "And a death cult."

"We should not be here!" James exclaimed. "No self-respecting Jew steps foot in Caesarea-Philippi, let along their biggest pagan temple complex!"

"Do you want to leave?" Jesus asked. "I won't hold it against you, if you choose to follow another rabbi."

"And go where?" Simon asked in consternation. "You have the words of eternal life! We believe in you because of who you are, but this—!"

"And who am I, Simon?" Jesus asked, breaking free of the stream of pagan worshipers moving to their left and right. Most went left to the Temple of Augustus, while a few went right toward the Court of Pan. Jesus went straight, cutting between the two lines of worshipers and moving toward the Gates to Hell. "I'm sure you've heard some theories."

"Herod is convinced that you're John, risen from the dead," Judas said, completely amused by this hairbrained theory. "Probably since he only heard about you after John's death, and you raised an army, only for it to disappear like so many spirits," he added, subtly reminding Jesus of the missed opportunity to dethrone Herod.

"Elias has been a common theme, especially since Nain, as he also raised a woman's only son," Nathanael commented.

"Elias, Isaias, Jeremias—any of the great prophets, really. The signs you do have exceeded all the prophets who came before, including Moses," Philip added. "Although people are naturally hesitant to place you on the level with Moses himself. Still, the parallels are fascinating. He parted the sea; you walked upon it. He gave the people bread from heaven, and you are the bre—ohhh..." he exclaimed in sudden realization. "You didn't mean that we should *literally* eat your flesh, but like the manna in the desert, you are the source of life! We must digest your teachings, let your life become just as much a part of us as what we eat. The Israelites survived exclusively on manna and would have died without it. We must see you in this same light. Is that it? There's no *real* cannibalism, right?" Philip asked desperately.

Jesus laughed. "Very good, Philip. It sounded disturbing at the time, but you all chose to remain with me even when you didn't understand. You won't always understand, but if you are patient and continue with me, some day you will. Well," Jesus said brightly, gesturing behind him to the gaping maw of darkness descending into the earth. "Welcome to the Gates of Hell!"

The huge cave at Caesarea-Philippi, which descended into the ground below a mountain of exposed stone was, according to all civilized people, one of the entrances to the Underworld. Those few bold or foolhardy souls who dared enter were rumored never to return. The entrance to hell was considered a sacred place, and a temple had been erected to Zeus, the king of the gods; Augustus, the king of kings; and a courtyard for the worship of Pan, the god of shepherds.

"Enough about rumors," Jesus said, returning to the previous subject. "Who do you say I am?"

"You are the Messiah," Simon said quickly. "Or 'Christ' in the Greek, since we're in a Greek city. You are the Son of God—the Living God, not these..." He gestured to the pagan temples.

"Yes!" Jesus said. "You've struck gold, Simon bar Jonas! You didn't hear *that* from any rumor, but from My Father. Yes!" He reached down and plucked up a rock. "You are as solid as this rock, Simon! In fact, that's your new name: Simon the Rock—or Simon *Peter*, since we're using Greek. It's been too confusing with two Simons, and we can't keep calling Simon a Canaanite. He's as much a Jew as any of us. You are this rock, *Peter*, and my synagogue—my church, as the Greeks say—will be built on *this* rock!" His eyes turned to the massive stone mountain, pressing down upon the dark passage below it. "And my church will crush the very Gates of Hell!" His eyes lit with the spark of fire that had first captivated Judas, before the flames burned down again.

"But for now," Jesus continued, "you must tell no one of my true identity—not yet. Tell them of my works, but do not tell anyone that I am the Christ. Other things must happen first. You need to know this, so you won't be taken by surprise: When I return to Jerusalem, the religious leaders *will* turn against me. They will seek to kill me in the worst way possible, and... they *will* succeed. But the third day, I will ris—"

"Stop it!" Simon—or Peter—cried in consternation as he planted himself in front of Jesus. "Don't talk like that! I know it looks grim, the way you've been received in some places, but it's not going to end that way! Don't even think that! You're the Savior of Israel! You are the conquering king!"

Jesus stiffened, and the fire returned, scorching Simon Peter. "Get out of my face, Simon. So quickly you change from *Peter* to *Satan*—from a solid support to an adversary! So easily you forget the words of God and return to rumors. Do you follow me because of who I am, or are you just interested in what I can give you, like the rest? If you *truly* want to follow me, get ready to die carrying the very thing that's going to kill you. If you're only here for fortune and glory, give it up. Seeking eternal life *will get you killed.*"

"So... we're all going to die?" John asked miserably.

Jesus's severity softened. "I said to be prepared to die, not that you will. Some standing here will not taste death until they see the Son of Man receive His kingdom."

"Master," Judas cut in. "I hate to interrupt, but that *pagan* woman is back." He cocked his head behind them where a woman stood watching. She seemed to have recognized Jesus by reputation alone, and had been following them off and on since their arrival in Phonecia. Jesus had wanted to give tensions in Galilee time to unravel. The only option was to go where no Jew would willingly go. Leaving Israel for Phonecia was the only way they could escape detection by the multitudes. Jesus's reputation had spread to the point that he could go nowhere in Israel without being mobbed. His plan had worked beautifully—until this pagan woman had recognized him and loudly started calling unwanted attention to their group. Having a woman follow you everywhere, screaming your name and lineage, was a terrible way to stay incognito. Jesus had initially ignored her, and the disciples had followed suit, but the woman was tenacious.

They had finally lost her in the busy marketplace on their way to the Gates of Hell, but now she had found them again. As soon as the woman saw that she was noticed, she started up her crying again and rushed toward Jesus to fall at his feet. "Please, Lord, Son of David, have mercy! My daughter is possessed, and I know what you can do! Please, my Lord, Son of David, have mercy!"

Judas smiled thinly at some pagan worshipers who gave their group a wary glance. A woman worshiping a Jew at a pagan temple was not something that happened every day. "Master, please!" he begged. "If she keeps this up, we will have crowds following us everywhere—crowds of *pagans!* If you order her to leave, she will be forced to go."

"City Boy is right," Nathanael said philosophically. "We can't have pagans following us. What kind of example would that set? You've got to get rid of her."

Jesus nodded slightly and turned an unfeeling gaze on the pathetic woman. "How do you know what I can do?" he asked her coldly.

The woman pointed a finger at Simon Zelotes. "I recognize him. The demoniac."

"Not anymore," Simon corrected.

The woman smiled shrewdly, recognizing that Simon had inadvertently confirmed her claim.

"My disciples are correct," Jesus told her, his tone unnaturally cold. "I was sent to find the lost sheep of Israel. I am Israel's shepherd. You claim Pan as yours."

"My Lord, *please!*" the woman begged, now practically shrieking. Any more ruckus and the Roman Guard would be summoned. Thankfully, loud shrieking was fairly common in pagan temples.

Jesus glared at the woman's hysterics. "You expect a man to steal the food from his own children's mouths so he can throw it to some filthy dog on the street?" He grunted in disgust.

Judas stared in consternation at this shocking reversal. They had all expected Jesus to show mercy on the woman. Jesus *always* showed mercy to the undeserving. Constantly, he brought the worst types into his own home, healed lepers, and generally heaped mercy upon every single pitiful creature he met. So much so, that the disciples were forced to constantly recenter his focus upon those more deserving.

Yet now, to see their master, who was always so kind, treat this woman with such pitiless disdain... It was shocking. No, it was horrible! Judas suddenly realized that as infuriating as Jesus's indomitable mercy was at times, it was one of his greatest forces of attraction. To see him exude such hatred and disgust to a poor woman, even a pagan, was strangely revolting.

The woman took the abuse humbly, not even denying the slur. "You are completely right," she said quietly. She glanced up to meet his eyes, betraying a boldness her soft words did not express. "But even the filthy dogs are allowed to lick the crumbs from the floor."

Judas suppressed a grin. The woman was sharp; he had to give her that. Still, Jesus's cold dismissal of her pleas was surprisingly galling. Jesus took his eyes off her to glance at his disciples, and their faces betrayed the same revulsion which Judas felt. Jesus nodded to himself and turned back to the woman with a deep laugh, rich and full of compassion. "My dear lady," he said, pride evident in his voice. "Your wish is my command. Your faith is an example to us all."

The woman thanked him quickly—her goal achieved—and left without another word. Perhaps she thought she had bothered them enough. She simply took Jesus at his word that her daughter was healed. Jesus turned back to his disciples with a pleased grin, and Judas realized with a start that they had been played for fools. Jesus had mirrored their own prejudice, allowing them to see for themselves how ugly it was. The woman was sharp, and Jesus had used her to cut them all.

"Rather bold of her to ask a Jewish deity for healing in the midst of all these pagan gods," Judas said, unable to stop a grin from forming.

Jesus smiled cheerfully. "I thought so! But I have sheep everywhere; not all pagans follow the call of Pan."

"You're not thinking of moving your ministry here, are you?" Simon Peter asked reluctantly.

Jesus laughed again. "Not today, Peter. It's time to return to Galilee," he said, his grin turning sly. "I think we've learned what we came here to learn."

For research notes, see chapter 33 in the reference section.

XXXIV

"Judas?"

Judas turned his head, looking for the man who had hissed his name in the crowded Temple court.

"Judas ben Joseph!" Judas said, recognizing Jesus's brother. "Where's your brother? Have you seen him?" It was the big day, the last day of Tabernacles, and Judas had no idea where Jesus was. Jesus had sent his disciples out again in pairs soon after their return to Galilee—not just the twelve, but others. Although Jesus's cannibalistic insinuations some months before had caused problems, he still had followers. He had now commissioned seventy of them to work in pairs, driving the Sanhedrin's search into an even worse frenzy. Jesus was keeping his location a secret and sending others to work in his stead. It was now the only way he could conduct his ministry without risk of arrest.

Herod was on the alert for large crowds, and the Sanhedrin had released an official summons for Jesus of Nazareth. They wanted him brought for questioning, but that was merely formality. If Jesus showed himself, the Sanhedrin would find him guilty by hook or by crook.

"Which brother?" Judas ben Joseph asked with a laugh. "James? Joses?"

Judas glowered at him. "You know which brother." He hesitated to even say Jesus's name here in the Temple's Inner Court. Jesus was on everyone's lips, but only in hushed tones among trusted friends. The Sanhedrin's spies were everywhere, and Herod's spies were everywhere else. It infuriated Judas that Jesus had allowed things to get to such a point without addressing the situation publicly. Judas understood the necessity of a low profile, but while Jesus had been hiding in Phoenicia, the Pharisees and Sadducees had inexplicably dropped their perpetual rivalry to face this new threat. It was disturbing news.

"Right, the bastard," the other Judas said sarcastically.

"Have some respect. He is still my master," Judas said coldly. "And he is *no* bastard."

"You actually believe that pile of *peripsema*? Never mind. Look, I like you, Judas. I really do. But he's my brother. Right? And maybe he has abilities that seem uncanny, but that's all it is. He's not—" He sighed. "You know, I tried to get him to come with us—actually do something as a family again? He said he wasn't coming."

Judas cocked an eyebrow. "Attendance is mandatory by Mosaic Law."

"Well, you and I both know he doesn't much care about that," Jesus's brother replied. "I told him if he wants to gain support, he can't keep hiding! It sets a bad image—makes him look untrustworthy. He shouldn't have anything to hide! That's what I told him, anyway. He gave some lame excuse about how it wasn't time yet." He shook his head in frustration.

Judas held up his hands. "It's a legitimate complaint! I don't understand it either. We had five thousand men ready to march on Herod's palace, and Jesus just... sent them home! Everyone is talking about him in whispers and murmurs, but talking nonetheless! Whether they believe in him or not, he's on everyone's minds. Many believe! He has the momentum to do whatever he wants, and the Sanhedrin is powerless. Herod is powerless! The throne of Israel is waiting, and he hides himself!"

The trumpets signaled the beginning of the water ceremony and the arrival of Annas. The two Judases' conversation stopped at the high priest's arrival. The aging high priest was returning from the revered Pool of Siloam, carrying the ceremonial pitcher of water. The same ceremony had been done for the last six days, but today was the high day: The Great Hosanna. The trumpets blasted twenty-one times instead of three, and the priests marched around the altar seven times instead of one. As the trumpets quieted, an ocean of palm branches rose from the crowd.

With precision crafted from years of practice, the priests and the crowd simultaneously burst into song: "Save now, we beg you, oh Lord, oh Lord, we beg you to send prosperity." It was a prayer for blessing, but specifically for water. If the autumn season was dry, the following year's harvest would fail. Tabernacles was a celebration of freedom from Egypt, but more than that, it was a week-long prayer for water, repeated every year.

It was also a prayer for deliverance. The Hosanna psalm was known to be a Messianic prophecy. Hopes were high that the Messiah would soon appear, yet none dared speak the name of Jesus for fear of the priests. Indeed, Jesus himself had stayed away for the same reason. What kind of Messiah feared the plotting of his own priests and hid from the very Temple he had cleansed less than three years prior? What sort of Messiah would provoke that kind of treatment? What sort of Messiah would allow it?

Jesus should be here. Judas knew the man's abilities—in some small way, at least. Jesus could have these pompous priests swearing allegiance in under a minute if he showed even a fraction of his true power. The man could walk on water, for heaven's sake. If he would only reveal his miracles publicly, in the Temple—instead of secretly, in every backwater village in Galilee—these priests would realize the truth. And if they refused, they would be priests no longer.

After the water ceremony's conclusion, Annas stood. It would be his last time officiating as high priest—at least openly—and though it was not part of the ceremony, it was common for the high priest to speak a few words after the proceedings in the hopes that his words would be remembered by future generations. So far, none of the countless speeches had quite struck the mark, but each high priest held out hope that somehow, their speech would be the one remembered.

Annas raised his hands to silence the crowd, and a loud voice broke the stillness. It was *not* the voice of Annas.

"If any man thirsts, let him come to me and drink! He who believes in me, as the scriptures say, out of him will flow rivers of living water!" All eyes turned to the voice. It came from a simple Nazarene who had climbed partway up one of the four massive pillars in the Women's Court, putting him in plain view of everyone.

"Well," Jesus's brother muttered. "You asked for it."

Judas almost laughed out loud with excitement. At last, Jesus was showing some daring, and like King David of old, he certainly had a flare for the dramatic. "Finally!" Judas said, producing a wide grin. Annas's face flushed with fury.

"Idiot!" Judas ben Joseph hissed under his breath. "They've got Levites at every exit! He'll get himself killed."

"Have a little faith in your brother, Judas," Judas replied. "The things I've seen him do... The Antonia Fortress couldn't stop him. Just you watch!" Judas slapped Jesus's brother on the shoulder and started pushing his way toward the Royal Stoa.

Annas signaled the nearest Levite officer. The Levites were the Jewish policing force within the Temple and handled all but the most extreme cases of insurrection. Even with such a brazen attack on the Sanhedrin's authority, they were reluctant to summon the Roman Guard from Antonia on a feast day. Romans did not care about collateral damage.

Jesus had been in plain view of all, including the Levites. There was no way he would be able to slip by them unnoticed. A pair of them moved on Jesus's location. The crowds collapsed into pandemonium as men argued whether Jesus was the Messiah, demon-possessed, or any number of possibilities in between. The mayhem hindered the Levites' progress.

Judas had no fear that Jesus was in any real danger. He would need to confront the religious leaders if he ever planned to ascend Israel's throne. Tabernacles was the perfect time, with all Israel assembled and all hoping for the coming Messiah. Judas pushed for the Royal Stoa, where the Sanhedrin met. Dressed as a rich Pharisee, he would gain a prime position for the questioning—if Jesus allowed himself to be taken. Either way, it was sure to be a show.

The crowd parted as Annas pushed his way to the high seat in the circle where the Sanhedrin met. Annas's son-in-law, Caiaphas, took the prime position on Annas's right, and the other seats filled rapidly. Not all of the seventy-one members of the major Sanhedrin were here yet, but only twenty-three were required for a formal hearing. There was twice that now. Nicodemus arrived, looking extremely nervous. He caught Judas's eye and nodded grimly. He was an ally, but Nicodemus knew openly supporting Jesus would destroy all his social standing within the Sanhedrin—possibly even his seat on the Council. He would have only one opportunity to cast a vote in support of Jesus, and he wanted to be sure he did not waste it.

The crowd parted again as a squad of Levites arrived. On ordinary days, there were only twenty-one Levites on patrol within the Temple. These were stationed at the five outer gates, the five inner gates, the inside and outside corners of the Temple, and three guarding the chambers of fire, hearth, and incense. That number was doubled or even tripled on holy convocations.

"Well?!" Annas demanded as the Levite police arrived. "Where is he? Surely, he could not escape. Why didn't you bring him?"

The Levite commander cleared his throat and shifted uncomfortably. "We let him go, Highness."

"You WHAT?!" Caiaphas, Annas's son-in-law, screamed. "Jesus of Nazareth has been summoned to the highest court of Israel to answer for breaking the Law—and now insurrection against the high priest—and you let him go?"

Annas pursed his lips at this. "You forget your place, Caiaphas," he muttered. "You are not high priest yet, my son. Why did you release the Galilean?" he asked, turning to the Levite.

"Apologies, Highness, but this man..." The Levite shook his head in wonder. "This man... No man has ever spoken like this man."

Annas's upper lip quivered in rage. "So he talked his way out of arrest, did he? Are you Levites, or are you as duped as the uneducated idiots who don't know the Law? Has any one of us—any ruler or Pharisee—believed in this... person? The rabble following that *raca* is cursed! Clearly, you are cursed as well."

Nicodemus cleared his throat, attracting glares. "Speaking as someone who *does* know the Law..." he said carefully. "Every Jew has a right to defend himself upon any accusation. Does our Law allow a man to be condemned before his trial?"

"Nicodemus! I had no idea you were from Galilee!" Nahum said mockingly. "Why don't you pay less attention to trial etiquette and focus more research on the fact that *no prophet has ever come from Galilee!* Prophets are called from Judea: God's homeland—not that backward excuse of a country."

Annas cleared his throat. "Since our only defendant was not arrested," he said through clenched teeth, "there is no point to continue. Meeting is adjourned. Samuel," he added, staring down the Levite with a hard glare. "If this Nazarene returns, you *will* arrest him."

Samuel shrugged. "Perhaps. You were elected to your position, Highness. We were born to it. If this Galilean breaks Temple Law, we *will* arrest him. Otherwise... deal with this problem yourself."

For research notes, see chapter 34 in the reference section.

XXXV

The Levites made good on their promise. Jesus returned to the Temple early Sabbath morning, and the Temple police let him in without a word. Pharisees were obsessed with the Law, and on the Sabbath even the scribes were prohibited from writing on any permanent surface, but the priests and Levites were exempt and were allowed to work in the Temple during Sabbaths and feasts.

With the Pharisees in the synagogues, Jesus taught in the Temple uncontested for the duration of the morning. When the Pharisees returned and discovered the betrayal of their own policing force, they were outraged. Judas was concerned they might summon the Temple Guard from Antonia to get rid of the troublesome Nazarene, but the Pharisees knew using Roman soldiers to fix a Jewish dispute would certainly turn the people against them. Jesus was a direct threat to their influence, but their authority was based in the Law. Going outside the Law would only undermine their authority further.

They were forced to change tactics. Jesus was constantly surrounded—now more than ever. The Sanhedrin would lose all credibility if they publicly took him by force without solid legal grounds. They had to humiliate him. They had to trick him into blatantly breaking the Law in a public forum.

Judas realized the cruel brilliance of their plan the moment he saw Annas and several leading members of the Sanhedrin dragging a woman into the Outer Court, heading for Jesus. It was obvious by the woman's disheveled dress that she had been caught doing something reserved only for the privacy of the marriage chamber. The Law required Jewish women to cover their hair while in public for modesty reasons, but this woman's long, dark hair was exposed for all to see. Judas wasn't sure whether she showed her hair willingly to advertise her "profession," or if she hadn't been given time to cover it. Her hair would have been extraordinarily beautiful if the Pharisee had not been dragging her by it.

The high priest pushed his way through the crowd surrounding Jesus, followed by the other Sanhedrin members.

"...does not abandon the lost sheep," Jesus continued, not even glancing at these intruders. "He leaves the ninety-nine, finds the lost sheep, and brings—"

"This woman was caught in the very act of adultery!" Annas snapped, cutting Jesus off. "She seduced a married man and was caught right in the middle of it!" He raised his hand, pointing out several Pharisees. "Here are witnesses." His demeanor calmed into a mockery of politeness. "Moses commands *in the Law* that adultery be punished by stoning, but... we ask *your* advice. What do you say?" he asked in an oily voice. They were asking Jesus to pass judgment, and tradition demanded that whoever passed judgment was required to throw the first stone himself.

The crowd turned to Jesus with bated breath. The Sanhedrin's devious set-up put Jesus in an inescapable position. Judas knew his master could never bring himself to condemn this woman to death. Jesus had a soft heart for sinners and outcasts and was remarkably sympathetic to women. Indeed, some of the man's disciples were women, which was an unheard-of breach in social protocol. But even if Jesus could bring himself to enforce Mosaic Law, he would then be arrested for murder. Only Romans had the legal right to pass an official sentence of death. Anything else was considered murder, and everyone knew the penalty for murder. On the other hand, if Jesus caved to his merciful nature, he would be publicly seen in blatant breach of Mosaic Law, and no Messiah would break the Law of Moses. The trick was perfect: either Jesus would be forced to break Mosaic Law and be proven a fraud and a heretic, or he would break Roman law and be crucified for murder.

It was far better for Jesus to be pitted against Rome than to break Mosaic Law. As much as Judas sympathized with the poor woman, her death was the lesser of two evils. Jesus had to stone her. Judas could see no alternate solution. The Messiah's purpose—at least in part—was to destroy Rome. Being an enemy of Rome came with the territory, but for the Messiah to blatantly pervert the very Law he came to establish... Both ends were horrible, but mercy would be far worse. Judas prayed that Jesus would make the hard choice and let this one sinful woman die to save the nation.

Jesus cast a scrutinizing glance at his intruders but ignored the high priest's question. This would only prolong the inevitable, as refusing to answer was the same as refusing to condemn. Instead, he stooped down, and with a significant glance to the high priest, began writing in the dust with his finger. He glanced again at the high priest, making sure Annas did not complain about him writing on the Sabbath. He also wanted to ensure that the high priest recognized his knowledge of the nuances in the oral tradition, which allowed writing, so long as it was easily wiped away. From his position in the crowd, Judas could not tell what Jesus wrote, but it couldn't have been more than a few words. He could see the high priest's face grow paler with each stroke of the finger.

Jesus finished his writing and straightened himself on the crate he was using as a chair, letting the other Pharisees read the short message. Annas's face grew hot, then pale again, and after a long moment of loaded silence, he turned and stalked away without a word. Judas and everyone else stared at the retreating figure of the high priest in shock. By abandoning the questioning, Annas was tacitly admitting the woman's innocence—despite the witnesses against her. With him gone, the duty of passing judgment fell to Amon, the oldest member of the Sanhedrin. However, if Amon passed judgment, he would be quietly accusing the high priest of making the wrong call. Amon would not dare disagree with the high priest, but neither could he openly give a verdict which opposed the Law. Faced with an even harder decision than Annas had faced, he followed the high priest's example, abandoning his comrades without a word.

The next in line was faced with an even worse dilemma, as Amon was now added to the list of elders who he would contradict if he chose to uphold the Law. He abandoned the questioning as well. The other members retreated, one by one, until the youngest had also turned and escaped from the clever trap.

Somehow, with a few strokes of his finger, Jesus had taken the impossible decision the Pharisees had thrust upon him and thrown it upon their own necks! The man was a natural tactician. He had been trapped in an unwinnable battle and had turned the weapons of his attackers against them. Judas wondered if the other disciples realized the absolute brilliance behind this turnabout, but there was no opportunity to ask.

Taking no time to gloat in this decisive victory, Jesus knelt down to meet the woman who still crouched at his feet, waiting for the strike of the first stone. She was totally unaware of the silent battle that had waged above her and cowered in expectation of a painful death.

"Sister," Jesus said quietly, lifting her chin. She met his gaze hesitantly, her eyes filled with tears and terror. "What's your name?"

Her brows drew down slightly in confusion. "Mary," she said, hesitant to give any further information which might bring shame to her friends or relatives—if she had any.

"Mary," Jesus repeated kindly. "What are you doing here?"

Her terror was replaced by confusion at Jesus's shocking ignorance of her impending doom. "I... I was condemned."

"Condemned by whom?" Jesus asked, drawing her attention to the suddenly vacant circle where the Sanhedrin had been. The crowd was still too shocked to move in and fill the gap. "Where are your accusers?"

Mary looked around in perplexity.

"Who accused you?" he asked again.

"I guess... no one," Mary said quietly, staring at the silent crowd that suspiciously lacked Pharisees. "Sir."

Jesus smiled. "It is against the Law to condemn anyone without two witnesses. Since they are not here, I cannot legally condemn you—nor would I. That life of darkness is behind you now," he said kindly. "Don't go back to it."

Mary lowered her eyes. "I must. I have nothing else."

Jesus gripped her hand and lifted her to her feet. "Yes, you do. I am here now. I am the light that will keep the darkness away. Stay in the light. The darkness will not overcome it."

For research notes, see chapter 35 in the reference section.

XXXVI

"Where are you from, Mary?" Judas asked, surreptitiously slipping a couple of barley cakes and an apple from Susanna's table into a fold of his robe. She often offered Jesus and his disciples food and lodging when they were in Jerusalem, but the others were elsewhere. Jesus had send Judas to escort the woman away from the chaos of the Temple to Susanna's, where she could get a decent meal in peace. Susanna's table was always open to friends of Jesus—even whores—and it was nearby. Judas had far better things to do with his time than escorting whores, but when Jesus commanded, even devils obeyed. It wasn't that he disliked the poor girl, but any of the other eleven could have brought her here while Judas sniffed out the Sanhedrin's next move. He had a feeling things were far from over, and it wasn't like any of the others were putting any thought toward what would happen when Annas and his sycophants came back for round two.

"Bethany," Mary replied as the two stepped into the busy street, heading back to the Temple. Susanna had cleaned Mary up and lent her a proper head covering. No one would recognize her as the woman the Pharisees had dragged through the Temple courtyard only that morning.

"I grew up in Bethany!" Judas exclaimed, pulling his thoughts back to his duty at hand. Worrying about the Sanhedrin was pointless until he actually had a chance to learn their next move. Until an opportunity appeared, he intended to be as pleasant and kind as he could to this poor girl. "You have family there?"

"None with any desire to see me," she said sadly.

Judas laughed in commiseration. "I know the feeling. But those feelings can't always be trusted. There was once a prodigal son who felt the same way. When he returned, his father was so happy that he ran to meet him."

"I can never return," Mary protested. "I would bring shame to my family."

Judas leaned closer. "If you haven't noticed, Jesus is a celebrity! He's constantly smothered by crowds. Let us take you to Bethany. People will be so busy talking about Jesus, they won't have time to talk about anyone else. I've seen it happen a dozen times."

"But my family..."

"Your parents will be angry at first, but they yearn for your return. Believe me." Judas had experienced that first-hand with his own father. They were closer now than they had ever been, and Judas still did not know how to feel about it. He hadn't spoken with his father since the healing.

"My parents are dead, sir," Mary replied. "I have a brother."

"I don't know much about brothers," Judas admitted, "but if anyone can solve this, it's Jesus. Regardless, there is someone in Bethany I want Jesus to meet, so you can travel with us."

"Do you still have family there?" Mary asked.

"My father," Judas admitted. "The only family I ever had. Watch your step." He stepped under the twin arches of the Double Gate and guided Mary up the uneven steps leading to the Temple Mount.

"Anyone I've met?" Mary asked.

"Not in person," Judas said grimly. "Simon ben Judah."

Mary gasped. "The leper! Oh, I'm so sorry! I couldn't imagine..."

"He's not a leper anymore."

Mary gaped. "What? You mean... Jesus? The rumors are true—what he does?" Judas nodded. "He healed your father; that's why you follow him," she mused.

"On the contrary," Judas replied. "I don't follow Jesus because he healed my father. My father is healed because I follow Jesus. I hope—" Judas froze mid-sentence as he stepped from the Double Gate. He could hear shouts coming from the Women's Court.

"...no bastard, like you! We have one Father: God!"

"If God was your father, you wouldn't be trying to kill me! *I* came from God. Your father is the devil, and you act just like him! He was a murderer and a liar from the start! All you do is lie! You say I'm a sinner? You've been trying to prove me wrong all day, and you have nothing!"

Judas knew that voice, but even if he didn't, only one man in all Israel would ever dare to brandish such bold accusations. Judas rounded the corner of the gate and immediately saw the problem. Jesus had drawn a less favorable crowd around him. Judas scanned the crowd for friendly faces, but the other disciples had not yet returned from the midday meal. Only John had stayed.

Judas didn't see a single Pharisee. Jesus had bested them this morning, and they were not about to risk another shaming so soon, but they were not above planting dissenters in the crowd. It looked like a dozen or so had taken advantage of Jesus while only John was nearby to support him.

"You're a Samaritan!" the ringleader said, using the worst insult he could imagine. "And you have a demon. Didn't I say that?" he asked his fellows.

Judas breathed a sigh of relief as Simon Zelotes moved up beside him. Of course the former *Sicari* would be drawn to any sign of trouble. "This could get ugly," Judas said. "Be ready in case Jesus needs an exit."

"You think *he* needs *our* help?" Simon asked, lifting an eyebrow.

Judas shrugged. "He could stop them all with a single word, but he prefers a quiet exit. Same thing happened in Nazareth. He nearly got thrown off a cliff. You know the best route out of here?"

Simon grunted. "The *Sicarii* make all their agents study the Temple so we can stop slaughters like the one Archelaus caused. I'll get him out."

"Speaking of the Underground, have they reached a decision?" Judas asked.

Simon shook his head grimly. "The *Sicarii* are in disarray. A few days ago, the Son of the Father was captured attacking a supply caravan, along with two others. The Romans know they have him, but they won't execute him until they've tortured some more names out of him. The *Sicarii* are desperate to get him out. No matter how much he believes in his cause, everyone breaks eventually."

"The Son of the Father is the heart and brain of the *Sicarii*. Without him, they'll fall apart."

"Which is why they are desperate to get him out," Simon said.

"They need *leadership!* Real leadership." Judas cast a meaningful glance at Jesus, who was still arguing with the malcontents.

Simon shook his head. "Jesus is just another pacifist to them. They prefer military to miracles. If Pilate wanted Jesus, they would gladly trade him for the Son of the Father. They want a war, and they have no interest in Jesus until he proves himself capable of starting one."

The conversation dropped as Jesus stood, signaling the end of the debate. "I know you are going to twist my words when you report back," he said, "because you are liars, and that's what liars do. But I will not lie, so make sure you get this part right: before Abraham was, *I AM*."

Simon gasped. "That's *blasphemy*—in front of witnesses!" he hissed.

Judas whistled. "Not for him. But they will say so." He started pushing through the crowd with Simon behind him. "I believe Jesus just started that war you mentioned."

"Blasphemy!" someone shouted, as Simon had predicted. "Blasphemy in God's Temple! Kill the blasphemer!"

"The stones! Pull up the stones!" another voice cried.

Judas shoved one man away and grabbed another by his cloak. The man spun, leaving Judas holding the empty cloth. Judas punched through the mob into the small circle around Jesus and John. "John, time to go!" he hissed, catching John's attention. The crowd was angrily pulling up the paving tiles, planning to bludgeon Jesus to death in a hail of stones.

Someone must have recognized Judas, as he suddenly found himself thrown into the center of the circle, cut off from Simon and their escape. Judas sprang to his feet as the first paving stone came flying at them but flattened himself again as it whizzed above his head. The thrower had hurled the flat stone like a discus, and it sailed past Jesus to smash into the opposite side of the circle, bowling over several men.

"There's our exit!" Judas cried, flying for the gap created by the fallen men. He pushed Jesus through, barely ducking another flying stone. "Move!" he said, snatching John and throwing him into the breach. Simon caught them at the other end, and Judas dove in after, using the stolen cloak as a shield to deflect a volley of smaller rocks and debris.

They reached the edge of the crowd with only bruises, and Judas didn't stop until they reached the Beautiful Gate, putting a wall between them and the mob. "Put this on," he said, draping the extra cloak over Jesus. "Keep your back to them, and with any luck, they'll be too busy pulling up the pavement to notice our escape."

"Head for the Lower City," Simon said. "We can lose them there, then slip out into Kidron through the Water Gate."

"Wait!" Judas said, noticing Mary still lingering in the Outer Court, all but forgotten in the mayhem. He beckoned her over. "We can't leave her here," he said. "I'm sure that mob would be all too eager to stone her as a consolation prize."

"What happened?" Mary asked, joining them as they crossed the courtyard and started back down the steps of the Double Gate. "This is not because of me, is it?" she asked in concern.

"Yes, what *did* happen?" Judas asked, giving Jesus a curious glance. "Are we going to address that?"

"I said what I needed to say," Jesus replied. "Where are the others?"

"Dining with Judas the tanner," Simon said. "We'll pick them up on the way."

"I think from now on, we should stay outside Jerusalem when we visit," Judas suggested. "I would hate to put any of our disciples here at risk by staying in their homes. They'll certainly be watched but hopefully nothing worse."

Jesus nodded. "I agree. There will always be some measure of risk, but we should lessen it when possible. Bethany is within a Sabbath day's walk, but not directly under the nose of the Sanhedrin. We will stay there."

"Yes!" Judas said, excited that Jesus's thoughts were mirroring his own. "We can escort Mary to her brother's house on the way." Judas was eager for Jesus to meet his father. Simon ben Judah was the only person who had the leverage to pressure the Sanhedrin. Without his help, Jesus's war against the Council would split Israel in two. The Messiah was supposed to unite Israel, not shatter it, and yet Jesus's actions were rapidly pushing Judea into a civil war.

"Mary is from Bethany?" Jesus asked. "Excellent! We can stay at her house."

"Master, I must protest," Judas began. "My father is—"

"I will meet with your father soon, Judas. Have patience. But there are matters of more importance. Mary's family will need time to adjust to her arrival. If they are also focused on providing for guests, it will make the transition easier. We should stay there—if you want me to stay, and if your brother allows it," Jesus added, glancing at Mary.

Mary stared at him. "I... I would not... You would eat at the same table as—"

"—a disciple? Of course!" Jesus said quickly. "I often stay in the homes of my disciples."

"But..."

"Do you think you are the only disciple with a dark past?" Jesus asked kindly. "Judas was a thief. Simon, a demoniac. John was... well, we won't say what John was. I have many disciples with dark pasts."

"But I am a woman."

"You are correct. Your point?"

"Rabbis do not take women as disciples," Mary said skeptically.

"I do," Jesus said.

"It's true; he does," John added. "Not just supporters—actual disciples."

"Speaking of disciples..." Simon said. Ahead of them, the rest of the twelve stood speaking with a beggar on the street—or rather, speaking to each other about the beggar. It looked more like an argument, though not as heated as the one they had just escaped.

The other nine saw them coming, and Simon Peter was the first to break away. "Rabbi, we need you to settle something: Reuben says he was born blind. Is he paying the price for something his parents did, or is it his fault? We bare no sin before coming of age, so it must be his parents' fault."

"But," Philip cut in, "it's unfair for him to pay the price of his parents' sin!"

"That mob will be here soon," Simon Zelotes said. "We have no time for this!"

"There's a mob? What did you do this time?" Nathanael asked without surprise.

"Is this common?" Matthew asked. "Inciting mobs?"

"More than you know," Thomas muttered.

Jesus held up a hand. "Reuben, your blindness is not your fault, and it's not your parents' fault, either. It's an opportunity."

"Master..." Simon Zelotes growled, as distant shouting grew closer. "We have no time for a sermon!"

"Patience, Simon," Jesus said, picking up a pinch of dust from the street, and spitting on it to make it wet. "We must work while there is light. When night comes, no one can work. So long as I am here, I am the light." He worked the dust into a muddy paste between his fingers. "Do you know where the Pool of Siloam is?" he asked Reuben.

"Of course!" Reuben said. "I'm blind, not stupid."

Jesus smiled. "Soon, you will be neither!" He smeared the paste on the man's eyes. "Go wash in the Pool of Siloam, and when you return, you'll see the light. We have to go, Reuben, but you'll see me later. Go."

Reuben nodded and started toward the pool. "See? All done!" Jesus said with a grin. "We'll take the Essene Gate out."

"All due respect, master, but that gate is on the opposite side of the Lower City! Water Gate is closer," Simon Zelotes protested, even as he started following Jesus.

"Which is where the mob will look first—and find an entire neighborhood full of people raucously celebrating their friend's newfound sight. Let the Pharisees' mob meet *my* mob," Jesus replied, eyes sparkling.

"That's... brilliant," Simon said, cocking his head. "But why the clay? You can heal with only a word. Why the extra steps?"

Jesus smiled. "Plausible deniability: Reuben hasn't seen my face, nor does he know my name. He can't identify me. When the Sanhedrin questions him—which they will—he can plead ignorance."

Simon chuckled. "For a pacifist, you are remarkably devious."

"Yes," Judas chimed in, as a forgotten question awakened in his mind. "Speaking of devious, what did you write in the dust to make Annas's face turn that particular shade of white?"

Jesus shrugged mischievously. "I noticed Caiaphas was absent. I simply asked where he was."

Mary's face reddened.

Judas sucked in a breath. "You don't mean..."

Jesus chuckled grimly. "Certain sins require *two* people, yes? Wasn't it strange that they brought only one person to be stoned? You know Caiaphas would never miss an opportunity to see me humiliated."

"It was a set-up," Judas realized. "Annas would never publicly condemn his own son-in-law. It would mean he made a bad choice in choosing his daughter's husband. But Annas would have hand-picked the witnesses. I don't get it. They wouldn't dare accuse the high priest's son-in-law."

"I know how hard this day has been for you, Mary," Jesus interrupted. "We don't have to talk about this."

"It's alright," Mary said quickly. "Annas's witnesses would have kept silent, but not me. The man who... I do not know his name. But I know his face. If he had been present for the examination, *I* would have recognized him."

Judas whistled. "That is an ugly secret the high priest will be desperate to bury—along with anyone who knows it. Mary's life will be in danger."

"No," Jesus said. "Mary's old life is already dead, and her new life cannot be taken away. She is a new woman, starting today."

Judas nodded sagely. "Plausible deniability?"

Jesus chuckled. "Something like that."

For research notes, see chapter 36 in the reference section.

XXXVII

Judas took a shaky breath and stepped into the empty market of Arimathaea. Jesus had decided to spend some time in Bethany, making sure Mary and her brother, Lazarus, were on good terms before he moved on. The other disciples had been sent out in pairs, as usual, but Jesus had paired Simon Zelotes with Matthias, one of the seventy, leaving Judas on his own. Judas had been putting this day off for a long time, and although Jesus hadn't specifically commanded him to come here, he knew the reason for his suddenly open schedule. Jesus knew the weight which pressed upon Judas's conscience and had quietly given him the opportunity to relieve it.

Judas had taken the opportunity. Still, his steps dragged slowly through the silent market. The vendors had all gone after the morning shopping. The place was vacant except for two lonely day laborers still waiting to be hired. They rested under a canopy, taking what shelter they could from the late afternoon sun. Judas planted himself beside the two stragglers. He had no Pharisees to impress, so he wore his worn traveling clothes. He blended in with the day laborers except for the glaring lack of callouses on his hands. "No work today?" he asked.

For men with no steady occupation or trade, the market was the gathering place to find a job working for anyone needing an extra hand. Work was easiest to come by in spring and autumn, when farmers needed more hands for planting and harvesting. The laborers rose early, waiting for someone to call on one or two, or half a dozen, if they were lucky. The unlucky ones were forced to wait for the next job, any job at all—if there was a next job. Once midday was past, the chances of finding work dropped to zero.

One of the men sighed by way of reply. They had arrived before dawn, waiting for work, only to watch their comrades be selected one by one or, failing that, giving up and going home. This pair seemed too desperate to give up.

"Two dozen men or more, this morning," the other replied. "The lucky ones got hired, the smart ones left. The idiots stayed." He sighed, too.

"Two weeks I haven't caught work," the first added. "I can't stand the look on my wife's face when I come home with nothing. Keep putting it off."

Judas knew that feeling. He had also been senselessly putting off the inevitable, hoping for an impossible solution.

"It's stupid, waitin' here. I could have been out digging wild onions, picking herbs... Would've at least had something to eat."

"Simeon said a guy comes here late sometimes," the first replied, picking idly at some dirt under a worn fingernail. "Hope is a stupid thing. You're awful late to be looking for work," the man added, giving Judas a once-over. "What're you here for?"

Judas chuckled nervously. "Waiting on that same guy."

He felt a stab of apprehension as he saw him. It had been three years since Judas had last seen Joseph of Arimathaea. Three years since Judas had swindled the man out of a significant piece of his fortune. Three years. It didn't seem so long. Judas hoped the man didn't hold a grudge. There was still time to leave before Joseph saw him. He could put this off a little longer. But no, like the man avoiding his wife's disappointment, it was senseless. Judas had put this off too long already.

Joseph entered the empty market, and his eyes glanced over the three workers, still hopelessly waiting for a job. Joseph was simply dressed, though the fine cloth betrayed his wealth. The man had simple taste. His eyes passed over Judas, then snapped back as he recognized his former steward. "*Judas?*" he said in unbelief.

"Joseph," Judas replied with a painful smile.

"Are you looking for work?" he asked, his face a mask of shock and confusion at Judas's audacity.

"No," Judas said, suppressing a wry grin. "I need to speak with you. Thought I'd find you here."

Joseph eyed him with disdain. He turned his attention to the other men. "You two. Are you looking for work?"

They brightened immediately, standing straighter, and doing their best to seem strong and eager. "Yes, sir!" one said, speaking for them both. "Any work at all! We are strong, and will work through the night, if need be."

Joseph nodded. "There is little daylight left, but you may work until dark. My estate is about a mile west. Follow the sun, and you won't miss it. Zedekiah will show you to your work. I will pay you what is fair."

"Yes, sir!" the men said in unison, and hurried off at a jog toward Joseph's estate. They didn't take the time to thank him, knowing they would see him again in only an hour or two, when the other workers would be paid and sent home.

Judas laughed dryly. "Same old Joseph," he said, shaking his head. "Still hiring workers at the eleventh hour."

"You have a great deal of nerve being here!" Joseph hissed. "Do you realize the—I could have had you hunted down and *crucified!* Thievery is a capital offense, and what you did... I could *still* have you crucified. Do you know that? I kept the records." He laughed in shock. "What desperation must have driven you back...!"

"I know!" Judas said quickly, throwing up his hands in surrender. "I know. And... I'm sorry. I don't need anything. I didn't come to beg. I... I came to apologize."

Joseph flinched. "You *what?!* Walk with me," he snapped, starting back toward his estate and motioning for Judas to follow. "I can't stand here wasting time."

"I know," Judas repeated, falling into step with his former master. "I never saw myself coming back, either, but... Can I be honest?"

Joseph gave him a strange look. "I doubt it, but there's a first time for everything."

"I knew you would not prosecute me. You're too nice, Joseph. You don't have a vengeful bone in your body! I gambled on your mercy, and it paid off."

"*That's* your apology?" Joseph asked.

"I... Well, no," Judas stammered. "I was skimming money to fund the Underground. I believed in the liberation of Israel, but I knew you would not approve." Judas hurried on, before Joseph could interrupt. "I thought your wealth was all the permission I needed. You could afford to lose it, and I could afford to take it and give it to ones I thought more deserving. When you found out, I panicked. I wanted to leave on my own terms. I knew you would never take the money back from your farmers. You could never bring yourself to kill their newfound joy—even if you had every right! I wanted to show you that your mercy would only come back to hurt you, but here you are, still hiring workers an hour from sunset. You're still paying them a full *denarius*, too, aren't you? Of course you are," Judas chuckled. "You never learn."

"This is the worst apology I've ever heard," Joseph said in wonder.

"I'm getting there. Don't rush me. I did prove a point, just not to you— to me. I'm sorry. It wasn't my money to take, and... you are far more deserving of it than I could ever be."

They walked in silence for a long while as Joseph mulled over this admittance. "You support the *Sicarii?*" he said at last. "Those terrorists are the path to destruction, not to freedom. You stole money from me to fund terrorists?"

"I... yes," Judas admitted. "I thought they were the only way to defeat Rome. They kicked me out when the money stopped. I was no longer useful."

"They kicked you out. That's why you're here," Joseph said stiffly, finding the catch he had been expecting. "Judas, I... thank you for your apology. But... you cannot imagine that I would ever hire you again! You understand that, don't you?"

Judas smiled to himself. Joseph thought he had come crawling back because the *Sicarii* had kicked him out. "I have a new master," he said. "When the Underground rejected me, it put me on a path to discover the true Liberator of Israel! Joseph, I found him—I found the Christ! Well, he found me, in a sense. Do you remember your visitor, the night I left?"

"Remember?! I cannot forget!" Joseph said. "You gambled too much on my mercy, Judas. I was going to have you arrested and lashed—probably killed. You stole from me for *three years!* I offered you mercy, and you spat it back in my face by stealing even more! It was too much, even for me. It was Jesus who finally convinced me to let you go. He said if I must lash someone, he would take the lashes in your place, because he knew of the theft and didn't stop you from leaving. He offered to take your punishment! He *insisted!* I could never put that punishment on a friend and a guest—especially an innocent one! *He* saved your life! *That* is what a true shepherd of Israel should do! *That* is the attitude of the Christ—not some *Sicari* who cuts a man's throat from behind. I hope you didn't come to ask for more money, because I will never support a cult of thieves and assassins—never!"

Judas suppressed a grin. "You think Jesus, the penniless son of a penniless craftsman—from Nazareth, no less—is the Christ?"

"I never said he *was...*!" Joseph sputtered. "I was just... I mean..."

"Because he is."

Joseph nearly tripped himself as his legs forgot to walk. "What?"

"Jesus of Nazareth! He *is the Christ!*"

"He is in *deep trouble!*" Joseph countered. "I don't know what he's been teaching of late—I never expected Joseph to raise a heretic—but Jesus has managed to burn every bridge between Pharisees and Sadducees alike! He's a lawbreaker! I don't know if the rumors about his... *powers*... are true, but no man can perform miracles through God's power if he breaks God's Law. If he is performing these signs, then he is using dark magic."

"He does not break the Law!" Judas countered. "He ignores the Pharisees' interpretations, but he does *not* break the Law! Only God can do what he does! The Pharisees argue over the letter of the Law, but Jesus understands the *spirit* of it! The Pharisees have tested him multiple times, and each time he turns their words against them. They cannot lay a charge on him, and oh, have they tried."

"It doesn't matter!" Joseph protested. "The Sanhedrin *hates* him! I have friends on the Council. I know their opinions. If Jesus is the Christ, he will have to overthrow the entire religious structure!"

"Not necessarily," Judas countered. "Jesus has the support of the people, and even some of the Sanhedrin. Nicodemus is an ally. Annas is the force behind the hatred, and he will be replaced soon—if he hasn't been already. My father has *very* good reason to support Jesus, and I'm hoping he can apply enough pressure to get Nicodemus selected as the new high priest. With Annas gone, we have a good chance of swaying the Sanhedrin to our side! Caiaphas will never support Jesus—for reasons unnamed—but with Annas gone and Nicodemus as high priest, we will have the leverage and the influence to silence Caiaphas."

"You haven't heard, have you?" Joseph asked.

"What?" Judas asked, a cold feeling sinking into his gut.

"Pilate ousted Annas two days ago. Caiaphas is his replacement."

For research notes, see chapter 37 in the reference section.

XXXVIII

It was winter before Jesus returned to Jerusalem. The Feast of Dedication was not one of the three annual feasts which required attendance, but it was an incredible sight. It hearkened back three-hundred and fifty years to the reign of the Maccabees. They had cleansed the Temple, rededicated it to God, and established a new Jewish dynasty. The feast was a time of celebration and great expectations for the Messiah to—like the Maccabees—overthrow Israel's oppressors and establish a new dynasty.

"Is this really a good idea?" Thomas asked. "After what happened last time?" Every window in Jerusalem was glowing. The entire city was an ocean of lamps and candles, especially the Temple, which exploded with light as the disciples emerged onto the Temple Mount from the dark stairway.

"I promised Reuben I would meet him. Susanna's messenger said he needed to speak with me," Jesus replied. "I am not in the habit of abandoning my sheep, Thomas."

"Yes, but *here*? Couldn't Reuben have come to Bethany?" Nathanael asked pragmatically.

"At least we'd be indoors," Thad muttered. The night air was cold. The sky had threatened snow all day, and there would surely be some tonight.

"There is nowhere more beautiful," Jesus countered. "And Reuben has a lifetime of beauty to see. I wanted to meet him here."

"There he is!" Philip said, pointing. "By the Beautiful Gate. Talking to some Pharisees."

The conversation looked heated, with several Pharisees barring Reuben's way through the gate. "Are they denying him entrance?" Peter asked angrily. "He's an Israelite! They can't do that!"

Jesus crossed the courtyard and stepped up to the men. "What's going on here?" he asked.

Reuben did a double take, and his eyes widened. He took a long look. "I know your voice!" he said in awe. "May we speak privately?"

"Let's talk by one of the fires under Solomon's Porch," Jesus suggested. He guided them to one of the large fires burning in a brazier near the Shushan Gate. "Now, what was all that about, Reuben? Why won't they let you inside? Were you made unclean recently?"

"You're *him!*" Reuben said excitedly. "You sent me to the pool!"

Jesus nodded. "I'm Jesus. Nice to meet you under better circumstances."

"I need your help!" Reuben said quickly. "I don't know what to do! I was summoned by the Pharisees. They were angry that I was healed on Sabbath, breaking the Law. I told them all I knew. Of course, I didn't know your identity, but who else could it be? They asked how a sinner could heal someone. I said you must be a prophet! They opened an official investigation to summon my parents. Well, my parents confirmed that I had been born blind, but they wouldn't dare say more."

"Why not?" John asked, leaning closer. "Why would they withhold information?"

Reuben leaned closer, his face illuminated by the fire. "After you interrupted the water ceremony—that *was* you, wasn't it?" he asked, not expecting any denial. "After that, things exploded. You were on everyone's lips even before, but after... Caiaphas—the *official* high priest—is excommunicating anyone who claims Jesus of Nazareth to be the Messiah. No sacrifices, no atonement... They won't let me in the Temple because I refuse to denounce my healer! I cannot pass beyond the Court of the Gentiles. In their eyes, I am no longer an Israelite."

Jesus nodded, his face a mix of pride and concern. "Does this mean you believe in the Son of God?"

"I believe in *you!*" Reuben said quickly. "Who is the Son of God? I will believe anything you say!"

Jesus shrugged humbly. "You're looking at him."

Reuben gasped. "Lord, I believe!" he said. "You are the Son of God!" He collapsed without hesitation, falling to his knees in worship.

The Pharisees guarding the gate had stayed at a distance, allowing Reuben some privacy for his conversation, but they could not ignore the blasphemous act of a man being worshiped in God's Temple. "You! What are you doing?" one demanded, stalking quickly over and glaring at Reuben in suspicion as he regained his feet.

"Why are you here?" another asked, turning to Jesus.

"I am here for judgment!" Jesus replied cryptically, glaring at the Pharisees' intrusion "To bring sight to the blind and to strike blind those who see."

"Are you calling us blind?" the Pharisee asked indignantly.

"If you were blind, I could help you," Jesus replied dryly. "But you insist that you can see, so the problem remains."

"The *problem* is that this man has been excommunicated, and we caught him trying to enter the Temple illegally," the Pharisee replied, pointing at Reuben with disdain, "trying to sneak in like a thief." Several other men had started moving closer, following the Pharisees.

"A thief wouldn't come through the door," Jesus shot back, raising his voice so that all could hear. "Shepherds enter through the door. A thief would climb up some other way. You think you can keep Reuben from finding forgiveness by blocking his way through a door? *I am the door.* Anyone who tries to reach salvation by another way is the thief," he said, glaring pointedly at the Pharisee, "who does nothing but steal, kill, and destroy. I have come to bring life," Jesus continued, gripping Reuben's shoulder, and looking into the man's sparkling eyes. "And lots of it."

"You're Jesus the Nazarene, aren't you?" the Pharisee said, narrowing his eyes. "No one else would have the gall to say such things!"

Jesus ignored the comment and turned to address the rapidly gathering crowd. Even at the Feast of Lights, Jesus outshone them all. "A hired hand doesn't care about the sheep, so long as he gets paid. You know the type: the moment a wolf appears, he finds himself urgently needed anywhere else. No sheep is worth dying over—unless it's *your* sheep. A good shepherd will die to protect his sheep. I am that good shepherd. It is my choice to die protecting my sheep. I can give up my life, and I can take it back again. I have that power. My Father has said so."

This maddening comparison threw the crowd into disarray as they struggled to explain the meaning of these words. The leading Pharisee, who had not met Jesus before but was already on the fast track to disliking him, took full advantage of the crowd's confusion. "Are you listening to this?" he asked in consternation. "Anyone claiming Jesus of Nazareth to be the Messiah will be excommunicated, and this is exactly why! The man is possessed, and his demon has driven him mad! Listen to this madness!"

"These are not the words of madness!" Reuben exclaimed, drawing the crowd's attention. "Can a demon open the eyes of the blind? Look at me! Look at me and see that I also see you! I was born blind! Ask the Sanhedrin!" he shouted, offering the Pharisee a direct challenge.

The Pharisee held up his hands to quiet the crowd. "Very well," he said, changing his manner to a patronizing sneer. "Let's settle this. These arguments have been going for months. How long will you let this play out? If you are the Messiah, tell us!"

"I *have* told you," Jesus said. "You don't believe me. You see the works I do and hear that I do them in my Father's name, but you don't listen because you are not my flock. Sheep follow the call of their shepherd. My sheep follow me to green pastures, where they will live in My Father's house forever." Judas recognized Jesus's appropriation of David's Psalm. Jesus was placing himself in the parable, not only as the shepherd but also as God's Son. Jesus straightened proudly. "You will never steal my flock. My Father and I are united."

"You heard the blasphemer!" someone shouted. "Stone him! Finish what we started at Tabernacles." The crowd erupted in a mixed cry of agreement and opposition but growing angrier by the second.

"Not again," John groaned, preparing for the worst.

"Wait!" Jesus shouted, bringing a temporary pause to the impending violence. "You have seen me work miracles, help the poor, give sight to the blind..." he said, indicating Reuben as an example. "For which of these things am I being stoned?"

"You're being stoned for blasphemy!" the Pharisee shouted. "You're putting yourself on equal footing with God Himself! It doesn't matter what kind of sorcery you perform!"

Jesus smiled shrewdly. "Did not Asaph, in the book of Psalms, say 'You are gods; all of you are children of the Most High'? The Law cannot be broken. Asaph called those who read the Law 'gods' *in the Law!* And you stone me for saying the same of myself? If it applies to those who read the Law, shouldn't it apply more to the one God sent to fulfill it? Believe me or don't, but my work speaks for itself. My Father and I work in unity. We are one."

The crowd was past the point of reason. Angry shouts arose, and a hail of rubble peppered them, causing a flash of sparks and clangs as stones struck the large brazier and the fire within. Jesus's words had only managed to infuriate the crowd further, but their response gave Judas an idea. With a swift kick, he threw his whole weight against the heavy brazier and bowled it off its pedestal, showering the mob with burning coals.

"Go, go!" he hissed, as the mob reeled back from the burning coals and cloud of ash. "Out Shushan!" The gate was only a few yards away, and they slipped away in the chaos. Shushan led to the Mount of Olives, away from the glowing city and into the darkness of night.

"Master, why must you keep starting riots in the Temple?" Judas asked. "It's becoming a bad habit. What's going to happen when we can't get you out? That's not the way to make friends in the Sanhedrin!"

"Caiaphas has power only because I allow it," Jesus replied. "Don't forget to whom you speak, Judas."

Judas nodded. "You're right; I know. I just grow concerned with this rising tension. Something must break eventually. I just want to be sure that what breaks can be mended."

Jesus chuckled and patted him on the shoulder. "Everything can be mended, Judas. Your recent visit to Arimathaea should be proof enough of that. But rest easy; we won't be coming back to Jerusalem for a while. Nice distraction with the brazier, by the way. That's no way to make friends in the Sanhedrin, though," he chided laughingly.

Judas grinned. "But master, is it not written by Solomon *in the Law*," he said, copying Jesus, "that we are to help our enemies by heaping coals of fire on their heads?"

Jesus laughed. "Why, Judas, I believe you're starting to catch on!"

For research notes, see chapter 38 in the reference section.

XXXIX

I t was good to stand at synagogue again without fear of being killed. Bethabara had welcomed Jesus with open arms—figuratively, since there was no actual room for open arms in the crowded synagogue. It was packed, pressed down, shaken together, and running over. Jesus had chosen to keep the inner circle of twelve with him and make a wide circuit through all the land of Israel starting in Perea and continuing anywhere that was not Jerusalem. John had started his ministry in Perea, and after his death, John's many followers were eager to learn of his predicted successor. Jesus had healed many over the last few days, and in a shocking twist, the Pharisees in Bethabara had offered Jesus the honor of leading the Sabbath service. They listened to his reading quietly. Too quietly. Judas expected an interruption.

It was the manner of interruption which he did not expect. The dark cloth over the synagogue door shifted, letting in a shaft of light and a gnarled form. It took Judas a moment to realize that the form belonged to a woman. She was bent nearly double with a severe hunchback. She had probably started for synagogue early, but her steps were so slow and labored that she had arrived late. Jesus saw her immediately and paused his reading to welcome her and call her to the front. She hesitated, surely not wishing to be ogled and displayed as an example of poor life choices, but after some kind urging, she complied, and the crowd squeezed together to let her through.

"What's your name?" Jesus asked.

"Debra," the woman replied hesitantly, staring at the floor, since it was the only direction she could possibly look, as bent as she was.

"How long have you been tied down this way?"

"About... eighteen years," Debra replied.

"So long a prisoner," Jesus remarked. "Such a terrible knot no man can untie. I can." He took the woman in his arms, and Judas watched her fold into his embrace as Jesus pressed her against him. No matter how many times Judas witnessed these miracles, he never ceased to feel the wonder. The woman stepped back in tears, but with a strong step. She took her place among the women, standing tall and straight.

"This is preposterous!" Caleb, the chief Pharisee said. "We have bid you welcome, rabbi, to do your healing work—despite the rumors, which I am beginning to fear are true—but there are six days when men should work!" He turned to the crowd. "Come and be healed on any other day, but not Sabbath—right in the middle of the reading!"

The woman's head dropped, and she shrunk back into the crowd.

"Do you have sheep?" Jesus asked sharply. His tall frame now bent with the weight of the woman's sickness, though the effect was quickly fading.

"Yes, but I don't see—"

"Did you leave them locked in your house, or did you send them out with the shepherd this morning?" Jesus asked.

"The Law allows—"

"Yes!" Jesus snapped. "The Law *does* allow, you hypocrite. You release your sheep on Sabbath but deny me the right to release *mine?* If it is right to release an animal on Sabbath, which has been tied for only one night, how much better to release a daughter of Abraham, who has been tied down for *eighteen years?*"

Caleb's face turned red. Judas braced himself for an angry tirade, but John the dunkard's relentless spiritual beatings had softened Caleb into a humbler breed of Pharisee, and Bethabara was not Jerusalem. "You are right, rabbi," he admitted, ducking his head. "I will remember this teaching."

This admission on the part of Bethabara's leading Pharisee brought murmurs of assent and admiration for Jesus's application. Jesus returned to the podium and back to his reading when another woman broke the silence with an excited cry, swept up in the crowd's enthusiasm. "Your mother's womb must be wonderful!" she exclaimed, unable to contain herself. "And her breasts! To produce someone like you, who suckled from them!"

It was now Jesus's face which turned a deep red at this bizarre outburst. Women were not to speak in synagogue, but Jesus's reputation for accepting female disciples must have dared this woman to risk it. Though why she had chosen such a peculiarly taboo subject was beyond Judas's ability to discover. The synagogue fell into an awkward silence.

Jesus cleared his throat and pursed his lips, working to summon an appropriate response to this inappropriate comment. "Well, no... actually," he said, clearing his throat again. "On the contrary, wonderful are those who hear the word of God and who keep it." He indicated Caleb, who had so gracefully accepted the earlier rebuke.

Caleb accepted the compliment and gave Jesus an approving nod at his adept recovery.

"You know," Jesus continued, raising his eyebrows and attempting to shake off the image the woman's outburst must have produced, "this generation..." He shook his head. "There is something wrong with this generation. They ignore the signs I do show, and demand others! Well, the only sign they're getting is the sign of Jonas, the prophet. Ninevah will condemn this generation, because at least Ninevah listened to Jonas and repented. But this generation was given someone greater than Jonas, and they don't listen. It is like a man who threw a great banquet, and invited all his friends..."

Judas's attention strayed from Jesus's teaching as another late comer stepped through the doorway, letting in another shaft of light. Judas's eyes nearly popped as he recognized the robust frame of his father slip into the packed synagogue and squeeze into a place near the back. Judas hated to become yet another interruption to Jesus's teaching—especially with such a receptive audience—so he forced himself to wait until Jesus had finished, his mind a whirl as he wondered what business had brought his father here.

He slipped out as soon as Jesus dismissed his audience. Jesus would be receiving a plethora of invitations as the crowd flocked around him, hoping to receive the honor of his company at their table. It was anyone's guess if Jesus would dine with Caleb, the chief Pharisee, as was socially expected, or in some hovel. Judas would place his money on the hovel.

"What are you doing here?" Judas demanded, staring at his father's strong jaw and healthy face. His hair was growing back quickly, and a short growth of beard covered what had once been the deformed face of a leper. The man held no evidence of the disease now. "You never traveled before."

Simon shrugged. "Fifteen years of forced quarantine will turn the worst hermit into a traveler. I came to speak with your master."

"Of course!" Judas said quickly. He had been hoping desperately for his father's belief but had hesitated to contact him again. His father had needed time—they both had. His presence here was a strong indication that he had made the right decision. With his father's influence, perhaps there was still a chance to push the Sanhedrin into accepting the Messiah.

"Jesus!" Judas called, catching his master's attention as he pushed his way through the crowd.

Jesus turned from his conversation and smiled, giving Judas's father a quick appraisal.

"Allow me to introduce Simon, a Pharisee of Bethany," Judas said, "and my father. Simon, this is Jesus." Judas knew his master preferred simple introductions to let people decide for themselves what he was or was not. James and John shared a significant look at the introduction. Judas had always been reluctant to share information about his history or family. The other nine shared similar looks. Thomas, their resident pessimist, shook his head grimly, while Philip gave Judas a dramatically encouraging smile.

"I knew there was a reason you liked me," Simon the Zealot replied quietly, nudging Judas in the side. "Same name as your father."

Judas rolled his eyes. "Half the men in Israel are named Simon."

"And the other half are named Judas," Simon replied.

"I am glad to finally meet you!" Jesus said, taking Judas's father's hand. "Judas has often commended your abilities of late." He gave Judas a flat look.

"The pleasure is mine," Simon replied politely. "I am told that I have you to thank for this meeting."

Jesus nodded. "Yes, Judas told me of your newfound health. It is good to see you well."

Simon nodded. "I was sorry to hear that I missed your visit to Bethany. I was away. I... I haven't seen the land of Israel with my own eyes for a very long time. Even a hermit can grow restless after fifteen years."

"I understand," Jesus said with an easy smile. "I am a traveler myself. But do not be troubled; I enjoyed the greatest hospitality while in your city. You can be proud of your city's kindness."

Simon grimaced. "Yes... I am aware of the details regarding your stay. In fact, that is why I am here; I bring a message from your... *friend*... Mary." Simon clearly knew of Mary's history and was reluctant to mention her. Still, Judas's father owed Jesus a great debt—a debt that could never be fully repaid—and he knew it. "She would have come personally, but she and her sister, Martha cannot leave. Their brother has taken ill. She begs you to return immediately."

"We must go back!" Philip said quickly. "You stayed with them for over a month! Lazarus loves you. The whole family loves you! And you love them! Didn't you say you felt more at home there than anywhere? You must go!"

"Hold on," Peter said quickly. "The last two times we were in Jerusalem, you were nearly stoned! Do you really think returning is a good idea?"

"Why not just command the sickness to leave from here?" Nathanael asked, catching at the most sensible solution. "You've done so before. There's no reason to risk your life."

"Actually," Judas's father interrupted. "That's why they sent *me*. It's true. The Sanhedrin's obsession has spread to Herod, and the Tetrarch has spies everywhere. They intend to kill you. but they would not dare take you from my home. You will be safe with me. It is the least I can offer you in return for what you did. We leave tonight."

Jesus shook his head thoughtfully. "I still have much to do in Perea. This sickness won't end in death; it's an opportunity for the Son of God to be glorified. I will come, but I must finish my work here. Return to Bethany, Simon. Tell Mary and Martha that I will come soon."

"All due respect, sir," Simon replied, "but trust me when I say that traveling there without my protection will be very dangerous."

Jesus laid a hand on his shoulder. "I thank you, but I don't need your protection, Simon. Please give them my message."

Simon nodded grimly. "Very well, but do not linger. The doctors don't think he will last long. If Lazarus was *my* friend, I would leave now."

"It is good advice," Jesus said. "Take it. Go. Give them what comfort you can. Do for him as you would for me. We will speak again in a few days."

"I hope you are right about this," Simon said. "If you are too late, they will never forgive you."

For research notes, see chapter 39 in the reference section.

XL

"She doesn't look happy," Andrew whispered as Martha approached, coming up the road from their home in Bethany.

"I thought you said Lazarus was sleeping?" Philip asked. "Those are mourning clothes."

"He *is* sleeping," Jesus replied, leaning closer so their words would not carry. "I'm going to wake him up."

"Shouldn't she look happier, then?" Peter muttered.

Jesus sighed in frustration. "Lazarus is dead," he said bluntly. "I can't be poetic at all with you, can I?"

This pronouncement snapped the disciples into silence as Martha paused a few steps away. "I heard you were coming," she said stiffly. Her eyes were dry, but the evidence of tears lingered, despite her efforts. She was a strong woman, pragmatic and stoic. Her face was prematurely lined with evidence of toil and trouble. She and her brother had eked out a hard living while Mary, their younger and far more beautiful sister, had left them to follow a different, though equally difficult, path. Jesus had brought Mary back from that dark path.

Despite Martha's tough exterior, she was struggling to maintain her composure while facing the man who had both restored her family and now,

233

by his absence, broken it again. As always, news of Jesus's arrival in Bethany had arrived long before Jesus himself, and Martha had come to meet them on the road outside the village before the crowds found him. "I don't understand," she said, her voice tight. "We thought Simon... He was supposed to bring you back!" she said angrily, her iron facade cracking. "Lazarus was *alive* when Simon returned! You could have—if you had come back with him... my brother would not have died."

Jesus said nothing but gave her a sad, sympathetic smile in response.

She shook her head. "I tried. I tried so hard to hate you, you know?" She wiped away a foolish tear, which thought itself brave enough to survive her hardened face. "You brought Mary back—back from her... I just got my family back! And then... *He should be alive.* Anything you asked, God would give you. I *still* believe that. Simon said... you *refused?* You would have been in time! You could have... Why?" she asked, desperate for any excuse to explain the delay. Of course, Jesus had none; he could have come, he just... hadn't bothered.

"Your brother will live again," he said kindly.

"I know," Martha said coldly. "I'm not a Sadducee. I know he will rise again in the Resurrection at the last day. That is cold comfort now."

Jesus stepped toward her and gripped her shoulders. "Look at me," he said, forcing her to meet his gaze. "*I am* the Resurrection. Whoever believes in me—even if he dies—he will live. Do you believe me?"

Martha softened—slightly. "Yes. I believe *in* you," she said, though Judas noted the slight difference in meaning. "I believe you are the Coming One."

Jesus nodded. "How is Mary?"

Martha drew her lips in a line and shook her head grimly.

"Bring her to me. I want to talk to her—away from the crowds."

Martha nodded stiffly and walked away with heavy steps.

"Good idea to have Mary come here," Peter said, once Martha was out of earshot. "It's dangerous enough being this close to Jerusalem. Lazarus was a known associate of yours. If Simon spoke the truth, Herod will have spies among the mourners. We could be putting them all in danger by being here—not to mention ourselves."

"You're awfully worried about danger for someone who swore to give his life for me," Jesus replied.

Peter huffed. "That doesn't mean I want to stick my neck out for no reason! We were almost stoned to death the last two times we were in Jerusalem, and that was *before* Herod got involved. I know you can outsmart the Pharisees on legal matters, but Herod doesn't care about the Law. If he thinks you're a threat, he'll kill you."

"Herod does not concern me," Jesus said.

"Maybe he should!" Andrew said, coming to his brother's defense. "If you took Herod more seriously, John would still be alive!" The comment was harsh, but the other disciples had secretly voiced similar opinions. Andrew was the only one foolhardy enough to say it to Jesus's face.

Judas knew the jab struck home by the pain which crossed Jesus's face. "You didn't have to come," Jesus said quietly.

"No," Thomas cut in. "No, we're coming, and that's that. Nobody is leaving. If you want to go and get yourself killed, we will be right there with you," he said in a strange bout of optimism. "That way, we all die together!"

"That's a cheery outlook," Philip muttered.

Thomas shrugged. "If I'm wrong, at least it's a nice surprise."

Martha's return with Mary stopped further conversation. Mary saw Jesus and broke into a run. She collapsed before she reached him. She fell to her knees and broke into awful, gut-wrenching sobs. Jesus squatted down and carefully pulled her back to her feet. The shock and pain turned to anger, and she lashed out, striking Jesus on the chest with clenched fists. Jesus took the beating in stride and wrapped his arms around her, pulling her into his embrace until she collapsed into it, sobbing.

Jesus cried with her. Judas watched in silence. He had often seen Jesus sad, but he had never seen the man cry. Jesus didn't explain, or try to inspire

Mary with future promises, as he had with Martha. Mary didn't need that. She only needed someone to cry with her.

The scene lasted for a long moment, until Mary's sobs finally quieted. "Why didn't you come?" she finally asked, her head still on Jesus's shoulder. "If you had been here..."

"I know," Jesus said kindly. "Where is he?"

"I'll show you," Mary said, pulling away and starting toward Jerusalem. Judas raised an eyebrow. Only the rich could afford a burial plot near Jerusalem. Pharisees believed in the resurrection and paid good money to afford stone tombs near the Holy City, so they would be near it when the Messiah came at the end of days. The poorer classes were buried in personal plots if they had the land, or in charitably funded mass graves.

"He spared no expense," Mary said, smiling sadly as they walked. "Simon the Leper—not that he is anymore, but he's been known by that name for most of my life. He purchased a private grave near Jerusalem, hired the best mourners... They are paid through the end of the week. You'd think Lazarus was a personal friend."

"I'm so sick of the noise," Martha groaned. "You'd think a family could mourn in peace."

"It's a sign of respect. He gave us great honor," Mary replied.

"I waited by the road just to get some peace," Martha admitted, giving Jesus an exasperated look. Despite their heartache, Jesus's presence was a balm against their wounds. It was impossible to be angry at Jesus for long—at least, for some. The Sanhedrin felt differently, but to the average Jew, Jesus was a symbol of hope. The Sanhedrin saw him as only a threat.

"Ugh, I can hear them from here," Martha lamented. "How can they be so loud that we hear them a mile away from the house?"

"They wouldn't..." Mary said as they passed around the side of the hill to the garden where the graves were cut into the stone. Judas recognized the place. Joseph of Arimathaea owned a grotto here and had given Judas a small fortune with which to purchase it. The area was peaceful, with richly manicured grounds maintained by a gardener, who was paid out of the exorbitant sums necessary to own a plot. Simon truly had gone above and beyond. "They would," she said as a large group of mourners came into view. "Those are our mourners, alright. They must have thought I was coming here when I left the house."

Jesus rubbed his face. "It's alright," he said, stifling a groan. He took a shaky breath. "It will be alright. I just won't be able to stay long."

Mary creased her brow. "Why not?"

Jesus stepped forward into the crowd. They parted to make a path for him. It was not just mourners; most of Bethany had turned out for the funeral. It was likely the most elaborate funeral the little Jerusalem suburb had seen in a long time. The professional mourners were raising an unceasing wail of anguish. People were forced to speak louder to be heard over it, allowing Judas to overhear snippets of conversation that otherwise would have been whispered.

"Has he been crying?" one asked, noting Jesus's tear-streaked face.

"I didn't know he and Lazarus were so close!" another replied.

"Oh yes," a third answered. "Jesus rescued his sister. Lazarus adored the man."

"Rescued from what, I wonder?" the first mused.

"Lazarus wouldn't say."

"*That's* Jesus? The Nazarene?" the second asked. "The famous healer? Truly tragic that he didn't come sooner..."

Judas passed beyond the hushed conversation and overheard bits of others following similar lines. Jesus was still the center of every conversation. "Let me see him," Jesus said as Mary stopped at the large, circular stone covering the opening. "Roll back the stone."

Martha's eyes widened. "The funeral was *four days ago!* He..." She pursed her lips. "Have you smelled a body that's been dead for four days?"

"What did I tell you?" Jesus asked. "If you believed, you would see God's glory. Your brother believed. Boys..." He nodded to the stone, and Little

James was the first to throw his massive weight against it. The stone rocked slightly but fell back into place. Judas found a pole to use as leverage and jammed it under the stone as the two Jameses pushed against it. The Jonas brothers added their weight, and with Simon's help on the pole, the six of them managed to get it moving. The others stabilized it from the other side until it cleared the opening.

Judas was again surprised at the extent of his father's generosity. The space was large enough for a family. A small opening led into a grotto with shelves on both sides. A strong, earthy scent came from the dry interior, but Judas detected no scent of rot.

The mourners had fallen silent, staring in shock at the strange spectacle of the men forcing their way into a four-day-old grave. Jesus lifted his eyes and spoke in the sudden stillness. "Thank you, Father, for hearing me," he said loudly, before adding softly to himself, "I know You always hear me, but there are people listening. I wanted to be sure they knew..."

Judas suppressed a wondering smile. The Pharisees often prayed the same words over and over or spoke as if they were addressing some unknowable entity which they hadn't yet decided was entirely friendly. Jesus always spoke to God as a son to his father. He always showed respect, but his prayers held a certain relaxed camaraderie that was strikingly hard to ignore. Judas had often heard rabbis refer to God as their Father, or the Father of Israel, but Jesus actually *meant* it.

"Lazarus!" Jesus shouted, causing Judas to flinch as the silence shattered. Jesus took a deep breath. "Come out!" All eyes stared at the tomb. The cemetery was deathly quiet.

A scuffling sound came from the dark tomb, followed by a thud and a loud curse. "*Skata kai aposkata!* What the... *Ow!* Who tied me up?"

Jesus suppressed a smile as a collective gasp came from the crowd.

A figure emerged from the tomb, cocooned in tightly wrapped burial linens designed for covering, rather than movement. Lazarus was on the ground, worming his way toward the light, his hands pinned to his sides and his feet bound together by the white linen. "Jesus?" he asked, his voice muffled slightly by the wrappings encasing his entire body, head to toe.

Jesus's face broke into the widest smile Judas had ever seen put there. "It's me, Lazzy. Sit tight! Your sisters will have you out of those burial clothes in no time."

"*Burial* clothes?!" Lazarus exclaimed. "Why in Hade—Was I *dead?!*"

"They'll explain everything. I can't stay. Herod has spies here. Be safe," he said, glancing quickly at Mary and Martha, who were too busy extricating their brother from his wrappings to notice anything else. The crowd pressed in quickly, eager to see the man who had so recently been dead and who had crawled living from his tomb after four whole days.

Judas and the others followed Jesus as he slipped away. The crowd was too focused on Lazarus to notice their exit. Everyone expected the man who performed such an extraordinary miracle to stay and soak up the well-deserved praise of his accomplishment, not run away in secret. Almost everyone.

Judas was the first to recognize his father following them through the olive trees. He caught them quickly. "That was incredible!" Simon said breathlessly, catching Jesus by the arm. "And *dangerous*. But if we act quickly, we can gain momentum before the Sanhedrin has a chance to spin it their way. Dine with me, and I will explain the plan. *You* could be high priest come Passover."

Judas listened eagerly. He had worked for this moment—ached for it. Simon had decades of dirty secrets, and decades of practice in exploiting them, and he was officially offering his help. Jesus was reluctant to take his rightful place on the throne, and Judas had failed to convince him. If anyone was capable of convincing Jesus to mount a revolution, or maneuvering him into it, Simon was the man. Judas had learned from the best.

Jesus smiled politely. "I thank you, Simon, but I have other plans."

Simon blanched. "You're not staying with *them*, I hope?" he asked, nodding his head back in the direction of Lazarus's family. "You'll only put them in more danger. Lazarus will have a target on his back already, but my influence should protect them. You *need* my help. I can place you where you want to be with *minimal* bloodshed."

Jesus cocked an eyebrow. "I want to be in Ephraim tonight. How much bloodshed will that take?"

Simon smirked. "You know what I mean. Herod is watching you. The Sanhedrin would arrest you if they thought they could get away with it. They're already excommunicating anyone who openly calls you the Messiah. Many would kill you outright if they had opportunity. Right now, your actions are leading Israel directly toward an ugly civil war like the one between Solomon's sons. That war split Israel in two. Is that what you want? I can make this transition as smooth as possible. You can usher in a reign of peace without such destruction."

"Alright," Jesus said in commiseration. "I understand your wish to help, and I praise your zeal. I will return to Jerusalem for Passover. I will dine with you on the preceding Sabbath, if that is agreeable. You may invite whomever you believe to be the most beneficial to our cause, and we will then discuss what exactly it is that I want."

For research notes, see chapter 40 in the reference section.

XLI

As promised, Jesus arrived at Simon's house the Sabbath before Passover. Judas's father had everything prepared for the grand feast in the large main house opposite the single-room guesthouse where he had stayed as a leper. The first thing Judas noticed were the new servants. Simon was still a Pharisee, after all, and he had released his Greek servants to again hire Jewish ones now that fear of his leprosy did not drive them away. Simon hardly gave his guests a glance as they arrived. He was focused on ensuring his new servants did their jobs properly and bounced from place to place with the energy of a child.

"Come on in," Judas said, giving his father a cold glare. Judas understood his father's distraction, but it was rude to not acknowledge the arrival of a guest—especially this guest. "I'll show you around. Sorry about the lack of proper hospitality," he muttered. "I'm sure a servant will be along shortly with water for washing."

Jesus and the other disciples followed him to a long, low table, where about a dozen other Pharisees stood waiting for the eldest to be seated first as a token of honor. Most had selected honored places near the head of the table, and they all gave Jesus wary glances or nervous smiles as he entered. Jesus surveyed the table and noticed Lazarus standing by himself at the tail end of the long table in the place of least honor. Judas waited several tense minutes for the arrival of the promised servant. Technically, he was as much a guest here as anyone, but he knew where the basins were kept.

The tension rose as no servant appeared, and Judas was on the verge of retrieving the water himself when Jesus simply gave up and moved to the table, unwashed. This gained several dark looks from the persnickety Pharisees and only increased the tension in the room. This dinner was Jesus's last chance to make allies within the Sanhedrin and prevent Israel from a bloody civil war. If this dinner went poorly, Jesus's rise to power would be far harder and more violent.

Judas consoled himself with the pitiful fact that at least Jesus and his disciples were not the only unwashed people here. Several beggars lined the walls. It was common for beggars to appear at banquets, hoping for whatever scraps remained, even at the homes of Pharisees, who were eager to appear generous even if they feared contamination. The beggars were never allowed to sit at the table, but beggars cared little for such social distinction so long as their bellies were full.

Judas was surprised to recognize Mary among them. Simon had taken a significant risk by allowing a woman of her reputation to be here. There was too much riding on this dinner for any surprises, but so long as Mary remained quietly with the beggars and did not intrude, it was socially acceptable. Perhaps her presence would not cause any more trouble than Simon's failure to greet his guest had already caused.

Jesus selected a spot beside Lazarus on the far end, opposite the head. Judas recognized several minor members of the Sanhedrin, but none of any influence besides Nicodemus. He was the only *Haber* present, and it was unlikely that he would retain his place among the Brotherhood for long. The Pharisees' wary glances were no surprise; each man knew the risk. Caiaphas would consider any meeting with Jesus as treason. These men were willing to risk what little influence they had by lending Jesus their support on the chance of rising in rank under Jesus, should he become the new high priest.

They feared Caiaphas, but if Jesus could gain the support of even a small number of Sanhedrin members, there was hope.

"Hello, Lazzy," Jesus said, nudging Lazarus. "Sorry about missing your funeral. Does this party seem a little dead? If anyone can answer that, it ought to be you."

Lazarus burst into laughter. "If anyone can fix that, it ought to be you!" he said. "Don't apologize about missing the funeral; I slept through the whole thing. Ah, it is good to see you again, brother. Thank you. For everything. I'm sorry we never..."

"It was my pleasure," Jesus said, smiling. "Truly. Where is Martha?"

Lazarus smirked. "Martha is helping serve," he said, leaning closer. "Mary was not invited, but she found a way in nevertheless. Simon fears her... *reputation*... in Jerusalem might cause problems, but beggars are allowed, so I talked Simon into letting her stay. Simon is concerned that some might recognize her from that incident at the Temple. Thank you for that. You saved her life, you know? Mary, she... she bought you a gift. Spent a fortune on it, but she wanted to. I know you don't like expensive gifts, but please don't turn it down? It would break her heart. It's just... We're all so grateful. This whole family... We're a family because of you."

Jesus caught Lazarus in a warm hug. "You're *my* family, too, you know. I'm glad you're here. I told Simon he could invite whom he wished, but this..."

Lazarus chuckled. "I only got a spot at the table because I'm something of a celebrity, thanks to you—and you see where I stand. You wouldn't believe the questions I've been asked! Not that I've been able to answer a single one."

Jesus glanced around the large table. There were more Pharisees here than disciples. "Should be an interesting party."

"Interesting" was not the word. Simon still had not greeted his guest of honor. Either Simon's new servants were terribly untrained, or Simon was intentionally slighting Jesus. Pharisees were sticklers for custom and cleanliness. Every guest was to be formally greeted and offered water to wash their hands and feet. Often, hosts offered olive oil as a cleansing balm. Simon had surely noticed Jesus's arrival by now but had offered none of these amenities.

"Well," Jesus said, glancing around. "I'm sitting down." He took a seat, gaining several stern glares from the other guests, who remained standing, waiting politely for the eldest to sit first. Jesus was hardly the eldest.

"Master," Judas hissed. "I know you don't care about social politeness, but this dinner is *important!* We *cannot* afford to make a scene. *Please!*"

Jesus smiled, glancing up from his seated position. "If they were so concerned with propriety, you'd think someone would have offered me water—or at least a greeting," he said through the smile.

"Simon is very busy, and he's been out of society for a while," Judas said, coming to his father's defense. "He means no insult." Judas prayed that such was the case. If Simon had only invited Jesus here to make a fool of him, they were in deep trouble indeed.

"Good!" Jesus said, shifting to make himself more comfortable. "Then neither do I."

Simon finally entered, stopping conversation and motioning for the guests to be seated—after an inquisitive glance at Jesus, who was sitting already. Lamps were burning, and the meal was set, ready for the Sabbath sundown service. Simon formally dismissed the servants, their services finished for the week, and they joined the beggars in waiting for leftovers.

As he waited for the meal to start, Judas's attention was drawn to Mary, who shifted in frustration, watching Jesus with growing distress. Clearly, she had taken offense on Jesus's behalf. Judas stiffened. Her presence alone was enough to upset the shaky truce Simon had negotiated between Jesus and these Pharisees. Some of them knew her history, and Simon would need to address it if he hoped to keep his reputation. Judas saw her break away from the line of beggars and approach the table. He gave her a hard glare. *She should know better than to make a scene.* He shook his head firmly. She gave him a pitiful, pleading look and burst into tears, rushing forward in desperation before he could move to stop her.

She is determined to make a scene! Judas clenched his teeth as she struggled with the wax seal on a large, expensive bottle which she had drawn from her cloak. Fighting through her tears, she finally broke the wax and withdrew the cork. The unmistakable aroma of spikenard filled the room as she poured a little on Jesus's head, anointing him. Then, with a determined set to her face, she set about washing his feet with the rest of the bottle.

The Pharisees sat in horrified silence as Mary worked, until she froze, realizing she had no cloth to wipe away the excess oil. There was a collective gasp as she pulled off her head covering. It was taboo for a woman to even *touch* a man in public, but to show her hair was a strictly intimate gesture. A man could divorce his wife over such lewdness. Mary's long, beautiful hair fell over Jesus's feet as she stooped to wipe them off. Jesus could have sent her away—should have sent her away—but he let the shocking spectacle continue.

Finally, one Pharisee reached the end of his tolerance. "*This* is the teacher you wanted us to meet?" he asked in disbelief, breaking the loaded silence. "And he... allows *this?!*"

Simon cleared his throat nervously. "Well, I'm sure if he knew—knew the kind of woman... He would surely..." he stammered.

Surprisingly, Jesus came to his rescue. "Simon," he said, as the shockingly intimate scene finally ended. Mary, now red-faced, moved to rush from the room amid a fresh batch of tears. "I have a question for you," he finished, catching Mary's hand. "Stay, please," he told her.

"Oh?" Simon asked. "Go on. Teacher," he said, confirming that Jesus was, in fact, the teacher who he had called the other Pharisees to meet.

"Let's say you loaned a thousand *denarii* to someone, and ten *denarii* to another," Jesus said. "If you forgave both debts, which man do you think would be most grateful?"

"The one who owed the most, obviously," Simon said, shrugging.

"Right you are! Now, consider: When I arrived, you did not welcome me at the door. You did not offer me water for my feet, and yet you have clean water here. Mary had no water, but she washed my feet with her tears and welcomed me as she would only do with close family. You have been a Pharisee your entire life—even as a leper, you kept the Law as best you could—and you offered me this dinner out of curiosity. Your guests are under no obligation to me. They owe me nothing. But Mary..." He smiled. "Mary owes me her life and her family. Yes, she has lived a sinful life"—he turned to her—"but that debt is forgiven. Your sins are no more." He gave Mary an encouraging smile. "Thank you," he said, tears appearing in his eyes. "Thank you for this gift, and for believing in me." He let her go, turning back to the shocked faces around him.

The Pharisees broke into quiet murmurs over Jesus's comment. Forgiveness of sins came through the Temple service—not the word of any prophet. Judas had witnessed similar conversations before, and they never ended well. The dinner had started poorly and would only worsen without a rapid change of topic. He cleared his throat, desperate to lead the conversation into any other direction. "Master, that was a full pound of oil," he said, struggling to find some safer topic. He had often heard Jesus decry the wasteful spending of the Sadducees. It was one of the few topics on which Jesus and these Pharisees might agree. "That could sell for a full three hundred *denarii!* You could feed a family for a year on the profits! Would it not have been better to sell the bottle and give the money to help the poor?"

John gave him a cold glare. The others never liked it when Judas openly questioned Jesus. They found it threatening. Not that John should complain; earlier that week, he and James had gotten their *mother* to ask Jesus to make them his chief advisers. That hadn't sat well with any of the disciples. Judas returned the glare. He had as much right to question his master as any disciple. That was what a *real* adviser did.

"She gave me a wonderful gift, Judas," Jesus replied. "Don't tarnish this. Simon purchased expensive oils for Lazarus's funeral; don't blame Mary for doing the same. She's early is all. The poor will always be here, but I won't be. I'm glad she didn't wait."

"She could have waited until after supper, at least," one Pharisee growled. "We are called to a higher standard. We are the shepherds of Israel! People follow our example! By allowing these sinners to mingle with us, we condone their behavior!"

"And your solution is to avoid them, make them feel unwelcome, and even drive them away?" Jesus asked.

The Pharisee made a face of annoyance. "Their *sins* drive them away. Is it our fault that they have refused to follow the true path? No. We are ever ready to guide those willing to follow. Let Satan drive his swine where he will. We must care for *our* sheep."

"Have you ever been a shepherd, Matthan?" Jesus asked the Pharisee. "No, of course not," he said before Matthan could reply. "It's a thankless, unclean job, requiring work in all weather and on all days, including Sabbaths—and you are called to a higher standard," he added sarcastically. "Thaddeus kept sheep," he said, nodding at Thad. "What happens if a sheep loses her way and leaves the true path? Does the shepherd drive her off—keep her away to protect the rest of his flock?"

Thad chuckled dryly. "No."

"No! A good shepherd will leave the others, even if he has a flock of a hundred. He leaves the ninety-nine and searches for the lost sheep, listening for her cry. He does not abandon her to the wolves. He finds her and brings her back. And when he returns, the village celebrates—not because the sheep ran away, but because the shepherd succeeded in finding her! A lost sheep cannot find her way back. She waits and cries out for the shepherd. It is your job to listen for that cry. These lost ones will not come to us. We must go to them."

"As you did for me," Simon Zelotes said.

Jesus nodded proudly. "And you will find that there is more joy over the rescue of that lost one, than from the ninety-nine who need no rescue."

For research notes, see chapter 41 in the reference section.

XLII

"And the father says, 'You are always with me; all I have is yours! You are right to condemn your brother's sinful acts, but he has repented! My happiness will not be complete if you are not also happy. My son was dead, and is alive again! He was lost, and is found!'"

Jesus finished this latest story and leaned back. The dinner had gone well, considering the dreadful start, and the guests had stayed late into the night, listening to Jesus and speaking with him on many matters of history and the Law. Judas had managed to keep Jesus from saying anything too offensive, and the several minor members of the Sanhedrin which were present had shifted from purely skeptical to—if not receptive—at least some level of neutrality. It was far better than outright hostility. Jesus had spoken on his future kingdom but had deftly avoided any hint about specific plans.

"What did the elder son do?" Nicodemus asked, gaining nods of agreement from the others.

"That is the question, isn't it?" Jesus asked, rising to his feet. "Are we quick to condemn those who have led a sinful life, or do we rush out to bring them home? Do we celebrate with the Father at the lost one's return, or do we drive away our brothers and sisters? Right now, it is late, and I am rushing out so they can bring me to *their* home. Lazarus, are you ready?" he asked.

Lazarus yawned and stood. "It has been a long day," he admitted. "I'm dead on my feet." He grinned sheepishly.

Jesus chuckled. "Not anymore. Simon, thank you for the honor of being your guest. Judas, you will be staying here, yes?"

Judas nodded. "Yes, master. That is..." He glanced at his father.

"Of course Judas is staying! You think I would kick out my own son—after *that* story?" Simon asked, chuckling. "Are you sure you cannot stay, teacher? I have rooms. We have not even discussed..."

"Thank you, but no. I haven't had a moment with Lazarus's family since his funeral. I want to stay there," Jesus replied, turning for the door.

"Wait, wait, wait," Simon said quickly, catching his arm. "Do you plan to attend Passover in Jerusalem? If you step foot inside the city, you will be taken. Herod is hunting you. He will have eyes at every gate. I would *greatly* recommend you not attend."

Jesus cocked an eyebrow. "Attendance is required by Law. You, a Pharisee, would recommend I break the Law?"

Simon smirked. "There is a provision in the Law for those who are unclean or traveling. I could bring you to the Temple in secret next month on the provisional day, when Herod isn't expecting you. With any Herod, it is wise to exercise *extreme* caution."

"It's true," Matthan added. "Caiaphas fears your actions will bring down the wrath of Rome. The high priest has prophesied that your death is necessary to save Israel from annihilation. Both the Sanhedrin and Herod are terrified of Roman repercussions if you attempt a coup. Whether you succeed or not, Rome will see the uprising as Herod's failure to keep the peace. They're looking for an excuse to replace Antipas with a Roman governor, like they did to his brother. Herod the Great killed his own sons to preserve his place on the throne. Antipas will gladly kill you to do the same. They will do whatever it takes to stop you. Simon is right; you should leave while you can."

Jesus turned to Matthan. "I do not fear Herod. You tell that whimpering *shū'āl* that while he is busy playing king, I have demons to cast out and people to heal. If that coward wants me so badly, he can come and get me. I have work to do. Besides," Jesus said, grinning wickedly, "it wouldn't be right for a prophet to die outside Jerusalem—breaks tradition. The Sanhedrin would never allow it." He sighed. "Ah, Jerusalem... The Holy City: she kills her prophets and stones her messengers. Now *there* is a lamb that does not want to be rescued. Well, Matthan, perhaps your advice is right. Jerusalem will not see me until she is ready to welcome the One who comes in the name of the Lord."

Matthan nodded. "Jerusalem has a poor record for welcoming prophets. Go in peace, then," he said, and stepped through the door. Jesus followed him out, and Simon dismissed his other guests soon after. Jesus had given them much to think on, but precious few plans to set in motion.

"Well?" Judas asked as the last guest took his leave. Peter, James, and John were also staying with Lazarus. The others had taken Simon's hospitality and were staying in his small guest house, where he had stayed while suffering with leprosy. The house had been cleansed and aired since then and was safe for guests.

Judas and his father were the only ones left sitting at the long table under the flickering glow of a few lingering oil lamps. "What did you think?" Judas asked, idly spinning an empty bowl.

Simon creased his brow. "What can I think? The man speaks with authority. He grasps the nuances of the Law like no other. He is highly intelligent and can outmaneuver the cleverest lawyer. He raises the dead, controls the elements themselves, makes food appear from nowhere, can heal with a word, and even bestow his power on others. Clearly, he has the mind of a military commander and the power of God, but he has no ambition."

"And...?" Judas asked.

"What?" Simon said.

"He is the Messiah!" Judas exclaimed. "Surely, *you* can admit that! If you don't, your own skin will cry out against you! You're no longer a leper because of *him*. You sat at table tonight with a man who had been dead *four whole days!* Even Caiaphas admitted that he does great signs!"

"His miracles are undeniable, I admit," Simon replied. "There are too many to verify them all, but I have verified many—not to mention my own, of course. His credibility is incredible. And yet, if he *is* the Messiah, why is he so reluctant to take his rightful place on the throne? It is deeply concerning."

Judas shook his head. "I struggle with that myself. But Moses spent forty years in exile before he took his place, and David waited years for Saul to die. Perhaps Jesus is taking the same route. I just don't know if I can wait forty years... I don't know if Israel can wait."

"The comparison is striking," Simon mused. "I did some digging. Did you know Jesus was born in Bethlehem? His family escaped to Egypt just before Herod had all the male children killed. Moses also escaped a mass slaughter of infants by being raised as an Egyptian. If the rumors about Jesus's conception are true, then Jesus was adopted into the royal line of David, while Moses was adopted into the royal line of Egypt. Moses cured snakebites and provided manna in the wilderness. Jesus cures many diseases and provided bread in the wilderness. Moses parted the sea. Jesus calms it with a word and walks upon it. Moses saved our people from Pharaoh. The Messiah will save us from Rome... Has Jesus killed anyone—a Roman?"

"What?!" Judas cried. "No! I mean, not that I am aware... But I've only known him these three years. Still... I couldn't imagine him killing anyone. He hasn't a violent bone in his body. Why?"

"I have a contact in the *Sicarii*. They are terrorists, but they have experience in close-combat warfare. I had hoped to sway them in favor of Jesus, but they dismiss his pacifism as weakness. With their leader captured, we have a rare opportunity to put Jesus in that role, but he is too passive to inspire them. We need Bar-Abbas. If we could somehow get him out of prison, we would earn his respect. He would have the brains and guts to handle the messy parts, and Jesus—as the Messiah—would be our cry of victory. Jesus could remain stainless. He would never have to turn his mind to war. Bar-Abbas could fight the Romans while Jesus kept his hands clean as high priest. Unfortunately, Bar-Abbas is in the Praetorium. It's impregnable—Machaerus alone is worse. Without him, the *Sicarii* are useless. I was hoping to convince Jesus to break him out. I am certain he could, if he only set his mind upon it."

"Forget it," Judas said, scratching at a scuff on the table. "He wouldn't even save his own cousin from Herod. He's not breaking anyone out of prison—he doesn't even defend himself! He just leaves."

"He'll have to kill someone eventually."

"What do you mean?" Judas asked. "Moses never lifted weapons against the Egyptians."

"Moses was banished for killing an Egyptian. If Jesus is to follow the same path, there must be some inciting violence which will force him to flee Judea."

Judas scoffed. "The Sanhedrin will provide that. They've nearly stoned him twice! The Sanhedrin wants him dead!"

"But he escaped?" Simon asked quickly.

"Obviously," Judas said.

Simon leaned back on his couch. He nodded thoughtfully. "He always will."

Judas creased his brows. "What do you mean?"

Simon leaned forward again as he organized his thoughts. "Moses should have died in infancy—Jesus as well. Moses should have been killed for the murder of the Egyptian, but he was exiled instead. He should have been killed the first time he returned to Pharaoh's palace—or a dozen times after! Jesus should have been killed when he ran the money changers from the Temple—and a dozen times after! If Jesus is truly the Messiah, he *will* escape. Moses did not die because he was prophesied to save Israel. How much more is the Messiah prophesied to save Israel? If Jesus is the Messiah, God will not allow him to die before his work is done. And if he isn't..."

Judas paled. "What are you saying?" he asked slowly.

"Any chance of swaying the Sanhedrin to our side is long past," Simon said dismissively. "This dinner was Jesus's final chance to prove himself capable of defeating Rome. He had the opportunity to give the Pharisees a reason to support him, and he spent the entire time telling stories. The Sanhedrin *will* keep trying to kill him. They will keep setting traps. He may escape, but as their desperation grows, so does the danger. There have already been attempts on Lazarus's life. Do you think it will stop there? How many will have to die because Jesus refuses to act? Make no mistake, Caiaphas will not stop. They will keep coming, and the longer Jesus eludes them, the more people will die. Eventually, he will have to face them. We have an opportunity to make that happen on our own terms—before someone dies."

"So what? Lazarus already died! Death means nothing. We may die, but we shall live so long as *he* lives!" Judas protested.

"Death is not the only threat in their arsenal," Simon replied darkly. "Jesus should be on the throne. The longer that takes, the more suffering will ensue."

"Do you realize what you're asking?" Judas said frigidly. "You want me to... I can't even say it!"

"I understand your hesitation, but be reasonable, Judas," Simon said consolingly. "This is the best way. By turning Jesus over to the Sanhedrin, you are protecting his followers—his family! Jesus must face the Sanhedrin eventually. You know this! Why not now? Why not on our terms, before something happens which cannot be undone? There is no risk!"

"No risk?" Judas cried. "To whom? *You?!*"

Simon raised his hands in a calming gesture. "To anyone! You agree to turn Jesus over in exchange for the safety of his allies. This keeps everyone safe! Surely, you do not believe these men pose a threat to Jesus himself! The man commands demons—storms! He will be in complete control. If you are right, they will celebrate you as orchestrating Jesus's rise to power, and if you are wrong, they will celebrate you for exposing an impostor."

"Jesus is *NO* impostor! How could you, of all people, even *think* that?"

"I would never have brought him to my home if I thought that!" Simon snapped. "I took considerable risk in associating myself with Jesus. I am still respected among the Pharisees, you know. Jesus *is* the Messiah—which is the only reason I would ever suggest this plan! I know your loyalty to him, and I commend it! Trust me when I say the Messiah *cannot* be killed."

Judas relaxed slightly, though still wary. "Prove it."

"*You* will prove it," Simon said, "but David himself predicted it: 'My flesh will rest in hope, for You will not leave my soul in death, *nor will you allow your Holy One to see corruption.*' *That* is a Messianic prophecy. David is speaking of the corruption of death. The Messiah cannot be killed because God will not allow it. The prophecies say so! He has a destiny. *You can help him fulfill it.*"

Judas wiped his face, which had broken out in a cold sweat. "What if you're wrong?"

Simon placed his hand on top of Judas's clenched fist. "Son, I know we haven't always agreed. You chose your own path, and your mistakes brought you to him. He brought you to me. Jesus is the Messiah. I am reminded every time my fingers brush a flower, every time I feel a breeze against my cheek, every time I take a full breath. You see it in my face, and I see it in yours! There is no question, no room for doubt. He is the Holy One."

"Then you realize the weight of this burden you place upon me. There is too much at stake. He is the *Messiah.*"

Simon nodded. "He is. But your reluctance comes from doubt, not faith. You fear because you are afraid you are wrong. If you believed, you would act! God's deliverance is assured, but it is far greater when we act *with* Him! Israel could have inherited the Promised Land forty years before if they had acted in belief. Instead, they languished in the wilderness, and the promise was delayed. Jesus *will* ascend the throne of David. The only question is if this will happen before or after Israel plunges into a brutal civil war. You have the chance to place Jesus on the throne *before* the bloodshed! Force him to confront the Sanhedrin. He will be victorious! Remove the waiting and the risk and move forward. The other disciples are fearful. You must do what they cannot—do what Israel could not, so long ago. It is your duty to be a Joshua! Do not let Israel suffer another forty years of exile."

Judas took a shaky breath. "We shall see how Passover goes. I will consider. If I am given an opportunity..." He paused. "We shall see."

For research notes, see chapter 42 in the reference section.

Part 4

XLIII

Judas felt a sense of urgency when he awoke on the first day of the week. Jesus had spent the Sabbath with Lazarus and his family, and Judas had spent the day brooding over his father's advice the night before. A second fitful night had brought him no closer to a decision, and he awoke to find himself alone with only a message to meet the others in Bethphage. He was too late for breakfast and decided to forego it altogether rather than wait for a servant to prepare something. He needed to find Jesus. Perhaps seeing the Messiah would provide some relief from his impossible decision.

Bethphage was less than a mile from Bethany. Bethany was on the southeast side of the Mount of Olives while Bethphage was on the north, about a mile east of the Temple. Judas was one of the last to arrive and found a crowd gathered in the small Jerusalem suburb. His addled brain took a moment to recall the reason: This was the day the Passover Lamb was selected. The ceremonial procession from the special stables in Bethphage to the Temple always drew a crowd.

Of course, there were thousands of Passover lambs. Each family was required to provide or purchase a spotless lamb, but *the* Passover lamb represented the family of the high priest. Without it, the high priest would have no sacrifice, and Israel would have no mediator. All the other sacrifices would be worthless. Temple lambs were raised near Bethlehem, but the best were brought to Bethphage for selection. The marketplace in Jerusalem could not hold all the countless lambs required for Passover. Bethphage provided a place for the overflow. Of these many lambs, one was selected as the official Passover Lamb and brought to the Temple with much pomp and circumstance to be placed in a special pen designed to protect the lamb from any injury. They always selected the lamb a few days before Passover, so there would be time to replace it should any mark be found upon it. It was essential that this lamb be absolutely perfect.

Why Jesus was here, Judas had no idea. Jesus had never shown interest in the event before, but Jesus must have selected this meeting place for a reason. He had a reason for everything, it seemed. As Judas passed through the throng of people waiting for the high priest's appearance, he was surprised to recognize many of Jesus's disciples here. He found Chuza, Herod's steward, with his wife, Joanna; Reuben, whose eyes had been healed by the clay; Mary, one of Jesus's female disciples from Magdala; Nicodemus, the *Haber*; half a dozen Simons, several Judases; and many more—all disciples of Jesus. The seventy had returned, but there were others as well, many whom Jesus had healed. Judas caught a glimpse of Matthias and Justus leading a donkey through the crowd in what appeared to be a specific direction. They were both dedicated disciples and often joined the twelve when they could afford to take leave from their work. Judas followed them.

"Hey, sleepyhead!" Nathanael greeted him, spotting Judas approaching through the crowd to where Jesus and his inner circle waited. "You made it! You've got to get up earlier, City Boy! Thought you were going to miss it!"

Judas gave him a puzzled look. "Miss what?" he asked. "I've seen lambs before. There's a reason we never bothered to watch the procession. Besides, the high priest won't finish inspecting the lamb until afternoon. What's the rush?"

Philip nudged him with barely concealed excitement. "Look around."

Judas saw nothing out of the ordinary except for Jesus inspecting the donkey. "What's with the ass?" he asked, raising an eyebrow. "I've never seen Jesus ride anywhere."

"Exactly!" Philip said. "He's hijacking the ceremony—stealing Caiaphas's thunder, as he did to Annas at Tabernacles."

"Hijacking the..." Judas paled. His heart fluttered, and relief flowed in. His father's plan would never need to see the light of day! The implication was unmistakable; Jesus was going to ascend the throne. "It's the ass! It's happening. Finally, it's happening! The king is coming."

Philip gave him a puzzled look.

"It's from Zechariah: 'Shout, oh daughter of Jerusalem,'" Judas whispered in awe. "'Look, your king is coming; He is just and brings salvation, lowly and *riding an ass*.'"

"'His dominion shall be from sea to sea,'" Philip finished, recognizing the quote. "I thought that was metaphorical. Do you think...?"

The crowd stilled as Jesus settled himself on the donkey. All eyes turned to him. He scanned the eager faces with pride. Matthias and Justus had turned the management of the donkey over to Lazarus and had taken their place behind Jesus with the other disciples. Mary and Martha stood nearby, their eyes gleaming as they gazed at their king. Jesus found Judas in the crowd as his eyes looked over his followers. "Judas," he said, catching sight of his belated disciple. "Right on time. Do you remember my banquet? You tried to inspire something then. I stopped you."

"Of course," Judas said breathlessly. Jesus should have been made king after the miracle of the loaves and fish, but he had sent everyone away, escaping his destiny. He had walked on the sea only hours later. He seemed to split his time equally between proving himself the Messiah and avoiding all responsibility that came with it. The man was a maddening dilemma. "How could I forget?"

Jesus's eyes sparkled. "I won't stop you now."

Judas needed no further urging. He turned to Mary with a wide grin and gripped her by the shoulders, caught up in the energy of the waiting crowd. "'Shout! Oh daughter of Jerusalem!'" he said, eyes sparkling. The time was now. "*Your king is coming.*"

Mary shouted. "'Salvation!'" she cried, quoting the psalm from the Great Hosanna. "'Salvation and victory!'"

The psalm was familiar to all. They sang it every year at Tabernacles. The nearest disciples quickly picked up the next line: "'Blessed is He who comes in the name of the Lord!'"

The crowd exploded in cheers. Coincidentally, it was the same cry which announced the arrival of the high priest and the Passover Lamb. The crowd was too big for any but the nearest to see, and most of the outliers likely assumed the shout signaled Caiaphas's appearance.

The procession ground into motion with a thunderous cheer. Palm branches rose in celebration. Coats and blankets quickly covered the street, so the lamb would not bruise his feet against a sharp rock and become blemished. Jesus's donkey took no notice of this precaution and moved forward placidly. When clothing became scarce, the crowd began stripping nearby palm trees, throwing the wide leaves in the street for the same purpose or raising them in the air as the cheering continued.

The road from Bethphage led straight to the Temple through the Shushan gate. The crowd surged ahead, continuing the cry, though now the cry had shifted to "Blessed is *the king* who comes in the name of the Lord." It was a subtle yet striking change. Several Pharisees waited outside the Shushan gate to escort the high priest and the lamb into the Temple. They smiled in pride at the swelling numbers of the crowd, which was far larger than ordinary.

Yet something about the crowd and the energy of the people put them on guard. They saw the man perched on a donkey where the high priest should be and pushed forward, demanding answers. Judas didn't recognize them, but then, he couldn't keep track of every Pharisee in Judea. "What is the meaning of this uproar?" one demanded, catching hold of Philip. The crowd ignored them, flowing around the Pharisees and through the Temple gate.

"The king is coming!" Philip replied, snatching the Pharisee excitedly by his shoulders and shaking him. "Salvation through the Son of David!"

The Pharisee turned pale. "Who would dare...? Who is this?" he demanded, pointing angrily at the figure seated on the donkey.

"It's Jesus, the prophet from Galilee!" someone called, having heard the question.

Philip nodded proudly.

The Pharisee pushed Philip away with a glower and fought the flow of the crowd until he reached Jesus, who sat calmly astride his mount, watching the Pharisee's furious approach with a demure smile.

"You must stop this!" the Pharisee snapped, snatching the donkey's bridle from Lazarus's fingers and bringing Jesus to a halt. "For a teacher to allow his followers to engage in such mayhem, distracting from the arrival of the high priest! Stop them, or someone else will!"

Jesus chuckled to himself. "If I stop them, these stones would take up the cry."

The Pharisee stiffened. "This is the *Temple!*" he hissed angrily. "It is a place of peace! It is to be entered with reverence—not revelry! Do you not understand what *day this is?* It is the day for the coming of the Passover Lamb! You have disrupted the peace!"

Jesus returned the man's hard stare. "You don't know the meaning of peace. The day is coming when this temple will be entered by soldiers who will cut down you and your children and not leave a single stone standing. Then no one will be here to take up the cry, because *you* didn't understand what day it was."

This troubling pronouncement caught the Pharisee off guard, and his grip loosened. Lazarus pulled the donkey's bridle out of the man's grasp and led Jesus forward into the Temple amid a new eruption of cheering from inside the walls. Judas passed through the gate a moment later, shaking his head sadly at the Pharisee. Their reign was over. They had no idea what today was.

Coronation Day.

He pulled to a sudden stop as he entered the Temple. The crowd continued on, pushing a path to Herod's palace, most likely. Jesus had pulled up short and let those who followed him continue to flow forward through the Temple and into Jerusalem. He was staring at something, and the dark scowl on his face made a shiver crawl up Judas's spine. Judas followed his master's gaze and saw the trouble immediately.

The market was back: the money changers, the sheep, the noise. Caiaphas had returned everything to the Temple. He knew the reason behind the move which Annas had quietly enacted after Jesus first cleared the Temple three years ago, and his first act as high priest was to bring it back. The man had a personal vendetta against Jesus, and this new affront was no surprise.

"'Place of peace' my foal of an ass," Judas muttered, listening to the noise flooding the crowded plateau.

The proud shouts of Jesus's entourage mingled with the haggling and bartering of the buyers and sellers. This would be a show, indeed. Judas recalled the last incident, and he knew this time would be far worse. Jesus had allowed the crowd to announce him as king. His coronation could not be far off. It was finally time for the scribes and Pharisees to realize who they had pitted themselves against. No longer was Jesus an unknown yokel from Nazareth. His name was in every conversation. The Sanhedrin had officially denounced him, yet the people still rallied behind him.

Judas turned, expecting the same raging fire as the first time, but Jesus's glower had turned to sadness as he surveyed the scene. Judas had to look closer, but yes, the man's eyes were filled with tears. Jesus watched the crowd continue to flow through the Shushan gate until they began to dwindle as the procession continued on through the Temple courtyard and out the other side. Only a few of Jesus's followers hesitated, waiting for him to continue.

Judas waited eagerly, ready to see the fury which had filled Jesus three years ago, as zeal for his Father's house had consumed him. It did not come. Jesus sent Matthias to return the donkey and spent what little remained of the afternoon walking about the Temple, waiting for Caiaphas.

The high priest entered with no fanfare, and he took the Passover Lamb to its pen without ceremony. He returned minutes later, flanked by several ranking Pharisees, who gestured to Jesus as the reason for the poor turnout. The high priest's face was an ocean of fury. Jesus had stolen his grand entrance. The world no longer followed him.

This was what Jesus must have been waiting for: a confrontation. Finally, Jesus was ready to face his enemies. After orchestrating such an entrance, Jesus could not simply leave—not after being hailed as king. Caiaphas marched toward him, flanked by pious Pharisees and armed Levites carrying bludgeons. Comparing Caiaphas's look of discomfiture to Jesus's bold gaze left no question as to which of the men was the rightful leader of Israel. Jesus waited, watching the high priest with a calculating gaze until he had crossed most of the distance. Then Jesus turned, passed under the Shushan gate, and left the Temple without a word.

For research notes, see chapter 43 in the reference section.

XLIV

J udas chased after the retreating king of Israel in total consternation. Half of him was relieved that Jesus was escaping Caiaphas's wrath yet again, but the other half was nearly mad with exasperation over the explosion of excited expectation followed by yet another quiet disappearance. Jesus seemed to take cruel joy in bringing his followers' hope to the edge of completion and then quitting at the very cusp of victory. It was maddening.

"Where are you going?" Judas demanded through his teeth, pushing his way past the other disciples to find some answers. "You did all that to just... just *walk away?!* You told me you would not stop me! Yet here you are, disappearing again! Running from your destiny!"

"Did I stop you?" Jesus asked calmly without breaking stride.

Judas coughed. "Well, no... But... We expected..."

"You won't always get what you expect, Judas."

"I expect to know what it is you think you're doing!" Judas said angrily. The shattered expectations, coupled with his sleepless nights, were starting to wear on his patience. "I'm sorry," he said, stifling his frustration. "I just wish you would explain your current plan."

Jesus took the outburst in stride. "Alright," he said. "My current plan is to return to Bethany, eat a light supper, and turn in early."

Judas bit back a sharp reply and part of his lip. "I mean, when will you take your rightful place on the throne of David?"

"Yes," John said, dipping into the conversation. It was likely that all the disciples were feeling Judas's frustrations. "You said the Temple would be destroyed! When will this happen? When will this age end and your reign begin?"

Jesus paused. "The Sanctuary must first be cleansed," he said by way of answer.

"You've already cleansed the Temple!" Judas replied hotly. "You could have cleansed it again if you hadn't walked away."

"You study the Law, Judas," Jesus replied. "Do you know the law regarding a plagued house?"

"Yes..." Judas said hesitantly. These questions always threw him off track. Jesus enjoyed deflecting from the topic, only to attack it from another angle. It was a particularly devious and useful talent.

Jesus gave him an expectant look.

Judas sighed. "If the owner finds a plague in his house, he calls the priest to inspect it. If the priest confirms it, the house is shut up for seven days. If the plague persists after seven days, the house is condemned. Of course, the rules go on and on, but those are the basics."

"The basics are sufficient," Jesus said. "There has been a plague in my Father's house. I discovered it three and a half years ago. I removed it, but now it has returned."

"What are you going to do?" Peter asked, trying to squeeze in between Jesus and Judas.

"What is the protocol?" Jesus asked.

"To first cleanse the house, and if the plague persists after a week, to officially condemn it. Those living in it must leave," Judas repeated, working to not be physically pushed out of the conversation by the bigger fisherman.

Jesus nodded, ignoring their squabble. Ever since the Zebedee brothers had talked their mother into asking Jesus to give them leading positions, there had been tension in the group. Judas tried to stay out of these squabbles, but if pushed, he would hold his ground.

"Today, I inspected the house," Jesus answered. "Tomorrow, we cleanse it. In a week, the house will either be clean or condemned and left desolate. All who enter will be made unclean, and He who lives there will be forced to leave."

He who lives there will be forced to leave.

The implication was horrible. The Temple was the house of God! Every Jew knew this. After fifteen hundred years, Jesus was giving Israel one week to purify their worship, or the Divine presence of God would leave His House. One week. Israel had one week to accept the Messiah, or God would be driven out of His own house by their plague.

The other disciples did not seem to grasp the significance of this casual reply, but Judas felt it straight through his heart. He had been angry with Jesus's hesitation—angry that Jesus waited to take his place on the throne—and now, the time seemed so short. Suddenly, he realized the dreadful possibility that Jesus might not ascend the throne at all. It was up to them. He had given Israel one week to determine if they wanted him or not. Judas trembled at the thought. Sons represented their fathers. To reject the son was to reject the father. Everyone knew this.

If Israel did not accept Jesus as the Messiah, they would drive off God Himself.

Judas had one week to convince Israel to accept their Savior, or all would be lost. Judas knew the Sanhedrin would never accept Jesus the Nazarene. The little pressure he had known after speaking with his father now grievously increased. The others had no idea. They were still focused on who would be the greatest in the coming kingdom. They did not catch the dreadful significance in the pronouncement. Judas no longer cared who would be the greatest in the kingdom. His sole focus must be on ensuring there was a kingdom at all. And he had only seven days.

"So," Jesus said lightly, as if he had not just mentioned the possibility of God's banishment and Israel's impending doom. "You were asking about signs for the end of the age? Make sure no one deceives you, for many will come with promises of peace and safety and will deceive many..."

For research notes, see chapter 44 in the reference section.

XLV

"**N**othing? Not a single fig? Why, you liar! No one will find figs on you again! Ever!" Jesus told the tree in no uncertain terms. It was hardly dawn. Jesus had awakened his disciples before the sun and marched them to the Temple without time to prepare a meal. They waited by the path in puzzlement at this dark pronouncement. Jesus was hardly one to hold a grudge—especially against a tree.

He dusted his hands and resumed his trek toward Shushan. "First he talks to storms, now trees," Little James mused.

Judas chuckled. "So long as the tree doesn't reply," he said, slapping the big man on the arm.

"You recall what I said yesterday about the fig tree?" Jesus asked, taking his place again at their head. "When the leaves spread, you know summer is near."

The disciples nodded.

"That fig tree is full of leaves, but not a single fig. It's lying about what it has to offer."

"Master, there are other trees..." Nathanael said with a dry chuckle.

Jesus nodded thoughtfully. "Yes," he agreed, mostly to himself. "There are. They can be grafted in. Alright," he continued, clapping his hands and turning to his army of disciples. It was not just the twelve; the seventy were here also. Jerusalem was filled to bursting for the upcoming feast, and Jesus had many supporters among the crowds. Yesterday, Andrew and Philip had even met some Greeks who had heard of Jesus. His fame was spreading to the entire world. "Does everyone know their roles?" Jesus asked.

The disciples nodded again.

"Let's go."

They marched themselves to the Temple gate. The Levites took a long look at the eighty-three men—some of them armed—and silently stepped aside. They knew why Jesus was here. The disciples filed through the gate in pairs and formed a semicircle around Jesus.

"Remember, we work *with* the Levites," Jesus said. "Not against them. We are here to preserve the Law, not break it. There will be absolutely no bloodshed. Any questions?"

"What about the elders and scribes?" Justus asked. "They've banned some of us from the Temple for believing in you. We should return the favor."

"Let's not follow their example. All worshipers are welcome," Jesus replied. "Temple offerings are to proceed as usual. But no buying or selling. Anyone carrying wares is to be stopped at the gates. Anything else?"

"Are you sure about letting Pharisees in? They will be sure to cause trouble," Peter said, stating the obvious.

Jesus smirked. "Let them come." He waited for other questions, but hearing none, he turned. It was early, but the money changers and sheep vendors were already here. The Temple was busy with commerce. With so many Jews here for Passover, many rose early to beat the lines. Jesus scanned the booths and shook his head grimly, then took a deep breath.

"*GET. THEM. OUT!*" he roared. He needed no whip this time. The memory was seared into everyone's minds. Jesus moved forward, flanked by eighty-two men. Some disciples split away to position themselves at the gates as they passed, while the rest moved forward like a wave, pushing everyone out. It was over in minutes. None resisted. As before, the money changers fled, knowing the result of hesitation. Judas was glad to not be among them. He moved forward proudly, happy to again see Jesus acting like the commander he was. He would take his place on the throne. He must.

Six days. Jesus's ultimatum placed the deadline directly at the end of Passover. The first Passover, some fifteen hundred years before, had seen death like no other night, and the lamb's blood was the only protection. Judas feared this Passover might see Israel receive a similar fate. The thought was dreadful, filling him with fear and anger. The idea that Israel's shepherds would reject their own Messiah through selfish pride was unthinkable. He found a release for his emotions in a money changer's table which he kicked. The table legs buckled, and shekels flew.

The Temple court fell silent as the last of the frightened vendors evacuated. "Alright, good work," Jesus said, not wasting time. "Now, let's get these tables moved out. Gather up the money and return it to the treasury. Place the tables in the storehouses and throw out the pens. There will be brooms in one of these outbuildings. I want the entire courtyard swept."

"What about the Temple Guard?" Judas asked, casting a wary glance at the Antonia Fortress towering over the northwest corner.

"The chief Levite is sympathetic to our cause," Jesus explained. "They will not summon the Romans unless we break Temple law. This time, they know me and trust my intentions."

"No sneaking away, then?" Judas asked. "No need to escape the Temple Guard? No more running?"

Jesus nodded grimly. "No more running. I'll be teaching here for the rest of the week."

Judas grinned, not quite believing the words. "No running..." He shook his head. "I guess I better get busy."

"Tally up all the money from the tables," Jesus suggested. "I want to be sure the count is accurate before we return it to the Treasury. We can't have anyone accusing us of stealing Temple money. Leave the heavy lifting to the country boys."

Judas laughed. "Sounds good to me." He set about gathering up the money from the changing tables and the ground, where much of it had been scattered, and adding it up on one of the abandoned ledgers. It felt good to work with figures again. There was rarely enough in the disciples' pot to bother with counting and never enough to need quill and paper to tally the sums.

He disappeared into his work amid the new hustle and bustle of movement, listening to the other disciples at their own work. It wasn't long before people again started to drift into the Temple—with quiet reverence at first and then with more confidence as Jesus welcomed them. He had a crowd around him in a matter of minutes, listening to his teaching. Many came for healing, and the quiet reverence broke with occasional shouts of joy.

All this noise was typical and did not break Judas's attention from his task. It was shouting of a different kind that finally broke his focus. He turned at the surprising noise: happy shouts in high, giggling voices. He chuckled to himself in surprise. There were children here. That was new. The Temple—besides being a den of thieves and cheating money changers—was considered a place of solemnity. Children were not allowed in the Temple until they were of age. Yet, children were here playing. They danced around Jesus, holding some leftover palm branches and repeating snippets of the Hosanna psalm. The giggling of children was something Herod's Temple had likely never before witnessed. The Pharisees would surely find something unsavory to say about it.

Another group caught Judas's attention. This group, less pleasant than the children, consisted of Sadducees who had been allowed entrance by the disciples guarding the gates. There was nothing surprising about angry Sadducees, but one in particular seized Judas's attention: Joseph of Arimathaea. Judas dropped his coins on one of the remaining tables. "Leave that one," he told Little James distractedly, without taking his eyes from Joseph. "I'll be back."

The group of Sadducees pushed their way through the crowd. The eldest eyed Jesus up and down with disdain. "Your disciples claim to work under your orders," he said, mostly through his nose. "You are no priest or Levite to decide what can or cannot enter the Temple. Who authorized this?" he demanded.

Judas moved up beside his old master. Joseph was a Sadducee, it was true, but he cared little for the minutia of the Law. Joseph left that to the religious experts. Why he was here with this group of hostile Sadducees, Judas had no idea.

"Joseph?" he asked. "What brings you here?" Surely, Joseph would not pit himself against the son of an old friend, but his presence was alarming.

Joseph shushed him with a hiss. "I want to hear his answer."

In typical fashion, Jesus did not answer. "I also have a question for you," he said. "John's baptisms: were they from God, or just a passing trend?"

Judas suppressed a snicker. This crowd was filled with many of John's former disciples. They, as well as many others, considered him to be a prophet of God, and his unjust murder had only solidified his status. If the Sadducees denied his baptism, they would lose all credibility. If they agreed with it, they would condemn themselves for rejecting John's teachings. The leader cleared his throat nervously as he recognized the dilemma. "We... we cannot say... for sure," he stammered.

Jesus grunted in mock surprise. "If you can't even tell me if a man's teaching is or is not godly," he said politely, "then clearly you are unqualified to determine what should or should not happen in God's Temple, and you have no right to question my authority. Therefore, I have no obligation to inform you. But," he added, looking directly at Joseph, "you are welcome to stay and learn for yourself."

Joseph ignored the offer. The group of Sadducees left to join their old rivals, the Pharisees, under the shadows of Solomon's Porch, where they could glower at Jesus from a distance and plot his demise. None dared do more. Jesus had too many supporters. Since the start of his ministry, he had healed countless people. That kind of thing was not easily forgotten, and family lines were long. The throne of David was his for the taking—if he wanted it.

Six days until the night of Passover. Six days for the religious leader to either accept or reject their savior. Judas knew already what the answer would be, and it cast a dark shadow of dread over the otherwise happy day. Jesus *must* take his place on Israel's throne by the final day, or God would desert His people, leaving only death in His wake. The celebration of Passover was a celebration of God's mercy, but that mercy would not last forever. Could the end truly be only days away? Judas shook away the dark thoughts. Jesus would take the throne. He must. He was the Messiah. It was his destiny. The alternative was too horrific to imagine.

Belief comes first; the miracle comes after. He had to believe.

Judas returned to his task of counting the spilled coins from the changing booths, but a hand on his shoulder stopped him. He flinched and turned to find Joseph behind him, eyeing him critically. "What are you doing?" Joseph demanded.

"Tallying the money to get an accurate count before we return it to the Treasury," Judas replied. He pushed back the feeling of guilt he always felt when thinking of Joseph. Judas was not that man anymore, but the guilt returned under Joseph's suspicious gaze. He had a right to be suspicious.

Joseph cocked an eyebrow. "Are you sure *you* are the best person for this job?"

Judas laughed nervously. "I am quite sure I am *not* the best person for this job. Jesus knows my history as well as you, Joseph."

Joseph hummed to himself. "Then he is a fool to trust you."

Judas shrugged. "I would have said the same three years ago," he admitted. "Jesus is no fool. It is not stupidity, but grace, which drives him. I know you've heard much evil about him from your fellow Sadducees. You should hear what he has to say and make your own decision. Offer him the same grace you offered me once. He will not abuse it as I did."

Joseph took a long and thoughtful look at his former steward. "You are not the man I fired three years ago," he said thoughtfully.

"You and he are not so different, Joseph," Judas replied. "I know how much money you've loaned out over the years to those with none, and I also know how little of it you get back. You give freely because you have abundance. Jesus has no money to give, but he gives his reputation. His reputation would be spotless if he kept better company. He gives his own good reputation to those who have none and receives slander and accusation in return, while we get a chance to become someone new. He takes risks on thieves like me, *publicanii* like Matthew, demoniacs like Simon, and yes, even whores. He dines with drunkards and gluttons. It's no surprise that you do not recognize me," Judas said, "because Jesus has replaced the man I was with himself, bit by bit. It's something you will never understand until you know him."

Joseph mulled over this information. "His family does not follow him."

"Not yet," Judas admitted. "But they are in Jerusalem for the feast. When he takes his place on the throne of David, they will kneel. It will happen soon. He's done running. You see how he teaches here and the Sanhedrin does nothing? Jesus fears nothing. Demons fear him. Storms obey his voice! *He is the Messiah.*"

Joseph grunted skeptically. "I appreciate your sincerity, Judas, but excuse me if I cannot take the word of a man who lied to me for three years. Joseph was a good man, and he raised fine sons, but the Christ?" He cocked his head questioningly.

"See for yourself!" Judas said quickly. "You have no reason to trust me—I know! Jesus will be teaching in the Temple all week. Stay! You will see which rumors are true and which are not."

Joseph ruminated on the question with a perturbed scowl. "I will stay long enough to ensure that you return *all* this gold to the Treasury," he said finally. "After that, we will see."

For research notes, see chapter 45 in the reference section.

XLVI

Joseph did stay until Judas finished his count. In fact, he stayed all that day. And the next. And the next. Jesus taught in the Temple up through the fifth day, and each day, Joseph returned to hear more. Judas knew Joseph cared little for the message of vengeance and retribution most Messianic teachers spewed. Jesus was the exact type of Messiah Joseph hoped for—once he got over the false accusations and rumors of his fellow Sadducees.

Unfortunately, Joseph's belief came too late to do much good. The days passed rapidly, and Judas found the deadline staring him in the face without any hint of remedy. Jesus had continued teaching in the Temple throughout the week without any apparent concern for the deadline. He had made no move to either persuade the Sanhedrin or overthrow them. Neither had they made any move to attack Jesus. Both parties seemed reluctant to make the first move, while the end of God's covenant with Israel loomed ever closer.

"This is nice," John said, nodding to himself as he glanced around the room. "Small, but nice."

"Why do you act surprised?" Thad asked dubiously. "You and Peter picked this place out."

"Well, yeah," John admitted, "but it was a storage room. Needed some cleaning up. The master of the house provided everything." He glanced in appreciation at the table, spread with food for the Passover.

They were eating Passover a day early, but since Passover technically started at sundown on the preceding day, it still qualified. Jesus had insisted on eating it with them tonight, rather than tomorrow. Judas wondered if this change of schedule had anything to do with the impending deadline. It weighed upon him like a millstone. Israel was staring its own doom in the face, and the other disciples joked and prodded each other in oblivious ignorance, vying for their master's attention.

Judas had no such luxury. He had a plan—the same desperate, dreadful plan his father had proposed nearly a week ago. The only way to avert the deadly crisis and save Israel was to overthrow the Sanhedrin before the awful deadline. The religious leaders were too scared of a revolt to make a move against Jesus, and Jesus was too kind and gentle to make a move against them. He seemed content to let Israel doom herself, rather than lift a hand in vengeance against her false shepherds. Jesus was too pure to do what needed done. Someone had to make the first move.

Sometimes, villains were necessary to do what good men could not.

Is that what you want to be, Judas? A villain? Jesus's voice asked from the halls of his memory.

I'll make that sacrifice if I have to.

He stood by his words. Jesus had recently told a parable about a master of a vineyard whose servants had mistreated his messengers. In desperation, the master had sent his own son, thinking that surely his son could make the wicked servants see reason, but the servants had killed the son. Jesus had asked the Pharisees what the result of this would be, and they had replied truly that the master would miserably destroy the wicked men. They had prophesied their own doom. Of course, the Messiah could not be killed. If anything, this week had proven it. The Sanhedrin was terrified of Jesus. Twice they had tried to stone him, and twice he had escaped. They failed utterly in outwitting him, so now they simply avoided him. Jesus had taught in the Temple unhindered all week. Still, if Judas was wrong, he would doom Israel to utter destruction—but they were heading there already. Someone had to stop them, even if it meant doing the unthinkable.

His mind was a whirl of fevered thought through the dinner. He hardly ate. He remembered none of the conversation and only snapped out of his turmoil when he saw Peter bolt from the table in alarm. "What are you doing?!" Peter cried, shying away from Jesus, who knelt beside a washbasin.

Judas slowly returned to himself and recalled that there had been no servants present to wash their feet, as was traditional. He hadn't thought anything of it. Jesus was hardly a traditionalist. Strangely, Jesus had taken the duty upon himself.

"You will *not* wash my feet!" Peter continued. "That's a servant's job! If anything, it should be John, who is the youngest, or Matthew, who is the newest. Certainly not you!"

Jesus pressed his lips into a firm line. "If you do not let me do this, then you have no business being here," he said coldly.

This shocking pronouncement was enough to shake Judas out of his fevered state. Jesus had never before threatened any of them with dismissal. He could have easily kicked them out of his group for a multitude of reasons, but he had never even hinted at the idea. Finally, he found an offense great enough to threaten banishment, and it was over *this?*

Peter was equally shocked. He stared at Jesus in disbelief for a tense moment. "Well—well, not just my feet!" he exclaimed. "If that's how it is, wash everything! My hands—my head!"

Jesus suppressed a chuckle. "Just the feet are sufficient, Peter," he said, hiding a smile. "They get dusty from the streets. You've already washed once today, so we'll get your feet, and you'll be clean—just not all of you."

The disciples shared a strange look. They had all bathed today. Little James lifted a thick arm and sniffed at his armpit. "Smells okay," he said with a shrug, glancing at Thad for confirmation. Thad made a face at his large younger brother.

Jesus set about the humiliating task which should have fallen to another. Judas endured it numbly. The humiliation seemed lost on Jesus, and because of this, it fell tenfold to the rest, who knew they should have offered to perform the task before supper. Each had waited for another to do it until dinner arrived with no washing. They were still too absorbed in the quiet battle for supremacy in Jesus's ranks and considered the servile task beneath them.

Jesus finished and returned to the table. He told them that there was nothing humiliating about serving others, and that servants were not inferior to their masters. Jesus was setting an example for them all to follow. Judas struggled to listen, but the exact words were lost in the tempest which tore at his mind. *Belief comes first.* Jesus must ascend the throne before the end of Passover, or Israel was lost. What fate was left for a people who had driven away their own God? The Pharisees had already given Judas the answer: destruction. He could not let that happen. As his father had said, if Jesus was the Messiah, there was nothing to fear. He would survive. He would ascend the throne. Judas believed it. He must act. The others did not understand. Even Simon Zelotes, who Judas had hoped to transform into an ally, would not understand. Simon had become more of a pacifist than Jesus. He feared what would happen if he took up the sword again. None saw the impending doom hanging over them. Judas alone bore this desperate weight. The fate of Israel rested solely on his shoulders.

"Judas."

He flinched upon hearing his name. His plan was surely written on his face, but how could he hide it? He wiped the cold sweat from his brow and glanced around.

"Judas," Jesus repeated, holding out a disc of unleavened bread dipped in broth. "You've hardly eaten tonight. Take this."

Judas took the sop numbly, but he had no taste for food. It turned to ash in his mouth.

"Something dreadful is on your mind, my friend," Jesus continued, his brow knit with concern. "We can't have you like this. We'll be alright without you for a little while. Whatever you need to do, go and do it." Jesus gave him a kind smile, which plunged into Judas's heart and twisted. "Just be quick."

Judas nodded, his head in a daze. He stumbled unfeelingly from the room. He nearly tripped in the darkness on his way down the stairs. It was only a short walk from the upper room to his destination. Both were in the Essene quarter in the southwest corner of Jerusalem. The short walk took an eternity. Doubts assailed his frazzled brain, but he fought them off, forcing each foot another step forward. Jesus would ascend the throne. God's prophecies could not be thwarted. Jesus was no man to be killed by the plots of his enemies: He was God's anointed. God would not let his Holy One see corruption. The prophecies said so. The prophecies were less certain about Israel's future. Israel's future depended upon God's mercy, and Jesus had given that mercy a firm deadline. Tonight was the last chance to save Israel from herself, and Jesus was too busy washing feet. Jesus would not go to the Sanhedrin; Judas must bring the Sanhedrin to him, force them into a confrontation that only one would survive. It was the only way.

Judas paused in the darkness outside Annas's mansion. By Jewish Law, the high priest was elected for life. Annas was still technically high priest, but the Romans had replaced him with Caiaphas. The Sadducees recognized Caiaphas, but the Pharisees still recognized Annas as the true high priest. Caiaphas hated Jesus and his followers to the core, but Annas was more subtle. He could see reason. Judas stood in the shadows for a long time. It was not too late to abandon his quest. He could return to the disciples and watch placidly as Israel faced her doom.

No, he could not. He must try. He must push forward in the face of madness and let belief create a way. Jesus must overthrow the religious authorities before the end of Passover or God's wrath would be unleashed, and this time, Israel would not be spared. Judas shuddered. He had to believe. He had to believe his plan would work. *Belief comes first.* He knocked on the heavy door leading into Annas's courtyard.

The door cracked, and a wary eye peeped out. "Judas?" the watchman asked. Or rather, watch*woman*. It was a maiden who kept the door at Annas's house. "What are you doing here? I have nothing new for you. Go away before you are seen," she said urgently. She was young and had always been kind to Judas. He thought perhaps she might even like him, after a fashion. Not that they had spoken more than a few words to each other.

Judas almost took her advice. "I need to see him, Debra. It's urgent."

"Malchus?" she asked. Malchus was one of Judas's spies. They had a tenuous friendship based heavily in the silver Judas paid him.

Judas shook his head. "The high priest."

She blanched. "You're serious? The high priest? Dressed like that?"

Judas had not thought to wear his Pharisee disguise. He always wore it when making contact with or near Pharisees. The high priest would recognize his face, but likely would not know him to be one of Jesus's disciples. He would know soon enough.

"It's a matter of life and death," he said in all honesty.

Debra gave him a look of concern, but opened the heavy door to let him in. "A matter of *your* death, you mean." She huffed. "I'll tell Malchus."

Debra abandoned Judas to solitude in the courtyard as she went to wake Malchus, who would then wake the high priest. It would not be prudent for a maiden to enter her master's bedchamber—especially at night. Each moment crawled on as Judas continued to fight against his own mind. He could still run—abandon his dreadful quest and let come what may—but he waited in the darkness.

Finally, he saw Malchus appear, bearing a lamp. "The high priest will see you now," Malchus said.

Malchus led Judas to a large chamber which probably doubled as a meeting hall and formal dining room. Annas stood bedecked in all his finery.

He could no longer wear the official robes of the high priest, but that did not stop him from looking the part. He eyed Judas's worn traveling cloak with disdain. "I was told this was a matter of urgency?" he asked after a moment of silence.

"My name is Judas, Your Highness," Judas said, bowing.

"Yes, you're a minor Pharisee from somewhere unimportant. I've seen you before," he said, waving a hand dismissively, before his face hardened in anger. "Why did you wake me at this hour?"

"My name is Judas *Iscariot*, Highness."

Annas's eyes widened slightly. "Judas, Man of Cities," he said. "A disciple of... *him. And a Pharisee?*"

"Yes," Judas said, smiling at the high priest's surprise. "You want Jesus. I know where he is."

Annas scoffed. "Am I supposed to believe that you would betray your own master?"

"Jesus publicly insulted my father last week." It was technically true and a plausible enough reason. "My father is Simon the Leper, a *Haber*. I learned from the best how to play both sides against each other. What will you give me?"

"Judas ben Simon..." The high priest considered. "Thirty Tyrian shekels."

It was insulting. Thirty silver shekels was about two months' wages—hardly enough to buy a good slave. A pitifully far cry from the king's ransom Judas had expected—for Jesus was the King of Kings. They should have offered Judas half the Temple to turn over such an enemy. This was when Judas was supposed to bargain. He should have reminded the pompous priest that Jesus had spent the entire week in the Temple, and they were too scared to touch him.

"Done." Judas refused to dignify the pittance with any negotiation. It wasn't about the money anyway. When Jesus finally confronted the Sanhedrin and truly became the Messiah, there would be no need for money. "But it must be tonight."

"No," Annas said emphatically. "Not during the Feast. It would cause a revolt. Rome is always on high alert during the feasts. We cannot risk it. Contact me after Passover, and we will make arrangements."

"No!" Judas said hastily. "It must be tonight!"

Annas eyed him skeptically. He still did not trust a disciple of Jesus to turn on his master. "Why tonight?" he demanded, sensing a trap.

"Because," Judas said, "tomorrow, Jesus ascends the throne." *Or Israel is doomed*, he added to himself, *and God will abandon us*. Desperate times called for desperately mad decisions.

Annas must have sensed the truth of Judas's words—or his belief in them—because his face paled. "Give me an hour."

For research notes, see chapter 46 in the reference section.

XLVII

"**S**icarii?" Judas asked, recognizing Ishmael, his old contact, among the men which the high priest had assembled. It was a strange group. Several ranking members of the Sanhedrin accompanied them as witnesses, including Amon, Caiaphas's primary sycophant, in case Judas did not make good on his promise. The rest were armed. Some were simple laymen, carrying whatever weapon came to hand. Judas noted several off-duty Levites carrying batons. It seemed not all the Levite police were pleased with the changes Jesus had made. Certainly, Annas knew which were loyal to him.

Ishmael and a select group of others wore swords and a lithe grace betraying their ability. They were from the Underground. Interesting that Annas, of all people, had contacts within their order.

"He's taking no chances," Malchus said with a shrug, noting Judas's glances at the mob as he led them through the streets of the Essene quarter and to the upper room. The night was quiet. It must be about the third watch by now. The supper had been late, and it had taken the high priest longer to muster his forces than he had predicted.

Judas scoffed. "Does he actually think Jesus is going to fight back?" he asked, before biting back his words. Yes, of course Annas expected a fight.

Judas hoped for one—hoped desperately. Violence was far removed from Jesus's nature, but there was a first time for everything. There had to be. Jesus must overcome the Sanhedrin and become the new high priest by the end of the day. The alternative was unthinkable. "Of course, why wouldn't he?" Judas said, answering his own question. It chafed at him that Annas had not come with them. Jesus should be dealing with the high priest, not his underlings, but Annas was too much a coward to come himself.

Judas ascended the steps to the upper room, followed by Malchus bearing a torch. Some desperate feeling inside Judas hoped that Jesus was not here. He could abandon this desperate gamble. But in his heart, he knew he could not. Jesus must face the Sanhedrin. Today. This was the only way.

"Remember, take only the one I embrace," Judas reminded Malchus, who knew Jesus only by reputation. "No violence. I want him brought safely to the high priest." Malchus nodded, and Judas pushed the door open. The torchlight revealed an empty room.

Malchus eyed him. "Well?" he asked. Unlike the high priest, Malchus knew how deep Judas's belief ran. Malchus was skeptical about his sincerity, but he liked Judas well-enough to let things play out.

"They should be here!" Judas said in surprise. "He wasn't returning to Bethany. He made specific... The garden," he said, snapping his fingers. "He goes there often."

"Which garden?" Malchus asked, still sensing a trick. Judas had no such trick up his sleeve, only a desperate hope that Jesus would reveal his power and embrace his destiny. Jesus was Israel's only hope.

"Gethsemane."

"That's the other side of the city!" Malchus seethed. "You'd better not be wasting the high priest's time—or mine."

"I want to find him as much as Annas!" Judas snapped angrily. "Come on."

They cut directly through the city. The narrow streets were empty, and the band of thugs which trailed Judas and Malchus passed without hindrance, save for the bark of the occasional street dog. They reached Gethsemane without incident, thanks to a few directions from Ishmael. The *Sicari* was used to traveling these streets at night and avoiding Roman patrols. Any Romans meeting an armed band of Jews at this time of night would naturally assume they had evil intentions. The Romans would not be wrong.

Gethsemane was quiet when they arrived. Judas had always liked it here. Herod's vast aqueducts gave it water, so even in dry months, it was always lush: the perfect escape from the dusty streets of Jerusalem. It was an island of tranquility set apart from the madness and crowds that had followed Jesus the last three years. Judas was bringing that madness with him—and worse. He felt like an invader, entering the garden against its will.

The entire band halted as a strong figure stepped from the shadows and stood in their path. The dark silhouette thrust a stab of fear into Judas's heart, followed quickly by relief. Jesus was waiting for them; he had not been caught by surprise. It was a good sign. Jesus was ready. He looked haggard but stood firmly, as if he had already won the first battle and was ready to face the next.

Judas stepped from the ranks and approached his future king, his heart pounding. "Hello, Rabbi," he said, letting the moonlight illuminate his face.

"Is this really how you want to do this?" Jesus whispered as the two embraced.

Judas made no answer. His mind and heart were fighting a desperate war. He did not want to do this, but there was no other way. Sometimes, villains were necessary to do what good men could not. He released his master and moved to where the mob waited. He could not expose his true allegiance.

Jesus eyed the assortment of weapons and quickly divined the mob's intent. "Whom do you seek?" he asked.

"Jesus of Nazareth," Malchus replied, signaling two men with ropes to approach.

"*I AM he*," Jesus replied. His voice was calm, but power flowed from the words, and Judas felt his legs collapse in undeniable response. He fell, unable to stop himself. Jesus's reaction was all he had hoped for. Finally, the man displayed his true power. Judas shakily stood to his feet and saw that the others had collapsed as well. The entire band had been struck down by only a word. They stood, collecting weapons dropped from numb fingers, and stared at this man who could command them as easily as he could a storm.

The other disciples had heard the commotion and had fallen in behind their master. Peter stood at his side, his long fillet-knife drawn. His eyes found Judas and locked on him with shock and rage. Judas expected nothing less. He had accepted the consequences. Sometimes a villain was necessary.

"Whom do you seek?" Jesus asked again.

"Jesus of Nazareth," Malchus repeated, his tone far less confident than it had been at first.

"I already told you I am he," Jesus said calmly. "If it's me you want, let these others go." He motioned behind him.

"Agreed," Malchus said. "Come willingly, and the others can go."

Jesus nodded and extended his hands. Judas saw Peter whisper something in Jesus's ear. Jesus shook his head slightly. Malchus motioned for two *Sicarii* to tie their captive, but the men hesitated. They had felt the power radiating from this man. Malchus growled. He snatched the rope from them and stepped forward, intending to bind Jesus himself.

Peter lunged, shooting into motion like an arrow. His long knife flashed for Malchus's throat. Malchus ducked the blade, and it struck him a glancing blow on the side of his head. Malchus shrieked in pain and clutched his head. Blood gushed from the wound.

Instantly, Jesus snatched Peter's hand as the rare but familiar fire ignited behind his eyes. "Stop!" he commanded, before anyone else could react and quickly turn this confrontation into a bloodbath. "Put that away!" His eyes flashed from Peter to the mob waiting to take him as their hands instantly went to their weapons. "Any man who draws a sword will die by one," he said threateningly. He turned back to Peter, rage boiling behind his calm demeanor as he rounded on his disciple. "Do you not think I could ask my Father, and He would send me twelve legions of angels or more?!"

Judas watched eagerly as the fire burned. Finally, the Messiah was coming into his own. Judas had never considered the possibility that the Messiah might conquer with an army of angels, but it made perfect sense. His heart leaped with excitement as he finally saw his plan begin to work. The doubts retreated. *Jesus can summon an army of angels.*

Then, as suddenly as it came, the fire disappeared. Jesus sighed in disappointment. "But how else could the scripture be fulfilled? It must be this way." The doubts came rushing back.

Malchus had dropped to the ground, where he sat clutching his head and moaning piteously.

Jesus dropped his gaze to the hurting man and shook his head sadly. "What did you expect?" he asked in sympathy. "You come out to take me like some wanted criminal, with swords and clubs? I've been teaching in the Temple all week and you never approached me. Here," he said with a frustrated sigh. "Let me see."

Malchus was in too much pain to hear anything Jesus said, but he gave Jesus a desperate look as the humble teacher knelt down and plucked up something from the dark grass. Judas cringed as he realized the dark object was Malchus's ear. No wonder the man was in pain. Jesus reached with his other hand and tenderly pulled Malchus's hand from his head, releasing a fresh gush of blood from the terrible wound. "Please," Jesus said kindly to the man who was here to capture him. "Allow me." He pressed Malchus's ear back to his head and closed his eyes. His face flinched slightly, and Judas knew Jesus had taken the pain on himself.

Malchus groaned, then gasped as the healing took hold. Judas watched this exchange with incomprehensible wonder. Even now, while a mob was here to take him by force, Jesus thought of nothing but easing the pain of others—even his enemies. It was insanity: beautiful, sublime, glorious insanity.

A cold stab of fear thrust itself into Judas. Jesus was like no other man. Judas's plan relied on Jesus's sense of self-preservation, but what if Jesus refused to defend himself? He shuddered and shook off the horrible thought.

No, Jesus must ascend the throne. Prophecy must be fulfilled. God would not allow His Son to die. It was impossible.

Jesus stood, placidly extending his hands to be bound. "Alright, go ahead while you can. You wouldn't dare touch me in the daylight, but darkness makes evil men bold."

Malchus slowly stood, picking up the rope, which had fallen in the attack. He carefully bound Jesus's hands, watching him with equal measures of terror and wonder. He relaxed slightly when he tied the final knot and no angels appeared.

As Malchus relaxed, Judas grew more anxious. Still, Jesus must confront the high priest. Neither Annas nor Caiaphas were here. It was natural that Jesus would allow himself to be taken to the high priest. That was where his true power would be revealed. This was only a sample. Judas forced himself to believe it. *Belief comes first.*

Malchus stepped back, and Amon stepped up. He motioned to the *Sicarii.* "Take the others. Kill them if they resist."

Judas lunged instinctively. "That wasn't the deal!" he snapped, snatching a handful of Amon's robes.

Amon shrugged. "I made no deal with you."

"*Run!*" Judas snarled between clenched teeth, snapping the disciples into action. The whole purpose of this ploy—besides saving Israel from annihilation—was to prevent bloodshed. The Council was to take Jesus in exchange for the lives of his disciples. Amon saw things differently.

The disciples scattered as the *Sicarii* moved in. After Peter's initial attack, the assassins expected a fight, and their defensive approach gave the disciples a head start into the darkness of the garden—all but John, who had been the closest to Jesus and was a moment too late as Ishmael rushed him. The *Sicari* caught the back of John's tunic as he fled. John struggled, but Ishmael held tight. In desperation, John tore out of the garment and left it behind, diving naked into the underbrush.

"Leave them!" Malchus said angrily, calling off the attack. "We have the shepherd," he added to appease Amon. "The flock will scatter." He sighed, exhausted by the stress. The right side of his robe was still spattered with blood. "And the wolves will find them soon enough."

Judas prayed those words would not come true.

For research notes, see chapter 47 in the reference section.

XLVIII

"Thirty pieces, as agreed," Amon said coldly, tossing a pouch carelessly in Judas's direction. Judas caught it and slipped it in his robe as he moved to rejoin the mob leaving the garden. "Where do you think you're going?" Amon demanded. "You've done your bit. We don't need you now. Go, or I'll put a sword through your throat."

Amon was unarmed; clearly, he meant Ishmael's sword. Both had stayed behind to fulfill Annas's end of the bargain, as arranged. Ishmael smiled menacingly and fingered his weapon. He would enjoy putting his sword wherever Amon directed.

Judas clenched his fists. He wanted to be there. He wanted to see it when Jesus finally displayed his true power. He wanted to see these men grovel. "Fine," he spat. He knew there was no arguing with Ishmael. The man had hated Judas from the very beginning.

He turned and left the men to their dreadful errand. He was near Bethany, and he considered returning there, but one of the other disciples had likely already given them the terrible news. He would not be welcome there—not until this was all over and Jesus sat on Israel's throne. Perhaps not even then. Jesus surely would not kill him, but it was unlikely he would retain his place among the twelve. Sacrifices must be made, and Judas was ready to accept the consequences of his treachery.

But he was not ready to accept Amon's cold dismissal. He turned his steps back to the upper room. He was relieved to find it still empty. Wherever the other disciples had fled, it was not here. He didn't think he could face them—not now. After Jesus had taken his rightful place, perhaps. Jesus would forgive him; he was sure—after he explained things. It was the only way. The man healed Malchus's ear, after all. He had no concept of grudges. The others...

He quickly stripped off his worn traveling cloak and dressed himself in his Pharisee's robes. He could talk Debra into letting him in, and he could blend into the background as another minor Pharisee. All the Sanhedrin's focus would be on their prisoner. Judas could observe unobserved. He slipped out and made his way back to Annas's house. He was certain they would take Jesus there to wait for dawn. The Sanhedrin could not hold trials at night by Judaic Law.

Judas caught sight of another dark figure trailing behind the odd mix of scholars and thugs sent to take Jesus. The man stayed out of sight but kept near enough to not lose track of the band's direction. Judas used what little skill he had to silently slip around the man and get a look at his face.

It was Peter. Judas watched him with renewed respect. Peter had fled like the rest, but he had returned. He had sworn to give his life in defense of his master, and Judas was proud to see him make good on that promise. If Jesus refused to display his power, Judas would need an ally.

Unlike Peter, Judas knew exactly where this mob was going, so he moved ahead. He reached Annas's house before the mob and knocked again on the heavy door into the courtyard. Debra opened the door a crack, and Judas gave her his most charming smile.

"Debra, let me in." She glanced up and down at his change of clothes, then around him to the empty street. "The others will be here soon," he said reassuringly. "I just came ahead."

She pursed her lips but opened the door to let him in. He slipped inside. The courtyard was empty except for several bleary-eyed servants waiting for orders around a fire to stave off the chill of the night. The master was awake; the rest of the house was expected to be as well. "He has called many of his friends from the Council. They are inside the grand hall," Debra said. "You will not be noticed."

Judas nodded. "Thank you. Oh," he pulled her aside, "someone else is coming—after the main group. His name is Simon Peter; let him in."

Debra pulled back. "You ask much of me," she said coldly.

"I know! I thank you for all you've done."

She pursed her lips again. "Is he dressed like you?"

Judas chuckled. "No, he's dressed like a Galilean. Please, what trouble can one man cause?"

Debra sighed. "Fine, but he cannot enter the house. He would be noticed. He can stay in the courtyard with the servants. Maybe he will go unnoticed there. I risk my job for you, Judas," she hissed in annoyance.

Judas would have embraced her if not for the social rules against it. He shouldn't even be talking to a woman in public, but it was hard not to with Debra. "I know," he said, giving her an appreciative smile before opening the door to the hall and slipping inside.

Debra was correct in her claim that Judas would go unnoticed. The grand hall was filled with chief priests and Pharisees from the Sanhedrin, as well as many Sadducees. Judas recognized enough to know that none of the men here were sympathetic to Jesus—quite the opposite. They spoke in low tones, which dropped to silence at Ishmael's entrance with another *Sicari*, leading Jesus between them. Annas took the central seat, and the two *Sicarii* brouht Jesus before him, still tied with the ropes.

They rushed through the formalities with sloppy disinterest. This was not an official meeting. They had to wait for dawn to officially condemn Jesus.

Finally, Annas got to the root of the questioning. "You were summoned because rumors have spread regarding your doctrine. Many say that you teach against Scripture and against God. What is your doctrine?" he asked.

Jesus cocked an eyebrow. "I've been teaching openly in the Temple for a week. You never even spoke to me. Now you want to know my doctrine? Why don't you ask your spies? They were there."

Before Annas could reply, Ishmael backhanded Jesus across the mouth. Jesus reeled but stayed upright. "How dare you speak to the high priest that way!" Ishmael snapped. Judas braced for retaliation, but none came.

Jesus returned to his position calmly. "Did I say something wrong?" he asked, turning meek eyes on Ishmael. "If so, tell me. And if not, why hit me?"

This quiet response only worsened the *Sicari's* rage. "You say you're a prophet?" he asked coldly. "Prove it." He pulled his wrap from his head and covered Jesus's face, tying the fabric around his neck to secure it. None of the elders made any move to stop this vicious maltreatment, and neither did Jesus. The pit of Judas's stomach twisted as Jesus continued to hold back his power.

"Wait!" A servant halted any further violence as he entered the door. "High Priest Caiaphas has arrived," he said, ushering in the official high priest and several attending Sadducees. In secret, the Pharisees still considered Annas to be high priest, but in any official capacity, they had to recognize Caiaphas. Not that it made any difference; both were equally corrupt and hated Jesus beyond measure.

Annas politely gave his seat to his son-in-law, letting Caiaphas take over proceedings. "What is the meaning of this?" Caiaphas asked, indicating the blindfold.

"This man claims to be a prophet," Amon said mockingly. "We were simply testing the claim."

Caiaphas's face turned up in a leer. "Excellent idea. Proceed."

All restraint vanished at the high priest's approval. Amon slapped Jesus across the face. "Who hit you?" he demanded. "Answer, if you are a true prophet!" Ishmael quickly joined, and then others, jeering at their Messiah to answer their hateful demands. Judas watched in growing horror at the onslaught. His mouth went dry, and his brow became wet in a cold sweat at the humiliation Jesus endured. Why? Why did he not summon the angels? Caiaphas was here!

The attacks continued. Finally, Judas could bear no more. He fled from the room into the cool night of the courtyard. Dawn was fast approaching, and the gloom was already disappearing from the sky above. He was breathing hard. His plan was failing. No! He *must* believe. Jesus would ascend the throne. There was still time. As long as the Messiah lived, Israel had hope. The Messiah *could not die!* Soon, Jesus must reach a point where he could endure no more.

Judas crumpled to the ground, unable to endure the strain. He rested against the side of the high priest's mansion and forced himself to ignore the cruel treatment he had condemned his master to endure. He was breathing hard, but not from any physical strain. The doubts assailed him worse than ever. He had wanted this, but not *this*. Time disappeared as his feverish mind battled between knowing he had made the right choice and feeling the desperate fear that he had not. Only time would prove him right. He had to believe. Miracles surrounded Jesus. He must endure.

A commotion near the fire broke through Judas's fever as a man stood up angrily. Judas's addled brain sluggishly recognized the man. "I swear by Hades, you *raca skubala*, I am not! If I have to tell you *ekfylos kovalos* one more time... I don't *know* him, *bar kassoris!* Use your ears, for God's sake!"

This bold statement was followed by a stream of profanity unlike any Judas had ever heard. Peter had snapped. The four fishermen had never been the epitome of politeness, but all had worked to curb their tongues since becoming disciples. Yet, if any situation called for such language, this was it. The cruel profanity happening within the house was far worse than anything Peter said without.

The door behind Judas opened at the height of this tirade, and Jesus appeared in the dim light of early dawn, still bound between the two *Sicarii*. His face was bruised and bloody, his hair askew from the beating he had received. The man stood battered but unbroken. Even now, Judas could sense an innate royalty steaming off the man. It was a royalty that Herod himself did not possess, judging from the few times Judas had seen the man. Herod was king, but Jesus was *the* king. His bruised face scanned the courtyard, and his eyes caught Peter's gaze.

Peter's face paled in horror at the sight of his master. He stared aghast at the treatment Jesus had received. The crow of a rooster startled Peter from his daze, and he fled with an anguished cry. Judas would have done the same, but he could not turn away. It was far too late for that. Judas's sole hope of redemption rested in Jesus's victory. Indeed, the hope of all Israel rested in Jesus's victory. Judas believed—the people believed. Once they witnessed the Sanhedrin's cruel response, they would see who was the rightful ruler of Israel. They must.

Judas stood, shaking away his doubts with renewed vigor. It was almost dawn. Jesus must stand public trial at the Temple before the Sanhedrin. Jesus was biding his time for the formal trial. His battered face was proof enough of his maltreatment. Annas and Caiaphas were only digging their own graves. Judas felt renewed hope with the break of dawn. The hour of darkness had passed. Jesus was finally facing the Sanhedrin, and he had all the evidence he needed to condemn them publicly.

It was Passover, and Israel's Messiah was here. It was time. It had to be.

For research notes, see chapter 48 in the reference section.

XLIX

I t was a sham. The whole thing. As soon as the barest hint of daylight arrived, Annas and Caiaphas had dragged Jesus to the Temple for an official condemnation. It had been too early for any people to be there except those of the Council who had been specifically called due to their allegiance to one or the other of the high priests. None of the witnesses which the Sanhedrin called had agreed with each other on anything. Jesus had said nothing. He hadn't needed to. The witnesses had failed all on their own. It had gone wonderfully.

Until Caiaphas had demanded by the name of God that Jesus answer if he was God's Son. And Jesus answered. Judas had ached for the final blow to the Sanhedrin's power, but it had not come. The Council had condemned him for blasphemy without a second thought. It was unanimous—mostly because Annas had summoned no one who sympathized with the Nazarene. Less than half of the full Council was present, but almost twice the minimum number needed for a verdict. At this point, they weren't even trying to appear unbiased. It was despicable. Still Jesus said nothing. Did nothing.

The Sanhedrin could not legally condemn a man to death, so they had sent him to Pilate. It was almost funny. A Roman would decide the Messiah's fate. The Jews, who hated Rome beyond belief, had placed their own fate in the hands of a Roman. Perhaps that was the key. Jesus was meant to defeat Rome. Perhaps this pathetic mockery of a trial was the catalyst that finally pitted Jesus against Rome *and* broke the power of the Sanhedrin in one blow. It must be.

Judas found himself again crossing from one end of Jerusalem to the other. Pilate had taken command of Herod's fortress as a base of operations when Rome deposed Archelaus, Antipas's brother. Pilate had governed Judea for years now, and most people simply called Herod's palace the Praetorium.

Caiaphas marched up to the heavy iron doors and motioned for a *Sicari* to beat upon them. The heavy doors swung open after a few strikes, and a squad of Roman guards appeared behind them.

"State your business," the first said gruffly.

"We demand an audience with the Praetor," Caiaphas said pompously. "A prisoner requires a hearing." He pointed to Jesus. One side of Jesus's face was swollen from the earlier beatings, but he bore the bruises gracefully.

"Enter," the Roman replied, motioning for his troops to make way.

The high priest smirked. "We cannot enter the house of a Roman without becoming defiled, and today is Passover. We must be clean to eat of it."

The Roman smirked. "Of course, Highness," he said, his words dripping with an oily politeness that smacked of mockery. "Wait here, then."

Pilate appeared several long minutes later, looking quite presentable after presumably being roused from sleep only minutes before. He was the ultimate authority for all Judea, but he understood the importance of staying on his prominent citizens' good sides. His white toga wrapped him gracefully and his signet rings were visible, but otherwise, the only indication of his rank came from his proud bearing. He knew how to present the appearance of a commander. He scanned the assembled crowd carefully, noting the two prominent men: the prisoner, standing calmly with hands tied and face bloody, and the recently appointed high priest, with torn robes and a sadistic glare. Of the two men standing before him, only one had the same quiet, commanding confidence as Pilate.

"What charges do you bring against this man?" Pilate asked in Greek, the common tongue of the realm.

"Most gracious Praetor," Caiaphas replied in his silkiest Greek, bowing humbly. "This man is a dissenter. He seeks to pervert our nation. He has spoken blasphemies and ignores the edicts of Go—He claims that taxation is theft! He tells people not to pay taxes to Caesar!" he said, quickly changing direction as he noticed Pilate's boredom at his original list of infractions. Pilate was a Roman and would only condemn Jesus for breaking Roman law.

Pilate gave them a disinterested glare. "So what? I don't know a single Jew who would disagree with his opinion. Should I charge him with being a Jew? Or is there something else?" he asked sarcastically. "Something illegal, perhaps?"

Caiaphas huffed. As a Sadducee and now as high priest, he had grown used to others groveling in his presence; Pilate's cold dismissal must have chafed him severely. "If this man were not a criminal, we would not have brought him to you!" he snapped.

Pilate's gaze whipped to the high priest. His eyes narrowed, but he allowed the rudeness. "Oh, good!" he said cheerily. "Clearly, you have a firm grasp of the particulars of the case. I'll leave you to it." He turned to go.

"Wait!" Caiaphas called after him.

Pilate paused.

"Only Rome has the power to enforce *capital* punishment," Caiaphas growled through his teeth.

Pilate spun, turning back to the assembly with curiosity. His eyes interrogated the high priest and then the prisoner in turn. Pilate had seen and sentenced many thieves, murderers, and dissenters. Jesus did not match the profile. Jesus was dressed well in plain but clean robes. He had the bearing of nobility—far more than the high priest. Judas could see Pilate turning over this case in his mind. In the end, his curiosity won.

"I will question him," he said finally, spinning on his heels and motioning to the squad of soldiers who manned the gate.

Two Roman guards took charge of the prisoner and led Jesus into the Praetorium while the others moved to push the heavy doors closed.

Judas moved to follow his master, but a Roman guard held up a gloved hand. "I wouldn't try if I were you, Jew," he said, a hard glint in his eye.

Judas shrugged. "Is the Praetorium not open to the public?"

The guard chuckled to himself. "Yes," he admitted, "but this is Pilate's palace, *not* the Praetorium."

"I don't care," Judas replied. "I'm coming in." If Jesus had taught him anything, it was that defilement came from within, not without, and that the Romans were nothing to fear.

The guard's lip curled up in a half-grin. "You've got spunk for a Jew." He chuckled. "But won't you be *defiled* for your holiday?"

Judas shrugged nonchalantly. "Celebrated it last night." He forced a smile for the guard's benefit.

The Roman grunted. "Alright, *posthon*, suit yourself." He opened the door enough to let Judas through. Judas wanted to be near Jesus when he finally unleashed his power, but it was also satisfying to hear the gasps of horror from the Pharisees as they saw one of their own slip into the Roman fortress.

Pilate slowly circled Jesus as Judas entered the palace courtyard. Pilate's entire focus rested on his strange prisoner. He hardly paid Judas a glance. "You're not the typical man I find brought to my court," Pilate said carefully. "You're... different. I've heard rumors about a Jewish king. Is that you?"

The directness of the question surprised Judas. Thankfully, Judas was not the one who must answer.

Jesus smiled slightly. "Did you figure this out on your own, or did you hear it somewhere?" he asked, avoiding the question.

Pilate caught a surprised chuckle in the back of his throat. "Do I look like a Jew to you?" he asked, spreading his arms. "Rome has no quarrel with you—I am not your enemy! Your own nation brought you here. You were condemned by your own Council! Jews are fiercely loyal to their own. You are one; you should know! The *Sicarii* murder and rob their fellow Jews as often as they attack Romans, and their countrymen still hide them from our patrols! Do you realize how desperate a Jew must be to betray one of their own—to a *Roman court?* I've governed this province for three years, and I've never seen a Jew turn in a countryman willingly—let alone the Council! The Sadducees, perhaps, if they truly hated you, but half the men out there are Pharisees! The only thing they hate more than Rome is... apparently, you. So again, I ask: Do you make yourself a king? Are you planning a coup? I know many Jews do not care for Antipas—nor do I. So what can cause this level of hatred? What have you *done?*"

"Well, I do have a kingdom," Jesus said quietly. "But not here. Not in this world. If it was here, my men would have already taken this palace, and I would not be standing bound before you. But it's not..." Jesus shrugged. If the man was under any strain, he certainly could hide it. Jesus appeared in full control, despite his bonds and bloodied face. It was a good sign. The words, however... Judas ignored them. His plan would work. It had to.

"So, you *are* a king," Pilate said quickly.

"You've said it perfectly," Jesus replied. "I was born to this. It's the entire reason behind my existence in this world; I must show people the truth."

Pilate grunted. "What is truth? The future is unknown, and history is decided by the victors. Truth often has very little to do with it. Who gets to decide?"

Jesus smiled wistfully. "That is the ultimate question."

Pilate nodded thoughtfully. "Yes," he said, more to himself than his prisoner. His thoughtfulness passed in an instant, and he spun on his heels, motioning to the officer posted at the gate. The guards swung the large doors open, revealing the chief priests and elders still standing outside, waiting for Pilate's decision with impatient mutterings. Judas found himself pressed against the wall as he sidestepped to avoid the swinging door.

Pilate raised his hands to silence the angry mutters. "I have questioned your prisoner and found him faultless. He has broken no Roman law. Without further evidence of wrongdoing, I have no recourse but to release him."

Judas stared in wonder at this pronouncement. Of course, as his father had predicted, Jesus always seemed to find some means of escape. But for a Roman governor to declare him innocent after his own people had condemned him... It was all backward; Jesus was supposed to save Israel from Rome, not be saved *from* Israel *by* Rome.

The outcry following this dismissal was unsurprising. What had once been a solemn Sanhedrin Council was quickly turning into a mob that made the attack at Nazareth look like the simple misunderstanding Jesus had called it. Pilate again raised his hands to silence the mob before they turned on him. "What did you say?" he asked, pointing out one of the elders.

"I said, 'He started his trouble in Galilee, and now he's brought it here!'" the man replied. "And it's true! His own town—"

"He's from Galilee?" Pilate asked, eyes lighting.

"Well, yes, he's a Nazarene," Caiaphas admitted.

Pilate sighed in what almost sounded like relief. "*Antipas* rules Galilee," he said in irritation. "Jesus is *his* subject. I have no authority in this case without his agreement." He waved his arm dismissively. "Take him to Antipas. You may have better luck there, anyway." He smiled coldly. "I hear he likes beheading innocent Jews when he's drunk."

For research notes, see chapter 49 in the reference section.

L

The arrival at Herod Antipas's palace was strikingly different from the arrival at the Praetorium. Caiaphas barged in without asking permission, followed by the other chief priests and elders. "We are here by order of Pilate himself," he snapped at the guardsman who tried to bar his way.

Herod was technically an Ishmaelite, and the Pharisees often referred to him as such in no favorable terms whenever Herod did something they didn't like, but Herod was also considered a Jew when it suited the Sanhedrin's purpose—like today. As a Jew, Herod's home would be safe to enter without becoming unclean. Caiaphas had seen the impression Jesus made on Pilate, and he was not about to risk the chance that Jesus might also sway Herod to his side. Caiaphas wanted to be there to sway the conversation in his favor.

Judas had slipped back in among the ranks of the Pharisees on their way to Herod's palace. Antipas had a smaller palace than his late father, but it sufficed for when he visited Jerusalem as he often did for the feasts.

"What's your purpose?" the guardsman asked. As a vassal of Rome, Herod had command of his own garrison. Unlike the Romans' sleek plates of iron and red skirts, Herod's troops had traditional bronze scale armor over short, white tunics and heavy helmets with a low brim. Herod preferred the traditional armor of the Hasmoneans as a way to separate himself from Rome in the people's minds. He knew the importance of being seen as a Jew by the Jews and being seen as a Roman by the Romans. It was a dangerous balance that he didn't always keep.

"We come from Pilate's court with a prisoner. He is Galilean, so Pilate cannot legally sentence him to death without Herod's approval," Caiaphas explained, smiling thinly over the guard's heavy spear, which he held horizontally to block them from pushing even further into the palace. The guard had judiciously planted himself in a doorway between two massive pillars so the high priests and their mob could not skirt around him should they try to enter Herod's personal chambers.

The guard sniffed. "I can see that. What's his name?" he asked in annoyance.

"Jesus of Nazareth," Caiaphas said irritably.

The guard leaned to look over Caiaphas's shoulder at the prisoner. "Is that the one who fed five thousand people with only two fish?" he asked.

A vein appeared on Caiaphas's forehead. "Allegedly," he snarled.

"Huh," the guard replied. "Wait here." He twisted his spear and took a step back, leveling the point at the high priest with a dark chuckle, and paused momentarily to be sure he would not be followed. Satisfied with the result, he disappeared down the hall to find the Tetrarch of Galilee.

Herod appeared before the guard returned, eagerly marching down the hall as his servants struggled to put the finishing touches on his attire. His various attendants dutifully followed. Judas spotted Chuza among them, his face pale. Herod was dressed in the Jewish style—if more elaborate. He loved pandering to his audience. When he entertained visiting Greeks or Romans, he wore the traditional Roman toga, but when he spoke with Jews or during Jewish feasts, he preferred to appear traditionally Jewish.

He pushed his servants off him and rubbed his hands together. "Jesus the Nazarene?" he asked, scanning the crowd. "Ah, of course." He spotted the man with his hands bound and face bloodied. "You: here," he said, indicating a place before him. "The rest of you..." He shooed the others away. They retreated reluctantly, giving Herod room to survey his visitor.

This was the first time Judas had seen John's murderer up close. The man was in his middle years. His hair was thinning at the top, and his face was beginning to loosen under the strain of strong wine, rich food, and opulent leisure. "Pilate sent you?" he asked, eyeing the prisoner with evident interest.

"For your official condemnation," Caiaphas answered. "He cannot—"

"Oh, but he can," Herod interrupted, holding up a hand to quiet the high priest. "Pilate can do whatever he wants." He grunted in pleased surprise. "He must have known my desire to meet you. Perhaps the man is more civilized than I thought. What charges have they brought against you?" he asked, sizing Jesus up.

"He stirs the people to rebellion and seeks to take your throne," Caiaphas answered again.

Herod pointed a finger and clicked his tongue at the high priest. "Let the prisoner answer, if you please," he said politely. He turned, giving Jesus an expectant look.

Jesus returned the look, his face a mask of placid calm, but he did not answer. Jesus had spoken to Pilate easily enough. Judas wondered what game Jesus was playing with the ruler of Galilee. He knew Jesus was more than capable of handling himself in verbal confrontations. He had learned at least that much after watching Jesus tangle the Pharisees in their own traps time and time again. He had some plan in mind; Judas knew it.

"If he wanted my throne," Herod continued, "he would have taken it a year ago when he had an army at his back. Isn't that right?" he asked, scrutinizing his silent prisoner. "You had five thousand men with you. You could have taken Jerusalem with even a tenuous grasp of strategy and negotiated your legitimacy with Rome after seizing control. The people would have welcomed you. They were not particularly happy with me after they heard about the... unfortunate incident... with your cousin." He licked his lips. "They would not have been upset to see me gone. Yet you didn't even try. Why?"

Jesus made no reply, and, oddly enough, neither did Caiaphas. The high priest seemed surprised at this information.

"Oh, you didn't know that?" Herod asked, giving Caiaphas a pleased smile. "Quite a strange feeling to discover you were moments away from losing your throne, only *after* the moment had passed. I've been wanting to meet you ever since," he said, giving Jesus a gracious smile which Jesus did not return.

"Then there are the miracles," Herod continued. "My court is filled with stories. My chief steward, especially, often heralds your abilities," he said, indicating Chuza with a wave of his bejeweled hand. "Show me."

If Jesus registered the demand at all, he did not show it. Herod took a calming breath at this affront. He smiled thinly. Like Caiaphas, he was used to getting his way. "I have private baths here—heated baths. Could you... walk across the top?" He chuckled at the nonresponse. "No, I thought that story might be false. Could you turn it to wine? Too large, probably. What about a cup?" He motioned to a waiting servant, who came forward bearing a golden goblet filled with water. He offered it to Jesus, then, when he got no visible response, he pushed the goblet into his hands. Jesus took it without any acknowledgment and silently took a long drink. He smiled in thanks and handed it back.

Herod took the cup, and his mood darkened instantly. "Is he dumb?" he asked angrily, turning finally to Caiaphas. "Or deaf? He says nothing. He acts a simpleton! *This* is the man who has gathered such a following? His cousin, I would believe, but this imbecile..."

Judas realized the ploy instantly. King David had acted a lunatic to escape Achish, the king of Gath. Jesus must be using the same strategy on Herod. Jesus had a plan.

"He is mocking you, Your Highness," Caiaphas said eagerly. "We are certain that this is the terrorist, Jesus of Nazareth. He often stirs up riots and mocks God in His own Temple! He not only wants to seize your throne, but God's throne as well! His blasphemies know no bounds!"

"Is this true?" Herod asked, turning back to Jesus as his temper grew. "Are you mocking me?"

Jesus gave no response.

"Because if so, I will make such an example of you that others will speak of it for *generations*." His lip quivered in rage. Jesus's plan was not working.

Still, he said nothing.

"He says he is the king of the Jews," Caiaphas said, striking home the point.

Herod's face reddened. "King of the Jews, eh?" he asked, nodding to himself as he stoked his temper higher. "We'll be sure to entertain him royally, then. Chuza," he said, turning to his steward, whose face was ashen. "Tell Captain Ahab that we have a royal guest, and he deserves a *kingly* reception."

Chuza's face turned a sickly gray. "Sir, if I may—"

"You may not!" Herod snapped. "One more word, and you'll join him."

Chuza shuddered and turned reluctantly away to perform his duty. "Take him to the courtyard," Herod snarled, summoning a guard. He turned back to Jesus, his face hot with humiliation. "You are no better than me. I can work miracles, too: I can make the dumb speak. You *will* talk—even if it's just a scream."

For research notes, see chapter 50 in the reference section.

LI

If a man had a conscience at all, he needed to beat it into whimpering submission to be a soldier in Herod's court. Some men took the job because it provided security for their family and a good income. Others, because they lacked the initiative or the skill to be anything other than a slab of order-taking muscle. But there were always a few that took the job because sometimes, they gained a rare opportunity to unleash the full force of their sadistic fury without risk of reprisal.

Ahab was such a man, and his squad was specifically chosen to compliment his whims. Herod had learned well from his father and knew the value of such men. Villains were sometimes necessary to do what good men could not. Judas's mouth went dry as he followed his master to Herod's courtyard. Unless Jesus finally found his spine and stood up to these men, this would be brutal. But Jesus would survive. Perhaps this was the cruel twist that finally pushed Jesus to the realization that Israel could never flourish with Herod on the throne. An Egyptian guard had pushed Moses to the edge. Perhaps a Herodian guard would do the same for Jesus. So Judas told himself.

"Herod wants to give you the royal treatment, eh?" Ahab asked, circling his victim.

The Sanhedrin had also come out to watch the proceedings and see if Jesus would break under Herod's finest. Judas was lost to their notice, as both Pharisees and Sadducees were far more eager to see the humiliation of their sworn enemy than take notice of anything else. Judas could easily have slipped a knife through Caiaphas's ribs without notice. Not that it mattered. Jesus was in Herod's grasp now. Still, it was a good sign that Herod did not intend to kill Jesus outright. It did not matter if Jesus was beaten or humiliated; so long as he lived, Israel had hope.

"You don't want to be wearing these rags..." Ahab continued, fingering Jesus's worn traveling cloak. He tore it off with a vicious tug, pulling Jesus off-balance. Jesus stumbled forward and would have fallen on Ahab, had the man not stopped the tumble by slugging Jesus across the jaw. Jesus staggered back but managed to keep his feet. He calmly returned to a standing position.

"Sorry, Your Highness," Ahab said sweetly. "Force of habit. Let's get you into something more regal." He motioned two of his officers to approach, bearing a faded purple robe which probably had once adorned the shoulders of Herod the Great but had not seen use for any serious purpose in a long time. Ahab placed it on Jesus's shoulders with mocking reverence and stepped back to survey his work. Jesus bore the humiliation stoically as the Jewish Councilors watched in silence. Ahab enjoyed playing to a crowd, and the crowd watched with expectant glee.

Judas was shaking. He was only one man. He could do nothing to stop this. He would only receive the same cruel treatment as his master. He was powerless to do anything but endure and hope—hope that his belief would be enough. The morning sun still gleamed. The day was young, and life still burned in the Messiah's heart. There was still hope. Prophecy must be fulfilled. Jesus had said so himself.

Ahab shook his head as he surveyed the mockery he had made of his true king. "You're still missing something. Herod wears no crown because he is merely a vassal, but you are the true king of the Jews, are you not?" he asked, grinning wickedly. "A king requires a crown! Bring the crown!"

The crown was a wicked thing, modeled after the leafy crowns of the Romans, but instead of laurel leaves, this was a leafless monstrosity of twisted vines with long thorns extending from all angles. Judas winced at the sight as Ahab wrapped his hands with a leather strap and gingerly took the crown from his accomplice. He lightly placed it on Jesus head, then pressing down through the leather, pushed the wicked thing into Jesus's scalp. He stepped back to survey his work.

Jesus still stood silently. His eyes watered from the pain, but he bore it nobly.

Ahab shook his head. "No, it's crooked." He twisted the crown, using the leather straps to protect his hands from the spikes digging into his victim's head.

Jesus shuddered under this new strain but rallied. His teeth clenched, but he would not bring himself to make a sound. Judas had been wrong; Jesus was far from spineless. On the contrary, he seemed practically unbreakable. He bore this cruel treatment with stubborn dignity when a single word could make it stop.

"Perfect!" Ahab said, standing back to admire his work.

A thick drop of blood crawled down Jesus's scalp to hide itself in his eye, trying to return to its rightful place. Jesus blinked it away.

"Here you are, Your Highness," Ahab said, placing a thin reed in Jesus's right hand. Jesus let his hand take the reed, but then let the hand drop back to his side.

"Well?" Ahab asked, turning to his officers. "Behold your king! Come, give homage to the king of the Jews!" The first stepped up, kneeling before Jesus, who watched this mockery with sad eyes.

"Bless me, Your Highness," the soldier said mockingly to the silent statue before him.

"Oh, the king rejects your request!" Ahab said sorrowfully, as Jesus failed to acknowledge the mocking soldier. "You'll lose your head for approaching the king without his permission!" he added with a laugh. He stepped up to Jesus menacingly, leaning toward his ear. "Do you want to take his head, majesty?" he asked quietly. "Or... mine, perhaps?" His face turned into a gloating smile. "I took your cousin's head, you know. You could return the favor."

Judas stiffened, but Jesus remained passive. "It was over quickly," Ahab continued, trying to get a rise from his silent victim. "Well, quicker than crucifixion, at least. The sword... it was dull, you see? Took a little longer than usual. Herod told me to sharpen it, but..." He shrugged in pleasant unconcern. "...I forgot." He turned his back on Jesus, then turned again. "No, I didn't forget," he admitted. "Truth is, I wanted him to suffer a little more. I didn't like your cousin. He was so full of himself—thought he could tell everyone else what to do. Acted like he was better than us. Acted like *you* do, but you know what?" His lip curled into a snarl, and he snatched a handful of Jesus's beard, pulling their faces together. He spat, splattering Jesus's face. The spittle mixed with the blood that had now drawn several dark lines on his face. "You're *not* better than me. You're no king. You bow to *me*." His fist smashed into Jesus's stomach, causing him to double over. "That's better," Ahab said, tossing away the handful of beard that had torn off in his grasp. "Bow to your betters."

Jesus straightened but still said nothing, nor made any move to stop the attacks. Ahab glared at his unbreakable captive, then turned back to his men. "Who else wants a go?" he asked. Several others stepped up and took their turns working Jesus over, trying to get him to break. Jesus refused. The beating was worse than he had received from the Sanhedrin, and still he did not break. The Sanhedrin's elders watched eagerly. Some even took part. They were enjoying this. As much as they wanted Jesus dead, they wanted him to suffer first.

Judas watched until he thought he could bare it no longer. Jesus was unbreakable, perhaps, but Judas was strained to the breaking point when Herod finally appeared and called a halt to the terrible beating. He took a look at his soldiers, who calmed themselves from the frenzy they were working toward and stepped back, leaving Jesus standing alone. Jesus's face was battered and bleeding from the beating and the crown of thorns, which clung to his scalp tenaciously with long claws that dug into and under his skin. His nose bled terribly, and his jaw was bleeding from the chunks of beard the men had viciously ripped away. Judas had seen no teeth escaping the bloody attack, but many were probably loose. Jesus was nearly unrecognizable. His skin was swollen and torn from the beating, but his eyes... his eyes still gleamed with calm nobility from their battered sockets. There was no fire. Jesus watched Herod with a serene sadness that seemed ignorant of the wounds.

Herod's eyes held the fire of a man whose honor had been insulted. Jesus stood before him, battered, bloody, but still unbroken. "Are you ready to talk, now?" Herod asked coldly, knowing he would receive no answer. Jesus failed to surprise the tetrarch, and Herod grunted to himself at the silent dismissal. "As I thought, such a clamor over nothing. Send him back to Pilate," Herod said with bored dismissal, turning back to his palace. "He has full permission to do anything he wants to this fool."

Judas sighed with relief. Herod could have killed him. He had the authority just as much as Pilate, but Herod saw Jesus as a toy which failed to work. Herod had enjoyed John's presence because John was bold. Herod would poke him, and John would respond. Jesus did not. Herod had expected miracles and, failing that, at least some fiery rhetoric about his sins. Herod took little enjoyment from needless torture, and now that it was clear even torture would not provoke a desired response, Herod had lost interest. He had no use for Jesus.

Jesus had faced Herod and survived—battered, bruised, and mangled, but alive. If Jesus was to allow this charade to continue, Pilate's court was the ideal location. Pilate was the only man who had treated Jesus with courtesy. The Jews had abused Jesus, mocked him, and condemned him, but Pilate saw him for what he was—at least partly. Pilate knew Jesus was an innocent man. He had no idea what to make of the simple teacher, but Pilate recognized an innate nobility that just might be enough to keep Jesus alive. It had to be enough.

For research notes, see chapter 51 in the reference section.

LII

A squad of Herod's personal guards escorted Jesus back to the Praetorium. These men were simply there to do their job, and they escorted Jesus with the same grim silence as their prisoner. They turned Jesus over to the Roman guards, who led Jesus into the Praetorium and denied entry to anyone else under Pilate's order. Judas had to wait outside along with the chief priests and elders where Pilate's guardsmen had left them.

The doors opened a few minutes later, and Pilate reappeared. He raised his hands to address the waiting crowd, which had swelled in number as people heard of the strange events from the night before, though it was still mostly comprised of Pharisees, Sadducees, and *Sicarii*—besides the various rabble that all mobs inevitably collected.

"Look at this man!" Pilate said. He motioned Jesus forward, who still wore the faded purple robe Herod's men had put upon him. "He has been beaten and humiliated, and for what reason? You accuse him of deceiving people, causing riots, and attempting insurrection, but I have questioned him at length in front of witnesses and found no evidence to support these accusations. Clearly, Herod went to greater lengths," he said, looking at the fresh wounds, "and also found no reason to condemn him. Herod has left the decision to me." Pilate sighed in frustration. "Although I find no cause to condemn this man by Roman law, I agree to scourge him and release him as punishment for whatever Jewish law he has broken."

This concession was not enough and only exposed Pilate's desperation to keep the peace.

Caiaphas saw the weakness and pounced upon it. "Death! Crucify him!" he cried. "Death to the blasphemer!" he continued, forcing his excitement onto the others until more took up the cry.

Pilate watched in shock at the Jews' bloodlust. "It is customary at Passover to release a Roman prisoner of your choice, in honor of the holiday," he bargained. "Shall I release this man, who is called the King of the Jews?"

"Not this man! We want Bar-Abbas!" Ishmael shouted, and Caiaphas instantly agreed, rallying the crowd.

Pilate's face turned grim, but he signaled a guard. The riot continued until the guard returned with a second prisoner brought from the Praetorium dungeon.

Judas had never seen the Son of the Father before, but he knew him instantly. The man was thin and dirty from months in a Roman cell. His tunic was worn, like his face. He moved with a lithe grace which all *Sicarii* seemed to have, and his face was calm. Not the serene peace which still radiated from the battered and broken face of the Messiah, but the calmness of a predator waiting to pounce. His eyes held the fire that Judas sought, and with a sudden lurch, Judas realized his terrible mistake.

Jesus was the true Messiah. Judas believed it with every bone in his body, but Bar-Abbas was the Messiah Judas had always thought he wanted. At the Gates of Hell, Jesus had spurned the pagan woman to show the disciples the ugly face of the racism which they had come to see as normal. When they suddenly saw Jesus act in such a way, the horror became clear. Now, the true Messiah stood side-by-side with a true destroyer: a man who had no desire but to throw off the shackles of Rome by any means necessary. Judas saw embodied in Bar-Abbas every trait which he had tried to force upon Jesus, and again, the comparison exposed the dreadful truth.

Bar-Abbas's cold eyes struck fear into any who looked there. In his fight to destroy the monster of Rome, he had become a monster himself. In his eyes was the fire of passion which could liberate Israel, with no room for compassion or remorse. He saw only Israel's freedom, and nothing would stand in his way. The contrast was shocking.

Clearly, Pilate hoped that others would also realize this important difference, and displayed Bar-Abbas to make the choice obvious. Bar-Abbas was no friend of the Sadducees, which made up an influential portion of the Sanhedrin. Some of the Pharisees might secretly admire the brigand, but his tactics had grown bloodier and more desperate since the beginning of the Underground. The choice should have been a simple one, but Pilate did not know how deeply the Sanhedrin's hatred for Jesus ran.

"Shall I release Jesus Christos, a teacher, or Jesus Bar-Abbas, a murderer?" Pilate asked.

And with that question, Israel was forced to choose their Messiah: both named Jesus, both claiming the title of "Son of the Father," and both so very different. The moment had arrived, as Jesus had predicted. War or peace: the choice was simple, but the choice was one which Judas had been unable to answer until now. He had wanted both, but only now did he see how truly opposed they were. It was impossible to have both. They were antagonists: savior and destroyer, Christ and Anti-Christ. The time was now; Israel must make her choice.

Judas took a breath to start the cry and sway the crowd toward the right choice, but another voice cut him off.

"Bar-Abbas! Give us Bar-Abbas!" It was Caiaphas. Like Bar-Abbas, he was set on destruction and cared nothing for the consequences. He was safe from Bar-Abbas's deadly reach and did not care if his fellow Jews were killed by the robber's assassins. Jesus must die. Caiaphas had prophesied it.

Other Pharisees took up the cry. Many were *Sicarii* sympathizers, and although they would never bloody their own hands, they didn't want peace with Rome. They wanted freedom from Rome no matter the cost. Whatever few people might have asked for Jesus's release, their voices drowned in the rage of the high priest and his followers. Pilate watched this outcry with growing unrest. He had only a tenuous hold on the people of Judea, who were always ready to revolt against a Roman governor.

He held up his hands to again silence the crowd, but they cried louder, until Pilate had no choice but to give in or risk a revolt. Reluctantly, Pilate gave his guards a sign, and Bar-Abbas left his chains for the safety of the crowd. Finally, with their chosen liberator free, the screams died down.

"What do you request I do with Jesus Christos?" Pilate asked when the shouting finally ceased.

"Crucify him!" Caiaphas cried, causing the crowd to again explode.

Judas knew the power of mobs. Once they had gotten a taste for blood, there was no stopping them—not without a legion of angels. *Why do they not come?*

Pilate paled at this demand and held up his hands to again silence the crowd. They quieted but only partially. "*You* take him, then!" Pilate shouted. "Punish him as you will if he has broken your law. I declare him innocent!"

"He is guilty by our Law!" Caiaphas shrieked. "Guilty and worthy of death!"

The mob shouted their agreement, happy to let Caiaphas do all their thinking for them.

"Why?" Pilate demanded, growing more desperate to find some way to both placate the religious leaders and save the life of their victim. "What evil has he done?!"

"He has blasphemed by claiming to be the Son of God!" Caiaphas replied angrily. "The Law demands his death!"

Pilate blanched. He finally realized the fanatical zeal of this mob and knew the only way to stop them was with violence. Caesar had torn Archelaus from his throne because of a violent incident on a Jewish holiday. Pilate had replaced him. Rome was not kind to rulers who could not control their people. He turned, leaving the mob to feed their own frenzy, and pulled Jesus into the Praetorium.

Judas slipped in the door. The Roman guards were too focused on keeping the mob at bay to care about a single Jew. Events were rapidly crumbling. The crowd had tasted the blood of man; there was no return. If Pilate chose to give Jesus into the mob's hands, only God could save His Son. The other disciples had abandoned their master in terror. Judas must witness this. Jesus might not be the warrior of death that Judas had once thought, but surely God would save His Son. King David had prophesied it. God would not allow His Holy One to see corruption. It had to be.

"Where are you really from?" Pilate asked, the minute he was away from the noise of the angry crowd outside his gate.

Jesus ignored him.

"Look, I heard how they accused you. You said your kingdom was not of this world. They say you claim to be the son of a god. I've never put much faith in gods. But I can sense something... *divine*... about you. You *are* a king, aren't you?"

Jesus made no reply.

Pilate snatched a handful of Jesus's purple cloak, before thinking better of it and stepping back. "You're not speaking to me, now?" he asked in frustration. "I'm your only hope here! Herod gave you entirely into my power. I can crucify you or release you! Give me something to placate this mob or I will have no choice!"

Finally, Jesus turned his bloody face on the Roman governor. "You have no power over me except what has been given to you," he replied kindly. "I understand the difficult position you face. The one who placed you in this position is the one who bears the most blame."

Pilate shook his head in wonder at this. His prisoner was already brutally beaten, facing death, and he was making excuses for the man sending him to it. "I need to think," he growled. He left, heading for the courtyard where large cases were usually decided when the Jews weren't so worried about being defiled. Judas shrunk back, fearful of being seen by his Messiah. Judas had betrayed his king. Judas had placed Pilate in this position. He bore the most blame. When all this was over, Judas could beg forgiveness, but not now. Not when his master's face was a mask of bruises and blood. Jesus waited patiently for Pilate's return, standing like a stone. Judas kept behind him. He could endure the disdainful eyes of the Roman guards, but he could not endure Jesus's gaze. Not like this.

After many long minutes, Pilate finally returned, his face ashen. He took a long, painful look at his prisoner. "My wife warned me not to get involved. I'll do what I can, but..." He shook his head and, for the third time, approached the large doors and addressed the waiting mob.

"This man is no threat!" Pilate said, trying once more to quell the mob. "He has broken no Roman law!"

"He claims to be a king! It's treason against Caesar!" Caiaphas said angrily. "If you release him, you will be guilty of the same treason! Caesar is no friend to traitors."

"He claims to be *your* king!" Pilate cried in consternation. "Do you realize what you're asking? You're begging a *Roman governor* to crucify *your own king!* Is that what you want?! Should I crucify your king?"

"We have no king but Caesar!" Caiaphas shrieked.

Judas blanched. Minutes before, Caiaphas had demanded the release of a Jewish terrorist who hated Rome, and now he swore his allegiance to it. The man was beyond reason. Pilate realized the same. He turned to his prisoner, returned to the courtyard by two Roman guards.

"There's no stopping them, is there?" Pilate asked quietly, gesturing in disbelief at the frenzied mob.

Jesus grimly shook his head.

Pilate's face turned pallid, and he signaled a servant. "Bring me water. I want to make this official."

The servant returned with a dish of water, and Pilate dipped his hands in it gravely. "I wash my hands of this entire affair," he said loudly. "You have the Temple Garrison at your disposal. Deal with your prisoner as you see fit. I take no part in this. I am innocent of this man's honorable blood."

Caiaphas huffed in disdain. "His blood will be on our hands. And our children's," he said mockingly, placating Pilate's guilt.

Pilate swallowed. "So be it," he said coldly. "Take him away." He turned to go, leaving Jesus to the bloodlust of the mob.

"Wait!" came a demanding voice.

Pilate turned back at the urgent cry.

Caiaphas held up a hand to stop him. "We have witnesses who heard you promise," he said. "A Roman governor cannot go back on his word."

Pilate creased his brow. "I will do as I promised. I release the prisoner into your authority."

Caiaphas's lips curled up in an evil smile as his trap sprung. "Yes, but you agreed to scourge him first."

For research notes, see chapter 52 in the reference section.

LIII

They wanted this to hurt. Crucifixion was the slowest and cruelest death the Romans could conceive, and it still wasn't enough. The mob wanted more. They had humiliated Jesus, mocked him, beaten him, thrust a crown of thorns on his head, and finally pressured Pilate into giving them the death they so desperately desired, and it still wasn't enough.

"How many lashes?" the Roman executioner asked. He was a sturdy man with bristling muscles projecting from all sides and a grim face that betrayed no emotion. Judas could tell that this man was here to do his job, nothing more. He had conditioned himself to not see men on his whipping post, only jobs to be done. He had likely lashed friends and comrades on that post. "Pilate instructed me to follow your orders."

Caiaphas considered the question. The Pharisees still refused to enter the Praetorium because of the Passover, but they pressed together in front of the large doors leading into it, waiting eagerly for the lashing to begin. Pilate had abandoned them, not wanting to witness the suffering he had refused to stop. Judas did not want to watch either, but he remained, unable to tear himself away from the impending misery. Still, he held out hope—mad hope.

"How many?" the executioner asked again.

Caiaphas's lip curled in a hateful smirk. "Thirty-nine." Forty was the legal limit, and often fatal.

The executioner nodded grimly and returned to his prisoner. Jesus was chained around a thick log, his purple cloak and worn robe stripped from him, exposing a bare back. The executioner raised the whip and brought it down. Judas winced, waiting for a miracle. The three Hebrews in Babylon had stepped unscathed from the fiery furnace. Daniel had emerged unharmed from the den of lions. Joseph had risen from the dungeon to the highest position in Egypt under Pharaoh. Israel had passed through the Red Sea into freedom. God must surely rescue His Son in similar fashion. A legion of angels would appear to intervene. Now was the time. Another second would be too late.

None came. The whip struck the bare flesh with a cruel crack. Then another. Then another. Judas succeeded in preserving his precious hope of divine rescue until the first strike landed. The cruel whip cracked, and so did his belief. Someone in the crowd started up a count as each strike bit the defenseless flesh. The mob picked it up quickly. Eight. Nine. Ten. The bare flesh tore under the relentless attack. The nine-tailed whip had bits of bone and sharpened steel tied into the strands, and the sharp points repeatedly lacerated the flesh over and over. Thirteen. Fourteen. Fifteen.

As the whip continued to reign unforgiving blows against the skin, the sharp cracks evolved into wet slaps as the skin was slowly flayed away, bit by bit. The blood mingled with the raw flesh and muscle. Nineteen. Twenty. Twenty-one. As each stroke tore away the flesh, it also tore away Judas's hope of rescue, bit by bit. Jesus was still alive—for now—but that was all.

No help was coming.

Jesus was in shock. He did not even cry out under the endless torment. His legs had collapsed, and he remained upright only by the chain which held his arms to a hook on the massive post. Twenty-six. Twenty-seven. Twenty-eight. The priests and the mob counted each strike with cruel glee. Some ventured unthinkingly through the gate, defiled in their thirst for blood. Thirty-one. Thirty-two.

The whip flashed back, flinging blood and flesh with each flick of the executioner's wrist. His leather apron and bare arms were splashed with blood, as were some of the overzealous Pharisees who had inched closer, all thoughts of purity forgotten in the vicious punishment of their enemy. "Thirty-six. Thirty-seven. Thirty-eight. Thirty-nine!" A cheer rose from the mob as the final blow struck. The executioner dropped the whip mechanically and left to clean himself.

Another Roman unchained Jesus from the post, and he collapsed to the ground where he lay completely still. He was dead. The Messiah was dead. The crushing weight of dreadful truth smothered Judas in a heavy cloud of impenetrable horror. The mob was finally quiet, staring at the still form as if they too were surprised that their hated enemy could actually be killed. A gasp cut the stillness as the bloody mass of flesh that had once looked human slowly stirred. The Messiah lived.

Jesus placed his hands on the ground, and slowly, painfully, pushed himself onto his knees, then to his feet. He straightened with torturous movements to stand gazing at the silent mob. His back was nothing but bloody ribbons of destroyed flesh, and his front was no better. The nine-tail was long; the cords often wrapped around the body to tear further into the flesh, and there were always a few strikes that missed the mark, striking the legs or the head instead of the back. The pitiful creature that stood before them could no longer be called a man, for every bit of his humanity had been stripped away—except for his eyes. Those terrible eyes. They still held only pity. Jesus had endured all this and still could not bring himself to hurt another human being. Judas knew he had the power. Jesus could kill them all with a single word if he wanted. But he didn't. Jesus was mad. They were all mad. Every one of them. The mob was mad with rage, Judas was mad with desperation, and Jesus was mad with mercy.

Pilate appeared as a squad of soldiers from the Temple Guard came to take possession of the condemned. True to his word, Pilate would allow the Sanhedrin to do what they wished, but they would have to use the Roman soldiers under their own command. He crossed the courtyard to meet them at the gate but kept his eyes down as he passed Jesus, not daring to look at the innocent man he had failed to save—not that Judas had any right to condemn him. Judas bore the most guilt; Jesus had said so.

Pilate carried three signs, one of which he was working to alter. He must have been planning to crucify Bar-Abbas and his two accomplices after the feast, but Jesus had taken the terrorist's place. It was customary for a man's name, origin, and crime to be written above him on the cross, so that all who saw the terrible sight knew the reason for the sufferer's misery.

Pilate finished his alteration and handed the signs to the Roman *decanus* of the Temple Guard. He turned, anxious to leave the dreadful courtyard and the mob filling it.

"Wait!" Caiaphas said hastily, catching Pilate's attention.

Pilate turned with a cold glare.

"What did you put on the sign? What crime?" Caiaphas asked, as if he had not condemned the man himself.

"Jesus of Nazareth: King of the Jews," Pilate replied coldly. "That's what you accused him of." It was the closest thing to a crime Caiaphas could pin on Jesus. The Sanhedrin desperately wished to overthrow Rome and establish their own Jewish dynasty but had ironically sworn fealty to Caesar in their desperation to convict their enemy. The Sanhedrin had made their choice; any who claimed the Jewish throne could now be executed by Rome for the simple crime of being king. It set a dangerous precedent.

"You should say that he *falsely* claimed to be the king of the Jews," Caiaphas said hotly, realizing the political trap into which he had fallen. The Sanhedrin had officially and firmly positioned themselves against Jewish independence, and Pilate knew it. In their desperation to kill their enemy, the chief priests had promised fealty to Rome and ended any hope of a

Jewish dynasty. To be a Jewish king was now a crime worthy of death by Sanhedrin Law. The Sanhedrin had demanded it, and Pilate had enforced it. The precedent was set, and now Rome could legally kill any Jew for the same offense without recourse. Caiaphas knew the mistake he had made and was desperate to change it.

"I said what I said," Pilate spat. There was no love lost between the Roman governor and the Jewish high priest. Pilate's eyes betrayed the regret he felt for caving to the Jews' demands, and he had found a small way to repay it. He turned, ignoring the high priest's protests, and disappeared into his palace.

The executioner returned, dragging two more condemned by their chains toward the row of crosses piled against the wall and allowed each man to take his pick of the selection. Each cross was equally terrible. It was the worst of deaths, used only on the worst of criminals. Often, the sufferer would linger for days, suffering terribly as their weight hung from spikes driven into the wrists. Breathing was nearly impossible, and natural response forced them to occasionally pull themselves up, resting all their weight on a third spike driven into the feet. The unbearable pain would allow them only time to take a shuddering breath, before sinking back to dangle from their hands, unable to breathe, unable to die—unable to end the unendurable suffering until thirst or exposure finally released the sufferer.

After their dreadful selection was made, Pilate's soldiers turned the three prisoners over to the half-legion of Temple Guards, who would escort the prisoners to their place of execution, ensuring their arrival without any foolhardy escape attempts—either by the prisoners themselves or sympathizers in the crowds that always followed the doomed to their inevitable end. Two Roman soldiers gripped each arm of the two *Sicarii* prisoners as the crosses were lowered onto their backs. They struggled futilely against their captors as another soldier tied their outstretched hands to the crossbars, forcing them to carry the cruel device or risk flogging by their escorts. Jesus, bloody and suffering as he was, accepted the cross without struggle as two soldiers lowered it onto his bleeding back. His knees nearly buckled with the weight and the pain, but he rallied and stood, even as the rough wood dug into the torn flesh of his back. The pain had to be excruciating, and still, no angels came to rescue him. The savior of Israel had been rejected, and he was going to die. He was going to let himself die.

Judas could take no more. He turned from the awful scene, seeking any kind of relief, knowing there was none. Some infinitesimal spark of hope still remained, a coal buried deep in the ashes of misery. Judas knew the coal would extinguish the minute it reached the air, so he buried it. He must get away. He had caused this, and he could endure no more.

He pushed his way through the crowd. News of Jesus's capture had spread, and the crowd had swelled. Rage and hate were no longer the only emotions displayed; now shock, horror, and simple curiosity filtered in as more people came to investigate. It was too late now. The sympathizers could do nothing. The sentence had already been pronounced.

Judas pressed through the milling crowd, shoving desperately to escape the crushing bodies and the equally crushing doom that smothered him from all sides. He passed two streets before the crowd finally started to thin. He was nearing the edge when he felt a hand catch his arm. He tried to pull away, aching for escape from the awful scene and the guilt pressing against his mind, but the hand gripped him tighter. "Judas! What's happened?"

Judas turned, fighting to hide his roiling emotions, and saw his old master.

"I just heard. Jesus was taken to Pilate?" Joseph of Arimathaea asked, concern lacing his voice. "What's he done?" After seeing Jesus teaching openly in the Temple all week, hearing of his arrest must be shocking.

"It's not about what *he's* done," Judas said quietly.

Joseph must have recognized the dreadful pallor on Judas's face. "You did something. Didn't you?" he asked, his face paling from the realization. "I heard he was betrayed by... You were trying to play both ends, weren't you?! You gambled on his mercy, as you did with me! I warned you one day your schemes would be your ruin, but this is worse," he said, clutching his head. "*What did you do?*"

"No!" Judas said, shaking his head miserably. "No, I gambled *against* his mercy. He said if he was not crowned king today, God would abandon Israel! He was doing nothing! I had to—I thought if he faced the Sanhedrin, he would finally take his rightful place. He said he was done hiding! I just— he won't even defend himself!" Judas shouted, his voice breaking in a cry of pain and anger.

"This is bad," Joseph said, shaking his head in disbelief. "No, what you did to me was bad. This is... This is *worse*. It's unthinkable! How could you—" Joseph clenched his fists and put an angry finger in Judas's face. "It should be *you* dragging that cross—not him! This will not go unpunished," he growled. "You may have doomed Israel, but you have certainly doomed yourself. You just *had to meddle!* You can't leave well enough alone! You owe your *life* to that man! The least you could do is follow his lead, but no! You think you can outwit the Messiah! He saves your life, and you take his." Joseph shook his head grimly. "This is unforgivable. Even for me. It took you three years, Judas, but you've finally found my limit."

"I'm sorry," Judas said quietly, barely a whisper in the suddenly quiet street. The mob had moved off, following the three prisoners on their agonizing journey to an even worse death.

Joseph spat in disgust. "Being sorry won't change this. I'm surprised the poor man is still standing. If he dies..." He shook his head. "It should be you with that cross. It should be you."

He turned without waiting for a response and started back toward the Praetorium. "Wait!" Judas called, suddenly terrified of being left alone—terrified of being abandoned, as he had abandoned his Messiah. "Where are you going?" he asked feebly.

Joseph closed his eyes and sighed. "To try and fix this mess—beg Pilate to reconsider. There is still time—hours at least—before he dies. Crucifixion takes time. I am a Sadducee, after all. Pilate has respect for us—for my wealth, if nothing else. There may still be hope for him—if not for you," he said, giv-ing Judas a look of grim loathing. "I do believe in him. I thank you for that, but this betrayal cannot be undone. I should feel sorry for you, but... you brought this on him. If he dies..." He smiled grimly, a weak, pathetic thing that betrayed more sadness than any frown could hope to convey. "I have a tomb nearby. He deserves better than a mass grave."

He turned again and abandoned Judas to his misery.

For research notes, see chapter 53 in the reference section.

LIV

Judas followed the crowd at a distance, pulling his *tallith* down to hide his face lest he be recognized again. Meeting Joseph had twisted the knot of dread tighter in his stomach. If any disciple of Jesus recognized him, they would either know his guilt—or they wouldn't. Both were terrible. If they knew, Judas could not bear to face their anger—or worse, disappointment—and if they did not, it would only drive his guilt in deeper.

He ducked his head lower when he passed Mary and several other women whom he recognized. Thankfully, their eyes followed Jesus. Judas did not dare look at their faces and risk seeing the tears he knew were there. He had done this. Israel was doomed. The Jewish leaders had condemned themselves, but it was Judas who had given them opportunity. Jesus had trusted him. Jesus was more than his Messiah; Jesus was his dear friend. Judas should have protected him with his life and instead had sold him for the price of a slave. Whatever doom awaited Israel, Judas deserved the greater portion to repay the misery he had already caused. And Jesus still had much more to suffer.

The crowd had swelled with sympathizers, though none moved to challenge the Roman escort. The people pushed up against each other as the front of the crowd stopped. Judas pressed in to see that Jesus had finally collapsed. He lay on the dusty street just outside the city gate, with the cross lying atop him. The Roman escorts knew better than to beat him. Jesus was at the end of his strength, and further punishment would do nothing. Of course, no Roman soldier would bear the humiliation of dragging the cross, so the squad quickly spread out to find a substitute. No Jew would risk it either. The cross was an instrument of death, and to touch it would make one unable to partake of the Passover. Even under threat of the whip, the Jews shied away from the Romans' demands.

The procession ground to a halt as the soldiers searched the crowd. Judas ached to volunteer. Joseph had been right in saying that he deserved the cross. Jesus had saved him from the cross, and Judas had repaid his master by sending him to it. Judas should take the full punishment or, failing that, at least bear the burden, but he shrank from the horror of it. Every eye would be watching him, knowing his guilt, hating him. He could not bear it. Jesus let the cross press his bleeding wounds into the dusty street, waiting for rescue that would not come. Jesus did nothing. He had accepted his fate. If Israel did not want him as their Messiah, Jesus was content to let himself be killed. He would not use his power to save Israel unless they wanted to be saved. No one moved to help.

The soldiers finally found an African in the crowd and forced the task upon him. He seemed ignorant of the social revulsion surrounding the cross and took the burden with little protest. Jesus rested for a long moment, breathing heavily, but a sharp word from a soldier roused him, and he painfully pushed himself back to his feet and started moving again.

The ghastly procession split from the road to ascend a low hill which overlooked the gate into the city. Guided by the squad leader, the African placed Jesus's cross in the center, taking the place intended for Bar-Abbas, the Son of the Father. The placement was important; the middle was always designated for the worst offender. The signs which the soldiers were nailing to the tops of the crosses would show all passersby that being the king of the Jews was a worse offense than thievery and murder.

A loud thud and an awful shriek cut the morning air as the executioner struck the first nail into one thief's wrist. It took four soldiers to hold down the naked man. His clothes had been stripped and would be divided among the soldiers as a perk for performing the grisly task of crucifixion. The executioner knew just where to place the nails in the hand so that the cruel iron would grind against the bones and the nerves but still hold the weight of the sufferer as the cross dropped into place. Each strike of the hammer brought a fresh scream, though each scream grew weaker as the poor wretch exhausted himself.

The executioner moved to the second thief, and a similar terrible play ensued while the soldiers lifted the first thief into position. A fresh shriek of unimaginable pain exploded as the heavy cross reached its zenith and dropped solidly into its hole with a jarring thud. The thief's screams continued until they finally dropped into terrible groans. The pain would not end.

Another awful shriek sounded as the second thief dropped into position. Judas could not tear his eyes away from the terrible scene no matter how he tried. Jesus was last; the Romans knew he would not escape, though they did not trust him so much as to leave him unguarded. Jesus lowered himself onto the rugged wooden surface and collapsed upon it with a painful gasp, extending his arms without complaint.

Whether he did so willingly or simply had no strength to fight back, Judas did not know, but the soldiers holding Jesus down did little more than keep his arm steady. Jesus did not resist, even as the nail pierced his skin with a hard strike of the hammer. It took four hard strikes of the hammer for the nail to hold, and still the man did not cry out. The other arm followed with the same dreadful precision, and the same awful silence. Judas winced at every blow, aching to change the horrible outcome of his ill-thought gamble. Jesus could do anything and did nothing. Their Messiah was letting himself be killed.

The cross rose slowly. Judas's every fiber waited in painful suspense for the sudden drop. It came. Jesus dropped with the cross, and his full weight fell upon the spikes which held him up.

Finally, his silent endurance could bear no more. His voice broke in a jagged cry. "Father," he groaned, forming his cry of agony into a plea for mercy. "Forgive them." His voice dropped into a painful moan. "They don't know what they're doing."

The words pierced Judas to the core. In the very worst of his agony, Jesus still pleaded for his nation. He *was* the Messiah. Judas knew it as he knew the certainty of his own doom. Israel was killing their Messiah, and there was nothing Judas could do to stop what he had begun.

A mocking cry responded to Jesus's misery. "Listen to him beg his father. Why doesn't his father save him, if he is truly the Son of God?" It was Amon, eager to mock Jesus in his desire to please Caiaphas, who stood beside him.

"Yes!" Caiaphas added quickly. "Show us a sign, if you are the Messiah! Save yourself! Come down from the cross. Would God let His Son be crucified? His death is proof of his blasphemy!"

Judas shuddered at the words. It was the same reasoning he had used to convince himself to betray his master and friend. *If Jesus is the Messiah, God will save him.* Hearing the same words spit at his suffering lord with such vitriol was a cruel dagger to his heart. Yet, the question was a legitimate one: How could God allow this? He would not let His Holy One see corruption— *would He?* Was God finally giving up on His people who had rejected Him at every turn? Was that even possible? Yes, the prophecies always hinted at the possibility of such a dreadful outcome. Even the priests had condemned themselves in Jesus's parable about the vineyard. Jesus had asked them to their faces what would happen when the servants killed the master's son, and they had answered that the father would miserably destroy the wicked men. They had pronounced their own doom. But the son still died...

Judas had reached the end of his endurance. Hearing his own empty rationalizations spat back at his master and friend snapped the final thread holding his shattered hopes together. His hope imploded, crushed by the dreadful weight of his own guilt. He had gambled the very fate of Israel on the grace of the Almighty and lost. God was not coming to save His Son.

Judas fled from the awful scene, staggering down the low hill in a daze of misery. He saw John moving up the hill toward him, dressed in his spare clothes and leading Jesus's mother by the hand. Judas reeled back at the sight, not daring to pass them for fear of seeing the pain of betrayal in their eyes. He could not face them. He let his *tallith* hide his face as he quickly spun away, letting them pass.

Judas broke into a run, fleeing desperately from the guilt and impending doom which followed his every step. He could not escape it, but if he ran fast enough, perhaps he could outlast it—for a time.

For research notes, see chapter 54 in the reference section.

LV

Judas ran. He ran for miles, away from the city and surrounding farms and villages and into the wilderness, until he could run no more, until the hate and loathing he felt toward himself and the Sanhedrin had finally burned up in his hopeless flight from his relentless doom. The coals still burned hot, but his exhaustion kept them from consuming him completely. Finally, he was alone. He could put away the cruel taunts and the awful screams of the damned and pretend they did not exist.

He lay against the hard ground, gasping for air, feeling nothing but his own emptiness. He was alone. He ached for someone to tell him that everything would be alright—that what he had done had not doomed Israel, that there was still hope—but he knew better. There was no one to help him, nowhere to turn. The disciples would never accept him back into their company, and rightly so. He did not blame them. His betrayal had cut them all through the heart, and it was a mortal wound. They would hate him, and he should be hated. Any friend of Jesus would loathe him for the traitor he was. The Sanhedrin had nothing but disdain for him. They had used him, and now that they had taken what they wanted, they would hate him as they did his master.

He could not return to his father. He knew Simon too well; his father would only smile deviously and remind Judas in cool terms that if Jesus died, it simply meant that he was not the promised Messiah, and betraying him into the hands of the Sanhedrin was simply eliminating another false Christ. Judas knew better. No amount of careful logic would ever convince him otherwise. He knew better. His father knew better also, but his father had more practice at lying to himself. Judas could not pretend that Jesus was anything other than the Promised One: *The* Promised One. The *only* begotten Son. There would not be another. The only Son of God was slowly dying, leaving Israel to their chosen fate, as God's mercy finally reached its end. No amount of clever rhetoric would ever convince him otherwise.

Yet, Jesus was *still alive*. God often worked by the thinnest of margins. He saved at the last possible second, when all hope was lost. He had let Pharaoh's army pin Moses and the Israelites between impassible mountains and an impassible sea. He had saved the three Hebrews only *after* they were thrown into the furnace. The absolute silence of the wilderness calmed his fevered thoughts, and hope glimmered again in his chest. The wilderness reminded him of John the dunkard, who was dead but still offered up his wilderness as a place of refuge. When languishing in prison, John had sent his disciples to ask if Jesus was the Messiah or if they should look for another. Jesus had simply told them to watch. He had healed many that day.

Jesus had not answered John's disciples. He had merely displayed his power. Why could he not display his power now? Still, others were working on his behalf. Joseph was speaking to Pilate. Despite Pilate's cowardly escape from the prosecution, there was a slim chance that he might still be convinced to intervene. Even so, Jesus was dreadfully wounded. The lashes would take a long time to kill him, but the end was certain without some miracle. Jesus had healed so many yet could not heal himself.

But Jesus did not keep his power for himself. He had bestowed it on others. Another could do what Jesus could not. Others could work on his behalf. There was a chance. Judas shakily stood to his feet and summoned anew a desperate energy, fueled by one single droplet of hope which momentarily cooled the inferno of dread. Jesus had given power to his ordained twelve. Judas was still a part of that number, whether he deserved it or not. He hoped he was. Jesus would not save himself. He was waiting to see if anyone came to his rescue. He was the Chosen One, yet his chosen had rejected him. None helped him. But Judas would help him. Even if his betrayal had severed his connection to the Messiah, there were other disciples. He had seen John at the cross. If Judas had lost his power to heal, he would convince John. Together, they could save their Messiah. If they healed their master, others would follow. Jesus would respond. He always responded to acts of faith. Like Caleb and Joshua of old, he and John could turn the tide and save Israel from rejecting what had been promised her. There was still hope for Israel. Her Messiah still lived.

Judas broke into a run. This time, it was not fear that drove him, but a renewed hope, more desperate than the last and more urgent. It was all he had, but it was enough. It had to be. His feet rushed over the jagged ground. He slipped on a patch of loose rock and fell, tearing his hands, but he felt nothing. There was too much at risk, and the slimmest thread of hope drove him onward. It was possible.

With every step, hope burned a little brighter. After seeing his hopes dashed to pieces time and time again, he had hope. He had a plan. There was a way to fix this. He kept moving. Another stone caught his foot, and he went down, smacking his head against a boulder. Everything went black.

For a moment, he thought he had passed out, but he still felt his body. He was blind. As he groped in the sudden darkness, his eyes adjusted enough to see his hands as he held them to his face. He was not blind; the world had gone dark. God had abandoned Israel and struck the sun. The thought thrust a new stab of terror into Judas's already battered mind. He pushed it down. Jesus was not dead. It was unthinkable for a man to die so suddenly on a cross. Crucifixion often took days to finally snuff out the life of the sufferer.

Judas had to see for himself. If there was the slimmest chance to save his master, he must try. He pushed on, fumbling stupidly in the darkness, feeling his way inch by inch. He knew he had to be close. He kept going, one careful step in front of the other for what seemed like hours, until he finally heard the sound of people: cries of terror and agony. It was a relief. At least he was not the only one trapped in this darkness. He had thought that God had cursed him for his betrayal, but no, he was not alone in his misery. The darkness had struck everyone. It was cold comfort. God had cursed Israel.

He pressed on. Finally, his reaching hands struck a long wall of rock. It must be Jerusalem. He used it as a guide, feeling his way until he felt a gate at an inside corner. There was only one gate like that on this side of Jerusalem: Gennath Gate, near the three towers. He must be close. Skull Hill was not far from the city. He nearly fell headlong into Amygdalos Pool on his way to the crucifixion site. He passed others now, feeling their way through the terrible darkness, trying to find their way back to the city. Judas pushed past them.

He paused on the road, unable to see where the trail leading up the hill connected to the roadway. He groped along the ground in despair. Someone tripped over him as he felt the roadway, trying to discover the path from touch alone. The man grunted as he struck the ground and released an angry curse. Judas thought he recognized the voice of Caiaphas, but he couldn't be sure.

Suddenly, a loud voice exploded over the blackness. Judas knew that voice. Jesus's words were filled with desperate misery as he cried out in despair. "God! My God! Why have you abandoned me?" He spoke in Hebrew, rather than Aramaic, the common tongue. Hebrew was the language of scholars—the language of priests. Judas shuddered. If even God had abandoned His own Son... Judas could not think of that. He followed the voice, using it to direct him. He found the path leading up the hill and crawled up it, feeling his way by touch and memory.

His hands reached a rough wooden post, and he groped up it, feeling for the man above him. He touched the feet, and felt the spike driven into them. The man above moaned in surprise and fear. It was not Jesus. Judas moved on, feeling for the next cross. He heard Jesus speak again.

"It's over," the sufferer said weakly. The words struck Judas with physical force, throwing him to the ground as the words in Gethsemane had done. The earth reeled under him.

First the sky, and now the earth itself shuddered at the horror which Israel had thrown upon her Messiah. The ground trembled under him like a rolling sea, and loud cracks broke the stillness as rocks exploded or were ripped to pieces under the terrible pressure. Judas gripped the cross in terror as the earth tore itself apart. It was the end; he was sure of it. First the sky and now the earth. God was abandoning them, and the earth would not survive it.

Then, as quickly as it had started, the violence stopped. The earth quieted, and the sky slowly opened to reveal blue heavens beyond the once impenetrable clouds. Judas gasped. It must be a sign. There was still a chance. He reached up, pressing his hand against the broken feet nailed to the cruel tree. He willed life into them with his every fiber, as he had done with his father, believing desperately.

Nothing.

Reluctantly, he forced his eyes upward to look at the battered and bloody body of his master. The corpse hung lifelessly from the nails. The breath was gone. Jesus was dead. And with his death, all the healing power he had given to his disciples was gone as well. Judas was too late. He had failed. In everything, he had failed. The Messiah was dead, and with him died all hope for Israel. Judas felt his final hopes crumble to ash as the horrible truth finally crushed him.

God's only Son was dead.

Judas had doomed them all.

For research notes, see chapter 55 in the reference section.

LVI

J udas had failed. Israel was doomed. Her Messiah was dead. She had no one to blame but herself. Judas felt no personal guilt for his nation's fate, but for his friend's... He had betrayed his friend—all his friends—and no matter the reason, it was unthinkable. There was no solution. Nothing he could do would ever change the devastation he had caused. All he could do was balance the scales. A life for a life. When hope died, only Law remained.

He temporarily pushed that out of his mind. First, he must reach the Temple. The pouch of silver weighed heavily on him. Thirty Tyrian shekels were easily carried, but these were stained with the blood of his master and the weight of the life they had so cheaply purchased. He must return the silver. He would have no need of it soon enough.

He was a traitor, and so he would be remembered. He could accept that. He was a thief, and so his history proved. He had betrayed his master into the hands of his enemies. He had murdered his friend. All was true. But his motives had been sincere. He had gambled and lost—lost horribly. Lost everything. But he had not done so from *greed*. The idea was revolting. Judas knew if he kept the silver, others would see it as the sole reason for his betrayal. He could endure being known as a thief and a traitor—for all that was true—but to be seen as a man who would betray his friend for *money*—for thirty pitiful silver pieces... No, that was unjust, and that was more than he could endure.

He reached the Temple Mount almost without knowing it, until his feet left the stone steps, and he looked at the wide plateau where Jesus had taught only yesterday—where Jesus would never teach again. There was no crowd today. A few people lingered, but the courtyard was practically empty. He turned back toward the Royal Stoa on his left, where the Sanhedrin held council, but it was also empty.

It was only then that he recalled the day: Passover. The holiday had been forgotten in the madness of the last hours. It seemed an entire lifetime ago that he had sat down to eat the Passover meal with all his friends. He had seen John at the cross with Jesus's mother, but the others had scattered. He wondered what would become of them now that their master was dead. They would return to their lives, perhaps, if they could—if life would even be possible after this.

It was afternoon, strange as it seemed. The hours of darkness had thrown the day upon its head. The Temple appeared undamaged from the massive earthquake that had struck the moment Jesus died. The Temple stood firm, but Judas had noticed several houses in Jerusalem that would need a carpenter. Israel would be short one carpenter from now on.

He entered the Treasury and saw a small group of people gathered to witness the sacrifice of the official Passover lamb which Caiaphas had brought from Bethphage less than a week ago. Jesus had stolen his crowd that day and again today. So many people had known of Jesus that news of his crucifixion had drawn away the entire city. Only the most pious of Jews were here to witness the Passover sacrifice. Even in death, Jesus drew a crowd.

There was something odd about the scant crowd. In his feverish state of mind, Judas struggled to find the reason. Men spoke in quiet huddles, muttering. Judas finally saw Caiaphas and his troupe speaking quietly with troubled expressions. It should have been time for the ceremony, but the lamb was nowhere in sight.

Distracted from his quest by this strange occurrence, Judas pulled aside a priest he was sure would not recognize him. "What's going on?" he asked quietly, matching the hushed voices of the other men.

The priest turned to him with a horrified stare and lifted an arm, pointing toward the Temple. Judas looked. It stood tall, towering over Judea from the Temple Mount as it always did. Judas had feared that Jesus's prediction of the Temple's destruction had been fulfilled at his death when the earth shook so terribly, but the Temple stood as immovable as ever. Except... the interior looked... odd. There was something... Judas gasped.

"The Glory is gone," the priest said.

The massive curtain which closed off the Holy of Holies from all but the high priest had torn in half, exposing the most sacred of places for all eyes to see. The place of God's dwelling was empty. God lived among men no longer. Today was the final day. The Jews had rejected their Messiah, and their God had abandoned them.

The prediction had come true. Judas's gut clenched as the horrible reality finally struck him. God had lived among his people for thousands of years, and in one fatal day, all was lost.

"You! What are you doing here?!" a harsh voice demanded. Judas turned to see that Caiaphas had spotted him. The high priest approached, dressed in his official robes and followed by his official sycophants. "You cannot be here!" he snapped. "You entered Pilate's hall; you are unclean!"

Judas angrily stalked toward him, causing the high priest to draw back. "I *am* unclean!" he cried. "Inside and out! I betrayed an innocent man. His blood is on *my* hands! I'm here to confess. And return the money."

He held out the money bag. Caiaphas eyed it skeptically but refused to extend a hand. It was blood money. Touching it would make Caiaphas unclean. The irony was lost on him. Caiaphas grimaced. "The few remaining Passover lambs escaped and fled during the earthquake." He smiled cruelly. "So if you come seeking a sacrifice, we cannot help you. If you feel as if *you* have done something sinful," he said, clearly displaying the lack of guilt on his own conscience, "you'll just have to make do on your own."

Judas felt a wave of anger wash over him at this cold dismissal. He didn't know what he had expected. "As will you," Judas said coldly. He pointed to the empty Temple. "Your house is abandoned." He threw the money at Caiaphas's feet. The bag burst, and the silver scattered over the stones in tragic memory of the man who had thrown aside the tables of the money changers and scattered the silver here before—the same man who now hung lifelessly outside the city. Judas abandoned it, leaving the blood money with Caiaphas along with a bitter glare of hopeless anger.

"Don't return until you've brought a proper sacrifice!" the high priest called after him.

Judas ignored him. He left through the Shushan Gate without a second glance. There was no salvation to be found in this Temple—not anymore. Jesus had saved so many, but no one else had the power to restore life. The Savior had none to save him. The Life Giver's life had been taken. Judas could do nothing for Israel or for his friends. They were all on their own—every one of them. The servants had killed the master's son. Their final advocate was dead.

Judas knew he bore the most guilt. His senseless meddling had destroyed Israel's last hope. When a man failed as miserably as Judas had, thrown away all shred of honor, and knew he deserved death, there was but one remedy. The only honorable solution was to remove the problem. Judas was that problem.

Roman generals who failed in their duty would throw themselves on their swords as a last, desperate act of honor. It was a Roman tradition that heralded back to ancient times. Judas had no sword, but he was no soldier. He could not live with his guilt, but he could still leave on his own terms. He could balance the scales. When hope died, the Law remained. After a life of trickery and failure, his final act could be one of honor. He abandoned the

Temple. There was no reason to return; God had abandoned it also. Judas had one final destination. He followed the path he had taken with Jesus and the other disciples countless times. His steps were heavy but solid. He could see his destination now.

It was a large tree with thick, spreading branches that had once provided ample shade. The tree still had a few shriveled leaves clinging to dead limbs, but these were in stark contrast to the vibrantly green fig tree it had been only a week ago, before Jesus cursed it. It was a fitting destination. In a single day, the life had gone, and the tree now stood lifeless. It had failed to offer any help to its Messiah, and so its Messiah had left it to die, cursed and abandoned.

The tree had simply neglected to provide figs. Judas had betrayed his master and brought death to his nation. He was doubly cursed. He found a low branch and pulled himself up. He was not a particularly strong or agile man, but he managed. He found a sturdy limb high enough from the ground to suit his purpose and jumped on it, testing its strength. This must be done right. He could not live to see another failure. He must do this one last thing right.

Slowly, he undid his belt. It was a long cloth braid, tied double, and strong enough to hold his weight. Careful to keep his balance on the limb, he slowly wrapped his belt around it and tied a strong knot. He fitted the other end into a noose and placed it over his head. There was just enough slack to allow him to sit on the limb with the rope snug around his neck. He tested the rope again to be sure. He had to be sure. His final act would be done right. He deserved death. He deserved a *worse* death, but he had no cross or sword. He had this rope, and it was enough. He would see justice done. He would cling to this last shred of honor. It was the last desperate act of a hopeless man. There was no gamble in this. He would not fail again.

He dropped from the limb.

For research notes, see chapter 56 in the reference section.

Epilogue

It started with the sound of an earthquake, an earthquake made of brass. A sound so deep and terrible that there was nothing else, only the deep tones of an infinite trumpet, vibrating in a perfect, dreadful harmony which shook the very atoms into motion. The trumpet expanded into a violent, inescapable symphony that should have shattered the earth and heavens, but instead of shaking them apart, it shook them together. They fell into place, melting together with the heat of a thousand suns.

The heat was unbearable. It exploded over him with awful intensity, filling his lungs with searing breath that rushed wildly to every fiber, burning with a hot, blinding glow. His eyes could not take the brightness, and he threw a hand over his face to hide himself from the source of that terrible light.

Judas stood on an unfamiliar hill, surrounded by nothing. The ground was scorched clean but burning still. Nothing grew here, except that overwhelming sound of countless trumpets that pulsed through every fiber of his being and continued onward toward an unimaginable crescendo. Finally, the burning flames eased enough that he could look for the source of the scourging light. He saw that he was not alone on this dreadful hill. Others were here, enduring the same bewildering shock. His eyes turned upward, squinting at the terrible brightness, and a new horror burst upon him.

He was alive.

He was different—strikingly different—but Judas knew him instantly. Jesus sat upon a glowing steed that shone with a white brilliance overcome only by the blinding light of its rider. The creature, which Judas could only describe as a horse, stood upon the air as easily as the ground and rushed with frightening speed toward the burning earth below.

He was alive.

The thought sent a thrill through Judas even as he realized the doom awaiting him. Jesus had returned, but gone was the humble Galilean. Jesus glowed with holy radiance. From his mouth exploded a hot beam of light so intense that it appeared a solid blade, and his eyes... his eyes burned with the fire Judas remembered so well, only far hotter—a thousand times hotter, and hotter still. An unquenchable fire that nothing could stop. It was the fire Judas had dreamed of and which now terrified him to the utmost. Jesus was here to conquer, and he *would* conquer. Judas's wish had finally been realized, but too late.

Jesus was not alone. Legions of angels surrounded him, glowing in incomprehensible patterns too glorious for the eye to process, but that was not all. There were others with him, shining men who rode on steeds of similar form and power. Judas knew that he might have been among them once, but it was too late.

Jesus's burning gaze caught Judas in its consuming light, and he shrank back, not daring to meet the terrible face which he knew so well. Jesus spun his mount, and the creature whirled with impossible grace, aiming straight for the traitor. Judas froze, not that it mattered. He knew he could never hope to outrun this supernatural steed, a far cry from the simple donkey Jesus had ridden before. There was no escape. He collapsed to his knees as terror washed over him. The King of Kings was coming for war.

The white-hot steed floated to a halt, hovering slightly above the ground, and the Son of Man dismounted, landing lightly in a burst of flame and light. He was dressed in shining clothes of glowing white, but the hem was soaked in blood. He watched Judas with glowing eyes. The burning gaze Judas had wished to see for so long now blazed with eternal fire, searing him to his very soul. Judas cowered, wishing for an earthquake to bury him and hide him from the dreadful light.

If Judas had ever doubted Jesus's divinity, it was inescapable now. Even his hair burned white with the glowing fire that washed over him and exploded from inside, lighting his eyes and mouth with even greater brilliance. Judas did not dare look at the holy face, and his eyes dropped to the hands, magnificent and horrible in their own right. Light exploded from jagged holes in each wrist. Jesus still carried the scars from his crucifixion. It was all the proof and more of Judas's guilt; his actions had caused those wounds.

Jesus paused a few feet from his treasonous disciple, watching him with those terrible eyes. Judas waited in agony for the dreadful blow, knowing that no punishment, however terrible, would ever compare to the horrible guilt he could never escape. He wished for the blow that would end his torment. None came.

"Hello, Judas." The voice was the same in some ways. Judas knew it as he knew his own, but it pulsed with energy. It was one voice and a thousand voices all speaking in absolute harmony. It was the voice of perfection—searing perfection. It was terrifying.

Judas cowered on the ground, waiting for the end, wishing for oblivion. The moments dragged on, and his spirit returned enough that he dared raise his head. Jesus still stood above him, radiating light and power. Judas could endure the interminable dread no longer. "We both know what I deserve," he said, his voice sounding cruel and harsh in his ears. It clashed against the perfect voice, breaking the harmony. "Do as you wish." He waited without resistance. Whatever fury the Son of God would unleash, he deserved it all and more.

"I will." The voice was filled with power, yet calm. Unyielding as granite, and as heavy. The voice could crush him with a single word. "Stand and face your king."

The command was impossible to resist. It forced Judas to his feet, though he ached for escape. He should not be here. His guilt and sin crushed him, pressing him into the ground, screaming for escape, but the voice of his king was impossible to disobey. Slowly, painfully, he raised his eyes to meet those of the man he had betrayed. They burned with eternal fire, but not so terribly as to overwhelm their expression. Judas was prepared for the fury he would find there. He had accepted his guilt and would face the consequences. He met the eyes and shrank back in horror. He had prepared for wrath but found tears.

The effect terrified him, and he froze, staring with indescribable confusion at the look of absolute pity.

Jesus smiled sadly, watching his evil disciple with unsearchable compassion. "I missed you," he said, his voice filled with longing for a lost friend. "There's so much you've missed, so much you would have done. The impact you would have had..." He shook his head in disappointment. "But I have found you now. That is what matters." His sad smile filled with pride.

Judas paled. "No," he said, shrinking back. He was familiar with Jesus's compassion; Jesus had interceded from the cross for those who had nailed him to it. The man was mad with it. Judas knew what Jesus was trying to do. "No, you can't do this!" he cried. "Not after what I've done."

"This isn't about what *you've* done, Judas," Jesus replied. "It's about what *I've* done."

"You were *dead*," Judas said in disbelief. "How...?"

Jesus cracked a familiar smile. "I'll tell you the whole story. Come with me."

Judas caught himself falling into their familiar camaraderie but fought it off. "No!" he said again. He had blood on his hands. He would not allow himself to get away with it. "I *murdered* you! Don't you see? I'm not part of your group! I'm a traitor. *I'm the enemy.* You can't save me—I don't deserve it!"

"I know you don't deserve it," Jesus said, knitting his brows. "So what? I don't save people because they *deserve* it. I save them because they *need* it."

It was strange, seeing such normal expressions coming from the glow-ing deity before him, but Judas's mind was not on such trivial matters.

"You should be with your disciples!" he cried. "Not some traitor! If you're tracking down a traitor, it should be to kill him—not save him!"

"The Good Shepherd leaves the ninety-nine to—"

"Shut up!" Judas shouted, clutching his head. "I'm not one of your sheep!" He paused, staring miserably at the man who still carried the scars of his death upon his glorified body. "*I'm the wolf.* I only steal, kill, and destroy. It's who I am!"

"That's not true," Jesus said in total denial. "You may have sold me to the wolves, but you are not one. You trusted too much in your own judgment when you should have trusted me! Yes, you made a terrible, painful mistake, but you are no wolf. Only terribly, desperately lost."

"Don't deny it!" Judas snapped. "I stole from Joseph—I stole from *you!* You didn't know, but I did. I *wanted* you to stone Mary! I wanted you to kill her to appease Annas! I'm not like you!" He retreated a step, shaking his head. "I can't do it. I can't be like you." His eyes watered, and the dazzling man before him blurred into a thousand beams of light. "I can't."

He had to escape. He could endure anger, rage, revenge, but this... The goodness was overwhelming—terrifying. He was beyond help. His actions were unforgivable.

"I know you can't," Jesus said, his voice full of sympathy. "That's why I came. The Good Shepherd—"

"I *know!*" Judas snapped, still retreating. "Please," he said, now begging. "Please just leave. I don't want you here." He only wanted to be alone with his misery. He deserved that. He could endure that. He could not endure this. "I can't be here. I murdered you! And your Father... I murdered His *Son!* Do you not understand how He must hate me? *I murdered His Son!*"

"My Father loves you more than I!" Jesus cried.

"Prove it!" Judas shrieked in agony.

Jesus threw his hands wide in desperation. "He sent me!" he cried, rushing for his lost disciple.

Judas fled, but the hands which still bore the holes from the evil nails caught him up and trapped him in a terrible embrace. The fabric of Jesus's robe glowed faintly, illuminated by the impossibly bright light from within. Judas did not dare look at the face as the two strong arms enveloped him.

"Let me go," he begged pitifully, straining futilely against the immovable arms.

"I won't let you go," the voice said, filled with undeserved sympathy.

"I knew who you were!" Judas said, his anger returning. "I *knew who you were!* And I *still* sent you to die! To betray a friend is unforgivable, but to betray *you*... No one can forgive what I've done."

"*I can.*"

Something broke inside him. Judas collapsed, bursting into gut-wrenching sobs. This terrible, unrelenting mercy. He could not comprehend it. It was unthinkable. It was indomitable.

"I've waited so long for this," Jesus said quietly.

Judas broke completely. Finally, he gave up. Faced with such unstoppable grace, he could do nothing else.

"Please, let me go," he moaned, still clinging to his misery like a shipwrecked sailor to the last piece of his broken vessel that he had dashed willfully against the rocks. There was nothing left, but it was all he had. He did not deserve rescue, but it was here all the same.

Jesus chuckled slightly. "Not until you bless me."

"I don't deserve this," he said feebly, even as he clutched the glowing robes with desperate fingers. "It should be *me* begging *you!* Not the other way around!"

"That thought did cross my mind," Jesus replied. "But that's not always how it works."

Finally, Judas pulled back, staring his master in the face with uncomprehending misery. "*Why?* Why me?"

"Lost sheep do not come to us, Judas. We must go to them. I told you that before."

"I don't understand," Judas replied. "How can you do this? For someone like me? You know what I deserve!"

"Why did the father wait every day for his prodigal son to return? It was not because the son was *worthy*. It was because he was lost—and because he was loved. *This* is my kingdom, Judas," he said, eyes glowing brighter. "Let me show you."

"You don't want me there," Judas protested.

"Oh, but I do," Jesus said firmly. "More than anything. Besides, I have a job only you can do."

Judas scoffed. "*Me?*" he asked skeptically.

Jesus nodded. "You are not the only lost son, Judas. There are many others like you. Others who died without hope—who have done unforgivable things. Sons and daughters of perdition. Lost sheep. They will not come to us."

"*You* want *my* help?" Judas asked again, still disbelieving, though the brilliant firelight in Jesus's eyes had finally ignited a tiny spark of long-dead hope.

"*Desperately.*"

Judas could find no words. "I don't know what to say," he said, half-laughing and half-crying, unable to find an emotion capable of expressing his feelings. "What will the others think? You are clearly insane, but James, Thad... Nathan? What will you tell them?"

Jesus smiled.

"I will tell them to celebrate, for I have found my lost sheep. I will tell them that my son was dead, and is alive again. He was lost, and is found."

"Are you really sure about this?" Judas asked, still unable to fully believe the hope that continued to burn brighter every moment.

Jesus lifted his nail-pierced hands. "Dead sure."

Judas laughed in disbelief. "You haven't changed a bit, have you?"

Jesus smiled. "'The same, yesterday, and today, and forever,' to quote your replacement."

Judas gave his redeemer a strange look. "My replacement?"

Jesus shrugged. "Someone had to pick up your slack. You'll meet him. You've missed a lot. I'll fill you in on the way to the banquet. Are you hungry?"

He was, strangely. "Famished."

Jesus wrapped his arm around his betrayer's shoulders. "Good. I've been craving a glass of wine for a *very* long time."

"I..." Judas began, feeling the broken pieces finally growing together as he spoke with his familiar friend. An apology was senseless. No words of gratitude were capable of expressing the infinite thanks he could never begin to comprehend. He did not have to beg. He was already forgiven. The grace was already there, waiting only for him to accept. "I've missed you, too," he said raggedly. It was all he needed to say. "What happens now?"

"We rebuild."

"Rebuild Jerusalem?" Judas asked.

Jesus shook His head. "Think bigger."

"The Promised Land?"

Jesus's smile grew into a wide grin, showing blindingly white teeth, and his already glowing eyes sparkled with uncontrollable excitement. "The universe."

For research notes, see the 'epilogue' in the reference section.

Thank you so much for supporting my endeavors to be a full-time novelist.

As an indie author, book reviews are absolutely essential. Reviews let other readers know which books are worth their time (and which aren't). Books with lots of reviews also get more advertisement time from website algorithms, so taking a few minutes to post a short review on Amazon (and elsewhere) is THE BEST way to make sure I can keep sharing stories with the world. Each and every review is greatly appreciated, and helps me continue doing what I love.

Thank you.

You can contact me or purchase books straight from the printing press (where I get a considerably larger percentage of sales) on my website at:

www.traitorbooks.com

References

Part 1 Reference Section

Chapter 1

As infamous as his name has become, almost nothing is known about the early life of Judas Iscariot. The same is true of all the figures from the New Testament. To blend these few facts into a convincing story, much of it must be based in assumption or simple imagination, but always with care to make it as reasonable and believable as possible. Although it is unlikely that Judas worked for Joseph of Arimathaea, it is plausible. As the appointed keeper of the money for the disciples (John 13:29), it is likely that Judas had experience as an accountant, so it is possible that he worked as a steward for a rich landowner like Joseph of Arimathaea.

Back to chapter.

Chapter 2

It is possible that many of Jesus's parables were based on real events and people. There is no evidence to indicate that the parable of the Unjust Steward, recorded in Luke 16:1–13, was based on the history of Judas Iscariot, but placing Judas in the story brings realism to both the parable and the characters of Judas and Joseph of Arimathaea while also keeping it solidly based in scripture.

Back to chapter.

Chapter 3

Some may balk at the idea that Jesus would even owe any debt, let alone that he would let Judas erase it without his master's consent. Some might even say that Jesus was complicit in the act, since he allowed Judas to escape. Although it is certain that Jesus would never lie on anyone's behalf, it is not unprecedented for Jesus to allow things that others considered sinful. And just because Jesus allowed the swindle does not mean he condoned it. The conversation between Jesus and Joseph is left to the reader's imagination, since this book is focused on Judas's perspective, but some hints about the conversation will be seen in chapter 10 and show that Jesus was not complicit in any deceit.

Back to chapter.

Chapter 4

Chapters 4–10 are based on the account in John 1:19–40. The Gospel of John does not name the other disciple who was with Andrew when they first saw Jesus, though it can be narrowed down some by process of elimination. We can be certain that it was not Simon Peter, Philip, Nathanael, or Matthew, who did not meet Jesus until later. Most scholars believe it to be John, but this is not directly stated. Though it was most likely a fellow Galilean traveling with Andrew, and not even one of the twelve, the possibility remains that it could have been Judas.

Back to chapter.

Chapter 5

According to Rabbinical tradition, men could not become teachers until thirty years of age. Since John was born six months earlier than Jesus (Luke 1:24–26), it is likely that his ministry started in the spring of 27 AD, six months before the start of Jesus's ministry in the early fall. This timetable also matches the four Gospel accounts.

Back to chapter.

Chapter 6

The character of Herod in the four Gospels is a bit confusing at first glance. Herod the Great was the first Herod: the same Herod who met the wise men on their way to Bethlehem and who later murdered all the male babies in that city, as recorded in Matthew 2. It was he who rebuilt and expanded the Temple of Jesus's day (known as Herod's Temple). Herod the Great had several sons, three of whom he killed, fearing a coup. These were Antipater, Alexander, and Aristobulus. His surviving sons included Herod Antipas, who ruled Galilee; Herod Archelaus, who ruled Judea until 6 AD when he was deposed by Rome for misconduct and replaced by Pilate as the Roman governor; and Herod Philip, who ruled Ituraea (Not to be confused with the disciple, also named Philip). It was Herod Philip's wife, Herodias, whom Herod Antipas stole, and which led to the terrible events with Herodias's daughter (Antipas's niece), Salome, as recorded in Matthew 14 and Mark 6. In the four Gospels, "Herod" is used for both Herod the Great, who reigned during the time of Jesus' birth, and Herod Antipas, who reigned during Jesus's adult life.

Back to chapter.

Chapter 7

Like Americans today, the beliefs of the Jewish people ran the gamut from the extremely conservative to the very liberal, but the three prominent philosophies were the Pharisees, Sadducees, and Essenes. One can make a loose comparison between Pharisees and modern conservatives, Sadducees with liberals, and Essenes with ultra-conservative outliers like the Amish and the doomsday preppers. Essenes were rarely seen and stayed to themselves, believing all other Jews to be corrupted by pagan culture. Pharisees desired a return to traditional values and were popular in rural communities. Often, they were seen as the ideal Jew. They kept the Law strictly and harshly judged any who failed to uphold their standards.

Sadducees held sway in large cities like Jerusalem, were often rich and influential, and saw the Law as merely a loose guideline which they could bend for personal gain. They often rubbed shoulders with the pagan Greek and Roman elites and worked to minimize or erase completely the dividing lines between Jew and Gentile. Essenes are not mentioned in the four Gospels, but Jesus made enemies on both sides of the Jewish political spectrum, condemning the false ideas of both with equal vigor. If we dare to follow His example, we will likely also receive hatred from both sides.

Back to chapter.

Chapter 8

The phrase "go the extra mile" comes from an ancient Roman law which Jesus alludes to in Matthew 5:41. Today, we see this as merely meaning to do more than is expected, but in ancient times, this phrase had a far harder meaning. To put this in perspective, imagine Jesus telling a Jew from the 1940s that when a Nazi Gestapo officer demands they carry his supplies and ammunition, the Jew was not to resist, but to carry these articles of war even further than necessary.

The Romans were an occupying force of enemy soldiers, hated by the Jews. The only group of people who invoke such a reaction today are the Nazis. The revulsion and shock this message would have brought only comes into perspective when compared to Nazi Germany. The idea that a Jew was to carry the very weapons their enemies used to oppress them was repulsive beyond measure, and Jesus's message that they should carry these weapons even further than absolutely necessary would have been received with horror. Yet such was the message of our Messiah. It is unlikely His message would receive any better reception today.

Back to chapter.

Chapter 9

The scripture which predicted, or at least inspired, John the Baptist's ministry comes from Isaiah 40, written seven hundred years before his life began. We can safely assume that John the Baptist, who was the son of a priest, was extremely well-educated, and came from a family that was, if not wealthy, at least not poor. This means that his odd wardrobe and habits were likely intentionally used to summon the imagery of an ancient prophet. Isaiah 40 is an excellent chapter to summarize John's ministry, both visually and as a call to repentance in the face of a Holy God. Interestingly, Isaiah 40:15 is also where the common phrase "drop in a bucket" originated and is still in common usage twenty-seven hundred years later.

Back to chapter.

Chapter 10

Since Andrew and his companion met Jesus directly after his forty days of fasting in the wilderness, it is certain that Jesus would have appeared emaciated. This reconciles the account of John 1 with the account of Matthew 3 and Mark 1. As usual, John's Gospel fills in a few details which the other Gospels neglect to add, clarifying what might otherwise appear as contradictory accounts. The fact that the four Gospels sometimes disagree on minor details is often used as evidence of their unreliability, but is ironically one of the greatest proofs of their authenticity. In fact, all truthful eyewitness accounts are contradictory, as any police detective will readily confirm. If the Gospels agreed on every particular, skeptics would be just as quick to point out (and rightly so) how impossible it is for genuine witness accounts to be identical.

Back to chapter.

Chapter 11

The *Sicarii* were the silent fourth philosophy of Jewish politics. They could be called terrorists or freedom fighters depending on your perspective. They focused mostly on silent assassinations of Roman political figures and influential Roman sympathizers. Although the *Sicarii* are not mentioned by name in the Gospel accounts and did not become a widely known force until after the life of Jesus, it is plausible that they formed far earlier and kept hidden until they had attained the support and numbers necessary to fight in the open. It was mostly their attacks which prompted the destruction of Jerusalem by Titus and his army in 70AD. After the destruction of Jerusalem, the last of the *Sicarii* took refuge in Herod's fortress, Masada. When the Romans finally breached the walls of Masada, the *Sicarii* had all committed suicide, preferring a quick death rather than falling into the hands of the Romans for crucifixion.

Back to chapter.

Chapter 12

The text which Judas recalls in chapter 12 comes from Isaiah 7:14, the context of which is a conversation between Isaiah and King Ahaz, the great-great-great-grandson of the infamous King Ahab. Ahaz is offered the opportunity to pick any sign he wants to prove the truth of the prophet's words, but Ahaz declines, not wishing to tempt God (unlike the Pharisees, who constantly demanded signs from Jesus). God responds by picking His own sign, mentioned in verse 14: "the virgin shall conceive and bear a Son, and shall call His name Immanuel." This beautiful name which God chose for His own Son means "God with us" and has been a popular name ever since. In the next chapter, God instructs Isaiah to name his son "Maher-shalal-hash-baz," which means "plunder speeds, spoil hastes" and has gained no popularity whatsoever. We feel your pain, Maher-shalal-hash-baz. We feel your pain.

Back to chapter.

Chapter 13

In 1st century times, a Roman soldier was paid one silver *denarius* per day. All coins were based on weight. Bronze coins were worth one eighth their weight in silver and were minted by local rulers, while silver coins were minted only by Caesar. The *denarius* was the lowest denomination of silver coins, and therefore the lowest denomination of coins bearing the likeness of Caesar. As the lowest, it was the most common coin bearing Caesar's likeness. This is why Jesus specifically asked for a *denarius* (called a penny in the KJV) in Matthew 22:15–22, Mark 12:13–17, and Luke 20:20–26.

The silver shekel was worth two *denarii*. The infamous "thirty pieces of silver" paid to Judas was likely paid in silver shekels. These thirty pieces would have been worth about sixty days' wages (based on fifteen dollars an hour and eight-hour days, this might have been worth about $7,500 today). One *denarius*, or half-shekel, was the cost for the yearly Temple tax which the collectors asked Peter about in Matthew 17:24–27, so the coin Peter found in the fish's mouth to pay for himself and Jesus would have also been a silver shekel.

Back to chapter.

Chapter 14

There is no record of exactly when or how Judas was called to be a disciple, possibly because Judas was already following Jesus when Matthew, Peter, and John were called. Given his plausible background, it is possible that Judas was a money changer and witnessed the first cleansing of the Temple, recorded in John 2:13–22.

There is some controversy over whether Jesus cleansed the Temple once or twice, since each Gospel account only records one cleansing. However, John places the cleansing near the beginning of Jesus's ministry and includes certain details which indicate that this was a separate event from the accounts of Matthew 21, Mark 11, and Luke 19, which all place the cleansing at the end of Jesus's ministry. It is probable that the first three writers did not feel the need to include both events, as similar as they were. John commonly included details that the other writers did not, while passing over that which had already been written. He places the Temple cleansing at the beginning of Jesus's ministry—totally separate from his account of the Triumphal Entry. This placement was likely intentional, indicating that these were two distinct events.

During the Temple cleansing, there were two policing forces at the Temple which Jesus would have needed to avoid: the Levites, which were Jews of priestly lineage and carried batons for ordinary policing matters within the Temple, and the Roman soldiers garrisoned at the Antonia Fortress. Records indicate that a legion of Roman soldiers was under the command of the Sanhedrin and remained near the Temple, likely in the Antonia Fortress, which was attached to the Temple's northwest corner, in case of riots or attacks from terrorist cells like the *Sicarii*.

Back to chapter.

Part 2 Reference Section

Chapter 15

There are several possible meanings for the name "Iscariot." It is far likelier to be a descriptive title rather than a familial surname, and one interpretation is "Man of Cities." It is impossible to say when Judas adopted this title, but since Judas is often considered the only disciple not from rural Galilee, it is possible that he was given this title by his less urbane peers to distinguish him from the other Apostle Judas (also called Thaddaeus Lebbaeus), hence his nickname in this book: City Boy.

The divisive reading which nearly got Jesus stoned in his hometown (as recorded in Luke 4:16–30 and specifically in verses 18–19) can be compared to Isaiah 61. Luke records Jesus's reading of Isaiah accurately for this very purpose. The city of Nazareth was extremely traditional and looked forward eagerly to the Messiah's destruction of Rome, as did many Jews of the time. For Jesus—a local carpenter—to claim this title while also deliberately skipping the vengeance against their enemies which they so fervently desired was a direct insult to everything they believed. Such a slap in the face, however innocent the words seem to us today, would have certainly been enough to cause the outrage which followed.

Back to chapter.

Chapter 16

Most scholars agree that Bartholomew (mentioned in Matthew, Mark, and Luke) and Nathanael (mentioned only in John) are the same person. "Bartholomew," a bastardization of "Bar-Tolmai," meaning "son of Tolmai" may or may not be connected to Talmai, King of Geshur, but it is a striking possibility. Other than what little is recorded in John 1, and a mention in John 21 that Nathanael did live in Cana, Nathanael's history is unknown to us. Artistic license is used here to give further significance to his calling. The events surrounding the Capernaum nobleman, however, are taken directly from the eyewitness account recorded in John 4.

Back to chapter.

Chapter 17

The calling of the four fishermen is recorded in Matthew 4, Mark 1, and Luke 5, while John's account skips over this event entirely. Matthew and Mark neglect to include the miracle of the fish, leaving Luke the only writer to record this event in its entirety. It is possible that Mark (which was likely taken from the eyewitness account of Peter) and John neglected to include the miracle out of humility or to avoid the accusation that they followed Jesus merely for personal gain. Matthew was not yet called when this miracle occurred and likely did not record it because he was not a witness to it. Luke saw fit to fill in the details of this important event and provide logical reasons behind why the disciples felt so compelled to give up their careers at the request of a perfect stranger.

It must be remembered that most Galileans were uncivilized blue-collar workers, in contrast to Judas's gentrified education. They were rough around the edges and had a penchant for coarse language. It is probable that some colorful words were borrowed from their Greek and Roman neighbors, as is common among linguistically diverse workmen, even today. So do not be surprised to find a smattering of Greek and Latin profanity in this book. In my defense, the Apostle Paul also uses Greek profanity in Philippians 3:8, and Jesus himself uses the feminine word "shūāl" to describe Herod in Luke 13:32: "Go ye, and tell that fox...". The context and cultural research both agree that this was an intentional insult. We have a similar insult in modern English based upon the term used for a female canine. Jesus also uses very insulting language throughout the Gospels, including fun terms like "generation of vipers," "whited sepulchers," and "you are of your father, the devil." Even though Christians should be careful in our language, perhaps there are times when coarse and even colorful honesty supersedes polite nicety.

Back to chapter.

Chapter 18

Like all melting pots, Judea was filled with people from other cultures: Greeks, Romans, and Samaritans, to name a few. Romans were polytheistic and often adopted the gods of the cultures they ruled to ensure peace with their subjects. Historical records show that some Romans kept the feast days and Sabbaths as the Jews did, while others even went so far as to denounce the gods of Rome and worship only the True God. These Gentiles were known as God-fearers and were welcomed in the outer court of the Temple. It is likely that the centurion mentioned in Matthew 8 and Luke 7 was such a man, especially since he funded the building of a synagogue in Capernaum. The Jews he ruled would have respected him, but he would still have been seen as an outsider. Even as a God-fearer, who kept the whole Law, he was still a gentile.

Back to chapter.

Chapter 19

The first known incident between Jesus and a demon is recorded in Mark 1:21–28 and Luke 4:33–37, and took place inside a Capernaum synagogue. These demons recognized Jesus instantly for who He truly was. It is often forgotten that these fallen angels were former coworkers of Jesus, and it is likely that they were once personal friends. Whether Jesus, as a mortal man, would have remembered them or not is a question which cannot be answered here, but they certainly recognized Him. We can also be certain that the same limitless love extended to fallen humanity is also extended to fallen angels, even though they refuse to accept it, for God *is* love.

Back to chapter.

Chapter 20

One point often repeated in the four Gospels, which is often lost in the retelling, is the vast number of people who constantly followed Jesus. We often see him depicted with twelve nondescript followers wearing nondescript beards and maybe a few hecklers—but this is not the picture the Bible paints. Mark 1:45 indicates that Jesus was so constantly swarmed that he could no longer visit any city, but had to hide in the wilderness, and people still came to him from everywhere. This level of fame is exhausting. It is likely that Jesus had precious little time to himself in the last three years of his life.

Back to chapter.

Chapter 21

Nain is a small village nearly twenty-five miles south of Capernaum. As with all genuine eyewitness accounts, the events recorded in the four Gospels do not match perfectly, and it is impossible to say how close together many of these miracles were, but Luke 7 records that Jesus arrived in Nain the day following the healing of the centurion's servant. If this date coincides with the events in Mark 1 and Matthew 8, it is safe to say that some extraordinary event must have driven Jesus to travel the twenty-five miles to Nain so early in the morning after such a long night of healing. Perhaps Jesus wished to escape the crowds or, as is imagined in this book, one of the disciples realized the level of exhaustion Jesus was enduring and tried to get him as far away as possible from the crowds in Capernaum. Whatever the case, we can be certain that the events recorded in the Gospels are accurate, even if the timeline is less certain.

Back to chapter.

Chapter 22

Leprosy was the most feared disease of the first century. Watching this first leper be healed was certainly a memorable event and is recorded in Matthew 8 and Mark 1. Luke chose to record an even more memorable event regarding ten lepers in Luke 17. Leprosy was highly contagious and terminal, and the response to it was mandatory social distancing and face covering. Jesus ignored the social distancing requirements of His day because He did not fear this disease. Likely knowing the censure He would receive from breaking these health and safety guidelines, He always cautioned the former lepers to not reveal how they had been healed. Even in the face of such miraculous healing, some still feared the disease more than they trusted the Healer.

Back to chapter.

Chapter 23

The calming of the storm is recorded in Mark 4:35–41 and Luke 8:22–25. Mark 4 records many more details, such as the time of day and the fact that there were other boats with them. The additional details make sense if this account is based on the observations of Peter, as many scholars think. This event would have certainly been more memorable to him, as a fisherman who lived his life on the sea of Galilee. This account also displays the level of exhaustion Jesus was under after dealing with such large crowds. The violent storms which the sea of Galilee is known for are not the type of weather that would induce sleeping. For Jesus to sleep through such a storm, He must have been exhausted.

Back to chapter.

Chapter 24

After Jesus calms the storm, Mark 5 and Luke 8 record a confrontation with a demoniac who lives in the tombs on the opposite side of Galilee in the land of the Gadarenes. Matthew's account (Matthew 8:28–34) obviously records the same event, since both are directly after the calming of the sea, but Matthew mentions two demoniacs in the country of the Gergesenes. Gadara and Gergesa were in the same area, and were likely used interchangeably to refer to the general region, but the number of demoniacs seems irreconcilable. However, Matthew often recorded details which the other writers might have left out to protect the individuals. Whether Mark and Luke simply forgot this second demoniac or whether they left him out to protect his identity, we cannot be sure. Inserting a memorable entrance for Simon Zelotes remedies this discrepancy and also provides an interesting history for an otherwise unknown disciple.

Like Judas Iscariot, the meaning of the title "Zelotes" or "the Zealot," which differentiates Simon Zelotes from Simon Peter, is unknown. It is actually unlikely to indicate his attachment to the order of Zealots (which did not become well known until later), and more likely that it simply indicated a level of enthusiasm that was impossible to miss, but we cannot know for sure. Also known as Simon the Canaanite, we can assume that Simon had some Gentile blood in his history. The full extent of this title's implication regarding his status as a Jew is entirely unknown, but there is no indication in the Bible that he was considered anything other than a Jew.

Back to chapter.

Chapter 25

The account of the healed paralytic is included in three of the four Gospels. Matthew 9:1–8 neglects to include the interesting fact that this paralytic was let down through the roof of a house, but this detail is included in Mark 2:1–12 and Luke 5:17–26. The texts do not say whose house it was that had its roof torn open. It could have been Jesus's own house. Matthew 4:13 indicates that Jesus had already made Capernaum his permanent home, and 9:1 indicates that this miracle happened in "his own city," which Mark identifies as Capernaum in 2:1. Often, the owner of the house is identified, as in Matthew 8:14 (Peter's house), Matthew 26:6 (house of Simon the Leper), Mark 1:29 (house of Simon and Andrew), Mark 5:38 (house of the ruler of the synagogue), Mark 14:3 (house of Simon the Leper), Luke 7:36 (the Pharisee's house), and Luke 22:54 (high priest's house). Several texts however, (Matthew 9:28, 13:1, and 17:25; and Mark 2:1, 9:28, 9:33, and 10:10) simply refer to "*the* house"—not "a house," but a singular specific "*the* house," whose owner is not specifically mentioned. All these texts seem to refer to a house in Capernaum, and no owner is mentioned. Since Jesus is already the prominent figure of the story, ownership is automatically applied to Him.

Despite the modern idea that Jesus was homeless, this is highly unlikely. Based on a simple reading of these eyewitness accounts, it is reasonable to conclude that Jesus owned a home in Capernaum. However, He did travel extensively and was probably forced to escape His home on many occasions to avoid the multitudes that followed Him everywhere. Perhaps He even gave up living in His home entirely, simply to escape the crowds that constantly swarmed Him. This might explain the remarks in Matthew 8:20 and Luke 9:58: "The foxes have holes and the birds of the air have nests; but the Son of Man hath not where to lay His head." Even so, there is clear indication that Jesus did own a home in Capernaum.

Back to chapter.

Chapter 26

The accounts of Matthew 9:9–26, Mark 2:14–22, and Luke 5:27–39 all place the dinner with Matthew (called Levi in Mark and Luke) directly after the healing of the paralytic. Matthew places the healing of Jairus's daughter directly after this dinner, while Mark and Luke place it after the healing of the demoniac (Mark 5:21–43, and Luke 8:41–56), placing the calling of Matthew much earlier in the narrative. Matthew, a Jew working as a Roman *publicanus*, was likely hated by his fellow Jews and viewed as a traitor to his race. He was likely denied entry to synagogue and most other aspects of Jewish culture. Even though he did not witness the healing of Jairus's daughter personally (of the twelve, only Simon, James, and John were present, which is why this book does not include the end of Jairus's story, since Judas did not witness it), it was likely the first miracle Matthew ever experienced, and therefore would have made a huge impression on him—especially considering that Jesus had just dined with him. This unbelievable act of solidarity with a *publicanus* would have received the same level of shock as a southern white minister dining with a black family during the height of the race riots of the 1950s and '60s. It is Matthew's timeline of events, therefore, which is likely the most reliable in this case.

Back to chapter.

Chapter 27

Even though women often take a backseat in modern depictions of the Gospels, the number of women mentioned in the Gospels is remarkably high for manuscripts of the time. Jesus taught parables which were inspired by (and related to) the daily lives of men *and* women. Some of His parables were about women. Women were recorded as the first witnesses of His resurrection, even though women were not considered reliable witnesses in Jewish culture. If the Gospels had been faked, the writers would have selected more reliable witnesses (men) to discover the empty tomb. Although women did have more rights under Roman law than Jewish law (especially free, unmarried women), conservative Jewish culture at the time saw women as hardly more than creatures designed to lead men into sin. Married women were kept at home if possible, and the most pious Jews would not even speak to a woman in public. Jesus ignored these traditions and often spoke to women—indeed, had women disciples. Luke 8:3 records Joanna and several other women as helping fund the ministry of Jesus and traveling with him. These were women of means, likely in positions of political power and more able to act autonomously through their connections to Roman and Greek culture, as opposed to the women married to more orthodox Jewish husbands. Most Pharisees did not even speak to their wives or mothers in public. To present one extreme example of Jewish views on women, there was even a sect of Pharisees known as "the bleeding ones" who would close their eyes in public to keep from even catching a glimpse of a woman, to avoid the risk of sinning by lusting after her. This often led to accidents and injuries as they would walk into obstacles or walls in their blind wanderings—hence the name.

Not all Pharisees kept such strict standards or had the same hatred for Jesus as their brethren from Jerusalem. Many of the local rabbis in the more rural towns welcomed Jesus. Capernaum and Bethabara are two examples of this, but in Jerusalem, Pharisees were stricter. The *Haberim*, or "Brotherhood," was the strictest and most militant sect of Pharisees in most matters of the Law. They kept themselves apart from all things which they thought might defile them and were likely Jesus's main antagonists during His ministry. The Apostle Paul was likely of this more militant and stricter sect of Pharisees, as he names himself a "Pharisee, the son of a Pharisee" in Acts 23:6.

Back to chapter.

Chapter 28

There were three annual feasts which required attendance in Jerusalem for all able-bodied males. These were Passover in the spring, Pentacost seven weeks later, and Tabernacles in the fall. The feast mentioned in John 5 is likely Passover. It is interesting to note that John mentions the Pool of Bethesda as "near the sheep-market." It is possible that the sheep which had been sold in the Temple the previous year had been moved near the pool to prevent further incidents like the one Jesus had caused.

It was a Roman tradition for the sick to be brought to pagan Temples where they could get some shelter at night. These were often removed to some less-noticeable spot during the day to keep the sick from driving off worshipers (and their donations). This explains why the paralytic does not simply stay near the pool constantly. His complaint that none will carry him to it makes far more sense under this realization.

The claim that an angel stirred up the water is a footnote inserted into the Gospel accounts later to explain local legends around the pool and isn't intended to be seen as a direct claim of divine intervention at this location. This claim was possibly invented to help reconcile Jewish and pagan beliefs about the pool, but there is no evidence to indicate that John (or Jesus) believed in the direct involvement of an angel at this scene. The fact that Pharisees were present at the pool is indicative that the site was not considered a de facto pagan site, but it is likely that Jews and Gentiles both frequented the area for different reasons.

Back to chapter.

Part 3 Reference Section

Chapter 29

The accounts in Mark 3:1-8 and Matthew 12:1-21 both describe the healing of a man's hand in synagogue as the incident which decidedly turned the Pharisees against Jesus. Luke 6:6-11 adds a bit more detail, even though it does not specifically mention a plot to kill Him, it does say that the Pharisees were filled with rage and discussed what to do with Him. The exact placement of this event is unknown, but it is likely around the second Passover of Jesus's ministry, in April or May, when barley is ripe, since Matthew and Mark both link this event with the disciples' eating of grain on the Sabbath. For the next two years of His ministry, Jesus was an enemy of the religious leaders, although Nicodemus is proof that He had at least one ally within their ranks.

Back to chapter.

Chapter 30

The identity of Judas's father will be explained more fully in the notes for Chapter 41. Although he is referred to in Matthew and Mark as "Simon the Leper," he is not treated as a leper, indicating that he is a *former* leper. His healing is not recorded, and it is entirely possible, therefore, that it was not Jesus who healed him, but a disciple. Matthew 10, Mark 3, and Luke 9 all clearly tell us that the twelve disciples were given power to heal disease, and this included Judas Iscariot. Knowing that Judas was given power over disease, it is quite possible that the healing of Simon the Leper happened through his own son, Judas.

The death of John the Baptist is recorded in Matthew 14:1-12 and Mark 6:17-29, and the surrounding texts indicate, along with a brief mention in Luke 9:6-9, that this happened during the time that the twelve were sent out in pairs. We know that this event had to happen fairly early in Jesus's ministry, because Matthew 14:2 and Mark 6:14 indicate that Jesus's fame had not yet reached Herod (Herod assumed Jesus was John the Baptist returned from the dead). If Herod had heard of Jesus before John's death, he certainly wouldn't have made this assumption.

Back to chapter.

Chapter 31

John had many disciples and was well-loved among the people. His death came as a shock and must have angered many against the injustice and cruelty of Herod Antipas. Their natural response was to look to John's cousin and named successor, Jesus. Matthew briefly mentions this in 14:12–13, while Mark elaborates further in 6:30–34 by saying that Jesus was too busy even to eat. Jesus escapes in secret but is found again almost immediately and, despite his fatigue, prepares an answer for their many questions that is both memorable and striking.

Back to chapter.

Chapter 32

The Feeding of the Five Thousand is possibly the most famous miracle of Jesus, but the cultural implications are often overlooked. Though it is called "The Feeding of the Five Thousand," this number only includes the men. Jesus provided food for far more people. Women and children were not counted, but the reason behind this simple fact is rarely discussed. Matthew 14, Mark 6, and Luke 9 all link the Feeding of the Five Thousand with the death of John the Baptist. Many in Israel viewed John as a prophet and knew that John believed Jesus to be the Messiah. As John's cousin, Jesus had the legal right by Jewish law to kill Herod in retribution, and many expected Jesus to dethrone Herod. This banquet in the wilderness was Jesus's response. Jesus separates the men and organizes them into companies of fifties and hundreds. Mark 6:39–40 includes this key detail, and the original wording is the same wording used for military formations. Jesus is assembling an army. It is no wonder that the crowd wanted to make him king, as recorded in John 6:1–21. Jesus clearly displays his ability to rule, provide for his subjects, and organize an army. Jesus was an heir to the Jewish throne by birthright, and John's murder gave Jesus a legitimate legal excuse to execute Herod and take his place on the throne. But Jesus's kingdom is not of this world, and his servants do not fight (John 18:36). This banquet sends a clear message to both Herod and the disciples of John in a profound and unforgettable manner: *Herod's throne is mine for the taking, but I am not here to take Herod's throne.* Unfortunately, the disciples do not get the message, and Jesus had to send them away so he could calm the overzealous crowd on His own.

Back to chapter.

Chapter 33

The cannibalistic remarks referenced in this chapter are recorded in John 6:47–60. They directly follow the Feeding of the Five Thousand and drive away many of the men who wanted to make Jesus king not long before. Jesus leaves Israel for a city that no Jew would ever dare enter—Caesarea-Philippi—likely so He can finally get a respite from the crowds of Jews still eager to make Him king. Matthew 15:21–28 and Mark 7:24–30 record the faith of the Syro-Phoenician woman, but they do not indicate any specific location. We do know that Jesus visited the pagan temple at Caesarea-Philippi, but it is unknown if the Syro-Phoenician woman met him here or in some other town in the area of Tyre and Sidon. This novel combines Jesus's discussion of the Gates of Hell recorded in Matthew 16:13–27 with the account of the Syro-Phoenician woman for simplicity's sake. All details of the pagan temple site have been gleaned from archaeological records of the area, which have confirmed the types of worship performed there. It is interesting that Jesus chose this site, surrounded by false gods (Zeus, the king of the gods, and Pan, a shepherd-type deity) and a supposed entrance to the underworld, to question His disciples about His identity as the true Shepherd and King of Kings, and also to predict His future victory over death.

Back to chapter.

Chapter 34

Luke 10:1–20 is the only account which mentions the sending of the seventy disciples. The exact timing of this in relation to the events of John 7 is unknown, but it is possible that Jesus sent the seventy out while He remained in hiding, as is mentioned in John 7:1. The conversation between Judas Iscariot and Judas, the brother of Jesus (*Jesus's siblings are mentioned in* Matthew 13:55 and Mark 6:3), as well as the other events surrounding the Feast of Tabernacles, is inspired by the record of John 7. Ancient traditions regarding the Feast of Tabernacles help to shed greater light on the significance of Jesus's words and their timing on the last day of the feast.

Back to chapter.

Chapter 35

John 8 is the only account we have of the woman caught in adultery, and it is a late addition to the original text. However, this does not mean that it is fictional. There are many reasons (especially if the woman in the story is Mary, Lazarus's sister) to keep this story quiet. The woman's reputation would have been tarnished considerably if this story was widely published. Later, after her death, it would have been safe to include it. There are several details in the story that indicate its validity, including the specific fact that Jesus wrote in the dust and that the Pharisees left eldest first. The exact message which Jesus wrote in the dirt was not recorded. We can only guess at what message would make these Pharisees abandon their quest. My personal theory is included in the next chapter.

Back to chapter.

Chapter 36

Like the previous chapter, this account is mentioned only in John. Perhaps, as Jesus had been in hiding, his other disciples were not present for these events and only John witnessed them. Perhaps they simply found other events more significant, or they thought the story might tarnish the reputation of one of Jesus's followers. John 8:13–59 and 9:1–12 relate the argument between Jesus and the Pharisees which led to him nearly being stoned for blasphemy, and the following healing of the blind man. Jesus clearly teaches that following God's Law is required to claim the lineage of Abraham. Being part of "God's Chosen People" is dependent on obedience, not bloodline—despite what many church leaders claim today. The men with whom Jesus was arguing were Jewish, yet Jesus boldly stated that their father was the devil, not Abraham.

Back to chapter.

Chapter 37

The identity of the man from the parable of Matthew 20:1–16 is unknown. Perhaps the story was not even based on a real person, but it provided another excellent backdrop for the fictional history between Judas and Joseph of Arimathaea. Is it likely that the parables from Mathew 20 and Luke 16 were both inspired by Judas's history? Perhaps not, but it is plausible, and adds biblical flavor to otherwise unknown personalities.

Traditionally, the high priest was to serve for the duration of his life. There is some confusion regarding the roles of Annas and Caiaphas. John 18:13 does reveal that Annas was Caiaphas's father-in-law, but their official roles are less clear. Luke 3:2 notes that both Annas and Caiaphas were high priests, while John 11:49 and John 18:13 seem to indicate that Caiaphas was made high priest in that year. Several theories exist. Annas could have retired and been considered high priest after his retirement, much like presidents in America still retain the title after completing their term. It is also possible that a schism had occurred and that the Pharisees and Sadducees each recognized their own high priest, or that Annas was ousted by Rome and replaced with Caiaphas. If this was the case, the conservative Jews would see Caiaphas as only a usurper and still consider Annas as the legitimate high priest despite his inability to make legal rulings, while the more liberal Jews would recognize Caiaphas as high priest in all respects. History sheds no light on this subject, but perhaps time will reveal the correct explanation.

Back to chapter.

Chapter 38

This chapter fills in the details regarding the blind man who was healed in chapter 36. The account in John 9:1–34 describes the healing and the man's excommunication as a single event, but verse 35 indicates that Jesus only heard about this later, so the later part of this story (John 9:35–10:21) has been placed in this novel with the account of Hanukkah (Feast of Dedication, or Feast of Lights) in John 10:22–39, directly after the account of the blind man's excommunication. Again, Jesus upsets the religious leaders to such a degree that he is nearly stoned to death. In my personal opinion, John 10:32 is evidence that Jesus possessed not only a sharp wit, but a rather snarky sense of sarcasm—and He is not the only Biblical character to have one. Matthew's mention in Matthew 2:23 that Jesus's home in Nazareth is prophetic because "He shall be called a Nazarene" is believed by some scholars to be an intentional pun. John specifically mentions in John 20:4 that he outran Peter on their way to the tomb. There is no reason to include this senseless bit of trivia unless it was intended as a playful jab among friends. Jesus consistently spoke in cuttingly sharp riddles, clever turns of phrase, and yes, direct insults, which are all so often lacking in modern retellings.

Back to chapter.

Chapter 39

Jesus's ministry beyond the Jordan is mentioned in Matthew 19:1 through 20:16 and Mark 10:1–31, and both texts indicate a slightly better reception from the Pharisees in this area. Since this is where most of John the Baptist's ministry happened, it is likely that his presence had some softening effect on the local synagogue leaders. Jesus was exceptionally well-received here, as John 10:40–42 also indicates. John gives us the most specific date for this ministry, placing it between the Feast of Dedication in December and before the Triumphal Entry during Passover week in the spring. Luke is unclear if the healing of the hunchback woman (Luke 13:10–17) or the odd remarks regarding Jesus's mother's reproductive organs (Luke 11:27–28) happened during this time, but the placement is plausible, especially since his rebuke to the ruler of the synagogue is taken with humility, rather than rock-throwing.

It is unknown what motive made Luke place the strange remarks of Luke 11:27 into scripture, but he felt them striking enough to gain a place. Perhaps they are intended as a divine reproof against the modern veneration of Mary to nearly—and sometimes equal to—divine status. Jesus treated His mother with love and kindness but was quick to counter any claim that she held any right to divinity.

Back to chapter.

Chapter 40

Again, John is the only account which includes any mention of Lazarus. In John, Jesus hears of Lazarus's death directly after the mention of his ministry beyond the Jordan, so it is evident that Jesus was near Bethabara when he heard the news. John 11:1 through 12:11 cover the entire story, including the dinner in Bethany at the house of Simon the Leper (see next chapter's notes). It is evident that the raising of Lazarus and the dinner with Simon the Leper are intrinsically linked. It also explains the extreme gratitude which Mary displays in John 12:1–8, which remains unexplained in the other Gospel accounts. John 12:9–11 also explains why Lazarus is not mentioned by the other Gospel writers: there was a plot to kill Lazarus. This plot would have certainly increased after Jesus's ascension. Mentioning Lazarus in the earlier accounts would have put him and his family in grave danger. By the time John wrote his account (which is clearly designed to fill the gaps of the other preexisting records rather than present an entire story on its own) there was no longer danger in mentioning names, so John includes these key details that help make sense of the other accounts. Lazarus and his family had either escaped Jerusalem or already been hunted down and killed by the time John wrote his account.

Back to chapter.

Chapter 41

A brief mention of James and John's request via their mother to gain the chief positions in Jesus's kingdom is included in this chapter. Both Matthew and Mark seem to place this either on the way to Jericho or while staying in Jericho on Jesus's last return to Jerusalem, likely only a few days before the dinner at Simon the Leper's. Matthew 20:20–28 includes the fact that it was their mother who made the specific request, while Mark 10:35–45 leaves her out of the narrative.

Simon the Leper is a character that must be pieced together from all four Gospel accounts. He is mentioned only in connection to this singular dinner. The accounts in Matthew 26:6–13, Mark 14:3–9, Luke 7:36–50, and John 12:1–8 all record the same event. Even though there are some differences, as is expected with eyewitness accounts, there are far too many similarities to assume they are separate events. This is the first appearance of this complex character, but from these four different accounts we learn that this man is called "Simon the Leper" (from Matthew and Mark), meaning he was a leper for some time, but his presence hosting a banquet indicates that he is a leper no longer, even though his healing is never recorded. Luke informs us that the host of this dinner was a Pharisee, but inadvertently gives us Simon's name in Jesus's reply (it is obvious from the text that Jesus is speaking to the master of the house). We can conclude then that Simon was both a Pharisee and a former leper—a difficult combination, to be sure.

Again, John's account fills in some of these gaps. He explains that Lazarus is partially the reason for this dinner, and John is the first to reveal the woman's identity. It is likely that the other writers wished to protect Mary's identity in connection to the history of this "sinner" who exposes herself publicly. By the time John wrote his account, Mary could have already been killed, or perhaps John simply decided that enough time had passed that hiding her identity was no longer an issue. It is impossible to say for sure. The last vital clue to Simon's identity is also in John, where Judas Iscariot is revealed to be Simon's son. The host of the dinner is not named in John, and some have wrongly assumed Judas to be the son of Simon Peter, since Simon–Peter is the only other "Simon" mentioned in John's account. It is only when we take all four Gospels together that the true picture is revealed. John neglects to mention Simon the Leper by name, but the other Gospels do. Jesus had upset and insulted countless Pharisees by the time of this dinner. The betrayal by Judas Iscariot makes far more sense when we realize that it was Judas's *father* who was publicly humiliated at his own dinner party, rather than some unknown Pharisee. Whether this is the true reason behind Judas's dreadful decision or not, it is evident that the writers of both Matthew and Mark considered the events of this dinner to be adequate reason for Judas to betray Jesus and make specific mention of it (Matthew 26:14–16 and Mark 14:10–11).

Back to chapter.

Chapter 42

The exact words of Jesus, as recorded in Luke 13:31–35 seem innocent to us today, but what meaning did they have in Jesus's day? The word for "fox" used here is "*shūāl*" and is feminine in the original text. It is certainly not used in a polite sense. Jesus was not saying that Herod was "foxy" or "clever" as we understand the word today. The most accurate comparison in modern English is a word which means "female dog," and when used insultingly, the modern version has a similar meaning. I have elected not to use it. The indication of the phrase is that Jesus considers Herod to be a weak, worthless impostor with delusions of grandeur and that Jesus has far more important things to worry about than a pretend king's impotent threats. He expresses this with colorful language that likely shocked the Pharisees just as much as similar language would shock good churchgoers today.

The Parables of the Good Shepherd, the Good Housewife, and the Good Father (briefly mentioned at the start of this chapter), as recorded in Luke 15:4–32 are a complimentary set. The first was intended to resonate more with men, the second with women, while the third sums them up and adds more depth and personality. It is likely that Jesus reused His parables often, which would explain why they are recalled so well in the Gospel accounts.

Despite them often being called the Parables of the Lost Sheep, Lost Coin, and Prodigal Son, the true focus of the parable is on the finder/rescuer, rather than the lost/rescued. In the last parable, the elder son has a right to be angry; the prodigal son's choice to abandon his family and spend his inheritance is not to be celebrated. But the prodigal son is not the focus of the story. The father does not ask his elder son to celebrate the son's poor choices but to celebrate the father's joy in his son's return. It is not because of anything the sheep has done that the village celebrates with the shepherd, but for the successful conclusion of the shepherd's search. It would have been an act of justice to punish the prodigal son for his poor choices and let him receive his "just desserts." The elder son is angry that justice is not served upon his younger brother, but doing so would also hurt the father, which would be equally unjust. Faced with two seemingly unjust solutions, Jesus profoundly and brilliantly presents mercy as the highest form of justice.

Back to chapter.

Part 4 Reference Section

Chapter 43

The triumphal entry would have been a memorable event in the minds of the disciples, who expected Jesus to ascend the throne like all Israel of the time. Its record can be found in Matthew 21:1–11, Mark 11:1–19, and Luke 19:28–44. Matthew and Luke leave no gap between the triumphal entry and the cleansing of the Temple, but Mark makes note that the Temple cleansing was the following morning.

The names of the two disciples sent to fetch the donkey's colt are unnamed, but they could have been Justus and Matthias. Peter indicates in Acts 1:21–23 that Justus and Matthias had been disciples of Jesus since His baptism by John. Although Jesus is typically pictured with only twelve disciples, He had many more. He ordained twelve, and later sent out seventy others, who must have been selected from an even larger group. Matthias and Justus were certainly of this number.

Back to chapter.

Chapter 44

The exact sequence of events during the final week is not completely certain, but most historians agree that the triumphal entry occurred on Sunday, five days before the Passover on Friday, which coincides with the Rabbinical tradition of selecting the Passover lamb five days before the Feast. Jesus would have then cursed the fig tree and cleansed the Temple on Monday, the following morning (Mark 11:12). Jesus must have left Monday night after dark, because the disciples discovered the withered fig tree Tuesday morning (Mark 11:20). The conversations with the scribes and Pharisees are harder to pinpoint, as Jesus taught in the Temple from Sunday through Thursday.

Remember that the Jewish day starts at sundown, so the Last Supper would have happened late Thursday evening, which was the very beginning of the first day of Unleavened Bread (Passover). The lamb would traditionally be killed the next day (Friday), to be eaten Friday afternoon before sunset, at the end of Passover Day, rather than the beginning. We can rationally conclude that Jesus ate the Passover dinner a day early (though still technically on Passover), because the scribes and Pharisees had not yet eaten the Passover lamb at the time of Jesus's trial on Friday (John 18:28).

Back to chapter.

Chapter 45

The second cleansing of the Temple is recorded in Matthew 21:12–17, Mark 11:15–19, and Luke 19:45–46. Mark gives us the most information and includes the fact that Jesus did not allow anyone with wares to enter the Temple (verse 16). This small piece of information tells us much. The many doors leading into the Temple Mount would have taken a significant force to continually guard. Jesus must have had many of His close followers nearby to enforce these rules, which would not have been possible at the beginning of His ministry, further indicating two separate Temple cleansings.

Another indication of two Temple cleansings is the remarkable similarity to the rules of cleansing a house of leprosy in Leviticus 14:33–57, which include an initial cleansing and emptying of the house, followed by an inspection, then a second inspection and a replacement of the unclean parts with new parts seven days later, and finally, if the plague still persisted, the complete destruction of the house. These same events happened in the same order with Jesus's first cleansing recorded in John 2, the inspection recorded in Mark 11:11, followed by the second cleansing the following morning. Jesus spent the rest of the week teaching in the Temple, but the hatred of the religious leaders persisted. Jesus then pronounced the house desolate in Matthew 23:37–39, just before predicting its destruction in 24:1–2, even alluding to the removal of the stones with similar phrasing as

Leviticus. At Jesus's death, the House of God was condemned and its Occupant evicted, as displayed by the Temple veil being ripped in two. The final destruction happened 37 years later when Titus's forces completely demolished the Temple to its very foundation—exactly as required by Levitical Law.

Back to chapter.

Chapter 46

The Last Supper is recorded in all four Gospel accounts (Matthew 26:17–35, Mark 14:12–26, Luke 22:7–38, and John 13:1 through 17:26), and each includes some details not included in the others. John, in typical fashion, only mentions the supper briefly, but includes the account of Jesus washing the disciples' feet after supper and an extensive record of Jesus's final words, which the other accounts leave out.

Judas did not witness Jesus's prayer in the garden, and so it is not included in this novel, but the account in the garden of Gethsemane can be read and compared from Matthew 26:36–46, Mark 14:27–42, and Luke 22:39–46. John does not mention Jesus's inner struggle in Gethsemane but cuts directly to Judas's entrance, which will be covered in the next chapter.

Back to chapter.

Chapter 47

Mark includes an odd piece of the story in 14:51–52 by mentioning a young man who fled naked. It is not mentioned who this man was, but if it was John, it would explain his absence during the trial and later appearance at the cross with Mary, Jesus's mother. He would have needed to return to wherever he had some spare clothes, and if this location coincided with where Jesus's mother was staying, he would have certainly informed her of the tragic abduction of her Son. However, this is all speculation and is impossible to know for certain. Jesus had many disciples, and it is possible that this young man was not even one of the twelve.

Because of the traditional ideas of "gentle Jesus, meek and mild," most Christians find Peter's attack on Malchus shocking, but it is interesting to note that Jesus specifically told his disciples to sell their coats and purchase swords at the Last Supper, only a few hours before (Luke 22:36–38). Two of the disciples already had swords, and Jesus agreed that two were sufficient. With this conversation fresh in their minds, it is no wonder that Peter was ready to put his weapon to use. The disciples asked Jesus if it was time to attack (Luke 22:49), and failing to receive a response in time, Peter takes the initiative to defend his master (Matthew 26:47–56, Mark 14:43–52, Luke 22:47–53, John 18:1–11). Jesus instantly intercedes to prevent further violence, but he does not specifically condemn Peter's defense.

It is also interesting to note the incorrect ideas tied to the phrase "he who lives by the sword shall die by the sword," which many assume to be a scriptural tenet, and which pacifists use to support their beliefs. However, this phrase is not found in scripture. The phrase which *is* in scripture is: "Put your sword in its place, for all who take the sword will perish by the sword." Matthew 26:52. This was not meant as a principle to be applied to all situations, but a direct command to Peter and the other disciples who wished to save Jesus through violence. Jesus knew that an attack against the angry mob would turn into a bloodbath, and Jesus commanded His disciples not to resist in order to prevent more bloodshed. It is not a principle which we must apply to all situations. Luke 22:38 is proof that Jesus expected his disciples to be armed and ready for combat, while Matthew 26:52 shows the importance of recognizing the right time to fight—and the wrong time.

Back to chapter.

Chapter 48

The trial at the high priest's house—if it can be called a trial—is recorded in Matthew 26:57–75, Mark 14:53–72, Luke 22:54–65, and John 18:12–27. John is the only account which mentions another disciple other than Peter, but this disciple is unnamed. Most scholars agree that this disciple is John, since it is found in his account. However, it seems unlikely that John, as a peasant fisherman from Galilee, would be known to the high priest, as John 18:16 indicates. It is therefore possible that this disciple was, in fact, Judas—especially since Judas was the entire reason that Jesus was there in the first place. As painful as the memory of Judas must have been to the other eleven, it is no wonder that he is mentioned only when absolutely necessary by the Gospel writers. It is possible that John wished to explain how Peter managed to gain entrance to the high priest's house but was reluctant to credit the feat to Judas. It is also possible that Peter only knew that a fellow disciple had gained him entrance and did not know his helper's identity. We can only speculate, but it seems likelier that Judas (who had already established contact with the high priest) would have been this unknown disciple rather than a fisherman from Galilee.

Back to chapter.

Chapter 49

The mockery of justice which happened at sunrise is recorded briefly in Matthew 27:1–2, Mark 15:1, and Luke 22:66–71. The exact details between the night trial at Annas's house and the official trial before Caiaphas and the Sanhedrin the following morning are somewhat blurred. It is entirely unknown if any of Jesus's disciples witnessed these events firsthand, or if they had to piece together the account from other witnesses (including Jesus, perhaps). As is common among truthful eyewitness accounts, the words and actions are remembered vividly, while other details, like the sequence of events, tend to be remembered with less clarity.

Back to chapter.

Chapter 50

Herod's involvement in the trial of Jesus is recorded only in Luke 23:6–12. It is possible that Herod was staying in the same palace as Pilate, since he was only visiting Jerusalem (as he ruled Galilee, not Judea), and any eyewitnesses would have been unable to enter. They would have therefore not known of Herod's involvement. However, it is far likelier that Matthew and Mark did not wish to risk Herod's anger by calling attention to his involvement. Luke, writing to "Theophilus," (meaning "friend of God," though it is unknown if this name was a personal title or a generic Greek term for any Christian man) was the only one who felt safe enough to indict the Jewish monarch, since he was writing to Greek Christians rather than his fellow Jews. The politics and social turmoil of the time were complex; if the other Gospel writers neglected to include Herod's involvement intentionally, we can be certain that they had good reason.

Back to chapter.

Chapter 51

Matthew 27:2–31, Mark 15:1–20, and John 18:28 through 19:16 place all the blame on Pilate and his soldiers for this cruel treatment, while Luke 23:1–25 seems to indicate that it was Herod's troops—not Pilate's—which mocked and abused Jesus. Luke does not mention a crown of thorns, but the other gospels all connect the crown of thorns with the purple robe (Matthew calls it a scarlet robe) which Luke does mention. Luke's account makes more sense, given Pilate's reluctance to sentence Jesus, but the exact details remain unknown. It is also possible that both Herod's and Pilate's troops mocked and abused Jesus. If so, Jesus would have endured this cruelty three times: in Annas's palace, Herod's palace, and Pilate's palace.

Back to chapter.

Chapter 52

The exact identity of Barabbas (or "Bar-Abbas," literally meaning "Son of the Father") is unknown. Some scholars claim that his name was also Jesus ("Jesus" in Greek or "Yeshuah," in Hebrew), which was a fairly common name of the time. The only information we have about Barabbas is mentioned in Matthew 27:15–26, Mark 15:6–15, Luke 23:13–25, and John 18:39–40. The most we know is that Barabbas had been charged with murder and "a certain rebellion made in the city" (Luke 23:19) while John 18:40 merely states that he was a robber. It is unknown if he was the founder of the *Sicarii* or simply some rebel, but he was notorious enough that all four Gospel accounts seem to expect the reader to know his identity by these scant facts. It is extremely likely that the other two thieves crucified with Jesus were co-conspirators with Barabbas. If Barabbas was the founder of the *Sicarii*, the possibility remains that the destruction of Jerusalem and the following massacre at Masada were direct results of Barabbas's release. This is mere speculation, but the Jews' bold promise of "His blood be on us and on our children" (Matthew 27:25) becomes far more significant if this critical choice between Jesus Barabbas and Jesus Christos is the direct cause of the miseries which fell on these same people and their children thirty-seven years later, in accordance with their wishes.

Back to chapter.

Chapter 53

Historians tend to agree that lashing was considered part of the punishment of crucifixion. Josephus mentions that scourging was part of a condemned criminal's punishment. It is possible that Pilate, knowing a man condemned to crucifixion was to be lashed anyway, suggested the lashing in the hope that it would be enough punishment. It is Jewish tradition that gives us the number of lashes for a condemned man, but the exact number is not recorded in the Gospel accounts. It is safe to assume, however, that in their demonic fury, the mob would have demanded the highest legal number of lashes.

Back to chapter.

Chapter 54

Criminals were sometimes tied to the cross and sometimes nailed to it. We know Jesus was nailed to the cross from the Gospel accounts (John 20:25), but tradition often displays the two thieves tied with ropes. This is unlikely, since the crucifixions would have been done by the same executioner, and it stands to reason that he would have used the same method on all three. The accounts of Matthew 27:32–56, Mark 15:21–41, Luke 23:26–49 agree that Jesus was crucified about the third hour (9:00am) and died about the ninth hour (3:00pm). John 19:17–37 mentions neither the timing of Jesus's death nor the three hours of darkness which preceded it. John mentions that the Sabbath was approaching (Friday evening), and that to prevent the men from suffering on the Sabbath, the soldiers were to break their legs. This would have prevented the sufferers from being able to raise themselves enough to take a breath, and they would have quickly suffocated. Pilate was shocked to hear that Jesus had died before this, since crucifixion was a very slow, lingering death (Mark15:42–44).

Joseph of Arimathaea is only mentioned in connection with Jesus's death (Matthew 27:57–61, Mark 15:42–47, Luke 23:50–56, and John 19:38–42). From these scant facts, we know Joseph was from Arimathaea, he was rich, a disciple, a "prominent council member" (on the Sanhedrin), and a "good and just man." John tells us that Joseph had kept his allegiance to Jesus a secret for fear of the Jews, but that at Jesus's death, Joseph boldly went to Pilate to ask for Jesus's body. By Roman law, any crucified criminal was denied the right of burial, so this was indeed a daring request—but Pilate agreed. Joseph donated his own tomb, while Nicodemus brought about a hundred pounds of spices for the burial. Both of these remarkable gifts could only be provided by very rich men. These few details—along with two of Jesus's parables—are the framework upon which the character of Joseph of Arimathaea is built within this novel.

Back to chapter.

Chapter 55

There is precious little information about Judas in the four Gospel accounts. He is mentioned only as one of the twelve (Matthew 10:2–4, Mark 3:14–19, Luke 6:13–16), or in connection to the betrayal of Jesus. Even in the lists cited above, he is named a traitor and mentioned last of the twelve, included only because he had to be. The shock of such a betrayal from one of their own must have been extremely painful for the disciples, and it is natural that they speak of it only when necessary. But what of Judas? The perspectives of the Gospel accounts are clearly seen, but little attention is often given to Judas's perspective. As a close disciple of Jesus, and after such personal proofs as Judas must have seen, it is absurd to imagine that Judas had any doubt about Jesus's identity as the Messiah. What motive, then, could have pushed Judas to betray the One who could save Israel? Greed is often cited as the source, since John 12:6 incriminates Judas for stealing money from the disciples' mutual funds. This claim of greed falls apart under careful scrutiny. Thirty pieces of silver was a pittance for such a betrayal, and Judas did not even keep the money. If greed was his only motive, his actions following Jesus's condemnation make no sense. Why Judas took money from the disciples' mutual funds is unknown. It is human nature to assume the worst of someone who has betrayed us, and the disciples were, after all, human. We can only view Judas through their eyes. As Nicodemus rightly said in John 7:51, we should not judge a man until we have heard his explanation. Sadly, Judas's perspective is lost to history. We can only speculate about Judas's true intentions, and ironically, many Christians today condemn Judas without ever considering his perspective.

The Jews expected their Messiah to defeat Rome in battle. They expected a warrior. It is ridiculous to imagine that Judas did not believe Jesus to be the Messiah, but like most Jews at the time, Jesus was not what Judas expected. It is entirely logical to conclude that Judas fully expected Jesus to retaliate—or at least survive. It is only after Jesus's condemnation that Judas vehemently returns the money. If he had truly expected Jesus to be killed from the offset, such a violent reaction to His sentencing would not have happened.

Judas's response, then, is unsurprising. The only person who might have forgiven Judas had been sent to die by his own actions. His close friends saw Judas as worse than an enemy, and the enemies with whom he had bargained saw him with only hate and disdain. Judas loathed himself for what he had done and knew there was no remedy. He was responsible for the death of his own Savior and the death of God's Son. From Judas's perspective, he had become the enemy of everyone: his friends, his Master, his enemies, himself, and even his God. Judas had murdered the only friend who might be crazy enough to forgive him. A man placed in such a terrible position is truly, inescapably lost. It is no wonder that Jesus calls Judas the "son of perdition" in John 17:12.

Back to chapter.

Chapter 56

The noun "perdition" is often associated with the idea of hell, or a state of evil which is impossible to remedy. Christians often use this phrasing as proof that Judas is forever lost and beyond hope of redemption. However, such is not the case. In essence, "perdition" simply means "a state of lostness," and is related to the French *perdu*, meaning "lost," or the infinitive form *perdre*, meaning "to lose."

Is this word proof that Judas is unsaved? No. The sheep, the coin, and the prodigal son are also lost. The coin is inanimate, but the sheep and the son are similar in that they do not wish to be lost. The son returns home. The sheep cries out. It is practically impossible to find a sheep in the wilderness if the sheep does not call out to its shepherd. The fact that the sheep is found indicates that it, like the son, desires to return. They are lost, certainly, but they do not *stay lost*.

Many people point to Mark 14:21 as evidence that Judas will not be saved, but this turn of phrase is used to express misery, not status of salvation. Job 3:3–13 uses this same imagery, and though Job suffered much, no one questions his salvation or the fact that his misery came to an end that was blessed "more than his beginning" (Job 42:12). John 17:12 may indicate that Judas is lost, but John 18:9 contradicts this. The most logical reconciliation between these two verses is that Judas *is lost*, but like the sheep and the prodigal son, he does not *remain lost*.

Matthew is the only disciple who records the end of Judas's life. Precious little is stated in Matthew 27:3–8, but these few details shed a light on Judas that is often overlooked. 1 John 1:9 clearly states that confession is the only requirement for salvation. The other Gospel accounts present only negative perspectives of Judas, but Matthew presents an interesting account of Judas's final act. Matthew clearly indicates that Judas expressed remorse (Matthew 27:3), openly confessed his sins (27:4), and made restitution (27:5). It presents a striking contrast to the chief priests, who respond to this heartfelt plea with disdain. They show no remorse, *but Judas does*.

An unrepentant and remorseless man would not have returned the money, and certainly would not have felt such guilt as to kill himself from intense regret. Is Judas's suicide enough evidence to condemn him? Tradition tends to make suicide into an "unpardonable sin," but there is no biblical foundation for this. Indeed, offering salvation for a man who kills another but denying it for a man who kills himself is neither fair nor just.

Is there a time limit on suicide? Is a man lost because he kills himself quickly with a rope or gun, while another man can be saved because he kills himself slowly with poor diet and lack of exercise? Both are fatal, and both a free choice, yet the typical church only condemns one of these. If a person knowingly drinks a liquid which they know will eventually be fatal, does it matter if it is arsenic, alcohol, or soda? Is God's ability to save reliant on the speed at which a poison kills? No, to place limits on God's ability to save is illogical and blasphemous. The only condition necessary to be saved by God is a desire to be saved by God. Judas's final acts appear to meet these requirements.

Back to chapter.

Epilogue

There is no absolute proof that Judas will be saved or that he desired to be, but based on the little information we have, there is a distinct possibility that Judas will retake his place among the twelve after the resurrection of the dead at Christ's second coming. The other eleven were no less sinful than Judas. All have sinned (Romans 3:23). We all require a savior, and although it is comforting to point to another as being worse than ourselves, we are just as guilty as Judas. Judas was called the "son of perdition," but we all fall into this category. We have all gone astray (Isaiah 53:6). We are all lost. But this is not the end of the story. Judas died without hope because his Savior was dead.

But Jesus didn't stay dead. And the lost sheep didn't stay lost.

Our hope is alive, and Judas's hope is alive as well, even though he doesn't know it yet.

"For the Son of man is come to seek and to save that which was lost."
(Luke 19:10)

Back to chapter.

About the Author

P aul Campbell is the author of The Doomed Disciple and the Callahan Chronicles series, as well as several short stories. He has many more books inside his head just itching to get out. Like most authors, Paul enjoys overused tropes like drinking coffee, reading mystery novels, playing a musical instrument, and writing about himself in the third person. He also has less popular hobbies like origami, collecting Lego® sets, and keeping the squirrels off his flying machine, which he hasn't flown since he crashed it. For more information about Paul Campbell or to order his books, please visit his website at *www.traitorbooks.com*.